I0772596

DARK ASCENSIONS

Issachon Book 1

CMOUR B

This is a work of fiction. All characters and events portrayed in this novel are either products of the author's imagination or are used fictitiously.

Dark Ascensions

Cover by Ron Smith
Formatted by Kingsman Editing Services

ISBN: 979-8-9882225-1-4 (IS)
ISBN: 979-8-9882225-5-2 (IS)
ISBN: 979-8-9882225-3-8 (KDP)
First Edition June 2023

www.DarkAscensions.com

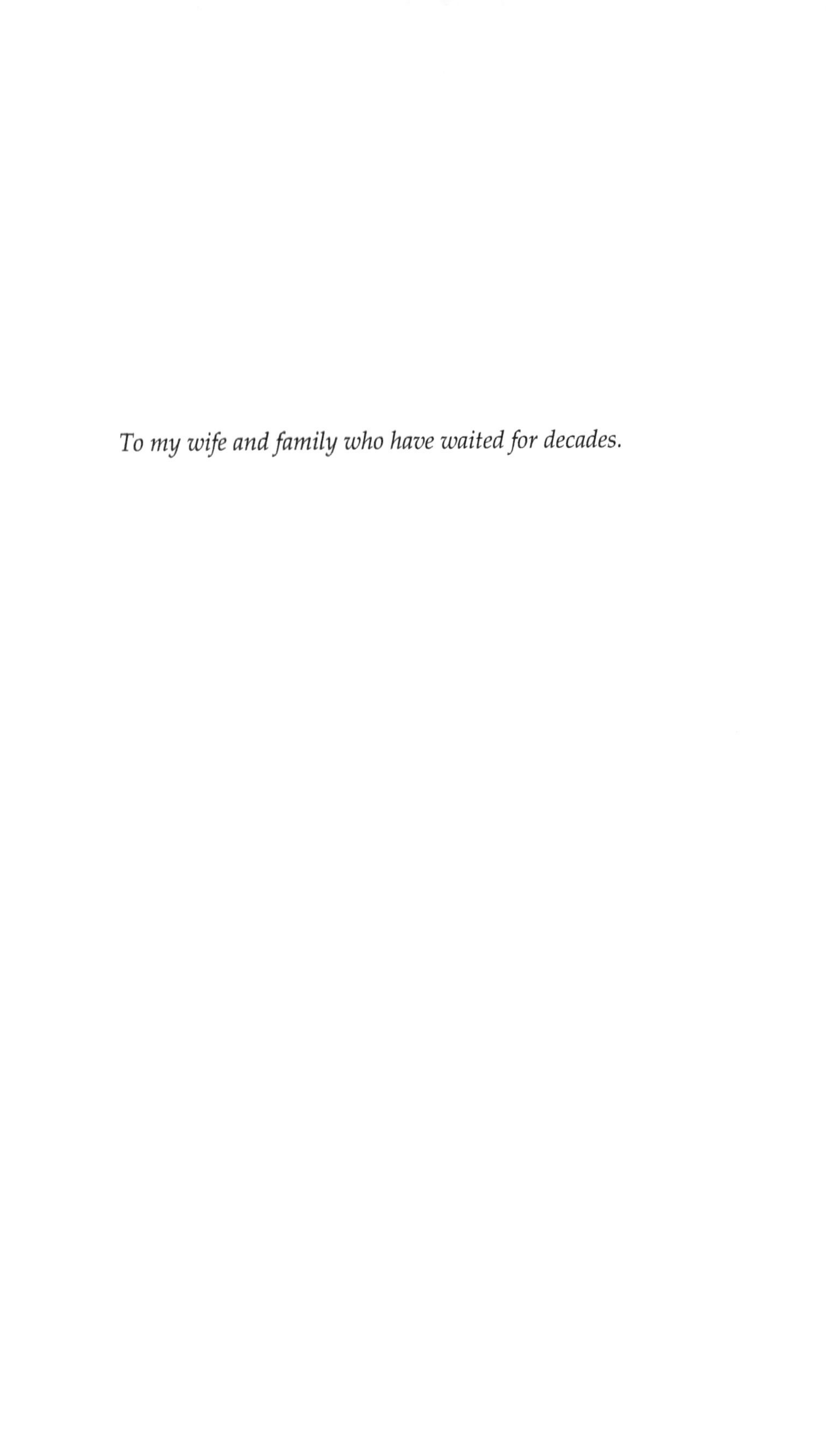

To my wife and family who have waited for decades.

Denton Street was dark, even with the moon hovering over the scene watchfully, which was right and proper for an October evening in Wisconsin. A slight breeze, appropriately in the west, kicked up swirls of leaves and detritus which rustled and murmured as they skittered and tripped down the street. Houses and shops set off from the street behind sidewalks and small yards punctuated the darkness with occasional light from fixtures mounted above porches or pouring through windows. A serene autumnal scene, as it should be.

The darkness and rustling wind made her sudden arrival less conspicuous, black clothes masking her further when she appeared in the deeper darkness a few yards back into an irrelevant alley. She immediately stepped forward from the alley to the sidewalk and looked to the right into the breeze that tossed her hair as the wind approached and fled. A block away she espied her destination; one of the more garish sources of light and an even more ebullient source of odors, necessary for her to smell and endure. She squinted and glared but set off against the prevailing wind.

Her step as she proceeded was precise but firm, each motion measured, each foot placed with care, not the graceful step of the dancer nor the controlled, deliberate gait of a royal procession. Instead, her steps had the careful and balanced poise of a cat stalking its prey, alert, strong, tense, even theatrical. A casual witness might have found the way she walked natural for a person who was so obviously athletic. A more focused viewer might notice the way she scanned her surroundings and call it paranoia. But the careful observer, who knew what to look for, would recognize that her every movement was deliberate and vigilant and call it prepared.

Not that anyone *was* watching, of course, the street was empty, and she knew it. She could sense it passively, with little or no effort; no-one was even looking out of the windows of the buildings that lined the street. Not that the buildings were empty, she could sense *that* too. Those not already asleep were winding down the end of their day and preparing for sleep or pursuing various entertainments that didn't include looking out at the street. She relaxed and grew tense at the same moment, remembering that it didn't matter who was watching out the window; the people she *could* see weren't the dangerous ones.

Across the street from her destination, she stopped for a moment in a darkened doorway to look in the windows of the hated establishment. She scanned the premises carefully and cautiously, gathering a sense of the several people inside. Then, care and caution given their due, she hastened across the street and approached the door with confidence. She reached, then hesitated on the threshold for a mounting series of throbbing moments, her hand lightly touching the doorknob. A dismal mental pallor draped itself across the shoulders of her mind as she pondered the anticipated but inconceivable pain and frustration of her next actions. She paused, sniffing the air disdainfully; the hated smell was strong, where she stood, on the safe side of the door. Her mind was rebelling at the thought of being immersed in the putrid presence of pizza. This was a disconcerting and novel experience for her, a person with such iron resolve. This made the experience doubly novel for her *because* it was disconcerting, further multiplying the tension to the level of being frustrating. It had been almost a dozen years since she had felt fear, and a dozen years since the last time she had entered a pizzeria. The two were connected.

Looking back, *that* evening, twelve years earlier, had started in joy, arriving with her two best friends, Shelley and Adrienne, laughing, talking about school and boys. There was soda and food, pizza, of course. The joy and food were brutally interrupted as something crashed through, changing her utterly and irrevocably. Despite the almost infinite and certainly all-encompassing power involved, somehow the smell of pizza became linked in her mind at that moment of power to the dreadful evil that she had become. Thus, the smell, confronting her at *this* moment, was tipping the scales in her mind and causing her to fear when there was nothing she *should* fear. She dropped her hand from the knob.

Stepping away from the door, she drifted a few steps, haphazardly, angling across the outdoor patio, empty at this time of night, stopping a few feet from the large front window. At her feet, the warm buttery light from the pizzeria window splashed onto the patio where it wrestled entwined against the ghostly sheen from the cold pearly moonlight that drenched the night. She stopped and wrestled, too, in a tumult of anguished memories, but above them all was the anger. In proper accord, she clenched her fists. She clenched them so tightly that her nails bit into her flesh, and a few drops of blood fell onto the ground where it mingled with her tears. Being here was ridiculous and inconvenient; she *shouldn't* be here. She spat in anger, feeling the loss of control, but concluded, upon reflection, that since she *was* here, she needed to focus.

She drew her arms up to her chest and hugged herself fiercely, a thin trickle of blood growing on her forearm. With a sudden cry, she thrust her hands down in a gesture of defiance and rejection, spreading her fingers with an almost audible snap. Then, she raised her arms above her head and closed her eyes, breathing deeply, the moonlight bathing her face. She sighed, the inner cleansing complete, the fear erased, the focus restored. No smell could assail her now; nor anything else; at least without a violent reprisal. When she opened her eyes, she saw the blood and scowled, banishing it and healing her hands. She strode to the door, opened it fiercely, and stepped inside. Only the unquenchable and ever-present anger remained.

As expected, the smell was multiplied a hundred-fold when she opened the door and entered, but now she was impervious. Instead of reacting to the smell, she took in her surroundings. The pizzeria was typical, a few people seated at tables with red-and-white checked tablecloths, parallel rows of booths along the walls, also with tablecloths catering with eager submission to the stereotype. A counter near the front for take-out orders, the kitchen at the back behind a service counter. Immediately before her was a small podium. As she approached it, a teenage girl emerged from the kitchen and moved quickly to engage with her, wearing a genuine customer-service smile and a badge that identified her name as Monica.

Monica's smile was no less and no more forced than on any other night, though this evening had been less busy and more tedious than some, which perhaps left her less affable and more fatigued, diminishing her buoyant personality. She looked at her newest patron as the door behind her eased to a quiet and soft close. Like many people who are regularly provided the opportunity to observe others at length, Monica appraised the woman who had entered. But despite her fears, she turned the volume knob on her smile to full and addressed her inquiry to the new arrival with warmth. "How many?" she asked, like so many hostesses, pretending that she couldn't count how many people had come through the door.

The woman turned her head slightly and her eyes narrowed, and she paused as if she were pondering whether to be sarcastic or humorous about the question. Instead, she said, "My name is Alystra. I am expecting to meet someone. Has anyone asked for me?"

"I'm sorry, nobody has asked for you." Monica's smile dipped a bit to align sympathetically with the news.

Alystra shook her head, not smiling in the least, "A table for two."

Monica lowered her voice confidentially, "To tell you the truth," and Alystra wondered if there were other reasonable options, "at this time of night, I am just here to greet people and take orders." She handed Alystra a menu. "If you want to pick a table, I will be over in a minute." She customer serviced a smile again and gestured toward the room vaguely.

Alystra nodded to her sideways and walked to a table near the center of the room where she circled it to the far side and sat facing the door. From the center of the room, she could most easily sense the other people in the restaurant with the least amount of energy expenditure. Facing the door would allow her to maintain vigilance against the most obvious avenue of assault, even though she had already sensed the door behind the kitchen leading into the alley. At this thought she looked around with a productive sneer; against most of her enemies, these walls would provide as much protection as a wisp of vapor.

At the thought of potential enemies and vapor thin walls, she squinted, a reflex more than a necessity. What she saw with her eyes during this exercise was nothing more than faint confirmation of a small slice of her greater view. She sent her mind swirling and wafting outward in all directions. Sensing each mind superficially for threats, she seized each motive, traced feelings and fears into the hearts of everyone within blocks. She built a web of passive awareness, which seemed unnecessary here on Earth. She found no relevant threat within the hundreds of meters she had probed. Earth was still a babe in the galactic cradle, untouched by the larger flow.

What she sensed, rather than any threats, were people winding down their days—watching TV; playing games on computers, phones, or boards; reading; or heading off to sleep. She also uncovered a few crimes, lies spoken, unspoken sorrows and brokenness, determination and conceit, passion and boredom, but nothing that was a threat to *her*, which was all that mattered. Then, having built a dome of awareness in all directions, she glanced around the room, to make her awareness a bit more personal and proximate. A young couple sat near the back of the room at a table near the kitchen, their minds engaged by each other and the evening they were sharing. Two men in the closest booth were arguing sports and the relative skills of athletes they could never hope to match. Alystra snorted and laughed inwardly but let her attention amble past. At a small table in the front sat an elderly man hunched over, of all meals, soup. He was eating hungrily and noisily, absorbed intently on the meal he himself was absorbing. She sighed and relaxed, though just a bit.

Monica came over, rattled off some specials, and offered to get her a drink.

Alystra paused, she had to think for a moment. *What beverages do they sell on this—my home—planet.* It had been too long since she had been here, though it was an absence that was only partially her fault. She dug deeply in her mind; something pungent, mere dirty water. "Just a cup of coffee," she spluttered, which surprised her since the last time she was on Earth she was only fifteen and had hated coffee. Of course, she had no intention of drinking it anyway.

As though Alystra were creating words, Monica's customer service smile faded in blank-faced confusion, quickly and valiantly her smile battled to regain control of her face, she replied, "I'm sorry, this is a pizza shop. We don't serve coffee."

Alystra was out of practice, so she didn't roll her eyes. Twelve years of no Earth drinks, or, any drinks, required Alystra to dig deeper, but an old favorite bubbled to the top, "Lemonade?" she asked.

"Absolutely, be right back." Monica, back on safe ground, hit her again with a beam of customer service and headed to the back.

As she waited, Alystra thought back to the note she had received that morning. It had been written on a small piece of vellum, *who uses vellum*, that had been impaled on a dagger and stabbed into the wall in the engine room of her ship. Hanging from the handle of the dagger had been a small silk bag that contained a single gold, jewel-studded amulet on a sturdy chain. The note had given her the address of this pizzeria, on *Earth*, and the time to meet, and one brief line, "I have news about Esdora!" The mention of Esdora had surprised her; she hadn't heard her stepsister's name in years, nor had she cared very much. She and Esdora had *never* connected, didn't *try* to connect, and probably never would. The other items, however, had really floored her, emphatically, painfully, metaphorically, and literally.

This forced her to look further back, remembering the dagger she had dropped six long years earlier in a place that was practically on the other side of forever; *64,280 light years away from here*. At the time she had been compelled by emergent factors to leave without retrieving it. Upon seeing the dagger that morning, at first, she had doubted. A frantic thought, her hasty summons from elsewhere, had caused the dagger sheathes that found their second home on her upper arms to crackle frantically in response as they materialized, one empty, the other . . . she emptied, pulling her other dagger from the sheath then holding them near each other, feeling the mystic affinity, the natural pull of weapons cast on the same forge by her uncle's hand. From the day he had given them to her she had felt their bond, and the spell between them was an old soothing music that she knew by heart. Having them together again renewed a sweetness in her mind that bore a powerful satisfaction.

But the amulet had held and released a hidden power that made her shudder even now hours later. After placing her daggers in their sheaths on her upper arms and banishing them again to a place of hidden presence, she had re-directed her attention to examining the silk bag. Thoughtlessly, she had then turned it upside down on her palm, forgetting everything she had learned concerning the unknown and the unseen. Her recent delight in having her dagger back had inclined her to be unguarded. When the amulet had fallen from the bag and touched her hand, reality had forced itself back upon her with a searing reminder. Looking at the amulet on her palm, she saw patterns on the central disk that looked like consuming fire. Indeed, she had been suddenly overcome with an unavoidable sense of conflict and danger. As she continued to look, the gems embedded around the edge of the face had begun to glow as if they were portals to the flame. It was at this moment that the amulet's hidden trap exploded. Images of power etched into permanence in her reeling mind, and she had fallen to the floor, unable to control her body. A phrase, "A future too dire" pounded like a heartbeat through the corridors of her fading consciousness. When she had awoken, it was already late, and she had had to rush to make the meeting at the pizzeria. She had cast a powerful ward around the amulet so that it couldn't touch her and thrust it back in the bag. Her hands trembling, she had opened a portal and fumbled her way to Earth and into the darkening evening.

Monica, standing to her left, placed a napkin and then the glass of lemonade on the table, saying something about the weather or maybe an upcoming parade.

But Alystra didn't hear Monica's statement. Something had broken through her dome of awareness and she jumped up to her right. Turning fiercely and summoning both of her daggers directly into her hands, she struck an aggressive stance in Monica's direction.

Monica looked at Alystra and screamed, stepping back quickly into a man who had just appeared behind her.

Monica was further startled, but Alystra was frantic. How had this man appeared, so suddenly and so close! Moreover, her mind cried, what is wrong with you! Why didn't you set a barrier around the table or the room? Awareness is never enough! Why are you being so careless? But she also wondered if she was being careless. She threw up a quick defense that was wavering slightly because of her sudden confusion, but nearly impenetrable, nevertheless. She also cast a hasty probe at the stranger that she felt bounce off him and scatter. Meanwhile, he was trying to calm Monica who disengaged from him and ran to the back of the room.

The stranger turned calmly, showing no notice of the probe Alystra had just smashed against him. Although, when he saw the daggers she held with the persuasive end in his direction, his eyes widened slightly. He approached a step, and when he reached her newly established defensive ward, he paused, looking at her with eyes that emphasized the question, "Alystra, please, can we sit and talk without all of these demonstrations?"

"Who are you?" she demanded, she scanned the room for additional threats. She chided herself, now she was *finally* at full readiness.

The man turned his head and looked at her sideways. "I would have thought that by prefacing our meeting by returning your dagger you would have met me without so much . . ." He paused, seemingly at a loss for words.

Alystra's voice was dark, "I could bring myself to be grateful for your generous gesture, and I am here, in part, in *gratitude*, I am also curious about your motives. I must be clear that bringing me here feels like a trap."

The man shook his head. "No, no trap, but I was hoping that this could be a friendly meeting." He spread his arms. He looked back at the table. "Could we sit down? I didn't realize my arrival would startle you so much. As you can no doubt tell by now, I am no mage, but I have several," he paused, rolling his eyes, "actually, scores, in my employ. The one who sent me here, well I had no control over the when and where, now did I?"

Alystra nodded. Now she understood. This man had merely appeared as a result of someone else's conjuring. Doubtless the unseen mage was testing her from afar, gauging her reactions. She laughed inwardly, let the fool try, no mage could ever best her, but at least they could have their mocking fun at her expense. She inhaled deeply and shot a quick trace around the room to collect the remains of the secret mage's spell. She had the scent of his style, and she would know who he was, and she could, no, she *would* reward him for his cheek. She also sent a more insistent probe to evaluate the man, confirming that he was no mage, although he did have a magical device in his pocket. It, though a curiosity, was not a threat.

The man reached his hand out and touched Alystra's ward, and then looked at her again. "Alystra, the other guests here are now watching." He raised his eyebrows and glanced around the room and toward the back of the room where Monica was frantically talking to the staff in the kitchen. "And you might want to do something about *her*."

Alystra didn't care but glanced quickly around the room without raising her eyebrows in the least and saw that the two sports guys were looking at her, approvingly, and with increasing attention, eyebrows at various levels. She laughed and withdrew her ward. It didn't matter anymore; she had spread a vast network of awareness and protection around her that no one else could penetrate without her instant knowledge. She also reached into Monica's mind and removed all memory of the man's arrival. Nevertheless, Alystra had learned, or rather *re-learned*, that she needed to stay alert, no more slips, no more slips *ever*. How many times had she learned and re-learned this lesson? Even being what she was, perhaps the weakness of human nature was still within her. *Why, oh why, must we re-learn the same lessons?* She banished the daggers.

The man sat down in the chair across from her, placing his hat on the table between them. "You have questions." He motioned to the chair she had been sitting in, and she joined him at the table slowly. "In fact," he continued, smiling, "you have already asked one question that I need to answer."

She scowled at him for a moment but sat down anyway. "What question did I—" but he cut her off.

"You asked me who I am, remember?" He smiled at her mischievously. "Right after you chucked that magical probe at me." He pretended to cough into his hand. "I haven't been the attention of so much magical force in years." Then he laughed, his dark brown eyes sparkling. "Fortunately, since I am not a mage, it is easier to thwart and protect me from some forms of magical attention."

Alystra ignored his comment; it was an odd thing to say anyway. She growled, "I am glad to see that you, at least, are enjoying this." She was growing tired of his thinly veiled hints. "Go ahead and answer."

"My name is Bendahrin, Bendahrin Casthay." He watched her for a sign of any reaction, but she gave none, so he continued, "Perhaps you have heard of me? *Bendahrin, etsit Palestre combit pneatarin?*"

This generated the response he desired. Alystra almost jumped out of her chair again. She was jittery. "How do you?" She started to ask, but then she paused, knowing the answer, especially since he had just told her.

"Of course, I can speak Parin," he interrupted, ignoring her dangerous glare. "I was born and raised on Palestre. Will you please calm down? If you had taken some time to look around a bit when you were there you would have heard of me."

"I was busy."

"Oh, yes, of course you were. All that training, yes, yes. Magic, bathing in the river-song of the Entaparion, of course." He paused. "I am an archaeologist, researcher, once a teacher, now a private academic. I collect many things, of course, and in Palestre I have immense holdings that constitute one of the largest private collections in the city."

"Holdings? What do I care about your collection? How do you know me?"

He snorted. "Be reasonable. Apart from the fact that your adoption was common knowledge among anyone in the city who paid attention, as well as your, ah, dramatic departure, I told you." He cleared his throat and leaned toward her over the table as though confiding a secret, "I am a researcher. I know many things, and information about you is one of the more *curious*, uh, commodities that I collect. I know quite a bit about you, perhaps more than most." He said this with what seemed to be an attempt at a casual air.

Alystra smirked, realizing that he was trying to make himself feel important. She was certain that if he *really* knew her, he would also know that information about Alystra was knowledge to be feared, and wasting her time was to be feared more.

And yet she felt increasingly puzzled rather than threatened or indignant; she had encountered numerous fools who knew her on opposite sides of a battle, but being researched as a curiosity was uncomfortably intriguing. "Like what?" she asked at barely a whisper.

Bendahrin smiled a sad smile and replied, waving his hands expansively, "Born here, meaning, on this planet, in Nebraska, a regional name, in a small, nothing town. Normal childhood, although very little is known about that, of course, and then, when you were fourteen you went with some friends," he paused, then added, his smile turning wry, "to get pizza."

She winced visibly and bowed her head involuntarily at the mention of the pizza parlor and that event. She remembered that night all too perfectly. The day, the date, the very moment of time was etched onto her heart like an epitaph in marble; a bitter cold monolith standing in wicked testimony of an irredeemable and uncaring change that had been forced upon her. She glanced back at him viciously, but he licked his lips and continued so her mind wouldn't dwell there too long. "You know what happened, and I need not mention it, but the end result was that you were changed. You became the Issachon, a primal evil. Some say this change was marvelous, others speak of it only with dread."

Alystra looked up at him and scowled, half standing and clenching her fists. "Who speaks—" The room dimmed at her icy words; the gasps of the other patrons clearly audible. She sat down, regaining control. This was ridiculous. He wasn't saying anything that wasn't constantly hovering before her mind. She *was* the Issachon, thrust of evil, a primal force or being. And being her, she cared little what anyone said of her.

In order to advance the conversation into warmer climes, Bendahrin interrupted, "I am not here to tell you about your past, nor to remind you of the path of destruction you have left behind you." He let his eyes drop, and it seemed odd that he suddenly seemed to be fighting back tears. "I know that no one can understand your torment, and I believe, sincerely, that it isn't your fault." Although he wondered, *Why do I know that, or think that I know?* He dabbed his eyes with a napkin he picked up from the table. "Please believe me that I feel for you."

This was absurd. She waved her hand at him with disgust. "I don't need your pity—"

"Oh, I know, I know." He held up his hands. "Ever since the change your very nature has not allowed you that weakness. That was not my point anyway." And he wondered how he knew *that*. He was confused by a compulsion that gave him confidence and insight that seemed to be sourceless.

He looked around the room as if searching for the right words, but she interrupted, "Forget the history lesson, let's get to this point of *yours* that is so clearly evasive to *you*; tell me what you collect! Anything I might care about?"

"Aaahhh," he said. "Are you always so direct? I imagine that is part of the change too?" She started to move again angrily, so he continued quickly, "Many apologies, no, it is my way of speaking, but yes, let me get to the point. I have purchased or found, among other things, the works of the master, Themlia. I have a number of his pieces in my collection."

Alystra looked at him with newfound but suspect respect. At the very least, this grabbed her attention. "My uncle? You collect his work?" It had been too long since she had talked to anyone, in a friendly way, the conversation was tossing her.

"Why yes. How do you ever think that I came by your dagger? I have had it for over four years." His smile was smug but seemed to carry a certain weight.

"How did you get it? I dropped it in a fight on—"

"The Bridge of Bolest. How well I know!" He laughed, dangerously interrupting her again. "And I will tell you that it sank to the very bottom of the ocean." He watched for her look of amazement and was not surprised to not be disappointed. "Ah yes. And let me tell you, the salvage operation to retrieve it was the *least* of the problems on that war-torn world." He stopped and looked up, stroking his beard, as though calculating in his head, then he mused, "Yes, that one cost me an enormous amount for such a small piece." He breathed a serenade of a sigh. "But worth it." His eyes were far away. He, too, was struggling to keep his focus riveted to the conversation.

Alystra watched him for a moment, seeking to understand him and his motivations. At that moment, Monica stopped by and asked him if he wanted a drink, and he said that he would have the same as Alystra, gesturing at the lemonade she hadn't touched.

Alystra pressed him about the dagger. "If it cost you so much, then why did you give it back?"

"I wanted to earn your trust. I hoped that we could talk. There are other bits of news that you should know, and I hoped this would open the door." Even as he said the words, he wondered why he had this motivation.

"Then you shouldn't have given me that accursed amulet. My hand still hurts from where I touched it, and a message is burned into my mind!" She leaned forward and gripped him with her eyes. "I have killed better men than you for less than that!"

In fear that was clear and eminently appropriate, Bendahrin raised his hands defensively and gave her a startled look. "What amulet?" he demanded. "I, well, my, that mage, the one who transported me here, used the dagger to attach the note, but that is all I know of!" He looked around nervously. The man who was eating soup had started coughing, and Alystra noted that he had glanced their way.

"This," she cried and grabbed the silk bag from her inside pocket. Turning it upside down she dropped the contents on the table. "This bag was hanging from the handle of the dagger when I found it!"

He leaned forward. Looking at the amulet on the table, Bendahrin saw a line of ancient runes inscribed around the edge and the pattern on the central disk appeared as an epitaph on a tombstone. Indeed, he immediately felt as if a dark but urgent voice was chanting words of a familiar ancient language in his ear, matching the words on the amulet. He nodded to himself in sudden awareness, the language was *thayrsis*, which was odd, since he had studied that language and the ancient culture from which it had sprung during a year of study on Cathlest, a non-magic world. He couldn't catch all of the words, but they were an imperative, second singular, and spoke of fear and hope. Despite this, he couldn't place the artifact. "I did not send it. I am sorry. I don't recognize it." He looked up at her anxiously.

Alystra narrowed her eyes. He could be telling an outright lie, he could be as perplexed as he seemed; what was his game? How could she tell without penetrating his defenses and digging into his mind for the truth? She could break through, no question, but he must already know that! In which case he'd be a fool to try and trick her. She relaxed for a moment. She'd take him at face value. And if he was a fool, honest or otherwise, the clock was ticking on his very life. On the other hand, if he hadn't sent the amulet, there was yet another new threat out there that had not revealed itself.

When Monica arrived with *his* lemonade, he was still examining the amulet carefully, without touching it. He looked up and asked, "It hurt you when you touched it? What happened?"

She reached out with the silk bag and grabbed the amulet. "If you didn't send it, then it is not your business. I will attend to it when I have time."

"Ok," he said, "back to the point. I gave you the dagger to earn your trust, so that we could meet and so I could warn you of some developments that might threaten—"

But she cut him off with a mocking laugh. "There is nothing that can threaten me! If you know me as well as you say, you should know that as well! As the Issachon I have no rivals and no fears."

He nodded his head. "Yes, yes, as you feel best. I am sorry that I wasted your time." He paused, clearly gathering his strength, and finally spoke very quickly, "At home, in Palestre, the Visionaries have seen you. You have come up in a number of recent prophecies and people are concerned about your influence. New forces are at work, mysterious and of unknown origin, and there have been threats and hints of various plots to undermine the government, even threats against the Melarth's life." He quickly cast about for a thread to grasp. "And if this amulet hasn't been enough warning, I will tell you that Esdora has returned after being away for a few years and openly proclaimed herself as a supporter of . . ." He stuttered, as though the words were hard to pronounce. "She has allied herself with Strenaus."

Alystra clenched her fists and hissed through gritted teeth. "Strenaus! The Palestrean Anarchist? Of *course*, she would, that . . . Ahh! Father would never allow." She paused. "No wonder she has been gone! But wait!" She turned and focused on Bendahrin. "Does this mean . . . ?"

He nodded slowly. "Please understand that as your older step-sister, she is currently your *Palaradin*, your clan-leader. At least as long as your father is missing. This makes you aligned unless you can prove distinction. But it also makes you a target, whether you prove your loyalty or not. This is the primary information that I came to tell you."

"I may not be born of Palestre, but my adoption is legal, and she can't . . ." Alystra was about to make a defensive statement when she felt the first trembles against her magical defenses. Multiple attackers were forcing their way through at the outer edges, and as her defenses crumbled other attackers began appearing inside the defenses. She jumped up suddenly.

Bendahrin looked up at her, startled and he began, "What . . ." The surprise was evident on his face. The other patrons of the shop were watching by now.

She turned on him fiercely. "Can you fight?" she demanded. Then she remembered who she was speaking with. "Forget that! Can you defend yourself? We have twenty seconds, at most. Quickly!"

He stuttered, "I-I have my passive defense that my mages—"

"That won't help you. Here." She took him by the arm and looked him in the eyes. She sought to know him fully and nodded, to herself. Then she put her hand gently but firmly on his forehead. She drilled through all of his defenses in an instant and grabbed hold of his mind saying, "Now you must trust me, in fact," and she sneered, "you have no choice, you are now mine, your other defenses are gone. Your destiny and life have been written and measured out." He gave her a look of disbelief, and she gave him a mocking smile. She spoke a quick and powerful binding spell. "This will allow us to communicate and work together as a team. But," she added with a short laugh, "This bond can never be broken. You had better hope that your words and heart are true!"

He touched his head, gently feeling the place where her palm had touched him. His mouth hung slack as he realized how quickly she had pushed through the defenses that a hundred mages had built for decades. *Her power is amazing!* and he reeled at the thought. Little did he realize that he had only seen the tiniest part.

Then he realized that she had thrust a small weapon into his hand. And at an instant thought from her he realized how to use it. "You made this?" he asked, almost stupidly.

"Of course." And she laughed. "You thought that you knew me, like so many before. But you, alone, will live to use your happy new-found knowledge!" She turned her back saying, "Stay behind me."

At this, she pulled out her sword, materializing it from her private universe into the shared universe of matter. A masterpiece of Themlia's craft, Brahtenla, the sword of duskfire, it gleamed with a pulsating energy, beautiful and deadly. Sparks and flame ran along the blade and as she settled into a ready stance, Bendahrin recognized another reason why no one had ever been able to beat her in any contest. The force from the sword itself was a pounding energy, but the force that came from her was manic and savage, terrifying and compelling. It flowed out from her in every direction like pulsing waves. At this the other patrons were terrified but didn't have sufficient time to react.

Switching Brahtenla to her left hand, she swept her right hand in a gesture and spoke a word of command, "Sleep!" and immediately Bendahrin saw that the patrons of the small pizzeria had indeed fallen asleep at her command and from his connection to her he saw that she had covered them with an impenetrable shield of protection. Indeed, he realized by seeing into her mind, she had cast everyone the same protection for *kilometers* around them. Was this mercy? Compassion? Concern? Mercy coming from Alystra? How could it be?

"Yes," she said, quietly into his mind. "Now you *begin* to understand!"

For a moment there was utter silence save for the mental rumble created by the pulsing waves of power that he felt coming from Alystra. She sent one final mind probe through her circle of protection and in an instant seized a mental picture of everything within several kilometers. And then the wall to their right burst as though a mountain had crashed through. At the same moment something ripped the roof away. Guided by her mental command, he turned and fired . . .

Bendahrin woke and was instantly confused. Lying on his side, he saw that he was in an unfamiliar room. Through an open door he noted shelves on the left wall, and the right wall was a row of massive windows, force-field glass, he recognized immediately. Partly from the faint glow around the edges, but more from the view: deep space. He was on a ship in space and moving at a tremendous speed from the way the stars were creeping past.

He rolled onto his back and felt a fair measure of deep and well-deserved aches and pains; although now he was comfortable, relaxed, even unexpectedly serene. "I certainly shouldn't be this calm," he mused aloud, "after what I've seen." And yet he did feel calm, a deep pervading warmth that worked its way to his very soul. He put his hands behind his head and allowed his mind to flit back to the battle, no, not to the battle, back to *her!* It was all about Alystra, the powerful Issachon. An unholy confidence hit him, and he realized in that moment that for the rest of his life everything would *always* be all about her. As that realization smothered his mind, he sighed a deep sigh of contentment and self-directed scorn. Then the battle raged in his memory. He had been there, in the room, surrounded by the maelstrom, watching in disbelief as unspeakable forces exploded in their fury all around. Alystra had stood strong, calm, and impenetrable as the waves broke upon her.

Suddenly he sat up. Like a bursting levee, the memories flooded him with a startling and painful clarity, as if his mind had, in that moment, decided to wake up and re-visit the memories viciously as a punishment for daring to examine them so casually. He buried his face in his hands.

"Twelve krends." She had said directly to his cringing brain as the horrors burst through the wall. Alystra and Bendahrin were surrounded, and the attack was fierce; each krend prepared with a battery of spells and physical assaults that were aimed, no, *focused,* with a single purpose —to destroy Alystra. Bendahrin remembered the assault to his senses, sounds that would have smashed mountains, and blasting energies that would have melted them first. Memories of chaos. He had never before seen a krend, for which he was now glad, but he knew, remembered somehow, that *even one* had the power to level a city. Alystra had dispatched twelve with casual effort. And then he realized from seeing her mind that the krends were just the advance guard, a mere skirmish line that arrived ahead of the main attack. Testing her, feeding the mind behind the attack with intelligence as they died.

From Alystra's mind he also sensed the main wave that was already upon them. This attack, he remembered, revealed what he thought was Alystra's real power. In every direction he looked claws were slashing, teeth dripping in snarling maws, blades, maces, armor; an endless barrage of reckless destruction. The ground shook ferociously, and the air thundered with waves all in the midst of a bewildering whirlwind of spells and curses directed against her, against *her,* always . . . against . . . *her.*

Their assault was reckless but Alystra had fought rock solid in the middle of the furies as an immovable tower of strength. As the enemies raged, she was sometimes a woman, full of strength and motion, and next she became a figure of living flame, dispatching her enemies with a mere sweep of her arm. At other times she became an abyss of utter blackness that swallowed the mystic energies thrown against her or a being of pure light who consumed her enemies as quickly as they appeared. She flew, she twirled, at times she leapt high into the air and scattered destruction at several attackers at once, other times she paused and held the whole battle with her mind, as though fixed in time, only to unleash a devastating and detailed counterattack. Her sword, alive in her hand, moved with the fluid grace of a choreographed dance. Every motion was smooth, refined and executed with confidence. She dispatched the first wave of assailants with what seemed barely an effort, and then she laughed, during the lull before the next wave, as she broke through and learned the identity of the one who assailed her. "Mendrem!" she cried. "I now know you! Your time is coming!"

The battle continued. At times the assailants circled and watched, probing for a weakness or rushing heedlessly; they attempted deceptions and feints, illusions and subtle attacks. Often the attackers combined for a concentrated attack or lined up to attack one by one, by one, by one. And that is how they died, either in huge groups or one by one, by one. Wave after wave crashed against her like an endless storm, but a storm of mere vapor against a pillar of granite. Again, and again, he experienced and felt the incredible power of her mind; her control was adamant, and her defenses appeared impenetrable.

In the end, after what seemed to be wearying days to him, she had stood at the center of destruction that fanned out for blocks and blocks in every direction—rubble, flames, debris sprayed into the smoky distance. She turned to Bendahrin and retrieved the weapon she had given to him. Although Bendahrin was trembling and shaken, her voice, when she first spoke was casual and smooth, "You, Bendahrin, are the only person who has *ever* lived to see me like that. But now," she paused and added, almost coyly, "put this into the circling mix of your vague understanding." As he watched with his wavering and fatigued vision, he saw the circle of destruction rebuilding and he understood why she had captured a mental picture before the battle. Within minutes she had rebuilt every structure in the circle of destruction, banishing the broken remains of her enemies. The pizzeria had re-appeared around them and she was dropping money onto the table to pay for their drinks which still sat on the table untouched. His last memory, as he passed out from magical assault and mental exhaustion and felt himself lifted in her arms, was her voice crying, "Awake!" and the patrons of the shop beginning to stir.

Bendahrin pulled his trembling hands from his face. The horror of his memories before his tear-filled eyes was replaced with Alystra herself who had entered the room and sat looking at him passively.

"I see your mind," she said. "And your thoughts and memories. You must understand that I have never, not once in twelve years, ever sought a battle with anyone." Then she demurred, "For the first year that claim might be slightly ambivalent."

He stared at her for a moment, then cleared his throat and looked around the room. The bed he had woken up in was built into the wall at the smaller end of a tapering, irregular suite. He stood, shaking a bit from his memories. Alystra backed away through the door as he exited the smaller bed chamber to enter the outer room. She steadied him for the few steps over to a table. He sat and put his head in his hands.

"So that you know, you have been asleep for about three weeks as you recovered from the battle."

Bendahrin's thoughts were less awake than he, so that claim took a moment to sink in, then he looked at her in astonishment, even more confused. "How did you, how did I?"

"My ship has medical facilities, and," she paused, not wanting to waste time on irrelevant medical explanations, "I am human. I know what humans need; magic closed the gap. I can assure you that right now, you will be fine, but you will also *feel* better when you have had something to eat. What would you like?" she asked.

Bendahrin was bewildered and looked at her with eyes that made his mental state clear. "Excuse me," he mumbled, shaking his head to clear his mind. "What do you have?" Then he paused, looking around, "and, where are we?" he added.

"You may have whatever you want to eat. Just name it." She was still passive, but her body quivered with pent up emotion.

He looked up at her with a puzzled look and stammered, "Uh, maybe, ju . . . just some bread and juice, something simple. I am still quite shaken." So again, still shaken, he shook his head to clear it.

She walked behind him, placing her hand on his shoulder. At her touch, he felt a tingling warmth spread through his body from the point of her touch until he was filled and calmed and soothed. At the same time a platter appeared before him on the table with a loaf of bread, some butter and jam, cheese, fruit, and a large glass full of juice. "I suggest some protein."

"Thank you," he said, looking up into her face, "Where did you . . ."

"I haven't wasted my time with culinary magic, so I stole it," she cut him off, "but let it suffice in your mind that the damage caused by this act was and will be minimal." His mouth dropped open in awe. She walked to the other side of the table and sat facing him. "I'll even send the empty tray, plate and glass back to their owners if that eases your mind." She added with a hint of sarcasm. "As for your other question; we are on my ship, *Lentoris*, traveling with all speed to our next destination, near the edge of the galaxy. Even though you are here, my quest continues."

Bendahrin started eating, watching Alystra with a wary eye. He had heard numerous stories of her life and wondered now at the veracity of them. Clearly, they all fell short and missed the extent of her power almost without measure. But they also spoke of her as a base animal of destruction; a mindless ravaging terror of cruelty and ugliness. He smirked inwardly with no small hint of terror, wondering in retrospect how he had even dared to meet with her in the first place. And yet as he looked at her, apart from her audacious and disarming beauty, she seemed serene and untouched by any mark of evil; certainly, her demeanor was not that of an uncontrolled destroyer. Her beauty was *indeed* disarming. Strong and athletic, slender but not towering. Her every movement was a perfectly controlled act of grace and poise. Her face was pure and angelic, with eyes of depth, seasoned by guile, wise, alert and yet tranquil. Her smile was the very image of charm and her hair was straight and smooth, cascading onto her shoulders, a rich auburn color that framed her face tenderly, sometimes with wisps of it flying in her face. Nothing of her features spoke of her power, nor that she was a terrible and terrifying warrior without match. As he examined her, he wondered why anyone would ever attack her, so great was her grace and attraction. He found her all at once alluring and captivating; her magnetism was palpable, her femininity immanent and intense. And yet she also seemed aloof and distant, like a star, brightly visible yet infinitely distant.

He withdrew his gaze with difficulty and spoke the first words that came to his mind. "Thank you for saving my life. I . . . I don't know how . . . ever to repay you."

For a moment her expression softened. She smiled and said, gently and with no contempt, "You would not have been in any danger if you hadn't been with me. And certainly, there is no need to repay, the cost was merely the price of a cup of lemonade, and I created the coins from memory."

He chuckled in response. "Your perspective is remarkable. I would think that you would be angry, frustrated . . . hmmm, maybe vengeful over that attack. Certainly your, uh, reputation seems to support a tendency in that direction, and yet you say that the cost was so small."

If he had intended to connect with her, this was the wrong thing to say. Her hard exterior came back in a snap that seemed to reverberate through the room. Her control, in some measure, diminished in that moment. "A powerful but foolish mage was he who attacked me. Mendrem is his name, and I will deal with him in time. *His* cost was enormous that night. A sizable army like that, well trained and prepared. Sadly, too many are able to field such a force, and by doing so he has proven that he is powerful and wise. And yet, as you heard me mention during the battle, I will take care of him soon. He will be building his futile defenses even now. Actually," she continued as though reviewing a seasoned masterpiece from the hand of an esteemed colleague, "A skillful attack. They were good, yes, very good. A thousand attackers employed over 7,000 different spells and combinations of spells in that one attack. Really impressive!" She nodded with an expression of professional appreciation; wistfully angry, smothered in *disgusted* appreciation.

He put his drink on the table, and his mouth fell slack, hundreds of questions forming, but one popping out with expedience, "You counted all the spells?" He sliced some cheese and stacked the slices neatly on a small dish.

"Of course!" she said with a laugh. "I had to counter each, didn't I?" She leaned forward and rested her elbows on the table. "I count the spells as a form of amusement, and I have developed a useful magic computation and memory system, required for many tasks, like restoring the town around the pizzeria—that is a combination of memory and time-shifting. Also, I use this magical mental math to enhance the drive system on *Lentoris*, increasing its speed capability. For years, I have pursued a galaxy-wide investigation, so speed, and therefore this ship, are indispensable." She stopped with a look of impatient concentration on her face.

The she pointed at him. "But, back to the battle. You aren't a mage, so you couldn't really see. *Your* experience of the battle was mostly what you saw and heard, creatures and men, women, flashes of light and blasts of sound. And what you saw of me was more dictated by your preconceived notions of who I am than by what was really happening." She smirked. "You could sense the power of the battle, but you couldn't see what was really happening. Each spell had a specific purpose, a limited target, and a specific measure of power. The complexity and interaction of spells at times like that are bewildering, to be sure. Let me try and simplify it this way: Imagine that one attacker tries to blind me at the same time another attempts to crush me physically and another merely slashes with a sword that contains a *shevreth planorim*, a cleaving spirit. Those three attacks could interact in countless ways. A portion of the energy could break off and numb my arm so that another sword attack can be pressed home successfully." She laughed. "Or almost successfully. Ha!" She paused so he could assimilate what she had said, then continued, "As I said, they were very good, they combined spells and manifestations and physical attacks brilliantly. Over 300 spells succeeded and hit me," she added darkly, and the room trembled and cooled perceptibly.

"But you seemed unharmed the whole time. I . . . I never saw you hurt at all!" he responded in disbelief.

Her voice turned harsh and the light and air seemed to fully disappear from the room. His hearing seemed diminished as though she was speaking to him from across time and space, "You can't imagine the pain I endured. The searing agony and dissolution of my soul that I experienced seemed an ageless torment in those mere moments. Earlier I said that there was no cost, but that wasn't true. The battle is *always* mine, but I pay dearly. Mendrem has great reason to fear."

She looked at him fiercely, "And not him alone!"

She stood and raised her hand, calling her sword, Brahtenla, to herself, its bright blackness and the power of its presence immediately filled the room. Bendahrin wondered irrelevantly how its presence could make the room both darker and lighter at the same time. Alystra examined the blade in her hand closely for a moment before continuing, "You had a substantial magical protection around you."

Bendahrin nodded. "Yes, my defenses represented a huge expense and the handiwork of quite a number of magical professionals. I hired countless masters from the guild at one time or another."

Alsytra pointed Brahtenla at him and he leaned back in his chair, his eyes wide, "Wasted time and effort. They built that wall of protection around you to protect you against magical attacks in general, but it seems to me that there is more." She advanced on him slowly, and he wondered with growing fear what she was thinking. "They, and you, perhaps, sought to protect against me specifically. You have been planning for a long time to approach me. Given my reputation, that is the most extraordinary level of foolishness I have seen from anyone. So, I have *questions.*" Her voice turned sour and wormed its way painfully into his mind. "Why, really, did you come to meet me? Not so that you could warn me about my beloved sister. How did you get *on my ship* to place that note, and my dagger?"

Alystra was coming around the table slowly and Bendahrin rose unsteadily from his chair, his head turning left and right. He glanced toward the door. Alystra saw and snorted.

"I am thinking . . ." Her look was sinister, her eyes burning into his mind. "You dared the danger so that you could steal this." She held out Brahtenla to him, and her eyes flashed.

With nowhere to go he backed away from the table, holding his hands in front of him, trembling, "Alystra, no, I didn't, really, I—"

She cut him off with a swift stroke of the blade, its tip passing near his outstretched fingers. "You want my sword?" she cried and, in that moment, twirled, slashing at him, the passage of the blade was an arc of sputtering flame. And yet she halted its motion just short of cutting the skin on the side of his neck.

He glanced slightly to the side at the fearsome blade, feeling the heat and cold, and a clammy deadness spread through his face. In that moment he sensed vividly the reality, the nature, of the blade, and he became more terrified than ever before in his life, knowing that the end of his life was a flick of the wrist away. The blade held a deadly power, a frightening and baneful will. It was barely controllable, an insatiable thirst. In that moment he glanced toward Alystra and saw in her eyes the strength that controlled the blade as she held it with an iron grip in her gentle hand. He also knew that she was somehow shielding him, even now, from the full measure of its dire presence.

She drew the blade back from his neck, whisked it behind her, and turned, dropping it on the table. He relaxed a moment and took a relieved step toward the table, but in that moment, she turned and grabbed him, pushing him against the wall, her arm firmly against his chest. She closed in on him and held him, her face mere inches from his. Looking into her eyes he felt once again her powerful presence. She seemed to surround him and envelope him. Being so near to her was breathtaking in a mixed way, both intoxicating and suffocating. Her touch filled him with a penetrating warmth and a sudden desire, but then he tried to avert his gaze. She reached into his mind and forced him to look in her eyes.

Then she spoke and it was a melody in his mind. "I broke through your paltry defenses to save your life, but I had to do something to you, something evil enough so that I could break through quickly and without hurting you. I make no apology for what I did," she paused, looking into his eyes, searching, "but you will forever be mine, our minds linked, your mind and soul will never escape my darkness." She winced and looked elated. "And worse," she finished.

Looking into her eyes he felt something new, something deeper and more powerful yet. He opened his mouth to speak, but she continued. "This will be a permanent bond between us, and a permanent mantle of protection over you. You will not need your army of mages anymore. But now you are mine." She pushed away and walked back to the table.

Bendahrin watched as she walked away and her words hung in his mind, "But now you are mine," seemed bad enough, but "my slave, darkness . . . and worse," wore the mantle of ominous finality. What would it mean for him to be linked permanently to a person who was known throughout the universe as a person of unspeakable evil? On the other hand, if she chose to protect him, he was probably about as safe as he could be. He walked toward the table, suddenly realizing that he was unsteady, and his heart was pounding in his ears. He wasn't sure what made his heart race more feverishly, being so close to death, or being so close to her. His mind dropped at his mental feet an even more conflicted thought, *what if those two are the same thing?*

She was already sitting at the table, smirking at him and enjoying his thoughts when he finally found his way to his chair. He sat down and looked carefully, but warily, at the sword on the table. Although it no longer flashed with fire and sparks, it still emanated a searing cold feeling of malice and power, and oddly, a purposeful joy. He leaned more closely to examine the ornate hilt, and Alystra held out her hand to stop him. "Don't."

"Yes, yes," he said, "don't touch it, I know. All of Themlia's weapons are attuned to their owner. And this sword," he looked up at her with stinging, teary eyes, "I have learned to fear."

"Let me guess," she said, with a half-friendly sneer, "you have some device that you think will allow you to pick it up, or enshroud it long enough for you to transport it home?" His fear swelled but he scowled, confused, but nodded. She shook her head and stood, raising her hand. The sword leapt from the table to her hand and she de-materialized it. "Bendahrin, you and the rest of the universe have a lot to learn about me. The arrogant presumption that you had, thinking that you could take my sword is the same as those who think they can defeat me in battle. That is why I have had little peace for a decade." She came near to him again, and he felt her presence more powerfully than before. "I kept you alive because you are the first person who has taken any interest in me for the past decade for a reason other than trying to kill me." Rolling her eyes, she chuckled. "Although wanting to steal Brahtenla isn't much better." She locked his gaze once again, but this time there was a different longing that he found there. Her next words came out under painful strain as though birthed from an impossible womb, "Bendahrin, what I really need is a friend . . ." The words hung in darkness, and she sat down again, her strength and energy ebbed. She paused and a moment of pain flashed across her eyes. "Do you know what it means to be lonely?"

He sat up straighter and stammered, "Well, yes, I suppose I've—"

"No," she snapped. "If you only *suppose* then you don't know true loneliness." She leaned toward him, and for a moment he thought that tears had begun to form in her eyes. "In a moment, in a single evening, in the blink of an eye, I was cut off from all my friends, from everyone I knew. Suddenly, instead of being a cherished member of my family, I was hated, rejected, and cast adrift. The pain of it has been an endless ache, an ever-present torment, and I have known that there was no hope, no joy to be found. I couldn't go back and feared to press on. I have passed through fear and unto anger and beyond despair, and even wished to die. And it wasn't only that I was cut off. As day passed to day, and weeks became months, I felt as though the person of value I had been would be utterly forgotten by those I had loved and the only echo that would remain was the passing rumor of my evil. So now I am the eternally unwelcome guest, with no hope of redemption. Forever accused and hated, forever cursed and unwanted.

"But you!" And she gave him an expression of utter perplexity. "Even under the wrong motivation, you are the only one, now, who has stood by me. There is something utterly *absurdly* audacious in your willingness to stand with me; you are utterly absurdly weak, no, *powerless*. But I thank you! You have lifted the corner of the page of what I thought was to be an endless burden of solitude."

Bendahrin wasn't sure what to do with these intimations. His normal reaction would have been to accept her gratitude and offer his continued support, but he did not want to come across the wrong way. Fortunately for him, Alystra was not able to dwell on relationships or gratitude.

Then she nodded slowly. "Yet, I think I can answer one of my questions. I assume that one mage from your platoons of mages placed the dagger and note in the engine room of my ship?"

Bendahrin, stammered, "I, uh, I suppose that is, well yes. Although it all seems suddenly so vague." He touched his forehead. "Why do these memories seem so distant?"

"Most likely it is caused, in part, by my abrupt burning away of their presence and work. We will think of that later." She stood and touched him gently on the shoulder and finished, "But now, come, you may not feel it, but you need more rest." She left his room, and he felt a wave of fatigue crash upon him, or maybe it was the loss of her energetic presence. He reclined in his bed.

Sleep seized him quickly, *like being eaten by a krend*, his mind winked at him as he passed from consciousness. His dreams seemed vivid and grassy and included premonitions of purple skies, shoppers, and halls of snoring injustice. It was one of those dreams he knew he had never had before, repeating itself over and over to grind away at recollection and coat him with a warm blanket of forgetfulness.

What am I doing? Bendahrin sat up and looked around the small bedroom suite. *No! What am I doing* here? His mind was filled with wonder as he pondered these two diverging thoughts. He felt confused awe that he had somehow been swept up in a dark maelstrom and landed himself on a ship in space with Alystra, which had *not* been part of the plan. *What was my plan? Why can't I remember?* Being with her was sufficiently terrifying, but he was also perplexed at what had transpired. *How had his happened?* Looking back, he realized, for the first time, that he had arranged to have himself transferred to Alystra's planet for a meeting with her, having made no plans for how he would return. If she hadn't taken him away, he would have been stranded. *Now,* that's *a strange providence.* Providence or not, he was confused and disoriented.

To his left was a washroom. Out of habit more than volition he stood and entered, deciding that thinking would proceed more smoothly during or after taking a shower. *The Issachon, the Destroyer. I am traveling with, well no, trapped with, a person who is a mythological legend of unspeakable evil.* His mind seemed to independently recoil from the attempt to consider his new reality. At the same time, he felt oddly comfortable, which, he assumed with fear, was something Alystra had done to him.

In his well-traveled method of organization, he thought through the three conspicuously meager groups of information about her with which he had to work. As he applied soap to its standard function, he shook his head at the first group. *I was there, on Palestre, when she lived there. Not that I had any interest in her magical studies, nor did I have contact with her. She was adopted by her father. I can't remember his name or anything else about her time there.* He shrugged and said out loud, "Until she destroyed half the city." Still, that wasn't much to go on.

He lined up the second group as the water rinsed him, faithfully and with no fuss. *Plenty of rumors. Destroyed planets and obliterated magical armies, wiping out whatever got in her way.* He paused and thought about his recent experience. *She certainly has the power, but I can't reconcile the rumors with the person I met and with whom I talked.* Bendahrin knew that he was up against an inconsistency, but once again he was frustrated that even the rumors, he knew, were scant and lacking in detail. As an experienced researcher, he wondered about the source of those rumors.

He picked up a towel that was hung on a towel bar which proved its worth and served him well as he turned his mind to the third group. *I don't know enough about the ancient stories and writings. How does one learn about timeless evil. Where is the academic research?* He kicked himself for his lack of intellectual rigor as only an academically minded person can. But the kick must have jarred something loose in his thinking. *There are no archaeological artifacts, are there? Has the Issachon ever been a person, or, in a person before? This is a topic for someone in religious studies.* Even as he stepped out of the washroom, a thought hit him that he verbalized for no one in particular. "There are temples for the worship of the Issachon." *Do they worship the concept of the Issachon, or the woman who now is?*

Opening drawers built into the wall he found his own undergarments and socks, and the closet was filled with his clothes, from his home. *How did she get past my security?* In immediate retrospect, he realized how absurd the question was. *She is one of the most powerful mages, or beings, in the universe, and I don't have magical or even mechanical security equipment in my closet.*

One of his mother's morning admonitions stomped into his mind, *orient your world!* Normally, when he had time to do so, he would think through his day under the fistful of categories and questions she had drilled into his head. But sometimes, circumstances seize any need for planning and force the normal considerations down a narrow canyon. He summed up his day quickly, *Find Alystra, discover where we are going, get some food. Oh, and get the layout of the ship.* This final t ask was a s afety imperative f or a nyone traveling through space, in case of emergencies.

He exited the bedroom area of the suite through the door into the sitting room, where he glanced at the furnishings. *Basic and func-tional, a desk, couch, some chairs, bookshelves with books.* He crossed the room quickly and exited through the outer door.

He found himself at the corner of two halls. He turned to his left and felt a painful mental fear from a wall of sudden disquiet. Approaching anyway, he saw that the wall was ancient stone carved with runes and intricate patterns that moved and changed, faded and glowed. He examined the characters to see if they matched any language or characters he knew or had ever seen. The longer he looked, the more mesmerizing were the coruscating patterns and shifting characters. He had flashes of awareness and recognition, and the best that he could conclude was that the words were a transliteration from one language to the language of magic. It was as though the wall were a dynamic spell book. He grew increasingly confident that he could speak some of the words, even though they would have no effect. At the same time, he had a growing sense of danger, so he backed off and turned away, ancient words tumbling through his mind. He shook his head to clear his thoughts, *I suppose that I should expect to find something magical and frightening on the Destroyer's ship.* He shuddered and turned back to walk along the other hall.

The floors were plush and the walls were all of a deep wood polished to a shine. The first door he passed on his right was stainless-steel, with a window. Through it he saw an immaculate medical examination room with countless drawers, sink, refrigeration, and the ubiquitous examination table and bed. He noticed a lingering hint of iodine. He had a terrible conviction that sad but necessary suffering had happened behind the clean and shiny door through which he gazed. He scowled. *How would I know that? A premonition or a memory?*

Continuing up the hall he passed two doors on the left leading into a library and sitting room. The walls were covered with shelves containing thousands of books. He scanned the shelves with envy, for as a collector of antiquities he recognized the condition and character of the collection, many obviously ancient, rare, or unique. *Wow! What a collection!* He also noticed, with a chuckle, that some of the books were cheap, trashy novels, and then noticed further, with a wince, that others were surrounded by auras of darkness, light, color, or moving shapes. One series of books was engulfed in flames, although the flames never burned any of the other books, nor the shelves. Curiosity seized him, and he reached out to touch the silver handle on the door; but as he drew near, he heard a gentle whispering of voices, beckoning and repelling, saying that the room contained glory and danger. But one voice rose above the rest and told him that this was not his time. The trashy novels didn't whisper to his mind in any fashion.

He drew back, and the whispering faded, then ceased, but his longing continued. He thought he knew for certain that his future and destiny would be wrapped up in tasting the delicacies of that room—or maybe that was just what the whispers wanted him to think.

Moving on, he passed a luxurious lounge on the right with tall windows full of moving stars. *Moving? If the stars appear to be in motion, we must be going somewhere at a tremendous speed.* He reached a T and noted an airlock with emergency equipment to the right. *Always nice to know where to go to get out.* He turned and followed the hall to the left. Three doors were on the left wall, but the entire right side was open, leading down three steps into what he saw was the forward observation room. Twenty feet across and hemispherical in shape, the whole front of the room was a curved sheet of force-field glass twelve feet tall. Off to the left was a console of holo-displays and controls that Bendahrin guessed was a pared down version of the bridge controls. The room contained a battlefield of comfortable chairs and tables, but what caught his attention was the black dome in the middle of the room, where the furniture had been pushed back. He had found Alystra.

The dome was about seven feet in height and had the appearance of an enormous soap bubble, except that the surface was semi-transparent black and dark gray, which moved in deliberate patterns over the surface. The interior of the dome was filled with dark gray clouds that matched the surface in movement and through the clouds he caught glimpses of Alystra standing in the center. Her feet were shoulder width apart, knees slightly bent, and her sword was in her hands extended in front of her. Bendahrin walked cautiously to the front of the dome and saw that the tip of the sword had just barely broken the surface of the bubble. From that point of contact, a thin stream of light flowed back over the dome until it reached the top where it shot straight back, across the hall and disappeared through an open door, where the stream of light terminated in a complicated computer console with a crystal memory drive that gave off a faint, pinkish glow.

He approached the bubble and the dark patterns coalesced toward him in a pattern that looked eerily akin to a huge eye. He gasped and recoiled two steps. For a moment he sensed that the ship had slowed slightly, and then his mind was slammed with an series of images, a complete visual tour of the ship. He felt Alystra push him back, gently and firmly, turning him toward the back of the ship, and then a most definite impact as though he had been kicked in the butt, accompanied by a sinister chuckle echoing in his mind.

Taking the hint, he turned and walked toward the galley, going back the way he had come so as to avoid the stream passing off the back of the dome. The galley was fully stocked and had enough canned, refrigerated, and frozen food to last him for months. The massive provisioning seemed ominous, but Bendahrin could do nothing to change his situation. Alystra had collected a variety of foods from all over the galaxy, with especial emphasis on foods from her own home on Earth or his home on Palestre. Bendahrin was unable to read many of the labels, but, having been raised on Palestre, the center of a huge galactic government, he was experienced at pulling together meals from diverse foods using nothing but the pictures. He was mildly dismayed at the lack of fresh produce.

He prepared himself something simple, which he ate slowly at the counter in the galley. He quickly discovered that the random spice he had chosen was far too strong for the random meat he had found, but he enjoyed the meal anyway. As he ate, he pondered his situation, wondering if he should be fearful or expectant. He mulled over in his head the various stories he had heard of Alystra, always distant, always ominous, and always rumors. There were never any close-in eyewitness reports, just reflections on shadows of events. He gave himself a mental note to ask her how everyone knew about her when there were no survivors; then he remembered the mage who had so recently attacked her—he had survived.

He thought back on his recent first contact with her. He could recall images of the battle, he could remember that they had discussed something, but the dialogue had gaps. He closed his eyes and concentrated on her and their meeting; and although he knew there must have been preparations for his trip to meet her, and a purpose, his mind gave him nothing. As though years of appointments had been removed from the calendar of his mind at the end, eradicating any evidence that they had ever been written on the page; he could remember nothing leading up to his meeting with Alystra at the pizzeria.

He remembered her accusation that he had approached her only to try to steal her sword. That line of thinking made him tremble with fear, but no memories or thoughts concerning his plan to do so came to his mind. At the same time, he couldn't remember anything concerning his plans to meet with her. He couldn't even remember the mage who transported him to her. He wondered if he had been used or betrayed, and Alystra's accusation about her sword seemed closer to the mark than ever before. He suddenly felt small and vulnerable to unknown forces surrounding him. At the same time, he carried a new confidence and a strange peace under her protection. He let the thoughts tumble in his mind for a few moments before concluding that he didn't have enough data to conclude anything.

He stood and placed his dishes in the autowasher and turned to explore the remainder of the ship, even though he had already been given a complete mental map.

Three weeks later he was starting to feel that the months of supplies in the kitchen were, indeed, an ominous portent. He had scoured the ship many times, poking into every corner he could, although there were some rooms that were locked securely. He had eventually entered the library and did not receive the same warning as before, although the voices still whispered and mocked his destiny. He had borrowed a few books that he had enjoyed in the forward observation room where Alystra always stood unmoving. Alystra's taste in books was eclectic. The majority of the books were spellbooks, relic sources, or books *about* magic and magic theory. He didn't waste time considering looking at these, even the ones that appeared safe. Although his language studies had afforded him the ability and opportunity to transliterate several of the magical languages to others, those tasks were always rather tedious for him, since he stood as a watcher at the feast looking in, unable to taste the goodness. He had found some books on political theory from Alystra's own world that she had savaged with notations. She had an extensive collection of well-worn and clearly loved history books, also from her world, and Bendahrin had focused much of his reading on these. Her library also contained a spread of cheap romances that were largely untouched, and Bendahrin left them that way. Math of all levels and all of the major sciences were represented by heavy textbooks. Finally, there was a large section of books on various hobbies: woodworking, fashion, fishing, and gardening. There was a smattering of fiction. Bendahrin was intrigued by the mix.

The port observation lounge was bathed in vague light and filled with an array of diverse artifacts on display. Bendahrin ambled through the displays early in the second week and examined the collection. There were scrolls and daggers and pottery, fragments of parchment, and figurines of stone, bronze, and marble. Bendahrin knew enough that he looked and didn't touch, even though many of the displays were open. He was passing a rack of dark and stained weapons opposite a row of stones that were in steel cages when he was smitten with a stealthy realization: the cases and displays were designed not to keep observers out, but to keep the artifacts in.

Almost as though a switch had been thrown, the room came alive with noise and motion. Bendahrin felt a swarm of playfulness and power, malevolence and benign wisdom, but he held his fear firmly and continued to walk through the room. *Magical artifacts are fountainheads but rarely have a will*, he reminded himself with little and receding confidence. And yet foolishly, as he continued, the spell and his confidence grew until behold, he saw a silver goblet filled with blood that bubbled and foamed. The stench made him dizzy, and he moved away quickly, but the rising blood-steam began to form into the figure of a man who beckoned to him with a twisted finger. Bendahrin turned but took two steps back. He was no mage, but he knew that he could not merely flee if summoned. He also kept his eyes riveted on the floor because he also knew eye contact was a sure way to be taken in. He could see two glowing eyes that wavered through the mist in his peripheral vision.

"Oh, yes! What is your name?" The voice slid through the air on a putrid line and surrounded Bendahrin in a slightly red glow.

Bendahrin winced but spoke clearly and carefully, "What is your aspect?"

The voice seemed to chuckle but showed some irritation. "What is your name? Let me help you."

Bendahrin felt a powerful tug against his will, his eyes flickered upward slightly, but he maintained his resolve. The formula was simple enough, questions could fly back and forth, and eventually your average magical being would probably get bored and stop wasting time. But if Bendahrin answered a question first, that gave the creature power, with unknowable results. He clenched his fists and took a deep breath. "What is your aspect?"

The misty form changed colors and settled its motion. "Oh, come now." The voice was soothing. "You are on my master's ship. I know Alystra, and why would I harm one of her guests?" The man of mists stopped for a moment. Then he continued thoughtfully, "She is probably in a seeking pattern now and you are lonely. So, let's talk. What is your name?"

Bendahrin felt absorbed and woozy. The appeal seemed so sensible. This was Alystra's ship, after all. He suddenly felt an overpowering self-esteem at being Alystra's guest, indeed, her *protected* guest. Pride swept through him. No one else had ever been on Alystra's ship! He had fought beside her as a trusted companion. He remembered his great valor and sacrifice in the recent battle. His feelings grew fierce and confident.

But then, and yes, it had been weeks, so he could most certainly enjoy a fruitful conversation with a stimulating and mysterious character. He *had* been lonely for so long, and after all, his name was scarcely some staggering secret. He saw himself comfortable and content talking with the stranger from the goblet.

But somewhere from the depths of his youth he remembered a repeated and silly chant, *"With one you aren't done, and two you aren't through. But you will be free, when questions reach three."* It seemed somehow silly and unnecessary. He *was* lonely, and he *was* an important guest. The argument clicked back and forth like a metronome in his mind, but suddenly stopped and he raised his eyes to meet his adversary. There was a jolt in his mind of recognition and fear, danger scraping at his mind like claws of steel, but he held the gaze and said, "What is your aspect?"

At once the tension passed, and Bendahrin could think clearly. A stampede of euphoria and relief thundered through his mind, and he sighed most audibly.

The man spoke again with a feigned voice that dripped of undeserved offense. "You don't trust me." He bowed his head in shame in a way that was clearly false.

Bendahrin glanced at him sideways in increasing *distrust*, but his head bounced back up again as the misty man continued.

"But yes, I commend you! You are the third person *ever* who has been able to resist my question. My demand is widely acknowledged as irresistible, but you escaped." The vapors paused. "So, now that we can talk freely, tell me your name."

Bendahrin shook his head. "No," he said. "We will leave *my* name out of this. But you can tell me *your* name."

The vapors stood still and there was a laugh. "Oh, Bendahrin, you are obstinate! I already know your name."

Bendahrin felt a chill that made him dizzy.

"Yes! Your mind is an open stage where I can dance. You see, I *am* magical and rare, so very rare. And I have a will because I am not a magical artifact. I embody the heart and blood of Kel-Purim." Their eyes blazed, and Bendahrin felt his mind drifting like a lost spirit. "You will not be free for avoiding three questions or three thousand questions. And now!" The embodiment of the heart and blood of Kel-Purim raised a misty arm and pointed at Bendahrin with menace.

Bendahrin closed his eyes and cringed most visibly.

A moment passed. Many moments passed with arms linked like a string of paper dolls dancing and kicking, mocking him.

Bendahrin opened his eyes and looked up slowly to see a most deliberate sarcastic grin displayed on the face of the misty man. "What? Now, what!"

"Oh, now nothing. You escaped, as I said, but that's because Alystra told me that you would be here. She asked me to make sure nothing here consumed you, but I figured I would try to have a little fun." Bendahrin scowled fiercely, but Kel-Purim continued mockingly. "You can't see it, of course, being just a wee bit blind to magic, but Alystra has wrapped you up tight with a huge, brown, knobbly frosting of protection that even I can't penetrate or ignore. Alystra went so far as to make it an imperative."

The blood in the goblet spluttered, and Bendahrin was hit with another face full of nauseating stench.

"And yes, you can call me Kel-Purim. That's my name, but I use the whole heart and blood thing because that's all that's left. It also seems more heroic, don't you think?"

Bendahrin was not to be taken in despite being well frosted.

"So, I can just walk away, heart and blood of Kel-Purim?" Bendahrin was taking no chances.

"Oh yes, of course!" The misty form nodded lamentably. "But be careful about getting too near that brown statue over there. Bredouk, he really wants to turn you into a bubbling torch of tar." Bendahrin turned, startled, and in that moment, the misty form approached him. Bendahrin turned back to find himself face to face with the bloody form. Kel-Purim seized Bendahrin by the hand. He raised his other hand. "This, is for you." A brilliant, white key, small but dense, appeared and he lowered it into Bendahrin's firmly held hand. When it touched, the key turned solid for a moment and then dissolved as though melting into Bendahrin's palm.

Bendahrin cried out in equal measures of pain and astonishment and wrenched his hand away. "What did you do that for?" he yelled, backing up a step and looking at his hand. "Where did it go?"

"Oh, you can just stop that yelling forthwith," Kel-Purim said with sarcastic indignation, throwing his head back pompously. "It isn't enough that I give you a warning about a real-life threat, but then you get uppity when I give you gifts." He pouted most obviously.

Bendahrin dropped his head into his hand.

"I gave you the key because you need it. And it never *went* anywhere. But you will have it, and that is all that matters." Kel-Purim arched up and over in a rainbow of stench and returned to the goblet where the blood roiled endlessly.

Bendahrin walked away slowly after one final look. He paused uncertainly for a moment before the statue of Bredouk. The statue was brown as Kel-Purim had mentioned, carved from dark brown stone the color of rich river mud. Bredouk appeared like a gruesome entanglement of a wolfish man and an alligator with a long alligator tail, six curved arms with ball-like fists, standing erect as if ready to spar. The human-wolf face glared at Bendahrin, and as he looked he thought he heard a deep growl. He moved away quickly and took the first turn past a transplanted dolmen. He pondered for a moment how Alystra had moved such a massive artifact onto a small spacecraft. His winding path led him past more extraordinary and beautiful displays but eventually he exited to the hall. Turning for one last look, he vowed to steer clear of this curious menagerie in the future. He knew in his heart, and blood, that he would break that vow more than once.

–|–

As the weeks passed, Bendahrin grew fatigued. Although the library and cinema were filled with countless diversions, the passing days grew heavy. He was accustomed to being alone, his interests and projects generally required long periods of solitary study. Properly prepared, his eventual excursions in pursuit of artifacts throughout the galaxy left him surrounded by hired hands with little personal connection. Even his academic and professional contacts were largely superficial. His enforced solitude on *Lentoris* without any projects or people forced his mind into the realms of life reflection. *Why haven't I put out the effort to build deeper relations? Were those projects an escape? From what would I be escaping? What was driving me that enabled me to live so alone?* In the end, he came to the frustrating conclusion that he was merely being melancholy and full of self-pity. *The truth is that my past life is receding and I am in a lull before an unknown future.* He couldn't tell why we wasn't wondering more deeply about whether that receding past life should bother him more.

From that time on, he spent long hours reading in the front lounge or gazing at Alystra with a mixture of longing and frustration. He was perplexed by her steadfastness and endlessness as the weeks passed. He never saw her move, flinch, scratch, or change her position. Even the tip of her sword remained as a fixed point as though she and the universe were frozen in time and space. But no, indeed, they were not fixed. Bendahrin had found his way to the upper deck with the crew quarters empty, and the small but efficient control room for the ship. He noticed that the controls were being moved and adjusted, and at those times there were minute adjustments of course and speed, or sometimes drastic adjustments. Alystra was not moving, but she was far from inactive.

Ｔhe weeks passed and eventually Bendahrin woke on a random morning to find Alystra standing in his room, watching him. Ominous delight burst into his heart, and he wondered in a muddled, barely awake way if his feelings for her would always be so mixed. She watched him passively as he stretched and rubbed his eyes. Her voice was a mixture of disgust and melancholy. "I don't know or remember the feeling of fatigue, nor that comfortable feeling of rest, but you seem rested enough."

He blinked his eyes at the intense light coming in through the viewport. The ship was no longer in space but was inside an atmosphere of deep blue skies and brilliant clouds.

"How do you do it? Go without sleep." He stood up and faced her, realizing how tall she was. He was just a hair over six feet tall, and he was looking down only slightly to meet her eyes.

"I use a constant flow of magic to nourish and recuperate my body. One byproduct of this exercise is that I don't get tired." She paused and sighed. "And, since you are already preparing more questions, yes, this constant effort does surround me with a low-level aura of evil, yes, I use it to feed myself and to take care of all other normal functions, including fighting off disease. And, also, yes, part of the reason I do this is that I don't want to be sleeping when an attack comes." She paused again. "This might satisfy your insatiable curiosity. I once practiced adding oxygen to my blood and removing carbon dioxide. I can sustain this when needed for any length of time."

Bendahrin nodded, and decided to not ask if she could have magic give her actual rest. Instead, he nodded again, toward the window, and asked the obvious. "Where are we?"

"We are at my home. I transported us and the ship here, about forty-six thousand light years, a few minutes ago." He began to ask a question, but Alystra had already searched his mind. "I am pressed for time here, so let me answer *all* your questions without you asking. Yes, under normal circumstances transporting us and the ship such a huge distance would yield a massive outpouring of evil." She sighed, even to her this same explanation was tiresome. "A few years back I created a stable magical space door in orbit around this planet that allows me to merely create an opening at one end, and I can come here. Less evil, not quite as fast as a direct magical move, but far faster than normal travel. The planet is Mellisahria. My city has no name, but I call my tower Nuans." She stood up and approached him, placing her hands on his shoulders.

He felt a rampaging surge of energy pour into him so that he stood up all of a sudden. He felt strong and alert.

"You have other questions for me, and it is time to show you some answers, as many as you can comprehend, and then . . ." She strode out the door, and he followed.

They passed the sterile medical room, the whispering library, and the silent lounge. At the end of the hall Alystra turned right and passed through the open airlock into brilliant sunlight.

Bendahrin followed her without a thought until he had gone about six steps from the airlock. Looking down he realized that he was on a tapering walkway about two feet wide and forty feet long, but the ship was hovering two kilometers in the air near the top of a slender tower; the city at the tower's feet and the mighty river that bisected it and then cascaded over the edge of a cliff at the tower's base looked two dimensional from this height. Looking forward, across the walkway, he was facing the massive structure at the top of the tower, a smooth disk a few dozen feet tall. Scores of meters in diameter, the disk curved away from him on the right and left. He stopped for a moment, immediately glad that he had been energized by Alystra. At this height, the expected fear attempted to sweep over him, and without Alystra's preparation, he knew he would have swooned.

She had stopped at the other end of the walkway on a wide

pavilion with a railing on it.

He scowled and clenched his fists. He strode forward and was immediately hit by a powerful crosswind which the ship had blocked. He repositioned his back foot to compensate and pushed forward, leaning against the wind which gave him the feeling that he was actually leaning *into* the wind and over the side of the walkway. He forced himself to walk and not think, but he made it anyway, and in seconds he was standing next to Alystra on the broad marble pavilion.

"You are toughening up already," Alystra said with a grin of malice.

"And I feel far less fear than I should! Is that your doing?"

She grabbed his arm and started directing him across the pavilion to a pair of glass doors. "Of course. You need to be aware that my protection isn't just passive or defensive. I am also enabling you to do more and be more effective on your own." She paused at the doors and looked back across the pavilion toward the ship. "If you had fallen, I would have caught you any number of ways, but I wanted you to start getting comfortable with the fact that you can do more now."

"Do more? Do you have something specific in mind?"

Alystra threw her head back and laughed, pulling him toward the door. "Many, many things. And most of them you won't like at all!"

The entrance through which Alystra ushered Bendahrin was on the second floor at the widest part of the disk. "Welcome to Nuans, my home." Bendahrin didn't know what to expect in the home of the fearful destroyer, but if he had given it some thought, he might have guessed what he saw: the place was empty. A labyrinth of marble hallways, high ceilings, staircases, empty rooms. He passed room after room with no doors, no furnishings, nothing.

"I haven't had time to build more than a few things here." She paused and rubbed her upper lip with her index finger. She turned to him. "No, I haven't *taken* the time." She shrugged. "You'll see my three finished projects."

Bendahrin wondered why she was saying so much.

She led him down several halls, and he stared in increasing despair at the emptiness. Although she clearly had a destination in mind, he kept slowing to look down the empty passageways hoping to see any sign of warmth and creativity to break the monotony of the empty gray marble. He was eventually stopped by rampant awe when they turned a corner and he was smitten with the view of one room Alystra had finished—the library. It descended into the floor below and reached to the top of the floor above, and it was suspended as if floating in the midst of an enormous cavern of polished wood. Walls and doors and shelves and floors made entirely of glass and lit with thousands of floating lights. Bendahrin could see that the shelves of books numbered in the thousands and the tens of thousands and more and were arranged in a maze of excitement. He stood holding an expression of unguarded appreciation, and Alystra even paused with him for a moment and whispered in his ear, "And it isn't glass." He turned on her in utter consternation. "Yes," she continued, "crafted from diamond and a wonder to be seen." He turned back, and his eyes glowed from the reflected light. "But for us, for now, we need darkness. She pulled his hand and drew him away into a tunnel of unnatural dark with heavy wood doors at the end. Bendahrin wondered why her need for darkness seemed suddenly so natural to him.

The room they entered was impossible. There was no clue to its size or shape because everything was a uniform blackness; not the blackness of a cave, but a deeper darkness of utter non-reflectivity, as though the room and everything in it absorbed light. Alystra and Bendahrin appeared lit but the light reflected from them could hit the eye and nothing else. Even as he walked, he felt no contact of his feet on the floor as though the impact of his step was somehow drained. When Bendahrin spoke, his voice sounded flat and toneless, as though the energy was being drawn out of the air around him. "This is a curious room."

"Don't talk," Alystra whispered into his mind. "Just think to me and I will hear it but try to keep focused so that I don't hear all of your excess and stray thoughts." She stopped and turned toward him, not really looking at him, because she didn't really need to, but she did want him to focus on something other than the fact that she was walking in front. "This is a room of perfect neutral energy. Every surface and even the atmosphere in here is magically energy neutral. Any sound you make will dissipate into the room and will require the room time to settle. Even the warmth from our bodies and our movement against the air are a moving cataclysm. You will see." She pulled him forward a few steps, and the surface changed beneath his feet. She grabbed his hand and placed it on an invisible railing; he bent to look at the railing but there was nothing that he could see.

"Please stop thinking about how amazing it all is." She searched a pocket in her jacket and pulled out the pinkish crystal memory drive he had seen on the ship. She jammed the drive into an invisible slot and began working the controls of an invisible control panel when suddenly she disappeared.

Bendahrin gasped. At the same instant the room exploded in sudden light. A galaxy of stars appeared beneath him in a display that was brilliant to the eyes.

Alystra's thought-voice came to him again, *"This is a complete three-dimensional map of the galaxy. The reason that I have it in a neutral energy room is that the room is only one hundred meters across, which means that with the whole galaxy displayed, this is a one quintillionth scale map."* Bendahrin was confused, and Alystra could tell. *"Okay, so math is not your strength. The point is that one angstrom of distance in this room represents about one million kilometers in the galaxy map. A hair is the size of a planetary system. A floating piece of dust could be light years across. For the kind of accuracy I need, a stray water molecule drifting through the room wrecks the display, a gust of warmer air from our breath is a disaster to the display."* She continued to work the control panel. The room shifted, and their position changed. The galaxy shrank to a size that they could see without looking all around, a few meters across. A star began to pulse close to the galactic center. *"This is where we are now, about eighteen thousand light years from the center of the galaxy."* Another star began to blink, about 120 degrees away from the first, and slightly farther from the center. *"And this is your home on Palestre. It is about twenty-two thousand light years from the center. And here,"* a third star joined the others, another 120 degrees away and halfway from the center, *"is my childhood home; we call it Earth. It is about twenty-five thousand light years from the center."*

Bendahrin couldn't even begin to comprehend the scope of what he was seeing. Nevertheless, he thought he was able to identify an important mismatch. *"But Alystra, I don't see why you are so interested in astronomy. This doesn't seem to reflect who you are."*

"Have I done anything *that has matched your preconceptions of me?"* The room changed again. They appeared to be moving at an unimaginable rate toward Earth. Eventually, they were positioned so that the single planet appeared, hanging in the blackness. It was

now the size of a fist with a tiny moon in its company. The stars had receded into the distance so that it looked like a starry night in every direction.

"This is Earth as it was on that night," Alystra began, her voice carrying the weight of sorrow and triumph appropriate to the memory. "I was transformed by a spell of immense power that traveled from an unknown source."

Bendahrin groaned.

"After my year on Henreth, and my nine months in Palestre, I returned to Earth and began to trace the path of the spell." A blue dot shone brightly from the planet. "This is where it hit me, after it went through the planet."

She paused, and Bendahrin gazed in the direction he thought she must be. As always, he had questions but held them close as she continued on a reflective academic tangent.

"Magic is a perplexing medium. It can be utterly chaotic, or severely structured. In either case, it is intensely personal, triggered by desire, but works according to patterns and laws that are adamant. And it is doubly odd that this is true whether the mage uses spells that guide it or release it, or if the mage just wills the magic into action." She chuckled. *"The same spell used by two mages will have the same result based on the spell's structure, but different, in some measure, based on the mindset of the speaker. Spells of will derive their character and effect from the strength of the mage."*

Bendahrin remained silent and tried to control his rampaging questions. Most of what she was saying could be picked up from any number of basic books on magic theory; a few he had read years ago, which was normal for a resident of Palestre. As the Issachon, however, her perspective on magic would be unlike anyone else's, and he was pondering her description: *perplexing medium.*

"Ultimately, in most cases, we can study the results of a spell and learn its structure, its nature, something of the originating mage, and how to duplicate it or reverse it. For all of its inherent chaotic nature, when examined, it is like a mathematical function that you can work in both directions. In fact, because the use of magic leaves the flavor of the mage and how magic was used, it is even better than an equation. If we start with the result, say the number eight, we can't really know whether that was the result of adding six and two, subtracting three from eleven, or multiplying two times four, you can see the possibilities are endless. Magic, to continue the metaphor, always contains the entire equation in the result."

At this point, Bendahrin could sense a mixed flood of emotions from Alystra that swept against him like a soothing, abrasive storm. She was caught in a moment of awe and anger, wonder and worry, disgust and determination.

"Continuing further," she continued, *"the obstacle to figuring out the magical event that hit me is the size of the equation. To understand it, even at the most superficial level, I need to trace it back, find the source, the mage or mages who cast it, and anything else about the source."* At this, he felt nothing but frustration from her. She sighed. *"Watch!"*

A mesh of thousands of blue strands appeared around the planet before them and trailed off in a direction away from where they were standing. Twelve loosely connected semi spheres of yellow lines of increasing size followed the blue tail. *"The yellow is the search pattern I followed at first, starting on the opposite side of the planet from where it hit me and searching the path backwards. What you see here is the search for the first two years. Because the spell-path was broken and intermittent based on the spell's interactions with other magical influences and even spatial anomalies, I had to search in a pattern - each yellow line represents a path I followed. The required search pattern was growing in size exponentially the farther I traveled from the planet."*

There appeared a vivid blue ribbon that wove and spun through space, appearing and disappearing and winding off in the general direction of Alystra's search pattern. *"This is the path of the spell that I discovered in the first two years. I quickly realized that I was facing two insurmountable problems. First of all, the spell-path drifted and dissipated with the passage of time which would eventually render sensing it increasingly difficult if not impossible. Also, just as an area of projection increases as a square of distance, my search patterns were quickly growing so large that I would never be able to finish in any reasonable time. So, I left the search to learn how to move at far greater speed, sense the spell more acutely and at any distance, and to conquer time. It is fair to say that I discovered solutions to all of these in differing measures. As I showed you a few minutes ago, I can move myself, my ship, and you anywhere instantly. That is not preferable because it leaves a nasty mark of evil. But I was able to find a solution that allows me to search the path of the spell."*

Bendahrin's thoughts that followed had no coherence as he tried to make sense of the infinite, but yet he landed in the most obvious spot. *"How did you do that?"*

Alystra laughed most decidedly. *"You really want me to explain how I conquered The Five Paths of Infinity? But no, you have seen my solution. The sphere I was in, it is called a Strentrian Bubble, named after the location in which I was finally able to create it. When I am in there, I can locate myself at any point in time, and the membrane is hypersensitive at an intensity and distance that is an inverse of how thin the membrane is. I, uh, acquired a ship that I was able to enhance to the speeds I needed and now that I am able to sense the spell at a distance of about two parsecs, I can trace the spell for enormous distances. I am still restricted by the formidable top speed of my ship, which is unleashed by the irreplaceable mathematical settings in the ship's drive. For that reason,* Lentoris *is utterly precious — a different ship would take years to program to match her capabilities. The only remaining limit is the volume of data that I can collect."*

She narrowed her eyes in a moment of concentration. *"Odd, I haven't thought of this recently, but I do know about a faster ship out there."*

She stopped for a moment, and Bendahrin nodded a vague comprehension lost in the complex math. Although he had a vague understanding of the size of a galaxy, he couldn't really grasp the scope of this adventure he had joined. Alystra didn't keep him in suspense. The galaxy zoomed out until the center half of it filled the enormous room again. *"Forget about the magic and technology and junior high math. Here is what I have found."* Against the background of the galactic panorama spread out before them in all directions, tens of thousands of yellow lines appeared with the accompanying blue ribbon. The work of the first two years surrounding the space around Earth was clear. From that point spread a tube of yellow search patterns that curved through tens of thousands of light years in a cornucopia of webbed lines chasing the elusive, blue ribbon. Although the path of the spell had headed out toward the galaxy rim at first, it had curved through an enormous arc and had passed between the location of Earth and the center of the galaxy.

Bendahrin followed the enormous pattern with his eyes and although he was not able to grasp the scope of the size, his experience with research gave him the ability to see the years of painstaking dedication that had yielded what he was viewing. He turned to look at Alystra in another of his moments of awe, but before he could think of an actual comment, the view had expanded until the whole galaxy filled the room again, and then he saw it. A fifteen-thousand light year arc of blue swept along the edge of the galactic rim and then shot off into the blackness away from the plain of the galaxy.

"I found this by accident a few years back, and I have traced it from time to time since then. The section we just completed is here." A section of the blue ribbon started to blink, and as it did, the view zoomed in so that the blue ribbon spread out before them. *"This represents about five thousand, two hundred light years of travel, which we completed in four weeks. In case you are wondering, I can't track the spell at the ship's fastest speed at all times, turns and obstacles take time."*

The back of Bendahrin's neck tingled in a way normally preceding a storm or massive cataclysm. Despite her fierce stonelike exterior, Bendahrin could see the signs of anger in the young woman before him. He wondered how being timeless affected patience, and he realized that even eternity needs to be endured a moment at a time. He reflected on the images of the enormous efforts he had seen, but the paths were disconnected and there seemed to be more ends than connections. He felt the weight of the task. Alystra's search to this point was incredible, likely surpassing the exploratory efforts of all of the rest of history, at least for a single person, but the universe was immense on a factor that even she had to chip away a piece at a time. His first impulse was to comfort her and express his pity, but he sensed she would have none of that.

The picture zoomed again, and Alystra pointed to the ragged end of the ribbon pointing out into the blackness. *"That is where we are going next."* They glared and stared at the faint blue against the lake of black for moments of wonder and fear and frustration and determination.

"Take my hand," Alystra said. He reached and found her in the blindness of neutral space. And they stood in a pavilion in the midst of a garden that circled around the top of the library. The sunlight was bright, pouring through a massive glass dome. Alystra turned to him and said in a whisper that barely contained the fierce anger, "Sometimes, to contain the evil, I hold it inside to release it in a controlled fashion. Eventually, it must be manifested." She scowled at the universe. "Make yourself at home. I will return." And she was gone.

–|–

There is an equation or formula where Goodness and Truth react, and the result is Beauty. It happens most naturally at the fingertips of musicians and painters and poets, where reflections of the deepest measure find expression and become alive in explosions of music and color and language. Take away the ultimate Goodness or pervert the Truth and expression becomes selfish and ugly, merely an inner expression; at best a haphazard mix of darkness or a cacophony of noise and cursing. Oh, the darkened mind yearns for beauty, but selfishness can never reach the heights. The universe, in contrast, lives this equation in endless ways, from the veins of a leaf to the dances of stars; beauty spreads across every tapestry, reaching into every corner, filling every space. It is bountiful and normal and requires no effort; fruit is what a fruit tree does.

There was a planet whose name was Beauty and life was everywhere. The sounds of the wind were a symphony, the colors and motion of flora and fauna were a painting in flux, and the voices of billions were raised in triumphant sonnets. For ages it grew and prospered and developed into a complex interlocking system in perfect balance. The perfection thrived in broad strokes and in minute detail.

But darkness expressed itself through hatred of beauty, and since it couldn't be conjoined, it refused order and rejected harmony; it must revel only in destruction. And so the moon, such an innocent spectator of the planet below, was thrown in violent hatred against its Mother, the sky was darkened by the surprised presence, and its passage was a tumult of flames. Its impact caused a shudder of such vehemence that the cry of death went up before the obliteration was complete. Alas, this was no mere accident of celestial mechanics. Although the planet broke in ways where tidal waves and earthquakes and volcanoes no longer have meaning because they fall so short, those death throes were nothing compared to the wrath.

The wrath came in a searing wave, the presence of darkness blotted out the sun. The rocks were licked up with searing power, the trees burst into ash, and the mountains flowed in streams of lava. But even the coming of wrath was no match for the coming of terror. It was a crushing presence that preceded the flames like a wave of stampeding insanity. Not one living mote was spared the sorrow of an exploding heart and annihilation was the only hope that any heart held. The Darkness swept over the tortured planet in paths of hate, leaving nothing but smoldering debris under its shadow.

In the end the planet was named Empty, or Void, or Despair and life was gone. The future of a billion songs was a destiny that was crushed, the culture and history of a million civilizations was a story aborted in the womb. Like any murder, it was the irredeemable expression of directed hate. It was perfect only in its senseless waste, but the Darkness also needs expression until it is finally, someday consumed by the light.

–|–

Bendahrin was examining a display of hundreds of different tiny flowers when Alystra returned. He heard a sickening crash and turned to see a figure of complete blackness kneeling on the paving stones nearby.

She was bent over on her hands, and she was breathing thickly, plumes of black mist pouring like torrents of steaming venom from her mouth. The paving stones were cracked and splintered beneath her, and the brittle sound of their continued breakage filled the air around her, which roiled in an attempt to escape proximity. Alystra's skin was thick and crusted and black as night. Bendahrin took a step toward her, but her voice boomed in his mind, *"Look away! Look away! Fool! And get behind me, or you will be destroyed."* She waved her arm and a chair appeared behind her, a few feet away.

Bendahrin felt a powerful yearning for death and yet refused to look. Hastening to sit in the chair with his back to Alystra, he felt the waves of terror and darkness pouring from her and yet he was somehow unafraid and untouched. How long he sat with his back to her, he could never know. But the twilight of the evening had appeared in the dome of the sky above the clear roof when he felt her hand on his shoulder. He glanced quickly at her hand to see that it had returned to normal, or at least, to what he thought was normal for someone who was human in part. He looked up and saw that her eyes were black and empty, dark orbs in a face of beauty. Her skin was painfully pale, but the color was returning, her hair was auburn again.

"My eyes will return last but eventually," she whispered. A single tear was weaving its way over the restored contour of her cheek. She knew his gaze in her mind and continued, "That is all I am able to express in the midst of the evil I have become." She looked directly at him and he flinched. "You know what I have done?" she asked, and he dropped his head and nodded. "This is why I must discover the source of the spell. I want . . ." and her voice stopped.

Bendahrin looked again to see that she had *been* stopped as if her breath had been removed.

"In my present state, I am unable to speak of hope."

As she continued to restore, they walked for a bit in the garden and talked. Her eyes returned.

Bendahrin noticed that the paving stones had been repaired as if they had never been damaged. At length, Alystra said she needed to do some research and suggested that he return to the ship as she hadn't prepared a place for him in the tower. She promised to wake him in the morning and walked in the direction of the library. He found his way to the open porch and crawled fearfully across the narrow path to the open airlock but felt at home when he arrived inside. He took food from the galley and another history book from the library to the front lounge and watched the sky and stars.

Bendahrin was soon lying on his bed in the ship. As he lay in the darkness, the windows of the tower shining outside the cabin window, he wondered who was more fatigued between him and Alystra. He knew that she didn't sleep, and yet her recent ordeal had both weakened her and made her wildly stronger. He thought about his home on Palestre and some projects he had left unfinished. That train of thought dropped him at a station where he pondered: what was he doing with her? What was she doing with *him?* She certainly didn't need him for this massive task of tracing the path of a spell. That made him wonder *why* she wanted him along for the ride, and that made him wonder if he should ask her to send him home. That thought gripped him with cold fear. For no reason that made any sense at all, he didn't want to leave her and didn't want to miss the adventure. As he drifted off to sleep, he thought about the future, and choices, and what he should do, in a swirl of sleepiness that left him with a fuzzy conclusion that hope depended on confidence that the future would align with expectations and desires, or something like that.

The glorious brilliance from the light of a new day was *not* streaming in the window, neither had Alystra come by to wake him. Bendahrin, therefore, woke with no assistance from the light or the Darkness. He sat up and gazed at the stars creeping by in the distance. Once again, they were on the move. He still had no concept of the size of the universe, but he imagined that if stars were moving across the window, they were "expressing traveling purpose," as his mother used to say. He thought that maybe he could ask Alystra about the ship's top speed.

He left his room and began to search through the ship. He circled the main deck level and didn't find her. When he passed the galley, he glanced in and noted that the shelves were filled again most ominously. Grabbing some fruit, he headed to the command deck. Alystra wasn't there, so he took the stairs to the bottom and found that the door was locked. Looking through the window he could see that the hall extended the length of the ship and, apart from a few lights, there was nothing to be seen. He had neither the desire nor the ability to force the door, so he moved on. Eventually, he found her in the one area of the ship he had never explored, the engine room where the ship's drive was housed.

She was seated at the massive control console, her eyes darting between three rectangles of light that were hovering in front of her, displaying rows and columns of numbers along with a few multicolored graphs. He watched her at this project for a while, wondering how she was communicating with the computer and periodically changing his attention by looking around the room or eating the fruit he had brought. To Bendahrin the engine room was nothing special. He had seen many before, and he wasn't particularly interested in technology. The room was a large cube, the height of two of the ship's floors. White walls, conduits, consoles with access panels, and, at the back, the shiny steel casings for the ship's drive system. As always, it was soundless.

Eventually Alystra stopped her work and turned to him, the hovering rectangles of light moved against the wall where they continued to display numbers.

"Is this what you needed to research?" Bendahrin asked as she stood and approached him.

"Certainly not." She scowled. "Whenever I get a chance, I add a couple thousand more decimals of precision to the formula or the base constant for the asymptotic drive." There was a beep behind her, and the rectangles of light disappeared. "Speed is everything, if I am ever going to finish mapping the remainder of the spell path."

Bendahrin took a bite from the fruit. "How do more numbers help the ship?"

"You and your math issues." Alystra stood up and walked toward the back of the room where a collection of complicated machinery was visible amidst pipes, conduits, and catwalks. From where she stood, it towered above her and descended below. She turned to a side wall and passed her hand over a small hole in the wall. "Incidentally, this is where your mage put my dagger." Then she turned to the machinery and gestured with her hand. "It's the asymptotic drive." Bendahrin nodded his head and she continued, "From the galaxy map, you have seen how far I need to go to find out what happened to me. The trail is long and my ability to search is always limited by speed."

Bendahrin, caught in the moment, interrupted dangerously, "Why don't you just . . . ?"

"Use magic?" Alystra finished, not even reading his mind in the wallowing obviousness. "Think, Bendahrin. I am the Issachon, so yes, I could trace the entire path in a moment, but imagine the scope of evil unleashed in such an act; an act that would, of necessity, span the entire galaxy, both in space *and* in time. How would that transform the galaxy? How would that transform me? Even now, I barely maintain the necessary balance at great personal expense.

"Anyway, to get past *your* interruption I will return to *your* question. Every asymptotic drive is unique, and the maximum velocity is an inverse function of a very complicated equation that controls the drive's proximity to the fixed singularity. At least, that is the way my drive works, other drives use proximity of multiple singularities, and even others use the function of impossibility angles, but that requires a theoretical baseline and projection points for the singularity. Cheaper but not so independent."

Bendahrin's eyes went wide, and he nodded. He had no idea how to respond, so, "Where did you learn this?" came out of his mouth.

She waved away his question. "I had to learn the math to program the drive to greater precision. But try this in that pathetic little mind of yours: Imagine that you are standing one meter from the wall. I ask you to step halfway to the wall, and let's pretend that stepping halfway increases my speed from one to two. And don't worry about the speed this represents. How far are you from the wall?"

"Half a meter."

"Right, or point five meters. Now take another step, halfway."

"Point two five meters." Bendahrin was confident of his math so far.

"Yes, and you can see that we have added another decimal place to the number that reflects the speed. But this reveals the problem with the asymptotic drive. Even you could probably do the calculations for the next few steps in your head, but eventually the number of digits in the equation gets so small, or so large, depending upon how you want to look at it, that it takes enormous levels of computation to produce the next small increment of resultant speed. Keep in mind, of course, that the actual equation of an asymptotic drive doesn't work this way. Each step of speed in your slow trip to the wall only represents a single additional digit of precision required. In a real asymptotic drive each 'step' of speed requires an exponential jump in precision. My drive requires about ten point zero one three *times* as many digits of precision for each step in speed. Without going into the details, I have one of the fastest ships in the galaxy because I have been entering levels of precision up to hundreds of trillions of digits. But that has taken me almost a decade to complete using my magical computation and memory enhancement, along with some custom-made interfaces with the ship's computer. That is why the ship is so important to me. It is worth more than everything else I have."

She stopped and looked around at the consoles and walls with a smile. "No, the data I have collected is even more important, but that data is stored in twenty locations throughout the galaxy. There is no easy way to backup asymptotic drive data remotely and no, I won't tell you why." She paused. "And no, there is no known or theoretical limit to the speed possible, the only limit is the amount of time you want to put in to enhancing the precision." She paused again. "Even you must know that calculating for asymptotic drives is a lucrative career path, yes?"

Bendahrin grinned and nodded his head. "Vaguely, yes. Palestre is a center of government and magic, not technology. So, I won't pretend that I understand, but it does seem like a lot of work." He looked around as if the walls were going to help him with remedial math. "So, what were you researching before?"

She turned toward the door. "My research was related to . . ." She stopped and almost instantly there was a tremor and the ship lurched, throwing Bendahrin to the floor. Alystra reached down, grabbed him, and in an even quicker instant they were on the ship's bridge.

"Impressive! They came out of nowhere," she cried, smiling but grim. Then, looking through the force-field glass that gave them a view around the ship of about 250 degrees. There was nothing to see, and she reached for the controls but stopped. "We have been overtaken by pirates of the B'Tark Stream. We need to act dumb. I can outrun their ship, but they have already transported three boarders."

Bendahrin was nervous, his face was ashen. "Are we in trouble?" He gasped.

Alystra glared at him in extravagant disbelief.

Meanwhile, he tried to remember all he could about the B'Tark Stream. He had heard as many horror stories about B'Tark pirates than he had heard regarding Alystra. This wasn't a surprise; they had been around longer. He knew that they used technology in amazing ways; in many ways they were able to duplicate what magic users could do. The rumors were that they were embedded with implants that allowed their teams to communicate and act as one. Their clothes were powerful computers that gave them control over energy and space. Hence, their ability to subvert other technologies for their own purposes was reported to be unmatched. As a rule, *most* people didn't even fight them because resistance regularly proved to be irrelevant.

Alystra was decidedly not most people. She waved her hand over the control panel, and it glowed faintly with an aura that spread in all directions. Bendahrin was about to ask how he could help when she grabbed him.

They appeared in the port observation lounge surrounded by Alystra's antiquities. He discovered that he had been dressed in a classy dinner jacket with tails even, holding a glass of brandy. "Stay here," she said, "and you will be safe. Pretend to look out the window, and if anyone comes, talk, stall—just bore them." He turned to look out the window, with Alystra's artifacts behind him. He was nervous, he knew of the B'Tark, and unlike Alystra, he *was* like most people, or, at least, felt that way.

Alystra had been tracking the location of the boarders and wanted to avoid them, so she turned invisible and ran from the room. Summoning her two daggers, Pehla and Teela, she seized them from their sheathes. Pehla she threw toward the back of the ship. In a streak it flashed down the hall and struck, impaled into the wall. She moved stealthily toward the front of the ship where she stabbed Teela into the wall at the opposite end of the hall. She sent a silent message to Kel-Purim in his chalice. Satisfied, she ran the remainder of the way to the forward lounge where she transformed, dressed in an expensive gown, her hair was full and beautiful, and in her hand, she held a wine glass, not too unlike the snifter Bendahrin held, *save* that hers was empty of wine rather than full of brandy. She stood in front of the window in the midst of the comfortable chairs, looking relaxed and wealthy. The attackers were, after all, pirates.

A moment later a man appeared behind her with a faint sound of displaced air. She started to say, as she turned, "Benny, I'd like another glass of . . ." But when she saw the intruder, she dropped the glass and gasped with surprise.

The man appeared as expected, like a high-tech soldier, black combat fatigues woven of strands of integrated circuits and energy transducers and covered with straps, pockets and weapons. The weapon he was holding was small but sinister and it was aimed at Alystra with threatening purpose. A woman appeared to his left and said a single word, "Finished," and the first man nodded.

"Where are your companions? We scanned your ship and know that there are five living beings on this ship, and none of them are animals."

Alystra had to stop for a moment to keep from laughing out loud. Bendahrin was, of course, in the port lounge, with dozens of other living entities, sort of, although only two were likely to be identified as such by anything other than magical means. The fifth was in the room at the back, next to Bendahrin's room. All of them were variously alive, and she chuckled inwardly at the thought of any of them as pets, especially Bendahrin.

"My husband went off to the galley for food, but who are you, and what do you want?" Alystra put on a voice that was as ditzy and sloshy as she could muster, given her natural impulse to just destroy them. At the same time, she was parsing their radio frequency and decrypting their linking codes. Magic had its advantages, but intelligence was the way to beat technology. She had to be careful, of course, so that they didn't damage the ship.

"We are soldiers of the B'Tark Stream and that is *your* last question. Where are the others?"

Alystra sashayed to a couch and reclined herself luxuriously. "Oh, as I said, my husband went after some food, I think." She continued to scan them aggressively, since she knew that their technology couldn't detect magic, which was an advantage that she had; magic could undermine, detect, hack, and interfere with technology in thousands of ways. Of course, one of the attackers could also be a mage; and if so, the advantage was more decidedly *all* hers.

The pirate who had spoken was clearly distracted by something he was hearing. The woman disappeared at about the time that Alystra had finished hacking their communications and had joined the stream of their data. She was immediately and temporarily fascinated by the sensation. Each of them could "see" what the others saw, and their visual perceptions were overlaid upon each other but slightly out of phase and with a slight color bias for each view.

These guys are loaded with great ideas! Alystra thought to herself. She marveled at the mental discipline and training required to use such an interface. She noticed that two of the borders were looking at the room next to Bendahrin's. Their communication came through as a multidirectional flow of shorthand concepts punctuated by keywords, rather than a typical language flow of distinct words and phrases. Again, Alystra was impressed with the prowess required to keep the thoughts linear and purposeful. Most of the time she had such a hard time with the jumble that came from Bendahrin's mind. She even had a stray idea that these pirates would be delightful allies and wondered what it would cost to recruit a team.

At the moment, however, she had to be careful not to show her hand because, after all, she could see that the one man was still looking at her directly. They were certain that there was someone in the room at the back of the ship, but the door couldn't be opened, and the wall was ominous and they were getting nervous. Their thoughts strayed to someone on their ship who could help—a mage—and aha! She caught a whiff of his name! Alystra filed it away and continued probing their technology, their suits, their built-in defenses.

As soon as she had penetrated their communications, she had cut off any external communication with their ship. At the same time, she had pushed her ship to top speed, a concern for the boarders since their ship was being left behind. Urgent calls were incoming, but the boarders, not hearing them and focused on taking the ship, were unaware; their time was running out faster than they knew. But that intelligence would also not be long in coming.

The view changed, and she saw that one of the pirates had transported herself to the control room. Upon arriving, she held out her hand and her suit flowed from her wrist and created a flat, black rectangle that she placed on the control panel. She watched for a moment and then the box disappeared, as though it had dissolved into the controls. Almost immediately, a small display appeared in the pirates' shared view. It looked like a simple program running to hack the computer controlling the ship. Alystra was again impressed by the simple power that allowed the pirates to blow through the security. If only they knew . . .

Alystra nodded as the other view changed. The third intruder had jumped to the engine room. At that moment the first man started talking to her, and she had a new appreciation of the advantage to having three independent yet linked minds at work.

"You must know that we are taking control of your ship. There is no point in putting up any resistance." Alystra could see that the third intruder, in the engine room, had created another square and placed it on the control panel there. After a few moments it disappeared, and a second small display appeared to the shared view she had hacked. Alystra wondered if she shouldn't investigate some of these tech fatigues in the future; not that she needed them, but gadgets always added that extra sense of wonder to any social occasion.

By this time, the crisis was moving to a conclusion quickly, and Alystra was having fun with the challenge of keeping up with all that she was seeing. Everything confirmed that her spell was working, so Alystra smiled at him for two reasons. "I am just sitting here."

The woman showed up in the forward lounge, and the communication between them centered on how the ship was secured.

Alystra's mind was racing at the flood of data. The two additional streams of data coming in from the black boxes had finished and one of the pirates thought a command to the ship's computer through the interface. It was an interesting combination of human language and simplified digital commands. Alystra took a guess at the intent and cast a sloppy but powerful spell that mixed with her earlier aura, the black boxes, her ship, their high-tech suits, and the pirate's minds. The ship seemed to slow, and the two pirates in the forward lounge with her nodded. She chuckled inwardly that even though they had a form of perfect secure communication they still allowed a little humanity to seep through; disciplined, but not disciplined enough.

At that moment, Alystra sensed that the other man had crossed the thread between Pehla and Teela, which would have alerted Kel-Purim. The view changed, and she could see Bendahrin slowly turning around, his face drawn and sweaty, but he was clearly trying to project confidence. Beneath the threshold of her concentration, she could hear him talking, and she knew her trap was working.

The three-way communication confirmed that the pirates had found Bendahrin, although they were still confused about the other three missing people. Bendahrin defended himself, vocally, and the pirate threatened him. The discussion went back and forth for a string of heated moments, and the woman suddenly appeared behind Bendahrin, in an attempt to subdue him.

Alystra almost laughed at seeing Bendahrin from the front and the back at the same time.

He struggled for a moment and then fell unconscious.

Alystra wondered for a moment if they had killed him, but she had heard the rumors of a B'Tark principle. "A live hostage is worth more than a dead corpse." Rather than trusting in the veracity of an adage, she tossed a quick probe to confirm his unconscious state.

The two pirates bent over Bendahrin and were about to lift him when a sudden twinge of fear hit them and they looked up.

The woman lept backward, her eyes wide, as a bloody cloud formed behind her partner. Before she could shout a warning or react, the cloud formed the vague shape of a man who reached out, or maybe the arm just grew, and stretched to touch the pirate from behind.

Kel-Purim struck and entered him.

Alystra was ready when the terror exploded in their minds.

The man in the room with her even looked in the direction of the port lounge, which made her think quite irrelevantly how amazing his situational awareness was such that he had so intuitively known the direction to his colleagues.

They cut the link to the man who Kel-Purim held, and their minds were released from the fear. She could hear their minds racing to a counterattack, so she removed the spell that was providing the fake data to their links, her deception having done the job. They quickly realized that they had been tricked and understood the serious nature of their situation; they had not taken control of this ship and their ship was far out of range.

Even so, the pirates fell back to their training, and their attack was simple, direct, and immediate.

Alystra saw herself doubled in their stream as the woman re-appeared. They put their weapons together, and Alystra sensed the final whiff of the intentions of their thoughts. Her spell was fast; their explosion was immediate.

6

The blast expanded in a ragged sphere from the source at about 320 meters per second. Alsytra's spell was faster, being instantaneous, but she was behind by the blink of an eye. In that time the destruction had spread about three meters, tearing a hole in the floor and ceiling and completely surrounding the two pirates in searing destruction. Alystra contained the blast in an impregnable spell of stopped time, and she was about to shift it outside when she realized that the man in the port lounge who had been captured by Kel-purim was gone, and the two other pirates had not been consumed, but rather had burned out their tech fatigues affecting their compatriots' escape; the chaotic, blasting release of energy from the explosion providing the necessary power that allowed them to send the other man the greater distance required. She held the moment for a while as she pondered this curious behavior. The explosion was an act of defiant sacrifice which she admired briefly with disgust. Then, inspired by their clever use of energy, Alystra, with a nod to the mysteries of alchemy, transmuted the remaining energy of the explosion into a gold coin in her pocket, a simple trick for a primal being. She walked from the room, leaving the two pirates hovering in time, and space, since they were suspended over the new hole in the floor. They could hang; she was more interested in Bendahrin.

As she strode down the short distance between the forward lounge and the port lounge, she changed her clothes and called to Pehla and Teela. The two daggers snapped into her hands with a sharp report, and she slipped them into the sheathes on her upper arms. She entered the port lounge and Kel-Purim greeted her with a triumphant grin. "Oh, yes! An exquisite ambush. Most exciting, and I haven't feasted on such a shock of fear in a long time. Did you get them?"

"One departed, but I assume you have that one."

"Oh, yes! I have nestled comfortably in his mind. My blood, his blood, what a mix. If he only knew what he carried, he might even be honored!" Kel-Purim said with a purr. "Do you have a strategy for me? Anything I should do?"

"Learn things," she said, and Kel-Purim smiled pridefully. Alsytra then asked, squatting next to Bendahrin. "Did they find out who I am?" Her ministrations to Bendahrin were effective immediately, and he sat up, looking dazed.

"Aha! Yes!" Kel-Purim said with enthusiasm. "Your boy did good, Alystra. Feisty! He kept that scoundrel occupied while I came out to take a look in answer to the alarm you set. He made up a good story, that one did, and it took two of them to take him down! And I was able to sneak up behind while . . ."

For a stretched moment Alystra looked almost patient. "And?" she said with a voice that was as flat and fetid as a surface of pond scum.

"Yes, see? You would never be able to get a job as a court jester," he said, with his arms crossed. "No, they didn't find out who you are. In fact, Rendall, who escaped, is even now explaining to the others on the ship that they never found out who the magic users were over here." He paused flamboyantly, stretching out his story, while Alystra sat in a metaphorical stew. Clearly Kel-Purim didn't get enough attention. "But that, of course, is because I was sneaky and hit him from behind in a careful ambush that I have had ready to use since before . . ."

"Enough!" Alystra passed from stew to anger with no metaphor attached. "We were just attacked. I don't have time for your typical tangents! Do you have anything useful for me, and no, you don't need me to clarify what I mean." She glared at him.

"Yes, well, you know," he said, pretending an air of nonchalance, "If my services don't satisfy you, you can always pour the blood back into the veins of its home and I can . . ."

Alystra sighed painfully, with obvious exasperation, and yet with a growing and smoldering hint of reluctant patience. "Stop baiting me. You know I can't do that. You owe me too much for rescuing you, and you remember the Selection *and* the Drought, they are both in abeyance. And besides, you don't fool me for a minute; you are in for the long game." She glanced at Bendahrin, who shook his head in confusion. "Your services are excellent, as you know, the veins can't receive you yet, as you also know, our work on *your* behalf is not done, which is your fault, and yes, I need to visit more often." She sighed. "But at the moment, what I need from you is some simple intelligence about our enemy."

Kel-Purim mocked her with a smile. "Ah, yes, oh, detailed One. Apology accepted." He snorted, and she fumed in return, partially for effect and partially because she *was* fuming. "And you are far powerful enough to get all of this intelligence on your own, if you really want to."

Alystra rolled her eyes.

"But," he continued, raising his hand, which made Bendahrin quail from the stench it threw off, "here it is: you were able to block their probes with the spurious data in your spell, which was all Rendall was able to take with him anyway. The memories of the interactions between you and they were largely inconsequential. Bendahrin seemed to capture your idea because he commented on his relationship with you in affectionate terms, and that was a delight to watch and muse over, so they think you are coupled and mated in your slippery and barely effective animalistic way. They did get some general data about the ship, energy readings, dimensions, and stuff of that kind. The visual data will make it easy enough for them to identify both you and Bendahrin. The focus of their attention, and even the current discussion that I am listening to is on Tored's Room and why the ship didn't explode. They were expecting to rush up and gather the other two from the wreckage. By now they realize that we have escaped, and they are concerned about getting their two stowaways back. Thus, endeth the salient information."

Alystra eyed him for a moment.

Bendahrin was both perplexed and in awe.

"Excellent," she said after a moment. "Keep an eye on him. Also, keep track of where they are going, and if there is anything that I need to hear, come and find me."

Alystra stood up and pulled Bendahrin after her. She walked through the collection, past Bredouk, who she patted on the rump, past the floating dolmen, toward the hall, and Bendahrin asked,

"What is Kel-Purim?"

"He is a very ancient creature that I discovered in a trap on an empty planet far from here. He was being punished, and I set him free, after a fashion. He carries a tremendous burden."

Bendahrin listened in part and felt confident that only some of what she said was true.

They arrived at the front lounge to find that the hole in the floor was completely healed, and the hole in the ceiling was almost fully repaired. Alsytra mentioned something vague about a spell and the ship healing itself and turned to the two pirates still suspended in time. She was about to release them when she turned to Bendahrin. "Do you realize that you have only been awake for about fifteen minutes? Would you like to get something to eat before we talk to these two?"

Bendahrin looked at her in wonder and then lifted his hand. "I have had something to eat." In his hand was the core of the fruit he had begun to eat what seemed now as so long ago. "What are you going to do? These men are pirates, and they should be turned over to the—"

Alystra laughed, with relish and malice. "Bendahrin, if I decide to turn them over to anyone, which I probably won't, that would be, for them, one of the safest things that could happen to them."

"But they attacked you!" Bendahrin could not have sounded more urgent. "Most people who attack you end up dead," he added without spreading any relish at all.

"True." She nodded, and Bendahrin thought that she winced as though truth caused pain. "But they didn't really attack *me*. They are pirates. They saw an independent and apparently unarmed and unguarded and helpless single ship and they did what pirates do. I am hardly in a position to judge them from some strict sense of morality. I was never in danger in even the slightest way, and," she paused and looked back to the pirates, "and I . . . may have reason to keep them alive, more than one reason if they can teach me about those curious computer clothes they wear, although I was gravely concerned about the ship."

"They're called combat fatigues. A person wearing them can do pretty much anything. Although countless military forces use them, they are a trademark of the B'Tark." He paused from the fashion distraction and returned to her concern about the ship. "What I fail to comprehend, I can see this is a pretty nice ship, to be sure, but considering you have endless wealth, power, and can go anywhere magically, and instantly, the ship doesn't seem all that important, really."

Alystra snapped, "No!" through gritted teeth. A wave of force blasted from her that threw Bendahrin a few yards backward to the floor where he was stopped by a large chair. "Weren't you listening?" The room grew hot as her impatience burned. "It isn't the ship, it's the drive! Programming the drive took years of effort. It is critical to the goal!"

She stopped for a moment and then shook her head, looking at Bendahrin lying on the floor against the chair, his arms outstretched protectively. His nose was bleeding from the impact, but he wasn't moving in his fear. She took a deep breath, and the room cooled. She walked to him slowly and grabbed his hand, raising him to his feet. He sat in the chair and summoned a cloth with ice.

Alystra squatted in front of him, first looking at him dispassionately for a minute, then, speaking dispassionately, "I am not able to apologize."

He nodded; his fear was passing.

"The years of effort required to program the drive is beyond price. No wealth can buy a ship like this because the drive is almost unique. With all the effort I have put into it, there is only one ship that has ever been built that is faster."

Bendahrin was still slightly dazed. "Okay, yes. The drive." He paused to touch his nose gently. "Okay, so where did you get this ship, then?" he asked as if his mouth were speaking for itself. Which, if he had been thinking about Alystra rather than his bloody nose, he might not have allowed his mouth to do so, all on its own, so to speak.

Alystra walked to the far side of the room and stretched out on a couch under the massive viewport. She waited until he had grabbed a chair and pulled it across the room to where she was, although not too near, she noticed. "Do you really want to hear this?" she queried him. "It is a most distasteful recollection."

"Can you summarize without all of the gory details?"

She raised her eyebrows. "Without the gore, there isn't much to tell, I'm afraid. But yes, I can summarize." She put her arms behind her head and looked up at the ceiling. "I was traveling to what I thought was a lead on my origins, but it was a trap. I was attacked, prevailed, and took the mage's ship, this ship, *Lentoris*. A fool name Krendt. I left him on a barren planet with no atmosphere, cursed with a thousand undying years. Fitting."

Bendahrin looked at her with cold fear edging to contempt and wondered how she could be so callous to the sufferings that she had chosen to inflict. As an abstraction he could conceive of her chosen punishment as just judgment for a person who got what he deserved. But his mind reeled as he considered the endless misery of a person forced to live without sustenance or even air to breathe on a planet that must be regularly frozen and scorched. Although he knew that even the best people are, by and large, selfish and uncaring, nothing in his experience could help him understand how she could feel so casual about inflicting such a horrendous existence upon anyone. Stupidly, and obviously without thinking, his mouth took off again in a horrible and disastrous tangent, "What a horrible . . . ! You . . . How could you . . . ?"

She sat up, looking at him fiercely, and her face was no longer amused, but angry and mocking. *Her* mouth spoke in contrast with perfect and steady deliberation. "You don't get it? You don't under-stand. But you will! Here, let me show you!" She stretched out her hand.

He screamed. His throat was scorching. He felt the world spin-ning; no, he was spinning, spinning, cycles, endless, endless cycles, cycles. His mind trying to focus . . . remembering was impossible, but yes, of course! No! Remembering was *unavoidable*! Wait! He cried halting; he had been here before, had always been here, joined to the pain. And a thousand times for each and every moment of a life that had been nothing but endless, remorseless, deliberate torment, the burning began, again and again, and yet again, each cell of his body burning! Not consumed, just burning. Flame and fire and fury filled every fiber of his existence. And the searing joined the searing knowledge, hopeless knowledge, hopeless endless certain-ty—a guarantee that the burning would continue forever added to the mocking despair that tore at his dejected mind; a broken mind, a tormented mind that reeled and writhed as the burning continued and continued and continued again and continued again and again for countless eons upon eons upon never-ending eons and he knew in his confident and relentless despair that there was no escape, no freedom, no mercy, because each following moment would be worse torment than the one before. And as his mind cried out again for the sweet mercy of final death, the flames mocked him by redoubling their torture, and he screamed into existence another cycle and another spinning cycle and another relentless spinning cy . . .

And suddenly he was back.

Alystra stood before him holding a glass of water. "Here," she said, handing him the glass. "You will be dangerously dehydrated."

He reached out to take the glass with both hands. His breathing was short and fast, and his heart was beating wildly. He took a short drink as she returned to the couch and sat facing him.

"Please understand that your average mage would consider what you just experienced pretty mild. In casting it, *I* had no intention to actually harm you, *and* I did not seek permanent damage. I only touched the shallowest surface of your mind, *and* the spell only lasted for the briefest time, mere seconds." She paused for a moment and waved for him to drink the rest of the water, which he did, obediently, his mouth now fully unwilling to opine in the slightest way. "In addition, I might add, I did not attack you physically, nor did I compound spell upon spell upon spell. In fact," she said, standing and approaching, "since you, unlike any mage, had no way of defending yourself, I entered and experienced the spell with you so that I could sustain you through it."

Then she stood and approached him and put her hands on his shoulders and gripped him firmly. A dark and powerful warmth spread through his whole body, and his mind was stormed by shadowy images of darker peace and chaotic comfort, all of his senses were filled as though with sweet but harsh smells and gentle sounds, and deep in his mind he felt the darkest hope. His whole body relaxed, and he felt his heart return to its regular rhythm; his hands and eyes became steady again.

"Please remember," she said as she returned to her seat, "that I endured days upon days of endless attacks; attacks that were full of malice, bereft of any mercy, and designed for my destruction. They held back not at all, and they outnumbered me by thousands. Their spells had been prepared in advance, designed for my utter misery and endowed with enormous power." Her voice caught, and for a moment she paused. "I was young and inexperienced, so I endured immeasurable suffering at their hands, at his hands." She clenched her fists and lowered her voice to a tone of terrifying menace. "No one has *ever* shown me mercy. I have been ambushed, tracked down, attacked, and hated only because of who I am, not because of anything I have ever done."

She stood again and approached him. Catching his eye, she said with a voice of finality, "We will not speak of this again. I make no apology for anything I have ever done, but I will not be lectured by you, or anyone else about what a horrible person I am." She turned and walked to the window, looking at the stars with a passive expression. "And in the midst of your self-righteousness, you might want to ponder what the universe would be like if I really *were* horrible."

Bendahrin gazed after her. He had never thought before what it must be like for her. In the years of hearing vague and misty stories about her, always from a safe distance, he had always viewed her as a terrible creature. He stood and walked toward her, wondering how to reach out to her; could he reach her? Was it even *possible*? Then he remembered the brief spell she had cast on him, and he wondered how he could even have the courage to be in the same room with her, let alone try to reach her.

He sighed and turned inward, thinking back over his life. He was an academic, at best just a glorified archaeologist and librarian. He had spent his entire adult life in his quiet study, attending lectures, visiting libraries, or at ancient dig sites. Naturally, he had become enormously successful over the years, and his wealth and prestige had allowed him access into the centers of society in the great city of Palestre. His wealth had allowed him to support his passion for collecting the armaments of Themlia and other odd, rare, and ancient trinkets. At the same time, he had never been particularly bold and as he fought to think back to his, non-rememberable, ridiculous plans to trick Alystra out of her sword, he wondered how the mages manipulating him had been able to overcome his natural fears.

In light of what had eventually happened, he was glad to not be a mere smear on the wall for his, what she called it, presumptuous arrogance, in the attempt. But now, standing with her, something stirred in his heart, a desire to be more than a spectator and observer. She was his real chance to become more than he had ever dreamed, and he might be able to help her at the same time.

Yes. I will find the courage to do this. I will be the one who shows her mercy. He even felt a tiny nudge of confidence despite the ever-present mocking laugh from the more practical side of his mind.

He approached her and stood by her side looking out the window. "I am sorry," he said feebly, and though he knew his words were true from the depths of his heart, his voice seemed to lack the power to match the decision he had made. "I have no idea, I *had* no idea, about what your life has been like. Is there anything I can do?"

She turned and stared at him, her eyes narrowed. Anger swelled in her at the impudence, but the sheer stupidity of his question stunned her. In her best imperious tone, she mocked him kindly. "I have no idea how to answer your question. It is a gesture unlike any I have ever experienced. Are you ready to commit to my choices, the path that is before me? I can't leave the evil behind even though I would wish to. And you, a person of no power at all, how can you help?" She turned back to the window, silent for more than a minute. She whispered to herself, "Oh, you will help. I have something you can do."

Bendahrin, not knowing what else to say, dredged up a question that had been burning in his mind, "Why?" he asked. "Why the endless assaults against you? All the stories point to," he stammered, wanting to make sure his mouth didn't blurt out something dangerous, "to you as the source of wanton destruction. You are depicted as a creature with an unquenchable thirst for destruction. But from what little I have heard from you it seems that you are the target and you are just defending yourself."

"I don't know," she said, shaking her head. "Well, no, I do! But it is just such an atrocious cliché that it annoys me." She took a deep breath to inhale some patience. "Some, those who know about the evil in me, have tried to destroy me to rid the universe of me. I guess they are being noble or heroic; mere errant or arrogant nonsense. Others have tried to prove themselves."

She moved away from the window and sat on the couch again. "You might not know this since you aren't a mage, of course, but the hierarchy among magic users is maintained by a semi-structured or chaotic process of challenging and defeating those more powerful, even if he or she against whom you put your strength is your trusted teacher. For mages, this is similar to some sports back on my home planet. The challenges can be formal or informal, although nobody actually keeps track of the rankings. To me, this practice is as idiotic as many others; some even think it is a way to gain power from the victory, and I, tragically, am at the top of the pile." She clenched her fists again. "Fools!" she hissed, and her eyes turned pale and deathly. "Their petty attempts to reach the top will only end in their destruction."

The room was aching under her angry determinations, but she soon relaxed and looked in his direction. "But, Bendahrin, you must remember that at the core, I am evil, worse than you can imagine. You must always remember that even now, I hold back the natural and insatiable urge to torture or destroy, even you, as a sheer act of will. When I am attacked and it is no fault of my own, I can gain formidable strength when I dispatch my enemies." She laughed. "No, I am formidable at all times." Then her voice changed, it sounded deep and hollow as though emanating from a long tunnel filled with a cold wind.

In response, Bendahrin shuddered with cold.

"In some ways, if I have no fools against which to test my strength with their futile assaults. I need to find my own supply of lifeless energy, for I, unlike them, *do* gain power in their demise. The hunger," and terror swept through the room as a painful wind, "will be fed, is always fed, must . . ." her voice caught, "must be fed."She sat forward with her elbows on her knees and she placed her chin on her clenched fists. Her eyes turned black and Bendahrin cringed with hope that she wouldn't look his way. She closed her eyes, and a black tear fell to the carpet where it burned and sizzled. Then her voice returned to normal.

Bendahrin moved his chair and sat close

She turned to view the intruders. "Let's see what our new friends have to say."

A lystra stood up and approached the pirates.
Bendahrin remained in his chair, not wanting to cause a stir. A moment later they collapsed to the floor but immediately jumped up, fists at the ready.

Alystra looked at them with no expression, and struck no stance, offensive or defensive. "I am impressed," she said, clapping her hands. "That trick to send your friend back to the other ship took me by surprise. But now," and she turned to gesture toward some seats.

They took that moment for a direct, physical attack.

Bendahrin gasped, but Alystra snapped a turn and grasped each of them by the throat. They both began to struggle, and one of them kicked out with a boot and caught her on the shin; she didn't flinch. Moments later they were both reaching to pry her hands away.

"Stop," she hissed, and darkness filled the room in a cloud of swirling fear. "I admire your courage and fortitude. But you are wasting my time. So, either stop or die."

This message seemed to get through, or the pirates decided that they would wait until later to try again. They stopped struggling, and Alystra released them immediately. They fell, stooping and coughing and rubbing their throats, but they showed no anger or defiance, which could hardly be taken as capitulation; they *were* biding their time.

Alsytra waved them over to the couch she had been sitting on before.

They moved and took their seats in docile form despite furtive glances roundabout.

"Let me make some things clear. You are on my ship, and *your* ship has fallen behind. We have some work to do, so you will be my guests . . ."

"Prisoners!" the man spat defiantly but dryly.

Alystra looked at them with mild amusement. It was impossible to calculate the speed at which she thought up ten thousand ways to annihilate him, but she kept her composure. "I suppose that you are angry, and your pride has been hurt that I caught you. But arguing over names and titles is irrelevant. I say, 'guests' and you say, 'prisoners' but both are preferable to 'corpses' which you could just as easily be. I would barely notice. Can we put aside the petulant posturing for a moment? Yes, in a sense you are prisoners because you are on a ship in space, and you can't just leave. If you don't like that, remember you came on board uninvited, so you are going where we are going whether you like it or not. From another perspective, we could call *you* 'stowaways,' which is, again, your own fault and choice. But I am not going to lock you up or torture you or anything else because *you just don't matter*. Everything that I must do demands my focus, and I am not going to babysit you. So, call yourselves 'hitchhikers' or 'travelers' if you like, but I say 'guests' at the very least because, at the moment, if for no other reason, you will be living in the former owner's guest quarters."

The two pirates looked at each other in a quick glance and Alystra knew their minds.

"In case you think that you are going to take over my ship behind my back, I think that we can drive that idea from your minds. Do you know who I am?"

The pirates looked at her with obvious contempt. Clearly, they did not recognize her, nor did they care. Bendahrin was fascinated by the dynamic in the room. On the one hand, Alystra was not the patient type, yet she was taking what was, for her, volumes of time with these two pirates, and Bendahrin wondered why. Alystra looked back at them with the hint of a smile, but the cold calculation of her mind was blazing in her eyes. First, she murmured, "Clearly you don't frequent the religious districts," and secondly, "Kel!" she barked, and Kel-Purim appeared hovering by her side.

"Oh, yes! You've called Me, and that means Something Special."

He looked at the pirates—one man, one woman, broken but defiant, seated on the couch, who, at his arrival, leaned back to increase their distance from him. They had already met Kel-Purim in their minds.

Bendahrin, in *his* mind, could see that they were not fazed by a beautiful woman, but a hazy, blood-colored man who floated in mid-air and who suddenly appeared when called was something to fear. *Ironic in six ways, as my mother used to say.* At that moment Bendahrin could see that the pirates had finally realized fully what level of magic was involved on this ship, but with Kel-Purim, they finally had something to confidently fear.

"Let's keep this simple. I am Alystra, and that should be enough."

The woman suddenly seemed alert, and Bendahrin wondered why.

Alystra turned to Kel-Purim. "These two are our *guests*. You will keep an eye on them. And Kel, do *not* look for some loophole." She turned back to the pirates. "You may have access to the hallways, the forward and starboard lounges, the cinema, and the library; though you need to be careful about what books you read. The galley is open for you, and you will pick your own quarters on the back section of the upper deck. If you mind your manners, I will drop you off at the location of your choice when I have time, if you mis-behave . . ." She turned again. "Kel? You may eat them, and I believe you know *exactly* what that means."

At this, Kel-Purim's whole body bubbled and the steam that poured from him filled the room with the putrid stench of rotting blood.

The woman's sudden interest in Alystra was easy to see, but Bendahrin couldn't tell whether she was fearful or whether she suddenly thought she had hit the mother lode. Her eyes were darting around in intense concentration. In that moment he could see the odd penchant for mages to challenge each other. A certain type of person would always see power as something to be challenged and conquered, some to prove themselves, and others just for the fight. He could see that the pirates were like this, and he wondered how long it would be before they became dinner for Kel-Purim.

"Do you have any questions for me?" She looked at each of them in turn. They didn't have any questions, or they only had questions that they were not inclined to ask, so she turned on a fake cordiality. "Your names?"

The two pirates looked at each other, and Alystra smiled. She already knew their names, of course, but she wanted to begin to gauge if there was going to be "trouble" as Bendahrin had asked.

They seemed to conclude what to do, and the woman bowed her head slightly and said, "I am Erin and this is my lord, Ver-Tark Jedra."

Alystra chuckled in her mind. On the scale from outright truth to careful deception, Erin had found the perfect balance between "my training always requires that I hold whatever edge I can" and "how relevant is it to lie in this situation." That is, the names were right, but she was the Ver-Tark leader. Since Alystra didn't care about their internal rankings and relationship, she went with the names.

"As I said, I am Alystra the Destroyer. You can read about me in the library or Bendahrin here can fill you in with endless bed-time stories about me." She gestured to Bendahrin haphazardly, who realized again that the woman pirate, Erin, was looking as though all her dreams had come true. "So, you know, since you already have a count of beings on my ship, the other living beings on the ship are Kel-Purim," and she nodded in his direction, "Tored, who you had better hope you never meet, and The Lynthe. It is stating the obvious that your best bet is to talk to me or Bendahrin. We are at the beginning of an extensive journey that will require some weeks of travel. We are leaving the galaxy to explore for reasons that you need not know at this time. Also, as I mentioned, you are free to enjoy the entertainments of the ship."

She paused for a moment in thought, and then added, "Probably, most of what you need to repair your tech clothes can be found in the workshop on the lower level." She raised her hand and a key materialized on her palm. She threw it to Erin. "I want you to make any repairs you can and be ready. Keep me apprised of your progress, and in fact, I will give you some ideas for improvements. Let me know if you need anything." She paused in a moment of determined calculation. Then, *"Oh,"* she whispered into the invaded privacy of their thoughts, *"I don't have time to waste with absurd attempts at sabotage or even more ridiculous plans to take the ship or escape. This is to let you know that I hear your every thought and desire and whim and know even the deepest eddies of your subconscious. We could be a team, but I warn you, there are prisons I can build in your minds that are worse than death."*

This final message clearly hit the mark; both pirate-guests, thinking that being a guest might *actually* be preferable to other imagined alternatives, sat up straighter, and yet, relaxed.

Alystra pointed aft and up and told them to make themselves at home, and she grabbed Bendahrin and they walked together to the port lounge where she kept her magical artifacts. Partway there, she turned suddenly to look at Erin and whispered, "How?" Then she continued with Bendahrin through the artifacts. She picked up an ancient stone box from a pedestal and held it with her hand on top. She seemed both perky and perplexed. What she said to Bendahrin was far from what he expected.

"This is *exactly* the pernicious problem with visions and prophecy. It is by *far* the least precise region of magic." She violently summoned a chair for Bendahrin, squeezing it carefully among the artifacts, and she gestured for him to sit. Then she began pacing and fuming. "Visions are a function of both the future as certain and the future as totally fluid. Unless some powerful being is directing the course of history, which happens, most views of the future are fluid based on innumerable choices and accidents, gravitation and rainfall, market forces and the wings of some butterfly. Obviously, the uncertainty goes up as our viewing distance into the future increases. If I tried to see the future occurrences of life on this ship tomorrow, the vision would be relatively certain, and, of course, I could act directly to make that vision come true or change it. If I try to see a month away, or a year, the visions become far fuzzier. Does this make sense?"

Bendahrin nodded and answered carefully. Her comments were basic theory, but he couldn't figure out why she was angry at the moment. "This is consistent with what I have heard, but why are you telling me this?" His understanding of visions and magic clearly outstripped his math skills.

Alystra turned, her enthusiasm evident in a visible change in gait which reflected her internal bouyant certainty. She opened the box from which a brilliant light flooded. Putting her hand inside, she scooped out a portion of the lightning bright fire. She placed the box back on the pedestal, closing the lid. Petting the flame absently, her hands radiated a pink glow. She raised her right hand and performed a circular motion with her palm toward Bendahrin. A disk of pink mist floated in the air between them. Then she continued. "Despite my disdain for visions in general, I don't want you to think that I am either unaware of the use or practice." Bendahrin nodded and shrugged and she continued, "Several months past, I cast a vision. I do it infrequently, and I don't use the results to guide me, but only to inform. If you like, I use visions as an advance insight that I can use to confirm a chosen path, once traveled, rather than to *find* the path. Like calculating the trajectory of something moving through space; given a knowledge of the gravitational forces at work, it is possible to calculate the trajectory of an object far in advance. Likewise, when the trajectory of the vision is later proven to be on track, reflection and evaluation of the original vision can be used to confirm that what you are seeing is true, in the real sense of the word."

She paused and breathed on the pink disk. A fuzzy image appeared of a solitary figure, walking but unsteady. The path the figure followed was fraught with apparitions, festivals and monuments, which Bendahrin imagined were metaphorical or symbolic. He assumed that the central figure was Alystra and that somehow, he was seeing a third person perspective of what she had seen in her vision.

Bendahrin watched as the lone figure meandered and crept, then climbed or tumbled, but the distractions and obstacles remained fuzzy. There were moments of severe action and sweeping parallels of kingdoms and epochs, but the path and the figure remained vague and shadowy. The scene changed and a crossroads appeared that seemed less vague, at least from Bendahrin's point of view. As "Alystra" approached and stopped, another figure appeared, and the crossroads resolved into a single path. The vision grew lighter and the pink edges began to glow more yellow, passing, by natural course, through a sickly orange on its way. The second figure approached the first, and the floating gave way to substance.

The two figures meandered farther most amicably, the path twisting into an upside-down translation, although gravity still did its required thing in the needed direction. Another crossroads approached, although vaguer than before, and two more figures appeared, where the background ground forward aggressively into a far spryer solidity. The four stopped in the road which had lost its juncture, and another figure or two approached. With this appearance, the entire spectacle became confidently solid and multicolored even as it disappeared. Bendahrin might have seen even more shadows or pairs of shadows approaching in the distance, but what he saw with certainty was the massive shadow of a spaceship that raced toward the growing group of wanderers.

"This is my reconstruction of the vision I had. And you see it, of course, only as I can reconstruct it. When I cast this vision, I was in a torrid frame of mind, and was casting about, literally and magically, in a moment of enforced patience. At the time, disgusted that I had even fallen to the weakness, I was ready to ignore what I saw, but my comparatively unique status as a primal force sometimes leaves me ensconced in a problem innate to my character. Even my mere awareness of a vision is dangerously provocative because, as I mentioned, '*unless some powerful being is directing the course of history.*'" She paused, clicking her tongue.

Bendahrin nodded with immediate understanding, this was like being back in primary school.

Alystra continued in confident frustration. "I am on the short list of those called 'some powerful being' and so, I should tell you, on a whim, I asserted my authority on the vision. Now I am trapped."

She paused to let Bendahrin think for a moment, his eyes fixing on Alystra's hand through the still hovering pinkness. "And then you showed up," she said quietly. "We will never know whether the vision tricked me into action, or whether I increased the likelihood of a possible future, or if the whole thing is still a coincidence. I can't ignore that after I threw power at this vision, you showed up, and now, two more are here. One, then two, as the vision showed."

Bendahrin nodded. "A problematic conundrum certainly. Did you force what happened by exerting your authority? I had been planning to approach you, I think, perhaps without knowing it. If our meeting is aligned with the first encounter in your vision, it seems reasonable to assume that I am here in fulfillment. But," he paused to scratch his head thoughtfully, "despite the fact that you took control of me in the battle, I am helping you willingly. At least I feel like I am willing on my own. These two pirates, if they are the next encounter in the vision, look as though they are ready to pounce on you at the first opportunity."

Alystra nodded. "And yet, as you have been recently thinking, you aren't even sure that you ever had any intention of stealing my sword, or whether it was an external compulsion, correct?"

Bendahrin nodded again.

"Who knows how long it has been since you have been directed against your will, if the idea was forced on you, or if you originated the idea and someone merely encouraged it. And maybe even that doesn't matter, whatever the path, you are here." Alystra banished the pink circle with yellow edges. "Even now, the reason you are willing to help is unfounded and directionless, and *partnering* with me was never part of your plan, your timid character would never allow it. Your immediate willingness was unexpected and suggestive, but without the vision, I would not have been very likely to meet with you that day at the . . . on Denton Street. You would have never had the opportunity to offer your support."

She slapped her leg. "You can see the weakness of visions. The fact that I *did* cast the vision and *did* decide to meet with you put you, put us, in a position that neither of us would have ever dreamed. And who knows, maybe you were a distraction and I *should* have been across the galaxy meeting someone else, but once I made the choice, and fixed the timeline, the arrival of these next two becomes even more compelling. So, whether my choices are making the vision come true or not is not only unanswerable, but it is also irrelevant. I am now exerting my power behind *this* destiny, whether I am following it or creating it." She clenched her fists in anger and trembled. "If I have faith in the vision, then the outcome will become the correct one whether it was meant to be or not. If I doubt the vision, then no outcome is the prescribed one and choices I make only matter apart from the vision anyway. Faith is enough to drive you mad, but doubt is a horrible companion on the road.

"Moreover," she said with a scowl, "I forced upon myself a painful personal conflict." She stopped and looked down, drawing her hands in protectively, her face troubled. "As long as I have been afflicted by inescapable evil, I have been terrified to rely on anyone else. The very thought of trusting someone, anyone, in any way . . . It was only in response to this vision that I was willing to meet with you, and yet the vision itself is forcing on me," she stuttered, "companions. By putting power into that vision, I have chained myself to one of my greatest fears; the fear that success may depend on the weak."

Bendahrin was not insulted by this, but rather, assured. Her doubts provided to him confidence that, so far, her obedience to the vision had led her against the grain of evil. His confidence, however, sought the answer that his mouth couldn't resist. "Did the rest of the vision reveal a good outcome?"

Alystra stopped with her mouth open.

Bendahrin nodded to prompt her to speak.

Finally she blurted out, "What makes you think . . . ?" She left her statement unfinished.

Bendahrin nodded and continued, "Thank you for the confirmation. I may not be good at math, but I have lived on Palestre all my life." He leaned back as she narrowed her eyes. "Visions are not generally about the journey; they are about the destination. If your vision was about whether you should get some companions, it isn't likely that the meeting of them would be revealed as an answer over time. I think that you have only shown me part of the vision."

Alystra laughed heartily. "And so, I *am* trapped. I added power to the vision through the choices I made, and *you* have turned out to be a surprise at every turn. You are right, I only showed you the part that pertained to this moment. Which means that I am more than trapped. I might have made the worst mistake of all! If you *are* the correct first choice for the vision, and the vision turns out well, then I have made the right choice. But if I threw my power behind you and made a bad choice, the outcome of the vision could possibly be overthrown. Either way, we won't know until we reach the end and see . . ." She clenched her fists. "I don't know what we will see."

Bendahrin waved his hand. "No, Alystra, you can't have it both ways."

This time she didn't even scowl.

"You were transformed, created, who knows, but, since you are the Issachon, you are evil by nature, and that, not the result of *your* choice. Somehow you are able to work against that overpowering nature, which is an impenetrable stroke of luck for the rest of us. Whatever you are or have become, the Issachon, conceptually, is an apocalyptic character, who, by nature, envelopes the universe in final destruction." He paused, licking his lips. "I am an historian, and researcher, so I have read enough and," he stopped, leaning forward and looking her in the eyes. "Don't think about this next question . . . just answer." He took her hand. "Could you destroy the universe?"

Her eyes went wide, and she nodded quickly, then shook her head, and he continued, quickly, to distract her.

"Somehow you, Alystra, are the *wrong* vessel for evil and somehow, you are able to make choices against your own evil nature, and even more. Maybe it is not *your* nature that is evil, the *Issachon* is evil incarnate in you. You somehow hold it at bay. It is more important than ever to find out how this happened to you. I see that now."

He let go of her hand, and she nodded thoughtfully. "I will go way out on a limb here and I will stop ahead of making conclusions. I now know the nature of the vision you sought, and you defied the Issachon in you in seeking it, which is why you can't show it to me. Moreover, you exerted your power on the vision to make it happen. But now we are in the worst place of all. You said it: 'what would happen to the universe if you used magic to figure out how you were transformed? What would that much evil do, spread across both space and time through the entire galaxy?' And now, you're telling me that you exerted your *power*, which is inherently evil, on a vision that could save or destroy the universe? Maybe the Issachon tricked the vessel. What would be the impact of *that* much evil?"

Alystra nodded but smiled, and her shoulders relaxed. "All true," she said, "but remember that exerting my power directly on the vision, which is mere possibility, even if I force it into reality, isn't the same as exerting the required power on the entire galaxy to discover my origin."

Bendahrin seemed lost in thought.

Alystra waited and after a handful of pregnant moments, he refocused on her.

"Sorry," he said, clapping his hands. "I was speaking my thoughts out loud. My original point was that the nature of the requested vision is one factor, the source of your power is another factor, but the one that really matters here is that *you* made a choice and exerted your power in support of an outcome, which I won't qualify for the danger such a discussion holds for you. The point is that now we *must* trust the encounters in the vision because of your *intent*. Whether the vision is or was right or wrong, or whether the universe will be destroyed, our only course is to put our faith in your choice and obey the vision . . ."

"As if we have a choice." Alystra finished the sentence for him. "And now we are faced with two reluctant pirates. As you said, you have, with no forethought, chosen to join me on your own. I could just change their minds so that they don't even *need* to make a choice about their presence on this growing team," she stuttered over the words as though even the concept of unity painfully derailed her thoughts. Bendahrin nodded knowingly as Alystra continued. "It might not require their volition, but just their skills."

Bendahrin shook his head. "Not likely, given the good versus evil nature of everything now surrounding the destiny you have empowered. We can't very well expect to produce a good outcome through the innately evil act of subverting someone's will. Such an act would go against your intentions." He paused again, and Alystra coalesced the lightning fire and returned it to the box from which she had removed it. Bendahrin allowed his eyes to wander and his thoughts to drift momentarily on some of the artifacts in her collection, frowning or smiling in response to what he saw. His gaze was caught by an egg-shaped stone hovering in a glass ball he hadn't noticed before. He continued vaguely. "The B'Tark Stream has not been a particular area of interest, so I can't think of anything that would help us to understand or penetrate their motivations. In the end, they will best be able to help us if they decide to follow you freely. More importantly, if we are seeking a 'good' end, it would be better if their motivation is something other than power or greed."

Alystra nodded. "We will need to ponder this, and maybe an answer will present itself." She paused for a moment, concentrating. "Thinking more immediately, we have another issue that is more pressing."

"More pressing than following a vision that might lead to the end of the universe?" Bendahrin asked snidely.

"Absolutely," Alystra threw back, with equal snide. "The pirates are here. Let's assume they are the two figures in the vision. Do we press on? Do we go back? Think about it. You have been with me for a couple of months. I partially ignored the vision and kept up with my travels because your appearance only provided a single blip in the vision. Now we have two points along the vision. Do we keep searching for what happened to me, or do we try to find the next figures in the vision?" She paused for a moment, then added, "please keep in mind that this is an enormous decision."

Bendahrin laughed. "Once again, you are trying to walk on both sides! When you confirmed just one answer to the vision, you didn't go out of your normal path to force it forward, why would you try to do that now? It is possible that the only way to make sure that you are following an unknown course is to totally change directions and continue as you were. The safest course is to stay on course with your original efforts and trust the vision to happen as it will. That is the safest course, at least until some clear change in the path presents itself. Whether you stay on track or don't, unless you *try* to force the outcome, which you could, with a correct vision, when followed, there is no way to either avoid its inevitable outcome nor to force it to happen any faster.

"The *correct* question is whether finding the answer you have spent the last decade searching for is still worth it, or whether it ever was worth the effort. From what I have seen, you have spent nine years, and the rest of the effort could take another forty or fifty or more. I can tell you for sure that I am not likely to live long enough to see the end of that, unless you can stop my aging." He paused for an uncertain moment, and she nodded with a roll of her eyes. "All right, so I could be here 'til the end of that journey. Are you sure that you even need to know what happened? The next figure in the vision will show up at the proper time no matter what you do. You just need to decide what the next *best* step is and leave the vision to itself."

Alystra scowled at him in anger, and Bendahrin felt it in the pit of his stomach. "Bendahrin, you have proven your worth to me today. The Strentrian Bubble allows me to search any time at any time, so if we don't find success moving forward, I can always go back to the search and I can promise that you will see the result. We will press on."

She began to walk from the room, but paused, as if a thought had seized her. Alystra stood still for some time, concentrating, then beckoned him to follow her. "Bendahrin, I want you to go retrieve our guests and bring them to the library." She walked toward the forward lounge.

As Bendahrin turned to head up the backstairs, he saw Kel-Purim appear with Alystra, who was talking fast. He turned past the galley and ascended the stairs to the upper deck. He called out as he walked past the few rooms that comprised the guest quarters when suddenly, he heard a noise behind him and turned to see Jedra leaning against the wall *outside* the room he had just passed.

"You're an interesting one," Jedra said, his words clipped and chewy. "No soldier, but she wouldn't need that. What? You her butler or cook?"

Bendahrin paused to look at Jedra without answering for a moment.

Jedra had removed his tech fatigues and was wearing shorts with numerous pockets, a sturdy shirt, and soft shoes, all of which had been under his combat attire. He was a heroic figure of obvious strength, not massive, but close; lean and taut. He was a few inches taller than Bendahrin, even leaning against the wall in a relaxed fashion. His face was stern, apart from his laughing eyes, which didn't seem to fit the physique. His eyes were startling and intimidating in a face that was unreadable, but Bendahrin felt that visage was the result of control, not from lack of an animating character, which was only hidden for suspenseful expedience. Jedra could crush him with his bare hands, and Bendahrin wondered what Alystra's protection would do about that. Oddly, the pirate, despite the external and obvious physical menace, worked hard to exude an effect of calm.

Bendahrin nodded absent-mindedly and said, "Alystra doesn't eat."

"I think," said Erin, who was somehow coming up the stairs *behind* Jedra, "that she doesn't eat *food*." Bendahrin was surprised to discover that she had been downstairs, since Alystra had sent Jedra and Erin upstairs before they had talked about the vision. She had similar attire to Jedra with the addition of a bright red sash that poured over her hip and down the side of her leg. She was Alystra's height and had long blonde hair, thick and currently tied up. She, like Jedra, was all muscle; not showy, but practical. Her face was alert, and her eyes carried a spark of something that was instantly compelling. Comparing her to Alystra, Bendahrin would say that Erin had the curves, but whereas Erin was disarming, Alystra's beauty was ravishing.

"She is voracious and feeds on something. But she is somehow beyond, now isn't she?"

Bendahrin, figuring that honesty made the most sense, and since he was an honest person anyway, chose to try it out on a couple of pirates. "She is the Issachon, a primal force of the universe."

Erin moved to stand next to Jedra. "Now, *everything* makes sense," Erin said sarcastically. Her voice was smooth *and* sharp, melodic yet cool. "A primal force of the universe, on a remarkably fast ship with some dumpy guy, out in the middle of nowhere, and about to leave the galaxy on a mission . . . one that I'm *sure* we would never understand, right?" She smiled caustically and batted her eyes at him.

He laughed and sighed. "I am not sure what you are expecting, but I can provide a simple summary that may guide you; if you really want to hear it. Alystra's mission is simple enough that anyone could understand it, and because of who she is, she will probably tell you her mind fully. Earlier when she said that you don't matter, she wasn't just being nasty. The fact is that we are all like mere leaves against her storm; none of us has the slightest impact on her or the slightest ability to stand against her. Or with her for that matter. Being secretive is, for her, irrelevant, and it turns out that you may matter more than she described." He gestured toward the stairs. "I think that may even be the reason that she wants us all in the library, if you please." He gestured down the stairs. "I warn you. She will meet *none* of your expectations but will confirm and embody *all* of your deepest fears. Did I say storm? Yes, we are in the storm that could well be the end."

As they started down the stairs, Erin responded, "You like to use a lot of words, don't you?"

Bendahrin was stumped about what to say but spoke anyway. "You are right. I do tend to say too much. But since you seem to have everything figured out, I'll refrain from saying more."

They entered the library to find that Alystra had provided a meal, laid out on the table with four chairs. She stood slightly to the right of the table. Erin's eyes swept the room, then she swept up to Alystra and stood facing her, leaving only a foot between them.

Bendahrin moved to the other side of the table in order to see them both, but Jedra stayed near the door, looking truculently calm and peacefully alert. Erin's face was fierce and frenzied while Alystra appeared bored. Bendahrin wondered why Alystra had allowed the pirate to get so close, and why she appeared so complacent. Alystra's eyes were locked on Erin's, and Erin's eyes were darting around Alystra's face.

The two women stood, unmoving, as moments stretched on and the tension rose.

Erin raised her left hand slowly to scratch her face.

Alystra's eyes dropped slightly, glancing at her hand, and Erin threw her hand to her left in that instant. Alystra followed Erin's hand with her eyes, and Erin struck with her right as her tech fatigues became visible and a blade shot out from the cuff near her wrist. Alystra's eyes were wide with surprise.

The blade seemed alive with motion, and Erin mocked Alystra as she started to fall, "Fool! Never underestimate the Stream."

Erin lowered Alystra to the floor, their eyes still locked, and Alystra gasped out through a mouthful of blood. "Mental discipline . . . amaz . . ."

8

Bendahrin's mouth dropped open, and he felt brutally light-headed. His knees felt weak, and he stared unmoving where Alystra had been, although he couldn't see her body because she had collapsed toward the table, which blocked his view. He vaguely realized that Jedra had moved silently to stand next to him, slightly behind and to the right.

"We assume we'll have no trouble with you?" He said quietly.

Bendahrin nodded in defeat, knowing that he had no choice.

Jedra, however, continued. "Is she dead?"

Erin spoke arrogantly as she rounded the table. "Pah. Too easy, blade fingers shredded her heart." She stopped in front of Bendahrin who was leaning heavily on the chair. "Now, let's see, what are we going to do with you? Prisoner? Guest? Corpse?" Her voice was full of nasty irony and mockery. "As a guest, *you* may have access to the hallways, any lounges, the cinema, and the library; though, I believe we have been warned to be careful about what books you read." She looked around the library greedily. "The galley is open for you, and you will pick whatever quarters you want, we won't be here long. If you mind your manners, *Bendahrin*, we will allow you to buy your freedom. If you misbehave . . ." She turned to Jedra. "Jedra? You may throw him out of the airlock." She focused her eyes on Bendahrin. "And I believe you know *exactly* what that means." She laughed. "This is a nice ship, a really nice ship, and you," she sneered, "you *just don't matter!*"

Jedra and Erin disappeared and Bendahrin assumed that they

had gone to the bridge or drive room to take control of the ship, and sure enough, in moments he felt the mild sensation of a turn in space. His knees finally gave way, and he fell to the floor. From this position it was easy to crawl around the table and kneel beside Alystra. The books in the library were no longer whispering about destiny, but he had no ears to hear.

He looked down at her face, angelic even in death. He gently closed her eyes and bowed his head for a moment, numb. He grabbed her hand, warm and soft and held it to his lips as tears dripped, dripped, dripped on her arm. His mind went simply nowhere as thoughts of visions—of fruit, fruitless discussions of asymptotic drives, and buying his freedom—bumped and jostled before him. His thoughts snagged on an image of her scowling at him when he had asked if they were in any danger.

In the end, the relentless thought that bubbled to the top was, *Get her off the floor! Get your friend off the floor.*

He wasn't sure if he could lift her, but he got his arm under her knees and he hugged her to his chest. Strangely, holding her close caused a stampede of feelings that he pushed away as newly irrelevant, but they taunted him about loss and loneliness. She was lighter than he expected, or his grief had made him strong, still, struggling to his knees, then to his feet, his first thought was to take her to the infirmary, but as he pushed his way through the library doors, he saw through the window into the sterile room and his mind raged for a moment in concert with his burning sentimentality that also raged against putting her in such a cold place. Of course, he could also hear Alystra in the back of his mind, mocking him for entertaining such silly thoughts. She would chastise him for being sentimental about her empty body.

Nevertheless, he proceeded past the infirmary to his own small quarters where he placed her on his bed as gently as he could. He fell back into the chair beside the bed, put his hand on her upper arm, and wept. He couldn't help but notice that her arm was still warm, and he looked through tears out the window at the hopeless stars that moved slowly across his field of view.

Many people in this situation might perhaps think of ways to overcome the pirates or re-take the ship, but for some reason, he wasn't over-worried for his own safety. The ship was familiar and unchanged, save for Alystra's lifeless body on his bed and the trail of blood stretching off to the library, and he could easily buy his freedom. Instead, he looked alternatively at Alystra and out the window, wondering how this impossible turn of events could have occurred. It had been less than an hour since he had been sleeping, in the same bed where Alystra . . . His thoughts were muddy, and they ambled around their discussion on visions from ten minutes earlier. Alystra had exerted power into the vision and then . . . what?

He stood up and went to the sink and worked to wash the blood from his hands, glancing over to Alystra and wondering how to clean her up. She didn't have quarters on the ship, and he had no idea if she had other clothes. Then he realized that he would never be able to undress her and put on fresh clothes, no matter what he might find. He walked to the window and looked out just in time to see another ship pull alongside. He felt the sense of deceleration and almost immediately; he heard the faint rustle of movement; he backed away from the window and looked down the hall to see a dozen new pirates who had appeared in the hall. They moved out with speed and precision, looking into and entering every room, Bendahrin barely noticed. He sat at the table in a daze as time passed.

Eventually he overheard voices and he saw Erin walking down the hall toward him with a man who looked very little like a member of the stream. His clothes were unkempt and sloppy; he fidgeted and bobbed at Erin's heels slightly bowed and cringing. She stopped at the door and glanced at Alystra. Her expression changed mildly, and Bendahrin was at a loss to identify the meaning.

She beckoned to Bendahrin and he followed her back to the library.

The man let him pass then entered the room.

When they arrived at the library, Bendahrin saw that one of the pirates was methodically looking over every book on the shelves, but left as soon as they entered. She gestured for Bendahrin to sit in one of the chairs at the table. He felt a swelling anger and decided to sit to the right, closest to where Alystra had been killed.

Erin sat in the chair facing the door and reached for some food, adding a mix of foods to her plate. "How nice," she said with a silent, ambivalent smirk. "The food is still warm." She gestured toward the food. "Bendahrin, eat! You may not get a chance for a long while, and certainly Alystra provided nothing but the best." She chewed and swallowed some delicious smelling meat. "I want to let you know what will happen next. My guess is that you have heard of the B'Tark Stream, and since the term 'pirates' is always used to describe us, we have a thousand lifetimes of reputation as ruthless and murderous."

"You murdered Alystra, so it looks as though the ruthless reputation fits precisely," Bendahrin said flatly.

"Yes," Erin quipped. "And I am imagining myself bathing in gold from the gratitude of the entire galaxy. I might retire and buy myself a few star systems of my own." She stopped and continued at the same time, that is, talking and eating respectively. "Come, Bendahrin," she said, between more continued bites. "This food is delicious."

Bendahrin could not have made a grumpier sound than the one he made at that moment. "I'm not hungry."

"As you wish. As I was saying, our reputation is really most annoying to us, we are rarely forced to the point of killing anyone—"

Bendahrin interrupted. "Rarely? That means nothing. No one is *ever* forced into killing someone else." His petulance had bubbled up to overflowing, although his statement seemed a bit hollow considering his recent associations.

Erin continued chewing, looking thoughtfully at him. She put her utensils down and leaned back in her chair. "Fine, let's forget about setting the context. You will believe what you want." She reached up and undid her sandy colored hair, allowing it to fall over her shoulders and over the back of the chair. She ran her hand through her hair, straightening it almost miraculously into beautiful perfection. "You are in a difficult position, and I want to help you through the process."

"Why?" Bendahrin countered. "What possible difference can it make to me, or for me? You certainly have no reason to care in any conceivable way."

"You are being obstinate."

"*You* just murdered my friend."

Erin snorted and shook her head. "Friend? How well did you even know her?"

Bendahrin scowled. "Friendship is a matter of heart and commitment. But fine! Erin. Provide your context."

"So, I shall." She leaned forward again and took a drink. Then, tapping the table for emphasis, said, "This is a business. You are inventory. We want your experience to be as painless as possible."

Bendahrin rolled his eyes but kept silent; he was starting to think that sarcasm or silence would lead to the same result, and he still didn't feel hungry at all. "Now that we have the ship, we will search thoroughly and inventory what we find. You will be asked some questions, under a truth spell, if necessary, in front of the officers. But most of all you will be the guest of honor at The Presentation, where we present our treasures to the division." She stopped and took a couple more bites of food. "Or in the case of the value of the ship, we might present before a larger venue. From what I know of you from a quick view of the records we have regarding Palestre, you are worthless as ransom, but you have sufficient resources to buy your freedom."

On any other day, Bendahrin might have taken offense at being described as "worthless as ransom," but he understood the meaning at once. It was the same reason that he was able to head off with Alystra for the last months. He had loose business associations and some casual relationships on Palestre, most predicated on his wealth, not on friendship. Nobody would ransom his freedom because he lived in a world of transactions where nobody cared about him as a person. He thought back for a moment and realized that perhaps he knew loneliness more than Alystra had contended.

His thoughts were interrupted when a man walked in. He didn't wear the black tech fatigues as the other pirates, and he was not in particularly good physical shape. He started to talk when his eyes fell on the rows of books. He started toward the shelves, whispering, "*The Pursuance of G-Gratheth* . . . an original of B-Bartorah's anthology . . ." His voice trailed off in wonder.

Erin cleared her throat, and he turned. "I apologize, O V-Ver, this," he gestured to the shelves, "these v-volumes, the artifacts, they are worth thousands of times the v-value of the ship. B-Beyond v-valuable, b-beyond priceless, b-beyond a treasure."

Erin began to speak, but he held up his hand, looking at Bendahrin. "You, B-Bendahrin from Palestre, correct?" Bendahrin nodded. He extended his hand, and Bendahrin shook it absently and suspiciously. "I'm R-Rish O'Flenk, I saw you on G-Garbear, a few years b-back. Your presentation on Portairen g-glyphs was fascinating. And, of course, your collection is a particular study."

Bendahrin rustled up as much snide and bile as his voice could muster without drowning. "You must stop by for a visit the next time you're in town."

Rish apparently missed the sarcasm, continuing vacuously. "Yes, I'd like that." He turned to Erin, who glared at him. "I apologize again, O V-Ver." With a slight, jerky, but sincere bow. "You await my r-report."

Erin nodded sarcastically, to the degree that nodding can be ascribed as such.

"The magical artifacts are astonishing, v-very similar to this library. Priceless and some are astonishingly dangerous and powerful. Many we can't touch, move or even approach. There is a powerful presence, a b-being in the port lounge, and one at the b-back, just outside the door. Far b-beyond me."

Erin was smirking, as if Rish embodied an inside joke, but she nodded patiently. "Alystra mentioned that there were three other beings. Kel-Purim, who we saw, Tored, and The Lynthe. And you can only identify two?"

Rish, who had winced at the mention of Alystra's name, nodded feebly.

Erin turned to Bendahrin and smiled. "We will find out what you know eventually. Kel-Purim, any ideas?"

Bendahrin shook his head. "I know nothing of magic," he began.

But Erin nodded to Rish who placed his hand roughly on Bendahrin's shoulder.

A palpable sound and racing pain crackled through Bendahrin, causing him to convulse violently like being electrocuted. This lasted for a few sloppy seconds; Bendahrin concluded that Rish was an amateur.

Rish lifted his hand carelessly. "Sorry, B-Bendahrin." He faced Erin. "There is no magic in this man. He has the r-remnants of a couple spells, still warm. They must have b-been recently lifted when Alys..." He stopped. "When she died." He knelt down next to Erin's chair. "O V-Ver," he pleaded, speaking frantically, "How, how did you kill her? She is *not* a mage, not *just* a mage. She is a primal force, one of *the* primal forces. One of the top *three* primal forces. This is serious!"

Erin scowled, seemingly unconcerned. "How serious, Rish?"

"End of the universe serious. Primal forces spring from, they are tied to the v-very core, the essence of existence. Necessary, b-but b-balanced, g-good, evil, *Peta* and *Issa*, in b-balance, magic, the universe continues. So much is unknown here. How a young g-girl b-became the Issachon is unknown, and, b-but, and nobody knows how this can even b-be. Drendard dwelling in a *person*? And you have killed her? Is evil dead? G-Gone? Or has it b-been released from the b-body, seeking? Did you see anything?" He turned to Bendahrin, seeking an answer from him, too.

Erin seemed more concerned about Rish's mental state than about the end of the universe, though barely. Maybe caring wasn't very common in the Stream, but Bendahrin was perplexed by her lack of concern. She nodded, trying to reassure him. "Rish, the universe is still here. Did you check the body?"

"Oh, oh, oh, yes. Her heart is minced." And so, he winced, most poetically. "I checked her out with flames and cold, tests of pain. I inflicted the b-body with horrors and soul exploration. Her b-body is an empty shell." Rish stared at the floor and held his hands together. His eyes were vacant, but a faint smile appeared on his lips.

Bendahrin noted his reverence. As a mage, perhaps he knows more of Alystra than others in the Stream.

Erin ignored him completely, pushed her chair back and stood up. "Rish, you are done here for now. We will need a concrete plan about what to do with the magical relics."

"Yes, yes, O V-Ver. I . . . I will work on it. I will most likely need the assistance of the division mages. And I warn you that even together, some of these r-relics might b-be b-beyond us. I strongly suggest," he said, bowing, "that we make the magic areas off limits, for safety r-reasons. In fact, the entire ship." He paused. "And I would like to make a r-r- . . . appeal?" He waited on her pleasure.

"Proceed," she said, grabbing more food.

At first, Bendahrin felt as though everything between the pirates held a heavy weight of stilted formality. As he watched, he realized that it was more likely to be a culture of fear and contempt, either attitude held by members depending upon whether they were looking up or looking down.

"I want to offer r-ransom for this live lot, B-Bendahrin. I b-believe that he has something from his collection that would, for me, b-be more v-valuable than the r-ransom, which I would g-gladly pay."

Erin frowned but nodded. "Granted, if you can cover it, you may make your appeal to the council and at The Presentation. Dismissed."

Bendahrin opened his mouth to speak, but Erin shut him down without a word. "Your time to talk is done for now. Follow me. Behind me, but don't *fall* behind." She grabbed her glass, drained it, and led him from the library and turned left.

Bendahrin glanced toward his room to see Alystra's body still on his bed. As they passed the starboard lounge, Bendahrin gasped to see that the ship was now inside the massive hangar of another ship. They headed out of the airlock and down a dozen stairs. He glanced back to see that another pirate had immediately closed the door and was welding a bar across it. Bendahrin wondered about the value of sealing the door when everyone seemed to be able to transport where they wanted with their combat fatigues.

Keeping honest people honest, he thought, as his mother used to say.

Erin led him at an angle across the hanger under Alystra's ship to a port that was in the middle of the wall. He noticed that two other ships were also in the hangar. He followed her through two or three turns. They passed numerous other men and women, and for the first time, he noticed subtle differences between the tech fatigues they wore and the ranks and insignias. The B'Tark Stream was clearly a military organization. Also, by passing so many, he noticed the salutes and deference paid to Erin.

They came to an airlock followed by a long tunnel, and another airlock. They turned left at a "T" and soon arrived at a spiral of stairs. Bendahrin followed her around and down, two, three decks. At the bottom, they continued in a direction that Bendahrin assumed, correctly, was aft, and they came to a door that Erin unlocked by pressing her hand against it. Beyond was a short corridor with six doors, and Bendahrin had a strong sense that behind these doors, if he could see it, would be plentiful unnecessary suffering and very little justice, though why a hall of doors should be so familiar made no sense.

Erin opened the second door on the right and gestured for Bendahrin to enter.

He passed through the door and turned to look at Erin bleakly. She made no expression or comment, though for a moment their eyes met, and Bendahrin sensed . . . something elusive . . . hope, or expedience?

She nodded slightly and closed the door.

Bendahrin didn't even try the door from the inside. Even if escape from the room was possible, he had no place he could go. He scanned the room that had the most basic of amenities—bed, table, chair, sink in a small shower, toilet. A recess held some bland clothes, but at least they were clean. He dug out an uninspired change from the meager selection and stripped to remove his blood-stained shirt and pants. And behold! He saw the blood, blackened in vicious streaks on the familiar cloth, and he froze in helpless awe and despair. The blood of Alystra was a paradox of pain and confusion. This affront was personal and a turning point for him and . . . for everyone.

For himself, as the tears stung his eyes, he reflected that he had only known her for such a short time, and most of that time, on the ship, they had rarely talked or interacted. And yet, he felt and knew that the passage of time meant nothing in this one friendship alone. No relationship with her could ever be casual or insignificant. She was gone, and even though her absence was like the disappearance of a *dark* star from his personal system, yet still, a *star* was gone, with the requisite gravity. The tapestry of his future had been shredded, and he felt the emptiness in full measure to the hole created in his heart. What loss! What waste! He had connected with the majesty and the woman, the terror and the warmth: Alystra. But now? She was beyond the door, hidden in that place of forever receding shadow. His tears fell on the streaks of blood, marring the hateful perfection of their message.

The turning point loomed before him, a behemoth that provided no comfort. The woman he knew was gone, but so was the *evil*. Even in the moments of his most overwhelming attraction, he had always been repulsed, and drawn, by the Destroyer, and this evil had been dispatched. Somehow, simply, and yet, *too* simply? How? Even Rish was baffled. How do you destroy the Issachon? Shouldn't they have sensed or seen the monster escaping the woman? How did this change the course of his future, indeed, the course of everything? Was the evil now gone? Or was it now released? Bendahrin shook his head in silent frustration. Freedom should taste sweet, even in his present situation. Incarceration by the B'Tark was far better than being chained to a prime evil, and yet his sorrow and emptiness revealed a heart torn by a towering absence; Alystra was gone, and something was dreadfully wrong.

He pulled on the clean garments and cast the bloody clothes into the corner with casual reverence. He sat down in the chair and chose the only sensible action: he wept for Alystra and his pain. With Alystra gone, guest or prisoner seemed irrelevant in the cells of the B'Tark Stream, and felt only marginally better than corpse.

9

Bendahrin tried, like so many prisoners before him, to assess the passage of time. Someone brought him some food, a nameless face who opened the door and rolled in a cart. He sensed the sarcastic hand of Erin on the first food delivery because the food was from the meal Alystra had provided, proof that *someone* had gone back into the ship. There was a large amount of food, several days' worth, and Bendahrin discovered that a refrigeration unit was built into the wall. He packed the perishables there and moved the fruit and bread onto the little table. The fruit alone could last him for a week. The cart had also contained some toiletries and hygiene products, which he considered a nice touch. He took his time emptying the cart. But as soon as he had removed the last item, the door opened, and the nameless face removed it. Bendahrin was thus confirmed in his suspicion that he was being watched.

The days migrated faithfully forward. Bendahrin paced. He slept. He ate. He pondered. Alystra was frequently in his mind, and he bounced painfully between despair and confusion, anger and relief. No answers, nothing made sense, and he knew that even if sense could be found, it wouldn't quench the sorrow. He paced. He pondered. He wept.

He had eaten scores of times and slept a dozen when the door opened and Rish came in with a box. He seemed far calmer than their last encounter, and Bendahrin guessed that this was from the colossal absence of the high-ranking Erin, Ver of the B'Tark Stream. At the very least, his stutter was gone. "I have a few items for you, and we have a few things to discuss. As you have guessed by now, we are observing you, so this discussion is not private, but it doesn't need to be." He started emptying the box onto the table. "More food and additional personal items that you might find comfortable. These," and he placed a stack of clothes on the table, "are your clothes for The Presentation. You will be told when to put them on. But I think that this will please you the most of all." He pulled a stack of six books from the box. "From my library, history, archaeology, and a few classics. I asked for permission to provide them myself. Normally you would have been appointed an advocate to discuss your comforts during your visit, but your situation has engendered a larger than normal level of interest from deeper in the Stream. In this case, I was eventually approved to be your advocate because of my ransom request."

Bendahrin wasn't sure whether to be pleased or not. He had dozens of questions, but he figured, rightly, that only certain information would be forthcoming. He kept his response specifically ambiguous. "And?"

"I am authorized to discuss three topics, from the ocean of issues."

Bendahrin was curious about this slip. Although Rish could only talk about three topics, he had now given away that there was an ocean of issues out there. Bendahrin imagined that "issues" meant "problems." Not that it mattered to him whether these issues or problems were a drop, trickle, stream, or ocean, since he just wanted his freedom. He wondered what kind of problems a ship of artifacts would cause. Snickering inwardly, Bendahrin wanted to say that the pirates would have been a whole lot better off if they hadn't killed Alystra and stolen her menagerie of trouble. "Go on," Bendahrin prompted, maintaining his ambiguous ambivalence.

"Shall we sit?" Rish gestured to the chair, and Bendahrin sat down.

For himself, he turned the box on its side and sat on it on the other side of the table. At this, the pile of clutter blocked their view of each other so they both laughed, then quickly transferred the items to the floor.

"One. Where is Kel-Purim?" Rish wasted no time.

Bendahrin had no answer. He stared at Rish blankly for an uncomfortable period of time.

Rish looked at him expectantly, and even nodded to prompt him.

Bendahrin seized the prompt and gobbled it up. "What do you mean? I don't understand the question."

"Kel-Purim, the magical being, red, bloody; you were in the room when Alystra told him to eat Erin and Jedra if they misbehaved. Where is he?"

"How would I know? You described the last time I saw him, no, wait." Bendahrin remembered. "Later, Alystra sent me to get *our* guests, and as I left, Alystra was talking to him. Ten minutes later she was murdered, but I didn't see him again."

"That's it?"

"What else could I know? You yourself painfully identified that I am not a mage, yes?"

Rish frowned. "That answer won't satisfy the officers. Was this what Alystra told you to say?"

Bendahrin had thought this answer over and over since he had been imprisoned. "Let me be clear. I have nothing to hide, *nothing!*" He looked up and around the room, as though he was directing his defense to hidden viewers, which was accurate. "I had a life. You know this, Rish, and there is nothing about that life that is hidden. My work, my career, I am sure that you have already scoured the galaxy for every detail about me. I met Alystra a few months back. I would bet you have already found the date. I don't remember the day, but I do remember *not* being careful or secretive about it. I traveled with her and learned a few details of her life, but only the smallest details. I barely knew Kel. He gave me a key; he tried to trick me, once. But now, Alystra is dead, gone. What little I know about her and her plans, and her stuff, has no secret value to me." Bendahrin spread his hands, a gesture of openness and resignation, ironically practiced universally by both honest people and liars. "And now that she is gone, why would I hide her ruined plans, or her irrelevant secrets, now that they no longer matter?"

Rish nodded, but demurred, "So, you claim you know nothing?"

Bendahrin snapped, "Absolutely, and I will prove my sincerity *and* ignorance. Alystra told Kel-Purim to eat Jedra and Erin if they misbehaved; they were there, they heard her instructions. Almost everyone would consider murder misbehavior, so, either she rescinded that order before they entered the library, or those two are still in danger. I don't think that much of anything could stop him if he was free to satisfy his hunger. Or, when she died, he was freed, and he had gone far away. Seriously, what else *could* I know?"

Rish paused, listening. Then he looked up and smiled a real smile. "Two. Your ransom has been set and I have received permission to redeem it for an item from your collection."

Bendahrin wasn't impressed, but he was always ready to learn something new, even if it was the inner machinations of the pirate economy, which was turning out to be more than just academic for him. "I am listening." Ambiguity was back.

"Obviously, it is a waste of time to demand a ransom for some people that we capture. In your case, you have no one *to* redeem you. When that happens, we work out a way for you to buy your freedom. Some people agree to work for us, like an indenture, others join us, if they have the skills, which you do not. But you have wealth."

Bendahrin snorted. "Absurd. There is no way to put a value on my collection. And besides, there is no way to know whether any item or group of items would sell, now or ever. As I said, 'absurd.'"

"Yes, most of our captives in your situation start with that perspective. Then we show them the market analysis, every major auction in the galaxy, trends, investors; our accounting teams are amazingly tiresome, but also astonishingly convincing. As you can imagine, we have substantial experience and regularly gain converts. And our accountants will show you that buying your freedom is really your best fiscal choice and the quickest way to get back to earning back what you lost."

Bendahrin was sickened by the crass, blatant greed. "So, how much do these *accountants* want?" His disgust was not ambiguous at all.

"No, Bendahrin, in this case, there is a better way out. I will buy your freedom from the Stream and all you need to do is give me an artifact from your collection."

"Any artifact?" Bendahrin knew that wasn't the answer, but he was fighting off disgust.

"You have a Teltarran Trough Totem, I believe? A few, in fact?"

"Several," Bendahrin answered, not realizing in his disgust that he had just pumped up his value in the ledgers of the listening accountants, and even this admission fell far short.

"Ah, yes, b-but I am interested in one from the B-Belstent dynasty, you do have one from that period, yes?" Rish was getting excited.

"Yes," Bendahrin said, "but it is not the most valuable totem I have. It is only about four thousand years old, I dated it by the serifs on the 'schweh' character in the bottom inscription." At least now he was becoming more engaged than disgusted.

"Yes," Rish said. "I r-read about that years ago. Phiss Laren claims that the serifs place it earlier, b-because of the oblique upper decorations that indicated a cultural move, closer to a spiritual awareness. His argument was convincing."

Bendahrin scowled for a minute at this distraction. "The oblique decorations could have been the result of—" but Rish suddenly sat up straight and cut Bendahrin off.

"Sorry, we can discuss this later. The totem, did you," he paused, trying to be casual, "did you open it?"

"Of course," Bendahrin said. "Its value can only be ascertained if you—" and Rish cut him off again.

"I know! What was inside?" he demanded, now his excitement had tipped his hand and his greed was bubbling to the top.

"Nothing," Bendahrin said. "That's why I say, it has very little value."

"Fool!" Rish slammed the table with his hand, "Those totems aren't decorations, they're prisons." He stopped and calmed himself. "I'm sorry, B-Bendahrin. The mage would put an ornate, carved doll, a character, in the totem until he had captured his enemy, then he would r-remove the doll and imprison his foe. Owning an empty totem might allow me to communicate with an ancient Teltarran sorcerer or sorceress!"

Bendahrin was stunned. He wanted to stop and count how many Teltarran prisoners he currently had in his collection. He even had double and triple totems, but he decided not to mention this. "I can buy my freedom by giving you an ancient sorcerer imprisoned in one of my least valuable artifacts?"

"Yes, pretty simple." He paused and looked at Bendahrin, again, with an expression of attentiveness and expectation.

"Do I need to answer right now?"

"No, and yes." His face looked suddenly official and blank, which might be redundant for those who like to be official. "At this moment, no, but, three, your review will be tomorrow, at mid-day. You will need to dress. I will come and get you. Standing before the officers, you will answer."

Bendahrin laughed sarcastically, "You, uh . . . haven't been a guest of the B'Tark. The light in this room never changes, and the little amenities, like a timepiece, perhaps? I have no idea whether it is mid-afternoon or midnight. Do you see my problem?"

"Simple. Dress now."

Rish picked up the box and carried it from the cell.

Bendahrin watched him go and felt an odd sadness. He pulled this feeling out and set it before him on the table to evaluate it while he changed clothes. He couldn't find it in him to care very deeply for Rish; he had known him for all of about ten minutes on the relationship clock, but Bendahrin felt as though there was a spark somewhere in the man that was being crushed and smothered by greed and this odd life as a pirate. He shook his head in silent frustration. People could be such fools. Allowing themselves to be enslaved by a lifetime of foolish choices, chasing one passion or another, never stopping to evaluate whether their choices were bringing glory or ruin.

The review clothes were a simple jumpsuit, which, when he zipped it up, immediately constricted upon him, not painfully tight, but skin-tight. He felt a bit awkward and thought that the light gray was overly somber. The day, the night, the morning passed as they did, and then Rish returned.

As they left the cell, Rish told him to walk behind and to try not to look around. Nevertheless, he had had enough time to think and plan, and his plan, to the degree that a prisoner can *have* a plan, was to comply, pay what was needed, and get home. The fantastic adventure with Alystra was over, and he wanted to return to his private, quiet life and cut himself off more than ever before. He began dreaming about his home on Palestre. He thought of himself sitting and reading in a chair by the large window in his second-floor library, sipping on a glass of three-hundred-year-old aged . . .

"In here," Rish said, opening a door for him.

Bendahrin turned to ask Rish if he was coming in, but when he turned his mouth open. Rish was gone. Bendahrin was angry for being a prisoner, and he was tired of surprises.

The room he entered was small and cubic, large enough for a loose semicircle of six people seated in chairs of odd non-uniformity with a single table near the center of the room. Bendahrin wondered if everyone brought their own unique chair. Comfort? Prestige? The walls of the room were a neutral blue, but the lighting came from eight lamps, spaced equally around the walls. Their light was dim, and Bendahrin wondered whether the purpose of the dimness was to make the proceedings more ominous or if the goal was to be relaxing. While his thoughts bustled back and forth irrelevantly between these conflicting purposes, he realized that understanding the purpose of lighting was probably a fruitless career choice for him, besides, his bustling thoughts quickly gave way to wandering thoughts, and he realized that they were merely trying to distract him from growing nerves. Despite this, he was able to find his way to the spot reserved for him, a simple chair behind the table at the center of the semi-circle. He stood behind the chair.

"Are you going to sit?" a languid voice wafted from the dimness.

"I will not do anything without explicit instructions. I don't want to offend by missing some detail of etiquette or protocol." Even Bendahrin knew he was just being defiant, but he wanted to pretend to be compliant even if he wasn't feeling particularly compliant.

Someone snickered, and another voice said, "Why?"

Bendahrin looked at the panel of faces. Three men and three women, tech fatigues, different insignias. Erin was third from the left, and Bendahrin wondered whether they were following a protocol or just sat this way by accident; they alternated: woman, man, across the room. The woman to the far left was dressed fashionably, hair, makeup, and composure perfect. Next to her sat a man who came across as all military. His uniform was pristine, but Bendahrin imagined that even his casual clothes would be starched and pressed to razor points. Erin was next to him, and Bendahrin thought that she looked bored and indifferent. The man next to her exuded an aura of mystery and cunning in suit, vest, and tie. The next woman was dumpy and disheveled, and Bendahrin wondered how long it had been since she left the front lines to support the bureaucracy. The final man was fierce and focused, and Bendahrin felt a twinge of fear as their eyes met.

"I guess my reasons would range between some confusion or fear about power and mercy. You have the power, I am hoping for mercy, and so I want to be as careful as I can be."

Someone *else* snickered at the word, "Mercy."

"In that case, sit."

Bendahrin pulled the chair out and sat, then slid up to the table. At this he noticed something on the table that he had somehow missed in the dim light.

He was about to wonder when someone said, "On the table is a *por-renvu*. It will help us to confirm your truthfulness."

The voice paused, and Bendahrin looked again at the item in front of him. It looked like a porcelain bowl with a silver lid; but looking at it his most fearful fears apprehended new levels of apprehension.

"Please take off the lid."

Bendahrin was not brave enough to simply inflict pain on himself, nor did he want to inflict pain on others as a matter of course and principle. "Does it hurt?" he asked.

Another chuckle, or maybe more than one, and a different voice spoke. "I don't know," the voice said. "I have never asked. You can let us know." This voice didn't seem to carry even the slightest touch of concern.

Bendahrin took a deep breath and reached for the *por-renvu* with no enthusiasm. He lifted the lid and placed it on the table. Immediately he felt as though a spike of light had entered his mind, cleaving it with surreptitious and irresistible finality. Although the sensation was disconcerting, it was certainly not painful. The bowl contained something alive that was both the source and the caster of the spell; Alystra would have been able to explain how one could be both. He was now surrounded by a yellow glow that created a sphere of haze. The semicircle of chairs was outside the range of the glow.

He spoke most confidently, "No, no pain, thank you." But there was more: as the spell washed over him, he realized that the pirates were clueless to the nature and function of the magic they were employing. In a sudden flash of clarity, a step beyond a mere realization, he saw the actual function of the spell, one that was purposefully and deliberately maintained by the bright creature in the bowl. This was no incidental, passive effect. The creature was working an ongoing magic for its own ends. Bendahrin asked, almost prompted by the creature in the bowl, that seemed to also be in a mocking defiant mood. "So, I am now unable to lie? I can only speak the truth?"

"No, Bendahrin," a new voice said, belonging to the man sitting to Erin's left, "that would be little help to us. The *por-renvu* casts a yellow light when you are telling the truth or thinking the truth. If you lie, the light turns blue, and there are countless shades of green in between. In that way, we can tell *when* you are telling the truth, which is what we want. More nuanced and free, likely to tell us more than mere truth."

From where he sat, Bendahrin looked out through the yellow haze at the six clear, vivid faces. From within the spell, their faces were different colors, too, and far more colors. In fact, the colors were further enhanced through the spike in his mind that allowed him to gather a far more nuanced insight into their thoughts, fears, motivations, and perspectives. Then another realization smacked him. Although the sphere of color showing his truthfulness only extended so far, all of those outside of this sphere were within range of the real spell. He smiled as his confidence stood up and strutted across his mind. It might have even laughed, since the odd protection of the spell that functioned to identify truthfulness on the part of the person inside the sphere was an almost irrelevant collateral effect of the *por-renvu*. In fact, Bendahrin sensed, from the entity in the bowl, that the yellow/green/blue lighting, although it functioned as the pirates described, was clever and deceptive, catering to the unknown purposes of the entity. He was shocked that none of the pirates knew the true nature of this magical presence, and then he realized that maybe they didn't care. He barely contained his laughter when he realized the creature in the bowl was deliberately making the yellow sphere smaller than the actual effective range of the magic to mislead *their* confidence. This spell was more useful to the person inside it.

"How long have you been traveling with Alystra?" The first question seemed absurd on the surface, but the irony was that Bendahrin could see the motivation of the question from the person who asked it—the woman to his far left. She was being evasive; the answer to the question didn't really matter to her, and he glanced at the faces, realizing that Erin was the only person who might have cared about the answer; oddly, not from the color on her, but from her attentive expression.

"We had only begun the most recent leg of our journey, a half-day out, when we were boarded and Alystra was murdered." He glanced at Erin, but she showed no expression.

The glow turned slightly green as he said this, so the suited man spoke caustically, "Why are you being evasive? You see? We can see that you are hiding something!" *His* color was angry, and Bendahrin could see, partially through the insight of the spell, that this man was a politician or lawyer type, sneaky, unprincipled, and conniving. He was also impatient and plagued with lack of confidence and fear of losing his memory. This spell provided lots of insights.

Bendahrin was awestruck. The creature in the bowl prompted him with an almost embarrassing level of self-awareness. "That was not my intention." The glow was solid yellow. "The question was ambiguous, and I wavered in which way to answer it. I will answer your ambiguous question the other *possible* way. I first met Alystra about sixty days ago, no, sixty days before she was murdered." The glow was brilliant yellow, which none of the pirates noticed as the indictment it was.

"Where is Kel-Purim?" This question from the man at the far right. Bendahrin saw him clearly, more analytical and methodical, a scientist, but still oddly self-serving.

Why is the creature showing me this?

"I thought you were listening to my conversation with Rish."

"Yes, but now we can see if you are telling the truth."

He looked across the tableau of faces. The spell showed him boredom and distraction, as if the questions were being asked for some reason other than obtaining an answer. He wondered if they were calibrating his answers against their favorite color of green. He sighed. "The last time I saw Kel-Purim was as I was moving to the upper deck on Alystra's ship. Kel and Alystra were together as they walked toward the library. Uh, no, Kel-Purim doesn't walk, he floats. The more important concern, as I mentioned, was the threat to Erin and Jedra if Alystra's command was still in place."

"Did you hear Alystra release Kel-Purim from that directive?" The fashionable woman asked the question as if she had read it from a script.

"No, which worries me." Although his glow stayed yellow, his comment raised the interest level to consternation or curiosity, among other more ominous and threatening feelings, and those, not directed against him.

"Why would you be worried by this?" asked the military man to Erin's right. He was surrounded by murderous anger, which

Bendahrin would have recognized even without the spell. He suddenly felt the first inklings of fear because of the volatility of the emotions in the room. He wondered at the nature of the hostility. It might have been caused by fear. He just didn't want any of the destructive emotional energy present coming his way.

"I have seen enough death to last a lifetime. Although I am not happy that Alystra is dead, I . . . I don't want to see anyone else dead, especially as food for a scary magical being."

Everyone in the room stirred.

"So, you want to protect Erin Flesson?" the man on the far right asked with a scowl, although many nodded, and the sentiment was expressed in other words barely submerged under breaths.

Bendahrin took a deep breath of his own and looked at Erin in disgust frosted with sadness. His response came slowly. "Despite my feelings, which are confused. I have pity for Erin. The weight of murder, like the weight of hatred, is its own well-deserved punishment. Alystra would, from the position of her own experience, not want to punish anyone on purely moral grounds, since none of us are perfect. For that reason, Erin has my pity, and I would wish her to change her ways. Although Alystra could not ever bear that sentiment, I lift that banner in her memory."

The room was utterly silent, and the creature showed Bendahrin a room of faces filled with petulant shame and hands blisteringly red in blood. Even so, their years of hardened practice and, moreover, practice hardening their hearts, smothered any remorse. One voice muttered, harder than the rest, "Only fools pity the strong." An accusation washed away by the next question.

"Who is Tored?" Fashionable asked in a way that tried to sound uninterested, but Bendahrin noticed at once that the volatility shifted. This was a topic that sparked interest and swept away most of the anger. He scratched his head, half ignoring the question since he had no idea. He was far more interested in whether the explosive situation in the room was political or personal. The psychology of pirate culture must be a fascinating study. What kind of alliance can possibly endure in a world driven by selfishness?

"I have no idea. The only time I ever heard that name, if it is even a name, was when Alystra mentioned it to Erin and Jedra."

Even though his glow was a bright, glorious, vivid yellow, the scientist, far to the right, challenged his statement's veracity. "You were on Alystra's ship for months! You expect us to believe that she never mentioned her other companions?"

Bendahrin wondered at this most conspicuously, at least as *he* saw it. In light of the yellow glow confirming his answer, he wondered about the nature of rational beings that led them to question the obvious whenever it doesn't support what they want to hear.

"Despite the confirmation of the *por-renvu,* I understand your consternation." He tried to say this in a way that didn't bring too much attention to the fact that they weren't paying attention to their own interrogation. "Although I was on the ship with her for a lengthy period, she was unavailable the vast majority of the time, focused on her efforts to track some dated magic through space. Of the sixty days, we spoke for less than a couple." He wondered if they would take the bait about her search. "Besides," he continued, "in the warm glow of retrospect, Alystra's mention of Tored and The Lynthe didn't give me the feel of 'companions' in the filial or friendly sense. My impression is that they were more of a threat than someone to break bread with. Even Kel-Purim, although talkative enough, wasn't someone you would *want* to spend time with."

"Alystra's ship seems the home to a number of threats." The statement was directionless and clearly a bid for information. Since it wasn't a question, Bendahrin wondered whether he should answer or wait. At the same time, the anger in the room soared, and most of Erin's companions, who seemed about as friendly as Alystra's, glanced at her. She remained serene and maintained a neutral color. Bendahrin wondered why Erin hadn't said anything.

"That, in my mind, is part of the risk of your profession." Bendahrin knew at once that he had said the wrong thing, especially since the glow maintained a steady, accusing yellow. For the first time, all of his interrogators moved and shifted as though uncomfortable. He was pressed with the stressful impression from their faces that the capture of Alystra's ship had caused waves in the Stream. The tension rose to a vivid spectrum before his spell-enriched eyes, when the dumpy woman raised her hand. She clearly had a massive weight of authority in the room because everyone immediately cooled before his vision and the room settled.

"Bendahrin," she said, lightly, "we have discussed, extensively, your worth. Your words to Rish confirm what we could learn about you, which was what we expected since you are not unknown by the populace of Palestre. But we are forced to wonder what is so special about you that would make Alystra take you on as a shipmate. Can you provide any insight into that?"

Bendahrin had not expected this question and could readily join with them in wonder. He pressed his hand against his mouth as he outlined his answer. "At first it made no sense to me, either. I am nothing *to* her, and yet, to summarize or paraphrase her own words, I was the first person she had met in a long, long time who wasn't out for her blood. She is, sorry, no, *was* not capable of friendship, at least not as many would consider friendship: her unwanted nature abhorred the warmth of feeling. But I had offered to help her, and she seemed to welcome it, perhaps, in part, because she had been alone for so long. On the day we were boarded, she also told me that she had seen my arrival in a vision. I can assure you that her interest in and acceptance of visions was generally met with derision. Why she chose to place confidence in this particular vision will never be known. Certainly, whatever outcome the vision may have revealed is at an end." Yellow with a slight hint of green. Uncertainty is like lying the longer you talk.

This answer generated a mix of emotions, exhibited to Bendahrin in a spectrum of toasty colors.

He rubbed his chin. "I don't know what you are looking for. Any value I had to her was something she chose to value. That is all I can offer to you." Yellow, yellow, yellow.

The woman to the far left asked, "Now, Bendahrin, could you describe what happened on that day? Where were you going? What were you doing when our team came on board? Then describe all of the events up until you were taken off the ship."

"As part of her overall plan to discover what had happened to her, she wanted to pick up a trail that she had discovered. I don't know for certain where that was, only that it was out of the galaxy."

None of them had the slightest interest in Alystra's journey of discovery, except Erin who was again leaning forward to listen.

Then he proceeded with the story of the boarding, from waking up and finding Alystra in the engine room, through til the time when he had walked into the library with Jedra and Erin. He carefully dodged the details of the vision by saying that he and Alystra had had a discussion about the vision that she had cast, and they flinched. Their colors were still apathetic, save Erin, still watching and colorless. He told the entire story with no interruptions until he reached the moment where Erin killed Alystra. This whole time, the yellow glow was steady.

Bendahrin was perplexed at the questions. They all seemed to be questions that could be answered by investigating the ship. But his contemplation was interrupted.

"Stop!" the military man said, impatiently. "How did Ver Tark Erin kill her?" Suddenly the color revealed agitation, interest, consternation, anticipation. Bendahrin had to be careful not to open his mouth in surprise at how vividly the spell exposed their blatant interest.

"As I understand it," Bendahrin said, hesitating, and looking at Erin, puzzled. Her color was a steady gray, unmoving. She was serene. "Ver Tark Erin stabbed Alystra with some form of blade that . . ."

"Stop!" This seemed to be his go to word. "First, you do *not* call her by her title, and second, we understand the technology—we know what she used—how could she possibly kill Alystra? Isn't she a super mage or something?"

The glow around Bendahrin wavered and changed, greening a bit. He had pondered this as endlessly as any thought he had had for his entire time as a prisoner. "I have little understanding of the nature of the Issachon. Certainly, I have read some of the religious writings, but they are legendary and ancient, full of portents and metaphors. I am not sure that a person has ever *become* the Issachon before, so there isn't anything to provide insights into the metaphysics of who Alystra was. Was she a vessel? Was there a joining? I have no way to tell."

Bendahrin had maintained a happy yellow through these comments, proving that he was, after all, a relatively guileless person to begin with. Of course, his investigations into the Issachon prior to meeting Alystra were largely superficial compared to the person he had come to know slightly, and he still couldn't remember everything from the period before meeting Alystra. The pirate panel displayed a spectrum of responses including anger, confusion, and fear.

"Forget about religion and the history books," said the suited man in the center—to the left of Erin. "You saw her fight, yes? She was formidable, as we have been led to believe from every story we could track down. How could a single thrust have bested her? After all that you have seen, how do you explain that?"

Bendahrin was puzzled exceedingly and sought to put the pieces together, but no amount of turning them around in his mind would make them fit. He had tried. "I have seen her fight, yes. Yes, one major battle, but it was a battle of force or strength. That battle was also tied to endless use of magic, and Alystra had, uh . . . ample warning." He looked at Erin, a mere few yards away, her face was utterly blank, and no color could be found there. He remembered Alystra's last words about Erin's mental discipline. "It seems that when Erin attacked, there was no magic, and no warning. As I understand it, the physical damage was so immediate that no reaction from Alystra was possible. But I must insist, and I think this is perhaps what you are trying to get me to admit, I would have never thought that she could be killed, but," he cocked his head to the side, "I would also concede that a quick thrust would be the most likely path to success, as we have seen."

"You were in love with her, weren't you?"

"No, of course not!" he retorted, but the sphere reached the deepest blue-green so far.

Once again there were chuckles and a slight gasp; the faces showed signs of both mockery and cynicism, but also unkind, grating pity.

Bendahrin was about to defend himself, when a familiar arresting voice took charge. "Stop! Who cares! So, it is your statement that she couldn't have been beaten, yet she was. Could she be subdued? Controlled? Was killing her the only option?"

"I believe strongly that killing a person, even harming a person, is *never* the only option. It is evil to hold such a thought." But Bendahrin stopped, witnessing dissension and discord. He looked from face to face, more slowly than before. The truth hit him, and his voice spoke, almost as if it were out of his control. "I'm not the one on trial here! You are questioning Erin's actions. *A live hostage is better than a dead corpse,* is that it?" The glow was now brilliantly yellow as if the magical being was casting a deliberate insult at the putative audience.

The discord disappeared with explosive immediacy; Erin was clearly no longer ambivalent, but still too hard to read. "We are not here to answer your questions. Could she be subdued?"

He was angry now, which made the glow waver greenly. "Alystra was a very complicated person, perfect evil, but conflicted.

She could have killed all three of the boarders and dropped their bodies into the nearest star without any amount of effort that would even be measurable—in fact, that would have made her stronger from what I know. Considering how precious her ship was to her overall designs, I am surprised that she wasn't more abrupt. Could she be subdued or controlled? No, emphatically no. Convinced? That was a possible alternative. She didn't listen very often, her purposeful and untrusting character made that difficult, but she was oddly able to act outside of her nature. We will never know whether a well-reasoned approach would have worked." He glared at Erin, who now looked hyper-bored.

There was a lengthy period of silence, and Bendahrin wondered if they were communicating in some silent high-tech way.

The man to the left of Erin now spoke again. "Bendahrin, as a rule, we don't ever want to kill anyone. Our *normal* activities are not bad enough to cause an official response, but when people die, normal operations become more difficult. When someone dies, we investigate what happened thoroughly. Our conclusions align with what you have told us. Killing Alystra was the only option."

Bendahrin was stunned and disgusted. He had never come across such a cold and calculating perspective; so carefully presented and justified as though they were merely trying to avoid an inconvenience. His estimation of the B'Tark Stream reached an all-time low; they avoided murder because it was a potential liability against the bottom line in their ledgers. Although he guessed that this should be exactly what to expect, this type of blindness accompanies those who are driven by selfish ends. They will now feel good about themselves because murder was necessary in this case, and they would all be smug in their conviction that they *normally* don't kill their victims. They would probably never realize the irony that the only reason they weren't *more* murderous was that it didn't support their already selfish ends. His thoughts were yellow, but he did not feel as though any words were necessary.

"One final question, simple logistics at this point: will you meet Rish's request to cover your ransom?"

Bendahrin looked bleak. "Yes, of course. I just want to go home."

"Then replace the lid. Rish will escort you back."

Bendahrin placed the lid on the *por-renvu* and stood to go.

10

The weeks passed. Bendahrin found himself thinking of Alystra, particularly her eyes that held both the storm and an odd calm. Thoughts of her and memories that felt far too distant often jumped him unbidden and unexpected. He was able to complete a book Rish had lent him, the *Ethareptikon*, an ancient epic that he had previously read in his university days. Reading the book left him feeling nervous. He had remembered the book being more ponderous the first time, but on this read he felt as though he was being swept along as the pages turned themselves. Enjoyable, painful, lonely, more days. Alystra was gone. Eating and sleeping passed the time and made it drag interminably. His dreams hinted at vacations and machinery. Rish stopped by. He and Bendahrin discussed endless topics of archaeology and places that Bendahrin had been but Rish had not. Invigorating, and more days. Sorrow layered on confusion. A new cart with food and then, a couple more books. Books that seemed too easy to read.

Bendahrin thought about his past, living in Palestre. He pondered his future, living in Palestre. He reflected on his collection and longed to be back among his relics and books and the comforts of his estate. He couldn't quite push from his mind that they were small comforts with Alystra gone. Rish came by when his duties allowed. Of course, he was never able to say anything about what those duties were. He asked endless questions about Bendahrin's life. Although Rish never mentioned his life, Bendahrin thought that Rish was in a trap that he wasn't able to see, surrounded by walls that nobody talked about. Lively, but sad; another book, another week?

Rish wouldn't even speak the next time he came when Bendahrin asked how long he would be in "this room." So, Bendahrin changed the subject and they talked through almost every chapter of Phiss Laren's *Digs on Laparian*, a thick textbook Rish had brought that Bendahrin had first encountered at a symposium on Laparian twelve years earlier when he had been given a copy of the original manuscript, heavily marked. Bendahrin told Rish to stop by someday and he would show him the notes he had taken in the margins.

Rish turned red and his stuttering showed up for an hour after this offer.

Engaging and frustrating, more meals and nights of sleep, the number of weeks was getting annoying.

He still wept daily, just as he should. And he fought internally for answers and found none.

His thoughts frequently trickled down the familiar furrows in his mind to Alystra. He concentrated 'til his head hurt on many nights, or maybe days, trying to figure out if she had said anything to him, a hint, or a clue. It made no sense to him; how could the Issachon *die*? Alystra, the woman, perhaps, but what happened to the evil? He somehow imagined that the release of the primal being would be a catastrophic event, but . . . nothing? She had died, almost silently, praising Erin's mental focus. She had survived horrendous battles and relentless attacks, all to be, what? Slaughtered by a tech knife? Absurd, but he had carried her lifeless, blood-streaked body. What had the pirates done with her body? That thought brought both unwelcome ambivalence and welcome, expected pain.

At the beginning, he had figured that his stay would be short, so he never made an attempt to count the days. Then, as a length of time had passed, he started counting how often he had slept, a bad way to mark time without an accurate timepiece. Sleep when you want, eat when you are hungry, read, think.

More eating and sleeping and weeping and reading blew past when Rish, breathless, came in for the last time. "This is it," he said, buoyant and expectant. "Time for The Presentation." He grabbed Bendahrin by the arm and pulled him through the door. "You will not need to do anything. Of course, you will be right up front."

They were bustling along corridor after corridor.

"The Presentation is a financial ceremony, one where the

commander of the victorious ship presents the value of the acquisition to commanders in the division. Considering the historic and enormous value of this presentation, there are some very important people here." He stopped himself, and he stopped Bendahrin, too. Then, grabbing his arm, he looked Bendahrin in the face. "I'm sorry this has been hard on you." He glanced at the ceiling. "Nobody monitors what is said in the halls, why would we? It has been an honor to meet you and talk. I will be standing with you in The Presentation since I made your ransom, barely worth mentioning, really. You stand with me."

They walked into the massive hangar that had been decked out for the celebration. Bleachers on two sides filled with hundreds of men and women who watched their arrival in silence. The decorations were ornate and *gaudy*. Bendahrin found them a bit repugnant, almost as bad as the event being celebrated. Alystra's ship had been moved to the center and was facing a dais at the front where two dozen chairs had been placed, slightly separated from a single chair, centered. All these seats were empty at the moment, but Bendahrin noticed that once again, like his interrogation, each chair was unique.

Rish was whispering loudly at his side, "The victorious crew oversees The Presentation, so each crew always tries to out-do previous presentations with more elaborate staging and pageantry. I was engaged to add some magical brilliance to the lighting and to make the victorious roars of the crowds sound," he paused, smiling smugly, "more heroic."

Bendahrin was saddened again at the superficial nature of this nonsense, and that a grown man could consider piracy and murder in a positive light.

Where is the victory in murder?

Bendahrin and Rish followed a path alive with lights that moved in waves to direct his steps. As they walked through the watchful silence, Bendahrin wondered why there weren't any victorious roars as Rish suggested. The end of the path stopped right under the nose of Alystra's ship, and Bendahrin immediately realized that he was part of the gift being presented, two pieces, big and little.

Erin suddenly appeared before him, teleporting to her place using her tech fatigues and the spectators burst into a thunder of appreciation. Then, one by one, each of the special dignitaries who had chairs on the dais teleported in, each to renewed applause, each bowing or waving, each seating themselves before the next appeared. Eventually only the central chair was empty and the audience settled into silence. The lights changed to a single spotlight aimed at the empty chair and the final man teleported into the immediate cacophony of appropriately heroic and victorious roars. The audience knew who demanded their praise and passed out favors.

The lights came back on to fill the room as this final arrival took his seat and gazed about the room, surveying the crowd. He raised his hand, at which the applause grew, if possible. When his hand went down, silence fell. His voice, when he spoke, though amplified through the room, was neither commanding nor powerful. It didn't raise your head or spirits with confidence or joy or a desire to obey. It was cold, pathetic, and jeering, paternal and patronizing, old but empty of wisdom or grace. "I am Velven Ostran, Prae Tark of Epsin quad, divisions two, five, eight, nine, eleven, and twelve. Seated with me are the Trae Tarks of my divisions to receive The Presentation and bestow commensurate gifts."

Again, his eyes wandered about, and Bendahrin wondered why the crowd didn't break into spontaneous applause.

"To whom do we address our reception?"

At this invitation, Erin stepped forward and spoke, *her* voice, however held a tone of command and respect, even Bendahrin felt himself standing straighter. "I, Ver Tark Erin Flesson, of the ship *Alaris*, stand forth to make a presentation."

Velven looked at her and smiled—coldly. Apparently, the official opening was over because he then spoke in conversational tones. "Ah . . . yes, Erin." His voice was positive, but vicious. "It is *such* a pleasure to be here, *again*, to see the success of *your* ship and crew." The word "your" was a growl. He paused and his nose twitched as though he was smelling something profoundly foul. Then he turned, gesturing to his left, but not taking his eyes off Erin, who glared back fearlessly. "And thanks to your Trae Tark, Polloni, for providing this fine concourse for our celebration today. It took us a long time to make arrangements for us all to be here, but we hear that *you* have something special to present, a once-in-a-lifetime find, is what I have heard."

Erin took a few steps forward, and the lights went down around the room lighting only *Lentoris*, which glowed. She began, "*My* ship," she looked at Velven, and he jerked forward in his chair, baring his teeth, and Erin smiled slightly. "Yes, my ship and my crew present our prize." She gestured upward toward the ship, and cried, "The ship, *Lentoris*, the ship of Alystra Alsatia of Palestre, a ship of hundreds of wonders and treasures. Hundreds of priceless treasures remain on board, and we have valued it as almost beyond measure!"

At this, the crowd thundered their empty approval.

The noise continued for what seemed far too long before Velven once again raised his hand. His voice was still cold and held its venomous edge. "And your captives?" His stare was now hungry, and some of the men and women sitting with him showed their emotions as well. Clearly this was an issue that had raised some power struggles at the top.

Erin didn't falter, but raised her hand for attention. "O Pre Tark and Trae Tarks, hear! Five captives there were, two aboard the ship remain unknown and awaiting those who can name them, one escaped and is lost to us, one stands here, ransomed by his value, and one perished at my hand."

The room immediately took this cue as an opportunity for gasps and a spread of incredulous sounds.

Bendahrin was disgusted and perplexed at the maudlin pageantry. His feeling was that this should have been worked out weeks ago, but maybe this was the time for final reckoning so that all loose ends needed to be hashed out one last time, for official and ceremonial reasons. This group was as fickle and tempestuous as teenagers. He wished that he had the *por-renvu* to provide more clarity.

Velven leaned forward, mocking, "And there was no way to subdue her? One woman, you want us to believe that she could not be tamed?"

Erin looked up at Velven and said with the finality of a mountain of granite, the slightest smile appearing on her face, "O, Prae Tark, no, Alystra can't be tamed."

At this there was a flash of blackness and a bolt of black lightning that shot down from above to a spot between Erin and Velven. A screech of a thousand broken souls tore through the room and blasted from the bolt of blackness like a shockwave, and she was there. Alystra stood facing Velven with her head bowed and her feet planted more than shoulder width apart in a circle of tortured and burned floor. Brahtenla was in her right hand, unsheathed.

Bendahrin stared in utter shock and wonder. He saw that several of the Trae Tarks had disappeared, along with the Prae Tark, but suddenly they were all back again, and their panic and fear were evident; he didn't need the *por-renvu* to see that being overpowered and forced to remain was an unknown experience for them. Some tried to stand up to flee, to no avail. He looked at Erin who had drawn a sword and lunged for Alystra, but she too was held in place. Bendahrin dared to glance around the massive hangar and realized that they were all held steady, of thousands, every last one.

Alystra slowly raised her head to look at Velven, and then she spoke and her voice was commanding and terrible, powerful and extreme. "Velven Prae Tark of the B'Tark Stream, Trae Tarks at his side. I am Alystra the Destroyer, your kind killed me, and I am now returned! The time of reckoning is upon you, and now I will make my demands. Speak!"

Velven's face was gray with terror and his body trembled in a way that was visible even at a distance. Despite his terror, Velven wasted no time, responding immediately from years of practiced deceit. "Oh, Alystra, who *we* didn't want killed, what do you want?" His voice now had no power or venom, it was thin and trembling within him.

"Three things, of which I give you no choice." She turned to look at her ship and at Bendahrin, and Bendahrin could see that she was entirely black again as he had seen her on her planet in the tower of Nuans, yet different, from experience he quickly looked away. "First, I will purchase my ship from you to make it worth your while, though you don't deserve my ransom price for what is my own. Second, with my ship, and all that it contains, Bendahrin, my companion, and Jedra, who attacked my ship, for whom I will pay the blood price." Alystra paused and glanced at Bendahrin, with barely a passing recognition. She turned to look at Velven.

"And your third condition?"
"We will discuss my third condition once an amount has been agreed upon and payment has been made."

Velven looked from side to side at the Trae Tarks who all avoided his gaze, cowards all, not wanting to get involved. He looked at Alystra, and winced. A steady black vapor poured from her body, head to foot and cascaded to the floor, rolling off in thinning billows. "The ship and treasures on board were, are, immensely valuable so setting a price—"

Alystra interrupted him with a voice of command. "Don't waste my time. I know their value better than you! They are mine. What price have you put on them? We both know that this has been determined. That is the paltry point of this Presentation, correct?"

Velven looked around him again. "Forty billion was our conclusion."

"Under-rated! But I will pay you twenty-five." She pointed off to the right on one side of the hangar, and a mountain grew in the darkness. "Count it later and use it well, and may you choke on each tiniest measure."

Velven looked to his left at the mountain, and a smile broke upon his face most involuntarily. "And your third condition?"

She turned to Erin, still unmoving with her sword pointed at Alystra. "Satisfaction! A duel. No magic, on my part. And I will kill her directly with my sword for her treachery."

Velven was clearly relieved and spoke with rising confidence. "I can't speak for Ver Tark Erin, but if you release her, let her speak in her own defense." A coward to the end. Bendahrin noticed that Velven didn't even speak a word of concern about Jedra or his cost.

At this, Alystra took her stand ten feet from Erin and slightly to her left, her sword point on the ground preparing for a parley. With an unnecessary wave of her hand to let the audience feel as though they had seen magic done, she released Erin, who moved as if she had never been stopped, slashing at Alystra with a howl. Alystra barely parried her first attack in time, and Erin pressed her advantage, thrusting and slashing furiously as Alystra backed away slowly before the onslaught.

Rish grabbed Bendahrin and pulled him back a dozen feet to get away from the combatants.

Bendahrin shook his head and realized that this was the obvious thing to do. He was dumbfounded and watching in awe. The swords of the two women were a blur in their hands, and Alystra was still giving way to Erin's attacks.

Erin had a vicious smile on her face as she came on, Alystra's eyes and face were still black, so no expression was there to be found.

Eventually Alystra backed around until they were just beneath the nose of the ship, and at this she held her ground. She steadied down and placed her left hand behind her back, looking as genteel as if she were in a fencing match, but this was the start of a prolonged engagement where the two women advanced and retreated in turn, testing each other's speed and defenses.

At one point, Erin pressed in close, forcing Alystra's blade to the side and she pressed inside her blade and slammed Alystra with her fist. At this, Alystra reached across and grabbed her by the throat and pushed her away so forcefully that she flew back, several yards. Erin's training was so automatic that even as she was being pushed, she drew her arm back and turned her blade, slashing up to slice Alystra's wrist. Then, instead of landing, Erin disappeared.

Alystra laughed, her voice thundering in the room. She turned slowly, her blade outstretched, looking for Erin's return, and sure enough, just as Alystra's head was turned looking in the same direction of the blade, Erin appeared on the opposite side of Alystra and took a slash at her back. With inhuman speed and agility Alystra turned, dropped down, ducking, and parried the attack, switching Brahtenla to her left hand to do it, with her blade slashing behind her. Then they entered a new phase, circling each other, and presenting short exchanges.

At this, Bendahrin realized that the room was filled with noise, the watching pirates cheered and yelled advice, encouragement, one group chanted, "Erin! Erin!" The Prae Tark and Trae Tarks watched intently, some joined in with the chant, others silent and grim, most, however, still tried to depart in vain, struggling against invisible bonds.

The circling continued, and Alystra, her blood dripping, returned to her stance with her left hand behind her. Erin was by now drenched in sweat, and Alystra had returned to her normal color, the utter black only remaining in her eyes. Bendahrin knew that Alystra could have ended this fight at any time and wondered why she was playing this game. They had been dueling for about twenty minutes, and Alystra gave Erin a simple salute with her sword and then bore in on her opponent. She attacked like a whirlwind, and for the first time she pressed Erin without stopping.

Erin backed away, fighting defensively, but soon the entire room could see that she was tiring, and Alystra, as always, hadn't tired at all, which, technically, *was* using magic. In a lull, that Bendahrin knew was Alystra toying with her, their eyes met. Erin's face showed a moment of fear, but then she bared her teeth and growled. Not that it mattered. Alystra was through playing. Now that Erin was slowing, Alystra took pleasure in slashing her arm once, twice, three times. She cut her face with simple parallel cuts.

Eventually, Alystra slashed her leg with a deep cut, and Erin, knowing that she had no chance of continuing the fight, vanished again.

The room went silent.

Alystra, unlike before, stood with her arms raised, her left hand still dripping blood that splattered on the blackened floor. She stood silently, waiting, and Bendahrin felt the waves of her cold majesty.

The tension in the room rose with a heat like an oven.

Suddenly Erin was there, crouching, again to Alystra's left, but as she thrust toward Alystra with her blade, Alystra's left hand swept down in a circle and back, parrying the blade with her arm and suffering a deep gouge.

Alystra continued the momentum and turned, plunging her blade into Erin's chest. Brahtenla passed all the way through, and Alystra, out of some nobility, approached Erin and caught her, lowering her gently to the ground, then she removed her sword and banished it. She turned to face Velven.

"Satisfied?" Velven asked, his face showing no concern, instead he seemed pleased.

"Let me be clear," Alystra pointed out at Velven then she turned in a full circle, pointing to the entire crowd, "I will take Erin's body for my own along with her possessions. I take Jedra Corbick, and his possessions. Bendahrin Casthay is mine, and he returns to me. My ship is mine. You won't need to open the hangar. But know this, I will not tolerate interference from the B'Tark Stream again. Make that clear to all. Next time, payment will be of a dreadful kind."

"Wait!" Bendahrin yelled, and at this, ran up to Alystra, who looked at him as if seeing him for the first time, ever. He said to her quietly, "Look into my mind. See what I want."

She looked as told and said, "Now?" She shook her head, but he nodded, eagerly. A small, ever so small smile accosted her face and she said, "Bestow it."

And in that moment, Bendahrin was holding a Teltarran Trough Totem, the one that he knew Rish wanted. He hurried over to Rish. "Here," he said, handing him the treasure. "I hope that someday you will be able to free yourself. In fact," he lowered his voice, "get word to me. That's all I need. Good luck." And he rushed off to Alystra.

Alystra was looking at Velven, who had stoically expressed himself and his cowardly fear by saying nothing and moving less. Alystra said, "And the gift to Rish is his from Bendahrin, who is mine." She pointed again to Velven, who raised his hand. "Are we met?"

Velven lowered his hand and spoke. "We have heard and received your terms, and this Presentation is final." His eyes darted off to the left at the mountain of treasure.

Alystra waved her hand, and cried, "You are released!" Bendahrin thought that she was being very showy by this point. Almost instantly, a group of thirty guards appeared around the mountain of treasure, the Prae Tark and all of the Trae Tarks vanished, most of the audience was gone. Clearly nobody wanted to have anything else to do with this catastrophic but unique Presentation and departed as expeditiously as possible.

Jedra was walking up to them, his face a mix of anger and despair.

He approached Alystra, ready to speak, when she held up her hand. "Say nothing."

And he stopped, bowing his head in defeated subjection.

Alystra bent down and picked up Erin's body. Bendahrin thought that the gesture was far too reminiscent of him carrying her and his confusion started to boil over. He was about to speak when she spoke into his mind, "*We need to leave. This situation is more volatile than it appears. I don't want to be forced to destroy any more of them. Hold your questions.*"

She walked to the rolling stairs at the side of her ship. In the wake of her steps her own blood mixed with Erin's on the floor. The airlock was suddenly open. Alystra placed Erin's body on the floor in the hall and walked back to close the airlock. Once done, she said, "Give me a moment," and she raised her hands above her head, stretching. There was a sickening lurch that Jedra and Bendahrin felt. She beckoned to them, and Bendahrin followed.

Jedra, however, knelt beside Erin's body and placed his hand gently on her arm.

Alystra turned and said calmly, "Please, Jedra, give me a minute and everything will be clear. Follow!"

Jedra stood dejectedly, his anger hovering at the threshold of exploding from him, but he walked slowly to join them, looking back once.

They walked past the forward lounge and both men stopped. They were in open space, moving fast.

Alystra said again, "I know you are both loaded with questions, but come here now."

The command in her voice made them both jump and follow her.

They entered the port lounge, and Bendahrin immediately felt the sense of motion and activity, Alystra led them to the massive dolmen, floating near the front of the lounge, on their right. She stopped before the opening between the rocks, Bendahrin and Jedra at her side. She turned to face the dolmen and called out, "*Thentrais, pheren moothnay Ohm Erin ofthet.*"

They could see right through the arch of the dolmen at the rest of the collection of magical artifacts behind it. After a pile of moments had thumped past, a mist formed and it took the shape of a person walking.

A moment later, Erin pushed through the mist and exited the dolmen.

Jedra gasped, and Bendahrin covered his mouth with his hand.

Erin approached Alystra as if no one else existed. The two women were face-to-face; their eyes were locked and Erin's eyes were darting around Alystra's face. They stood, unmoving, as moments stretched on. Erin raised her left hand slowly to scratch her face. She held it there for a moment and then, right when Bendahrin couldn't stand it any longer, Erin and Alystra burst into laughter.

11

endahrin stood somewhere outside of the mirth in a land that
was both confused and approaching angry.

Jedra was even further from the mirth, having landed in a
conflict of warring loyalties.

Erin seemed to be ensconced in a *flood* of mirth, which further
confused and conflicted both Bendahrin and Jedra.

Bendahrin was experiencing another new layer of Alystra after
months of confinement, and although he knew that Alystra had
somehow magicked a crazy solution for some reason, he was feeling
the heavy weight of weeks of loneliness and sorrow and broken
hopes and new expectations. Jedra was forsworn for life to Erin,
which, to him, had always been a place of duty and comfort, certainty
and known expectations. At the same time, Jedra had never known
life outside the restrictive confluence of the Stream's tributaries of
loyalty, subjection, restrictions, and rewards. Minutes before, he had
dwelt in a confident future of life in a tunnel, but now his eyes were
opening to the possibilities of vast horizons. Those same minutes
had taken Bendahrin from a future hope of bland serenity among
his treasures, but now he felt as though he had been flung back into
the troubling and unpredictable maelstrom of Alystra's epic destiny.
He felt a loss at something he wasn't sure he hadn't wanted, for the
benefits attached to a far-flung life of wonder. Jedra was not sure, but
he felt he was losing the safety of a known drudgery for the freedom
of self unleashed.

The mirth evaporated in a blink as Alystra reached the limits that joy could enter her presence without a swift and unpleasant intervention, and Erin was startled at the change, but still smiled gently, holding a happy, new, grateful expectation. Alystra turned and looked at Bendahrin, seeing him and attending to *his* attention with prompt immediacy. She stepped over to him and grabbed his two arms. She looked him in the eyes, and started, "Bendahrin, I—" she began, but he scowled, and quickly raised his hand to her mouth.

"I know," he whispered, "you are sorry. I know. Please don't say it. I don't want another world to die." He shook his head slowly.

Then she did something that might cost a hundred worlds in future weeks, but she couldn't find herself to care. She threw her arms around him, and whispered back, in a moment that might have been tender, had not more worlds been at stake, "Yes, Bendahrin, you know me."

The crushing warmth of this embrace might have worked some deeper evil in Bendahrin, but, as she held him, he felt exalted. She had broken a bond, broken *another* bond, through which a greater humanity had escaped. Bendahrin knew the cost would be high, but the end had never felt so hopeful. At the same time, her embrace washed away the past months of confinement; the fears he had endured were chased away, the loneliness obliterated. As always, a simple embrace held its own relational sway, and Alystra had a power that was ultimate.

She released him, though they held each other's arms for a moment, and through a haze of heady affection, he said, "This was your solution, yes? The way to secure the vision?"

She nodded and pursed her lips. "As I said, 'you know me.' Clever, yes? Do you like it?"

"Ha!" he replied, pushing her away gently, rolling his eyes and shaking his head with disgust. "Couldn't you have come up with a solution that would have left me at home? How many months was it, anyway?"

"About two, maybe more. You want to hit me, don't you?"

"Absurd! You wouldn't even feel it, and I am sure it would hurt me. And you might accidentally lose control and react to the attack and I'd end up on some lifeless asteroid." He laughed, then sighed. "The vision secured, destiny forging ahead, balance temporarily restored, but as expected, if you had a solution, of course it wouldn't be simple or painless."

"No, not simple at all, but effective." And her cold stone exterior was back. "Now come! We have an overdue meal to complete."

At that, she turned and pointed across the ship in another irrelevant gesture and they were there, in the library, and the table was set, as before, richly adorned, with fare plentiful and varied. Alystra gestured, and she sat in the chair facing the library door, Bendahrin sat on her right, Jedra across, Erin in the final seat across from her. "Please eat," Alystra said. "And I will start to answer your questions."

"The secret here is the dolmen," she began. "If you enter it, with the correct incantations in Erin's case, or, for me, with the right attitude, the dolmen will create an exact duplicate, a dolmen construct, of the person who entered. As long as that doppelganger is away from the dolmen, the original can control it, seeing what the duplicate sees, feeling what it feels, a perfect experience from afar. The irony and benefit of the dolmen as a solution for our situation, is that its function was perfect to satisfy our need. The only way to exit the dolmen, it turns out, is to have the construct return to the dolmen and enter it, or the construct must die."

Bendahrin turned to Erin. "Now, I understand why the *por-renvu* couldn't extract your feelings!"

Erin sat up straight and she looked at Bendahrin, her eyes wide. "What do you mean?"

"The creature, in the ceramic bowl, you do know there is a living creature in there?" Bendahrin didn't wait for her response. "When you and those other Stream people interrogated me."

She nodded slowly.

"The spell the creature casts, it does reveal the truthfulness of my words, yes, but the person in the sphere can see the emotions of everyone outside the sphere in enormous detail. You were totally gray, emotionless, but that's because you weren't you."

Erin laughed. "So, the person interrogated has the advantage." She laughed again, slapping her knee with enthusiasm. "I wonder why nobody has ever communicated that before?"

Bendahrin shrugged. "I have a feeling that is part of the spell. I don't think that I would be able to tell you, if you were still part of the Stream." He turned to Alystra. "How in the world did you learn about this dolmen?"

"I ran across it during my travels. Part of the function of the Strentrian Bubble is that I can sense magical events and relics more acutely from within. It drew my attention, so I stopped and studied it. Although it is potent and complex, the spell is straightforward. Enter, activate the spell, send out your doppelganger. When I found it, there were a dozen mages inside."

"Are they trapped?" Erin asked, curious but indifferent.

"Impossible to tell. Since their senses are limited to what they gather through the doppelganger, there is no way to communicate with them. I suppose that some may be living the good life, somewhere, and don't want to age or die. Other doppelgangers may be prisoners, or trapped, unable to return, or to die. The original may never exit the dolmen." Alystra paused to allow the oddity of the situation to sink in. "It is the same risk Erin and I chose to affect our plan."

Jedra and Bendahrin both had different questions, but Jedra was faster. "When did you enter the dolmen, how long have you been a fake?" He looked at Alystra, and he looked at Erin, compounding the ambiguity of his question; who did he mean by, "you?"

Alystra, who was always precise beyond what was necessary most of the time anyway, blew past the ambiguity by choosing to answer in the plural, "We both entered the dolmen at the same time, just after I sent Bendahrin to the upper deck to bring you down for our meeting, here, the first time."

This time, Jedra and Bendahrin had the same question, although Bendahrin held his first question firmly. Irrespective of the firmness, Jedra was still faster, "But, how did you . . . oh, Ver Tark . . . what made you choose to do this?"

Alystra stood up, gesturing to Erin to field this question since the "you" was no longer ambiguous.

Erin took a bite and chewed quietly for a moment, not really collecting her thoughts, but re-ordering them. "First and foremost, Jedra, I am no longer *your* Ver Tark; I am no longer a Ver Tark at all." Jedra began to protest, but Erin stopped him. "Jedra, my Ver son, for this final moment."

He gasped, his face turned white.

"I release you, utterly. Alystra has paid your ransom; and to the Stream, I am dead. We are free." At this, she stood up and walked to him, taking his face in her hands and holding his gaze with hers. "We have fought the final engagement of our old life. I have sworn my loyalty to Alystra." She looked to Alystra. "And if Alystra says the word, you are free to go, where you will do as you will." She returned to her seat.

All eyes turned to Alystra, who shook her head. "Never! Don't put this one on me. You are all free to go whenever you want. Bendahrin has a unique connection that can't be broken, but I make no claim over either of you. I certainly don't *need* any of you, but if you want to accompany me on my journey and destiny, I . . ." she shuddered.

Bendahrin finished her sentence, "She welcomes you."

Jedra absent-mindedly stirred some meat into a sauce that was certainly purposed for vegetables, and when he spoke, his voice was uncertain at first but grew in conviction. "I was captured to the Stream as a youth and entered the training as one who couldn't be ransomed. My strength proved my worth, and since I have little memory of any prior life, I can only remember my life of loyalty to the Stream. But oh, Ver . . ." And he stopped, proving that he was a whole lot sharper than a mere tool. "But, Erin, I would rather continue to serve with you here than leave."

Erin smiled. "Then serve as equals and we will put the past behind us."

Bendahrin figured that this was a good time to sneak in a question. "I, for one, will not leave. I have made my commitment and I fear that I know the danger. But, Alystra, you and Erin were in the dolmen for two months?"

Alystra laughed. "No, my construct was dead within minutes, as you saw and what an odd sensation that was." She put her hand to her chest where Erin's blade had entered. "No, I left the dolmen within minutes of your departure from the ship. I discovered that you had moved my body, and that was another surreal moment, seeing my own dead body. I had forgotten how perfectly the dolmen's duplicate copied the original. No, I have spent much of the last two months at Nuans, although I also took time completing my plans with Erin, and I watched you all the time, Bendahrin. Following the plan was important, but if you were ever in danger, I would have immediately jumped in to remove you, Jedra, and Erin's construct, and I would have recalled Kel-Purim.

"And before you ask," she looked at Bendahrin but called elsewhere, "Kel, you may return!"

At once, Kel-Purim was floating beside her, his rotting blood stench ruining an otherwise amazing repast. "Ah! Yes! You called me! What a *fun* time I have had. Are we done? We succeeded, didn't we? Hello, Bendahrin! Ha, I watched you, all locked up. Think of that the next time you avoid visiting me. And Jedra is here, and Erin, ha ha, you died. What fun!"

Alystra wasn't even annoyed at Kel's puppy-love enthusiasm. "Yes, Kel, you have done well, release Rendall, and give him some happy memories to replace the reality. And return to your chalice. I will come by to feed you."

Kel disappeared.

Bendahrin tried to wave away the stench and pushed his plate back. "Alystra, what did Kel do? What was this plan? What did *you* do on Nuans for two months? How did you and Erin formulate a plan so quickly? When did you even have time?" This last question was the one he had been holding.

Alystra seemed at ease and not the least bit grumpy. This made Bendahrin more nervous than anything, but he figured it was a temporary lull in her rampaging life. "Questions, questions, questions! Sit back, enjoy the food. We have some time. For now, I don't feel the pain of urgency. Let the story unfold. I will begin to allow Jedra the one missing piece for him." Alystra turned to Jedra, and Bendahrin turned to his food. "Jedra, know that Erin and I have spoken dozens of times in the past two months to pull together a plan to gain your freedom and hers. Part of this is in fulfillment of a vision that I had."

At this, she summarized the vision for Jedra, who seemed to accept it more easily and with fewer questions than Bendahrin. He also seemed immediately receptive and submissive to the vision and his possible place in it.

Alystra ended, "As you can see, your arrival was, to me, a fulfillment, but I needed to affect your freedom and convince you to leave the Stream. That is where Erin will pick up the story."

Erin seemed to have mastered the skill, uncouth to Bendahrin, of being able to regale others with stories while she ate, and so she began, chewing, "I have been in the B'Tark Stream twenty-five years. My parents were both members of the Stream, and both of them died when I was two. I was raised in the Stream, served on various ships, pirate and mercenary . . ."

She stopped, looking directly at Bendahrin. "And I wanted to mention . . ." She even pointed at him. "Seven years ago, we were approached to do one job, to steal something from your collection, but no amount of stealth or technology could get us inside, so we couldn't take the job. I would guess that the party that wanted to hire us hasn't given up."

Bendahrin nodded slowly. "Do you remember what they were after?"

"No. The Stream avoids operations on magical worlds. Technology against magic is a losing proposition. The only reason we considered it was the size of the payoff. We investigated and did some preliminary recon. We didn't take the job and didn't get the details."

Bendahrin poured some wine. "Perhaps I need to increase my security."

Alystra shook her head. "Don't bother. My protection of you extends to your home. I never told you since you haven't been there. All of your stuff is safe. Back to the story."

Erin started eating again. "I was aggressive and moved up the ranks. I slept in a bed of wealth. But life wasn't a pleasure. Wealth and no place to call home. Command with loneliness. Unity that was oppression. The celebrations, the rules, the training, the discipline, the ranks and rewards; nothing but control. I knew this, of course, but for a long time the adventure and the danger kept reality at bay. And it is enticing. The wealth, the power of command. But it didn't take long before fear started pushing out the excitement. Life in the Stream was more dangerous than our piracy. I'm not sure whether you noticed, during the presentation, Velven was cold toward me. Hold that! He's *always* cold. But he hates me with special vehemence. The second ship on which I served, *Estresh,* was a doomed ship that was destroyed in a debacle that was embarrassing to Velven. That disaster was how I was promoted to the command of my own ship, *Alaris.*" She sighed and shook her head. "Ever since then he has wanted me dead and I have been looking for a way out."

Bendahrin buttered a cheesy muffin.

"For years I looked for a way to escape—but even our internal history informs us that people only rarely escape the Stream." Erin continued, "To sum up, we attacked this ship and were captured. Alystra identified herself, and threatened us, but also mentioned teaming up, in our thoughts. So, I thought back, 'how?' and we began our plans."

Bendahrin nodded slowly and swallowed. "I remember, back then, when Alystra told you her name, you suddenly became alert. I thought that you were excited by the potential of having a chance at Alystra's riches."

Erin grinned. "Potential, yes. I have tired of empty riches."

Alystra spread her arms and held them outstretched. "We planned, the plan succeeded, now we move on. The Stream thinks that Erin is dead, Jedra has been purchased, and we are ready to turn our attention to the future. First, gifts." She reached out to Jedra and Erin, and in each hand she held a small flat box. "These are replacement power sources for your suits. These hold several hundred times the energy of what you are accustomed to, and we will adapt your suits with some additional technology, and magic, that will enhance what you can do."

The two ex-pirates took the gifts and turned them over and looked at them for a moment before they both placed them down. Bendahrin noticed that Erin put hers down first and Jedra followed her lead. Rank and service sometimes take time to fade.

Alystra continued. "Your possessions from your ship are in storage on the lower deck, although you won't be able to fit all of it into your rooms on the command deck. I have rearranged the bulkheads so that you each have a suite of rooms upstairs."

Erin scowled and shook her head. "I don't want any of those old symbols of my slavery."

Jedra nodded.

"We can sell it all if you want. Our ongoing objective may require us to go two different ways, and you will need a ship. I can use magic to send Bendahrin anywhere, because of his connection to me. You will need to get where you need to go the non-magic way."

Erin shook her head. "Even all of the wealth I possessed couldn't buy a ship to keep pace with *Lentoris*, and I won't revert to piracy again."

Alystra grinned massively. "Any amount of wealth we need is a trifling thing, as you saw at The Presentation. Besides, for your ship, we only need to buy a class one drive controller and replacement bridge controls that will be able to connect to an old, almost ancient design: with maybe some other parts. Custom and secret work would be expensive, of course, and I will need to do some magical repairs . . ." She let the smokey ambiguity hang in the air.

Erin leaned toward Alystra, scowling in perplexity. "Class one? Ancient? Do you have a ship in mind?"

Alystra's grin spread even more bountifully. "How would you like to be captain of the *Ascension*?"

Erin jumped up and walked across the room, turned, and strode back where she leaned on her chair looking at Alystra, her mouth open.

Jedra stroked his chin.

Meanwhile, Bendahrin scratched his head with consternation. For him, *Ascension* was only a footnote to recent galactic history, in a field that didn't interest him anyway, and he collected *truly* ancient artifacts. Nevertheless, what he lacked in enthusiasm and understanding was amply flattened by Erin's almost crazed attention.

"Do you know where the *Ascension* is?" She shook her hands vigorously, as if wiping away her own question from the air. "Of course, you know where it is that's obvious or you wouldn't have offered or suggested that I can be the captain of the *Ascension* but how did you find it?"

Bendahrin interrupted her question. "Wait! I only vaguely remember the *Ascension*. What is it?" And he, too, stopped himself in his own elder statesman way. "Yes, obviously it is a ship, but what makes it *so* important?" His voice and words, in contrast, punctuated for particular emphasis.

Jedra, whose taciturn nature was not to be outdone by haste or clarity, laughed and gestured to Alystra attentively. "You were saying? The *Ascension*?" Now his focus was intense. "I'm listening." And his questions didn't need to be amended.

Alystra rose from her chair and stood behind it with her hands on the back. "The *Ascension* was the first ship with a proximity-based asymptotic drive, although the drive concept had been tested extensively. During its maiden voyage there was an accident," and then it was Alystra's turn to turn back on her words, "No, not an accident, a poorly calculated lack of control that led to an unprecedented burst of acceleration and velocity. The test was going as expected, and suddenly the ship disappeared. The test telemetry was cut off, lost to distance, as soon as the ship was gone, so there is very little evidence of what happened. The scant records show that the power curve of the drive spiked suddenly."

She stopped for a moment to allow for the inevitable interruptions, which, for once, didn't come. "I have examined the few moments of test records closely, and I know what happened, but that is not relevant to our discussion, although we will need to postulate and test carefully later when we repair the ship. For now, what matters is that the joint corporations of Prevaria, and families of lost ones, searched extensively for about fifty years to find the ship, or the remains of the ship, or debris from the ship, or any evidence that the ship ever existed, and found nothing anywhere at the departure point or anywhere along the last known trajectory."

Bendahrin, with his characteristic, unquenchable curiosity had already held off his interruption as long as he could. "I love the idea of such an important historical relic, an old ship like this must be worth a fortune, and it would certainly be an epic, historical find. Certainly, technology has come a long way in the past half millennium. It would certainly be an interesting ship, but it would be an old, old, interesting ship that might not even function." He gestured back to Alysta.

Erin laughed, and Alystra smirked. She leaned forward shaking her head. "Here."

A glass of smooth, red wine appeared, with some after dinner chocolates, before Bendahrin.

"Drink, eat, and listen. I will tell you the importance of the ship and its uniqueness, and how I found it." She pinched herself, continuing, "Last time I checked, I was pretty thorough."

Bendahrin conceded to the power of wine and sarcasm in such proximity.

Alystra continued. "The *Ascension* was a prototype unlike any other. Because of the novelty of the new drive, the entire ship was over-engineered and over-designed for strength and power. As its disappearance proved, the drive was so powerful that it couldn't be controlled. The disaster convinced ship designers that delving into engines of that kind was nothing but trouble so that no drive like it has been even considered since that day. Designers and builders alike even have a name for it that has carried down to this day, '*Ascension* limits,' which no one dares to cross in their designs for ships or asymptotic drives. Some of the more colorful engineers use the phrase, 'the *Ascension* Wall of Fear.' The bottom line is that less powerful drives are sufficient for crossing the galaxy as needed, and the market doesn't want more, so there is no reason to go further; building ships is a business, and the subsequent designs met the needs of the *actual* bottom line."

Alsytra glanced at Jedra, who grinned. "But there is more to the story than that."

At this Erin and Jedra shared a knowing look and Bendahrin's curiosity peaked and was piqued.

Alystra held him off with a look and raised hand. "Yes, you probably are the only person here who doesn't treasure the details of the *Ascension* close to your mental center as we do. The *Ascension* accident also caused an enormous inquiry because of the loss of two famous and influential researchers; Porter Shopp, an astrophysical engineer, and Talia Themblen, the legendary military mathematician, along with their development teams. The entire project was carried out by one of the larger shipbuilders on Prevaria, and, as expected, they worked extensively to limit the consequences of the disaster, which included, among other things, that the designs had 'disappeared,' but it is also likely that the design details, for security reasons, were maintained on the ship itself anyway, along with the designers themselves. As for those left behind, the company paid extensively for their silence."

Bendahrin took another sip of his wine, and only Alystra, who could, and did, walk the pathways of his mind, would ever know if this was a sign of impatience or interest.

"The speculation, of which there are whole shelves in libraries filled, circle around three foci: the design of the drive, maneuvering capabilities, and the type and disposition of any weapons on board."

At this, Erin broke her silence, and her voice was passionate. "The B'Tark have been around for thousands of years. We have an extensive archive of unique intelligence gathered, so you likely don't know this." She paused and her enthusiasm was replaced with flaming disgust. "Of course, we used our insights to manipulate governments, disrupt trade routes . . . enough!" She paused again, and her disgust turned back to spirited fervor. "One of the engineers, paid for her silence, was captured by the *Rheumist*, a ship of the Brith-ten quad. She was broken and despondent, her husband, *and* son had been on the *Ascension*, and when she was captured, she decided to join the Stream where she rampaged up the ranks to captain her own ship and she, and her crew and ship, *Thalodis*, preyed on the region around Prevaria with a vengeance. For some reason, and I suspect it was out of love and respect for her son and husband, she only once broke her silence, during repairs on her ship that had been damaged in a fight. Her words were, 'If only I had *Ascension*'s omnis—they were asymptotic, too.'"

Alystra nodded vigorously at this addition to the story. "That would certainly hint at the scope of the ship's maneuverability." She directed her next comment to Bendahrin. "A ship in space doesn't fly like a bird or a plane, since there is no air. The main drive only 'pushes' in one direction, if you like, so to turn, you must rotate the ship to point the ship in the new direction of travel. Omni-directional thrusters, or omnis, are set at the corners of a ship to make it pitch, yaw, or roll to point the ship whichever way the pilot wants." She paused, suddenly realizing the implication. "With asymptotic omnis you would have the ability to thrust the entire ship in any direction without even turning, and potentially at speeds above the speed of light. That would be a formidable advantage in combat!"

Erin nodded.

Bendahrin was still not much engaged by science or technology, so his lack of interest continued flamboyantly. "Wow! How wonderful. Wouldn't it still be easier to just buy Erin a ship?"

Jedra looked at him in utter disbelief, and Erin shook her head, laughing quietly, but Alystra nodded and shrugged. "Of course," she conceded. "That would be easy *and* easier, but there is more going on, which strikes my thoughts. I didn't tell you the full extent of my vision, and it is filled with unmistakable images of armed conflict. And also, during your months as a guest of the B'Tark, Erin confided in me of reports of B'Tark ships being captured and turned from their loyalty. If we are seeing a growth of conflict, it seems well that we should capture and possess the most formidable warship ever built, for our side, maybe?"

Bendahrin sighed. "Oh yes, I am perfectly cut out for armed conflict," he said, not even attempting to hide *his* sarcasm. "But I suppose that having a *second* ship against the entire galaxy might help. What do we need to do?"

"No," Erin said, emphatically using her "captain in charge" voice. "How, Alystra, did you find the *Ascension*?"

"Don't you believe me?" Alystra began, but she was unperturbed. "An odd cross section of events, as with most coincidences." She paused to order her recollections. "I was working to create the Strentrian Bubble, which encompasses, time, distance, gravity, speed, magic, and several other factors, when I read in an oblique footnote about the disappearance of the *Ascension* and how it had shaken nearby magical constructs and efforts at the time. That didn't make any sense to me when I read it, and it still doesn't, but I was struck by the largely irrelevant speculations in the midst of some real science that showed the spike of energy and speed at the moment of the disaster. My exploration of the spell that had hit me required speed *and* the Strentrian Bubble, so it caught in my mind. I have worked with the drive on the *Lentoris* extensively, and over time, after I had completed the bubble, I put the two together and headed to Prevaria, which, by the way, is where we are headed now at all possible speed.

"So, yes, I have seen, through the use of the Strentrian Bubble, the *Ascension* accident." She stood and concentrated for a moment, the library dimmed, and an image, as if projected in three dimensions on the air, appeared in it. "This is my memory of the event from within the bubble. I traveled to the location about two years ago. I needed a break." Against the endless deep blackness, four ships were visible. "The large one, slightly above and to the left," Alystra said, "is the main construction ship, *Parder*. Slightly closer to us, and to the left is the company's observation ship, *Marfere*—a glistening star of wallowing opulence. The executives and investors and some top Prevaria government officials are aboard, about forty people. The smallest ship is a transport, a shuttle, and of course, *Ascension* is in the middle. Although there were only twenty-two people purported to be on board at the time, *Asension* can hold seventy-eight, with a mere nine as crew. Here we go."

Bendahrin, who knew the least about *Ascension*, gazed at the ship, and for a moment, his vision seemed to be especially brilliant and focused, as though the contrast or vibrancy had been turned up in his brain. Despite the odd sensation, he seemed compelled to ignore the sensation and to pay close attention. He pondered the ship. The designers, despite the utter pointlessness, had given the ship wings on the sleek cylindrical body, curved and tapered, graceful, sensual and soft. Any weapons had been integrated smoothly into the contours of the ship's body and wings, and there were enough massive force-field windows to qualify *Ascension* as a cruise ship. Suddenly, the ship was gone, no warning, no slow build up, no flash of light or warning; it looked as though the ship had just disappeared. His vision faded and returned to normal.

"I watched the accident from a dozen angles, I infiltrated and watched pre-voyage run-ups, design team discussions. I followed engineers through the halls, watched them sleep. I even watched the drive from its arrival through to the accident; I watched *this*, from the bridge." The view encompassed the entire bridge crew from the front of the bridge; orders were given and received, monitors were checked, buttons pushed, the navigator wasn't even looking forward when the drive was engaged . . . calm, methodical.

They were gone.

Alystra sounded flat. "As you can see, there was no surprise, no intrigue, no reason, an insanely powerful first attempt, but they weren't ready. An accident, really, which leads me to the conclusion that the only issue with their ship was that their control systems were inadequate to the task of controlling an overly engineered drive. They pushed the singularities too close and produced an explosive level of speed in the most powerful drive ever created. So, let's see where the ship went."

Jedra raised his hand. "Alystra, can we see that bridge view again?"

Alystra's eyebrows went up, and the view of the bridge went back up as well, then Jedra went up in serial fashion and walked right up into the image. "In the Stream, I studied bridge infiltration." He glanced sideways, at Bendahrin, then Alystra with an apologetic expression, and Alystra smirked. "Systems, communications, command," he pointed at each station as he mentioned. "This is the captain, Archer? I think, and his first officer, Stemens." He smiled; his eyes were bright and childlike in enthusiasm, which showed that he had read some of the books on the shelves of speculation

Alystra had mentioned. He pointed into the projection. "This is Talia, Talia Themblen, at the tactical combat station. But who is this?" He pointed to a tall and slender woman, standing close, directly behind Talia, who, unlike everyone else, wore an expression of fierce concentration; concentration directed at Talia. "I know everyone in the ship's crew. Everyone! But I can't place her. This means there were twenty-three people on the ship." He looked at the stranger intently for a marching string of moments, and then walked away with a scowl of concentration on his face.

Alystra watched *him* for a string of heartbeats and nodded her head. "It is possible that we will be able to investigate this mystery when we board the ship." The image vanished. "When I first followed the path of the *Ascension* it took me about five months. *Lentoris* wasn't as speedy back then, and I am only going to show you some of the critical moments." The image re-appeared, and Alystra showed the ship from the back, motionless. "The speed was astonishing, the ship traveled over seventeen-hundred light years in under eight seconds, which is why it appeared to disappear. Of course, I had to travel the distance at the fastest *Lentoris* could go, manipulating time as I went. But, to save you the months, I'll show it to you at real speed." From motionless, the ship was next moving at inconceivable speed, stars were lines and blue-shifted almost into invisibility; even the background radiation was visible as it piled up. At one point, the stars streaked to the left and the ship started spinning around in the direction of travel. A second later, the ship stopped, and Alystra's view of it showed the ship tumbling end over end slowly.

Erin watched wide eyed, and Jedra leaned forward with severe focus. It was Bendahrin who asked the obvious. "What just happened?"

Alystra shrugged, but with a knowing smile streaked across her face. "Guesses?"

The background hum of the ship was all that could be heard as the three tried to figure the answer.

Bendahrin sipped his wine; he had no guesses. Jedra walked around the table again to view the image more closely.

Erin was puzzled at first, but her eyes darted, watching the scene. At last she said, "I've heard of this, but it is so rare, was that a field strike? Was something nearby that the *Ascension* hit?

Alystra nodded and pointed at Erin. "Exactly! Two somethings, though not nearby, which is why no one has been able to find and claim the ship. Let's finish this story and get to work. Every asymptotic drive generates a powerful field around the ship, strong enough to deflect deadly debris, and, of course, space dust, both of which would destroy a ship moving at multiple factors of the speed of light. These days, designers control the size of the field to keep it as close to the ship as possible, but for *Ascension*, the drive's explosion of power created a field that was enormous, billions of kilometers across, and it hit objects in two planetary systems.

"The first was an empty asteroid in space that altered the ship's course by about seventy-three degrees and thirty degrees off the galactic plain and kicked it into a roll, but still at almost full speed. The second was a gas giant that it hit miraculously close to dead on. *That* impact crippled the drive, somehow, sending the ship tumbling through space at sub-light speeds, but fast enough to escape the gravity of the star. Back then, close to the time of the accident, for all those searchers, the technology was so new, having little idea about field strikes, they assumed that the ship followed a straight trajectory, and so they never looked more than—I don't know exactly—a dozen degrees off the starting trajectory. The *Ascension* is heading away from that gas giant at a reasonable speed, but it is very far from the planetary system and tumbling through interstellar space."

Erin sashayed to her seat and sat to the front but leaned back, laughing. She seemed intoxicated by the possibilities flooding the room.

Jedra, too, was lost in thought, standing away from the table.

Alystra banished the floating image and sat back at the head of the table.

Bendahrin showed no outward enthusiasm, nor boredom, but pushed on with his unending earnest quest to have a question for every moment.

"This sounds like a lot of effort for a ship, but the ship seems to bear the weight of such an effort. Shouldn't we investigate it more thoroughly first before we buy parts to fix it? What if we buy a bunch of parts and arrive at the ship and realize we are missing something critical? The ship has been floating in space for over six hundred years."

"Excellent!" Alystra snapped sharply, her face distorted with an evil grin. "Your ignorance will make you the *perfect* buyer when we get to Prevaria. We can use that to help disguise our true intentions. We will have you pretend to be a wealthy investor who wants to start a salvage company, and you want to buy a control system that will fit any ship you could *ever* find. No one should suspect that you are after the *Ascension*."

Bendahrin looked at her blankly, thinking slowly. "Let me guess," he said with vague apprehension. "This is one of those things that you said you had planned for me that I won't like at all, correct?"

The view from the balcony of the Extranta Hotel's executive top floor Epoch was enough to make a heart defibrillate from the floods of beauty, grandeur, and stupidity. The hotel staff called the accommodations an Epoch, for some reason pronounced "ay-po-sh." It was a three-story complex of bedroom suites, conference rooms, lounges, and custom eateries that sat atop the 1,400-meter-tall helix hyper tower in the center of Dardel, the capital, which meant, of course, the financial center of Prevaria. In order to maintain the proper balance, the staff would eventually tell Bendahrin that the hyper tower, pronounced correctly as "Hah purr," was right on the planet's equator so that standing on the balcony, one could see the fastest sunrises and sunsets on the planet, phenomena that apparently added to the experience in some *way* that some *how* would slip by Bendahrin no matter how many times he had it explained. The three floors to which he had access were a labyrinth of opulence and color, a beautiful museum-like landscape of exotic wood, stone, metal, glass, light, and shadow, all cleverly laid out with streams of water that sometimes floated above, forests of trees, even roaming animals and birds. Each view was a surprise, each room a new adventure, all ensconced in a flood of technology that was always present but never visible or obtrusive. Some rooms were all curves, others all sharp angles, halls were subtly angled, mirrors placed to enhance a view, and everywhere, sculptures and images and paintings and art. Bendahrin would come to feel that the layout was as much psychology as architecture. And he felt utterly ridiculous.

He was wealthy by almost anyone's standards, but this ... place was riches pressed and expressed to absurdity. It took him a few nights before he realized that the entire city, stretching for dozens of kilometers around, was designed to enhance *his* view, from *this* balcony. No other buildings came close in height, and even those blended into the display, and somehow moved. At any time, night or day, the city was a clock that showed *his* personal time, aligned to the time of his home; a home on a world, ironically, that they had made up. The psychological impact to Bendahrin was especially face-slappingly apparent when he discovered the whole city was a display of millions of colored lights that changed to fit whichever mood he felt or the music *he* chose to play in *his* suite. He was told that if he wanted to watch a movie, or match the city to the sunset, or the weather, the entire city would comply as a huge display screen. He had suggested that he'd prefer to read a book, and the steward asked for a title. At that moment, he was too embarrassed to select a name. This event had further surprised him, for he had learned that someone on the staff was always nearby, oppressively attentive, but never visible, so that if he merely turned suddenly or his *breathing* changed, someone would be at his elbow with an offer to assist or provide whatever he needed, or "eh comb oh date" his every wish.

Of course, Bendahrin's opportunity to be disgusted had been initially on hold. When they had first arrived at Prevaria, he and Jedra stayed on the ship, far from the planet, for three weeks while Alystra and Erin "scouted and prepared." As part of the plan, they had decided that creating the most confusion and providing the fewest answers was the best course of action, all while spewing rivers of riches as an irresistible distraction. In this way, hopefully no one would ask the right questions and identify the real reason for their visit. His part, now that he and Jedra were finally established in the Epoch was to fill *Lentoris* with equipment, tools, components and manuals, but as he looked over the railing down to the city, his crushing concern was what had happened to Alystra and Erin. Their disappearance wasn't part of the plan. As a result, his mind wasn't dwelling on playing his role, it was seated firmly in the starboard lounge on *Lentoris* where weeks earlier they had all worked out details of the plan to get what they needed to repair *Ascension*.

–|–

"I'm not an actor!" Bendahrin said, "My ignorance, about which Alystra was so maliciously excited, may make me perfect in some way, but I don't think ignorance has ever made anyone more proficient at fooling experts." He was seated in a chair with the massive force-field windows to his right.

Erin chuckled. She was leaning against one of the windows so she could easily look out at the stars or into the room where Bendahrin and Jedra sat. "Prevaria, where we will go to purchase what we need, is a center of shipbuilding, and a hub of technology and industry. The smartest engineers and designers in the galaxy work for the massive corporations that run the planet. This is to our advantage. The planet is a nexus of intellectual brilliance, accompanied by greed and a lust for power. You will be an enthralling unknown, but since you can't give away our true goal through any technological hints, your flood of opulence will overwhelm any attempts anyone makes to figure out why you are buying so much."

"Misdirection." Jedra added. "Throw so much wealth around they don't even look at what you're buying with it."

"But even that cloud of wealth will not be sufficient. We will need to make everything about Bendahrin farcical and even repellant." Alystra said as she walked into the room.

Bendahrin gasped. "What happened?"

Alystra had made her hair brilliant white and changed her face. Her nose was pointier and her features more aged with wrinkles and saggy cheeks. She had changed the shape and color of her eyes. Instead of her normal black clothes, she wore a shapely but professional rose-colored dress. "I have been to Prevaria, so I expect that no amount of money will be able to hide me when their computers compare my face to previous records. I will be Bendahrin's personal assistant, Marian Thorpe."

"I've never been to Prevaria." Erin said. "The Stream is big on secrecy and we, uh, *they* purchase ships and supplies through hidden channels." She paused, looking at Alystra's dress. "Seeing your outfit gives me an idea, though. Most of our combat fatigues come from Prevaria. We can probably purchase a selection that are designed as dresses. Then I would be armed." Bendahrin suspected that she would have felt uncomfortable if she were not armed.

Alystra nodded slowly. "This is a research and shopping trip, not an invasion, but yes, we need to be prepared for anything. And matching dresses styled to look like a uniform will work to add another distracting nuance to our boss. Jedra will need combat fatigues in matching colors too, since he will be Bendahrin's valet and personal security. He would be expected to be wearing them."

"Colors? Really?" Jedra shook his head.

"Yes, colors. Rose, sky-blue, emerald, pale yellow. Anything that will stand out and call attention to Bendahrin's odd propensities. We are well-paid servants in his circus, and he insists on specific colors on different days." She moved to face Bendahrin and gestured for him to stand up. "Erin, you will be Dahna Solis, and you can keep your face since you are unknown. Jedra, you keep your name and face, but Bendahrin, you must be untraceable, and, ironically, you are known, even though only in obscure archaeological and academic circles. So, let's take a look at you."

Bendahrin was in his mid-thirties with the bare beginnings of thinning brown hair. His mother had always called it warm-brown to contrast with his sister whose hair was dark brown. He wasn't obese, but the early signs of too many days eating with a book rather than hiking or other exercise were beginning to show in the expected places. His face was what some might call rough and ready, with heavy brows, strong cheeks, but with sad hazel eyes that were especially engaging when he was speaking or smiling. Because of his numerous academic years among ruins, he preferred sturdy clothes in earthy colors with adequate pockets that were still dressy enough for an unanticipated conference and comfortable enough to lounge with a book.

Alystra grinned. "We need to make you absurd, almost mad in appearance. We want everyone who sees you to be befuddled by the glare of your swank, and slightly repulsed." She began to walk around him and as she moved, he changed. His hair grew long and braided in a long single strand, a silvery color, streaked with dark green. His clothes changed into an over-stuffed suit with lighted stripes that looked almost like a comical military uniform. Erin snorted with laughter, and Jedra slapped his knee.

Bendahrin scowled, and Alystra agreed. "Yes, let's give you a new face, just like that." She paused and a nasty grin appeared on her face. "This will probably feel strange." As they watched, his head, indeed his whole body shrank and his face became more pinched and angular, and the scowl was ingrained to his features. She gave him a yellowish blond, pointy beard on the tip of his chin.

"Now that's nauseating." Bendahrin said, his voice somehow higher and raspy. "And my eyes!"

Alystra raised her hand and she presented him with a pair of black-rimmed spectacles with thick round lenses. "I will restore you when this is over." She stepped back and a full-length mirror appeared so Bendahrin could see the transformation for himself.

Bendahrin was astonished. He was utterly unrecognizable. He reached his now smaller hand to his face and opened his mouth in awe and disgust. "At least my face accurately shows the anger and distaste I am currently feeling." He turned to Alystra, "This ship had better be worth this level of humiliation."

Erin walked forward, trying to contain her laughter, she put her hand on Bendahrin's shoulder and suddenly both she and Bendahrin started coughing.

"What?" Jedra jumped up and approached but stopped suddenly when he hit the smell.

Alystra smiled at Bendahrin. "I figured that a strong defense of cologne would keep people from questioning you too closely. And your name for this shopping trip will be Chesleth Preller!"

"You are enjoying this far too much." Bendahrin said and Alystra laughed.

But they were ready for the absurdity to begin.

–|–

After depositing a mountain of galactic currency at the Dardel Corporate Trust Bank, Dahna and Marian rented the Extranta's Epoch where they made a huge fuss of re-arranging items and making preparations for Flen Preller's arrival, insisting that he would find certain arrangements and sculptures and colors intolerable. They arranged catering and scheduled and hosted three weeks of extravagant parties atop the Epoch with lights and glamor and glitter and bottles of rare wines, tables of odd cheeses, servers with dainties, and delicacies consumed amidst quiet private conversations carried on lilting or ominous live music, peppered with half-promised hints and innuendos, lingering smiles, and any allurements they could contrive. Rather than merely sending invitations, the gatherings were treated like a conference or trade show where any person connected to space or shipbuilding technologies were encouraged to attend. In addition, specific invitations were forwarded to, and several meetings were "arranged" with, top executives from the major corporations so Alystra and Erin could figure out the best possible sources for the equipment they wanted, always hinting that they were the ones who would most likely sway Flen Preller and lead him where to buy. In an odd accommodation, signs went up around the city tracking the countdown till Preller's assumed arrival.

These events were exhausting and exciting for Erin, and objects of infuriating danger for Alystra. Each party required focus, concentration, and subterfuge, dodging commitments and limiting useful information while being endlessly pleasant and polite while proffering promises of purchases. Erin called these machinations, "uphill opportunities," but Alystra was tortured by hours of patient kindness and attention to those she called in her own mind, "annoying targets." It didn't help that most of the time they were outnumbered by forty or fifty to two.

As they desired, many of the conversations turned highly technical, and both Alystra and Erin had to pretend they didn't understand ships or their systems or asymptotic drives. Other times the conversations turned into fishing expeditions to ferret out Chesleth Preller's home planet, his source of income, where he was, or why he was delayed, or any number of other secrets. Alystra found these conversations painful, but Erin turned these into opportunities to create fantastic fabrications. One young woman, pretending to be an engineer, tried to find out the name of Preller's home planet, and at the mere mention of his planet, Erin launched into a lengthy twenty minute re-telling of a fictional vacation she had taken with Preller's executive team to the mountains on the planet's south continent complete with the resort's picturesque location surrounded by snow-capped peaks, the scenic forests and rivers, and their daily activities; hikes, meetings, massages in the spa, and several meals they had all eaten on a terrace against golden sunset sparkled mountains. In the end, the "engineer" walked away so bamboozled, it wasn't until she listened to the recording later that she discovered she had heard quite a bit, but not the planet's name.

The non-pretend engineers were the most fascinating and

helpful, with very little prodding they would provide extensive technical details, the latest advancements, hints, tips, and suggestions. Once again, Erin's love of deception and intrigue made her a master at drawing out useful details with a simple smile and an innocent, "Really? Remember, I am in finance, so how would I . . ." Alystra frequently dug into the minds of those with whom she conversed using magic to learn, and master, more than just the facts, but the deeper understanding that only years of experience can convey. In the end, most of their late evenings were tied up writing notes of the most valuable intelligence gathered.

"So, what are you here to buy?" was a question that should have been simple enough, but for the Issachon, the fortieth iteration in a single evening required epic levels of self-control to guarantee the person asking the question survived to prattle on another day. Each questioner also felt duty bound to point out all the flaws in Chesleth Preller's plan. "Salvage is an honorable trade, most certainly," one pompous, bilious, and rotund gentleman pontificated. "Mr., uh, Flen Preller seems most enthusiastic."

"This venture has been one of Flen Preller's dreams since boyhood. He has waited long for the opportunity to outfit his small fleet of ships with the tools, equipment, and staff required to rescue ships in danger throughout the galaxy." Alystra explained.

"Yes, most noble, truly noble," pompous added, nodding vigorously enough that he spilled small sloshes of his drink onto a plush carpet of wildly chaotic colors. "Although there are already numerous, and I hasten to add, *contracted* and highly successful networks of seasoned salvors providing rescue coverage in all sectors of the galaxy. As mentioned, and, young lady, this is *important*, so heed my words, these companies already have contractual arrangements by territory or with shipping companies. In that closed environment, what does, uh, Flen Preller intend to do?"

Comments like this challenged Alystra in new ways. Although she was never tired and never slept, the temptation to yawn at these moments, purely as an act of flagrant honesty, was crushing. Instead, she imagined the annoyance plummeting from the balcony of the Epoch and demurred evasively, "There are always more ships that need assistance; Flen Preller *always* finds a way." Answers of this kind never satisfied the questioner, an offer of more drinks or food could usually provide the needed distraction to overthrow the need for further evasions. The more persistent and "not hungry" she would hand off to Erin, who was as much a well of duplicity as Alystra was of magic.

One evening, when the Epoch was full of fanfare, food, questions, and pressure, Alystra found herself chased and badgered by a persistent and unquenchable reporter one of the smaller news teams and unable to redirect the woman to Erin, who had been cornered by three high-ranking, high-pressure politicians. Erin, seeing the growing danger as she spoke with high-ranking one-through-three, kept a furtive eye on Alystra from across the room, watching with increasing alarm as the unwitting reporter hounded the vexed Issachon. Eventually, the woman yelled at Alystra, who turned slowly.

Erin was on the verge of panic, but she couldn't escape the trio who faced her. She saw Alystra talking slowly and deliberately, but Alystra was quickly surrounded by a crowd that seemed curious at first but also interested in the more revealing questions the reporter was asking.

Erin was soon lost in watching the crowd swallowing Alystra, and the high-ranking squad turned, confused, to watch with her.

The reporter was up on her toes, increasingly aggressive to Alystra, enjoying the attention, and, like a wolf with her teeth in its prey, tasting blood.

Alystra, to her credit, was still calm, answering slowly, but Erin, who knew, a little, what to look for, could sense the room growing warmer. She excused herself more aggressively and pushed through the crowd, thinking frantically how to intervene.

When she had closed about half the distance, the entire room flashed white and then went totally dark. Erin stopped, and suddenly they were in a closet on the floor below the gathering.

Alystra leaned back against the wall. "I guess I don't need to tell you; that was me," she growled, then laughed. "Right now, there is no power in the city. I couldn't hold it in any longer. Not sure how long it will be for them to fix it." And she was gone.

Erin paused for only a minute to prepare herself before she exited the closet and found her way up to the next floor in the near total darkness. Normally she would have used her combat fatigues to provide a light, but she didn't want anyone to see her using her fatigues in any way that would potentially reveal to them her distinctive Stream style. Besides, she wasn't in a rush and wanted to think about what she would say to her guests.

In the end, she needn't have worried. When she arrived on the next floor, most of the people were being guided by diligent and effusive Epoch staff to the elevators, which were somehow still working, or working again.

Alystra's doing? I wonder if Alystra filled their minds with the proper herd mentality to get them out of here. Or more likely the affluent power brokers didn't want to remain without the glitter and entertainment.

Erin greeted numerous people as they departed. "Yes, we will surely invite you back," and, "Yes, what a surprise! Does the city lose power often?"

The floor was soon empty, and the Epoch staff exited with stilted apologies.

Erin went out to the balcony and watched the darkened city. Lights could be seen on vehicles, some buildings had emergency systems, individual light sources appeared in countless places. She watched the stars for a few minutes, and the Entrata burst into life and light again. She turned to see the Epoch staff spreading out through the floor to clean up. She turned back, and as she continued to watch, power returned to additional sections of the city. Before long, all of Dardel was fully lit and Erin read from the massive city-clock that it was late enough that she went to her room, locked the door, and went to sleep.

The following morning, Erin found Alystra sitting on the balcony with two officials from the city and a representative from the Entrata who had come to apologize for the inconvenient power loss.

"The whole event was totally inexplicable, and, of course, inexcusable," one of the officials was explaining, a man of girth, but, at the moment, no mirth. "Circuits tripped, grids taken offline, backup systems disengaged. Hundreds, all throughout the city." His eyes were wide and surprised. "Perfectly timed, the outages coincided perfectly—utterly inexplicable. We suspected sabotage or a coordinated attack, but there was no damage, nothing broken, or even out of place."

Alystra smiled sweetly. "Were there any perpetrators caught on your excellent security systems?"

None of the three caught the sarcasm, they were so deeply immersed in the practice of privacy violation that the connection fluttered by without notice. Three heads shook emphatically, and Mirthless continued, pointing at Alystra for emphasis.

"We had teams review security records from countless critical locations, and we found nothing to explain the event. As I said, which perhaps you had missed when I said it earlier, inexplicable!"

Alystra nodded to them and stood up. "Well, that is all quite exciting. I can't tell you how happy I am to hear that there was no damage. That is good news."

The three stood and started for the elevator when one of the other men turned, "We certainly hope that this, so unfortunate experience, hasn't changed Mister Preller's desire to buy, to, to come and enjoy our hospitality."

"I am certain that *Flen* Preller remains eager to complete the purchases of his intention."

The three men smiled and turned to go with appropriate pomp. Alystra turned to Erin and rolled her eyes. Erin was smirking brightly.

As Alystra had alluded to in her comment about security, the entire Epoch was a flagrant violation of privacy: Alystra had identified early on that their every conversation was being heard, watched, and recorded. On the whole, this was to their advantage since it helped them to project a pretended lack of awareness that would likely put the listeners into a deeper confidence in their belief that they had the upper hand. Additionally, their inane babblings about the "soon to arrive" Chesleth Preller and his idiotic notions which were whispered in confidence would likely become cherished intelligence among the many listeners.

Erin, who was already cagey and misleading, took great delight in making conflicting promises. The challenge was that they could never speak in private, which meant their only conversations were through shared thoughts with the advantage of immediacy, but the utter lack of cadence a conversation enjoys.

After one night of swapping lies and hints with a group of wealthy bores, in which there were more financiers and fewer technicians, Alystra threw herself into a chair that was far less comfortable than it looked. "I'm exhausted!" She lied for the watchers and listeners. "What do you say we create our own change of pace and take a walk?"

Erin, who *was* tired, perked up at the opportunity. "How

affluent! Should we first protund the middle? Or just run it." She was laughing inside as she thought of the geniuses trying to figure out whether her made up words were another language, or some kind of code, and if so, what it meant. This role stroked her love of the theatrical.

They quickly entered the central private elevator that went down the center shaft of the tower rather than following the spiral path of the helix; less scenic, but faster. Their descent was uneventful, but in the private lobby they were met by several hastily assembled staff eager to offer transportation and suggest destinations and any other services required. Apparently walking was rare or confusing, so they were accosted and worried all the way through the main lobby and out into the street, where, it turned out, many people were walking.

They looked left and right and took a random direction, moving quickly in the chaotic light and darkness cast by the massive helix tower stretching above them. The noise and bustle were suddenly cut off, and Alystra spoke, "Erin, I was so close to disaster again tonight!" She sighed and gestured to the right, and they headed in the indicated direction. "We are in a bubble of obfuscation; we can talk freely, and the people following will hear nothing but the street noise around us."

Erin took a deep breath and jumped into the air, then walked a few quick steps. "Sorry," she said, turning and looking sideways at Alystra. "This is the first time I have walked freely in years. I'm feeling a bit exuberant."

Alystra nodded and mumbled something about "barely free in this jumble" but nodded, allowing Erin the personal enjoyment for some minutes.

They turned at a few random intersections always angling away from the massive helix behind them.

Finally, "We are being followed, of course."

Alystra laughed, pleased to have a companion with a similar stretching sense of situational awareness. Bendahrin was always lost in thought and as dense as a slab about certain things. "Seven people on foot, four vehicles, eleven drones, and a dozen viewers and cameras from the tower itself," she said flatly. "At least out here we can talk freely, although I am sore pressed from the temptation to knock them all out and depart, just to cause them the resultant confusion."

"I wonder whether they are watching us for our safety, or merely out of fear that we are skipping out on paying for the Epoch?"

Alystra shrugged. "Who cares? We have met almost everyone we need; we can bring Bendahrin and Jedra down in a few days, and then we will be done with this wretched prison. Everything here is too contrived. Next time I'll just fix the ship magically and deal with the impact of that choice later."

They continued easily through a few dozen blocks, talking of the day's efforts and comparing notes on the people they had encountered. They arrived at an intersection with a narrow, one-way street with fewer pedestrians, though it was still bright. In Dardel there was no such thing as a dark street, unless the view from the Epoch balcony required it. They proceeded along the narrow street, and about eighty meters from the intersection, Erin was busy pre-empting Alystra's thoughts with plans for the next day, when the street went black, not like a power outage, but like being plunged into ink. Sounds sliced through the darkness, people closing in quickly, a vehicle approaching, and suddenly, as if in a small sphere, light appeared in a tight area, several men were surrounding them on the street.

Alystra looked over at Erin and couldn't have been more excited to see that Erin had kept her head and had neither fought, nor fled; she was attentive and aware, no more.

The man to Alystra's right gestured to a door opening on the vehicle that had approached silently and spoke in a tone of threat and deference, "Inside now."

Alystra glanced at Erin and nodded quickly before ducking in through the open door.

One of the men climbed in the front, turning to Alystra and Erin, and one of the men climbed in the back with them, Alystra glanced out as the door was closing and saw the others swiftly disappear into the blackness.

She nodded. "Nicely executed," she said quietly.

The next instant the vehicle was streaking across the sky and a quick glance behind showed the massive helix shrinking swiftly.

Alystra turned to the man seated far too close for comfort. "Where are we going?"

He grunted listlessly, and looked out the window away from her, out the window and into nothing. "You will find out when we are ready."

Alystra glanced at Erin, and they shared twinges of smiles. Clearly, he had no idea. The two of them against the three gave them a thousand-to-one advantage, but if the price of knowledge was a few insults, they would and could endure insults and more. Nevertheless, they planned silently, in thoughts, wordlessly, and out of cunning.

By distance and speed, their trip was long, but fast. By the time they were touching down, the sun appeared to be rising, until, that is, they *had* landed, and they saw the sun continue to set before them. They had chased through the night and crept up *behind* the sun into a later evening. By any estimation they had flown about a third of the way around the planet in a dozen minutes. The vehicle had landed in the grass next to an enormous, sprawling house that spread over a dozen acres surrounded by lawns, fields, and a tended orchard of fruit trees. In the deepening shadows, they were led through a ground level door into a garage of vehicles. At the back side a heavy metal door stood open and they passed through it, down a clean, well-lit tile hallway, turned left, past a number of doors 'til the third on the left. They entered and the silent grunter closed the door behind them. There was the sound of heavy locks slammed into place and footsteps walking away. The room was small with a couple of beds and comfortable chairs, a toilet room and sink, not ominous save for the door with no exit. There were two sets of comfortable sleep clothes.

Erin started to speak, "Well . . ." when Alystra stopped her in her mind.

"Nothing, say nothing. Tactical?"

"No imminent threat. Eight people visible so far, three-story structure, large, but open. No cover around the house. No weapons visible, but many potential weapons evident. A subtle fortress. Nothing we can't handle."

Alystra put her hand on Erin's shoulder and thought back to her. *"Good, there are eighteen people here, but you are right, we have only seen eight. I sense purposeful strength, and the presence of a constant flood of ethical lawlessness, but toward us there is nothing. I have found the man in charge, but he is fully occupied. They were working under orders to grab us if they had a chance, but we gave them the chance when he wasn't ready. At this point, we wait, in fact, sleep if you want, no, I want you to sleep. Who knows what tomorrow holds?"*

Erin nodded. Fatigue was crowding her from all sides anyway, so she removed her boots, dressed quickly in the clothes provided, and laid on one of the beds, smiling at Alystra, who touched her head. She was asleep at once.

At that, Alystra placed wards at the ends of the halls to alert her if anyone approached.

–|–

On *Lentoris*, Bendahrin was settled into a chair in the forward lounge to enjoy a book and a glass of *Tala-rupe*—a carefully-mixed drink that had layers so that the flavor changed slightly as the glass was drained. A chapter at its end, he glanced through the force-field glass at the barren surface of the greenish-gray asteroid upon which *Lentoris* was parked. Hiding on an asteroid had been Erin's idea, close enough to arrive quickly, far enough away that nobody would know where they came from. As he gazed out, the beauty of the stars captured his attention for the hundredth time, and he pondered the timeless question of whether beauty implied design. He had read too endlessly in ancient and insightful literature to fully escape the wonder that was so regularly lost to people blinded in the glare of advancement and technology.

How does the interminable battle between good and evil make sense if there isn't design or purpose to the universe? Without a purpose, there is no reason to choose good over evil. His thoughts so distracted him, more even than his book, that he scarcely noticed when Jedra approached.

"My Flen Preller?" Jedra said, mostly in character but slightly mocking.

"Bountifully! What is your communication?"

"My Flen, it is time for us to go."

At this, Bendahrin jumped up and headed to his quarters which had been filled with the wardrobe and accouterments of his upcoming role. He dressed the part, applied the vapors and jewels, and prepared for the grand act.

Their passage through planetary customs and the landing on the western landing platform of the Extranta Epoch were expedited by officials at all levels of government. Even though the hotel enjoyed special treatment at most times, the landing of Flen Chesleth Preller was so highly anticipated that records were set satisfying Jedra's request for landing instructions. When they finally landed, Jedra turned defensive and Bendahrin turned on the fop.

14

Erin woke up to find Alystra watching her.

"The people here are awake, so we should be ready for the next move soon," Alystra said into her mind. "We need to not speak of anything important, yet. Although I sense no malice or threat, we are now being watched. Odd, what I sense most from our host is mixed anticipation of something exciting and a fierce protectiveness. I could dig deeper, but we will find out his intentions soon enough."

Erin took the prompt to speak of nothing important and pretended to be normal. "Good morning," she said. "Has anyone come in?" Alystra shook her head, and Erin was sure that she knew more; not that she would *say* anything out loud after warning Erin to say nothing important. They waited for only a few minutes before they heard someone coming.

The door was opened, and a woman led them to a lavish bathroom, where they were given time to shower and offered a change of clothes, which neither of them donned—preferring to wear their combat fatigue dresses now that events were moving. They were then led out through the garage, rounded a garden, and climbed some stairs to an open terrace where an old man was standing beside a table that held a spread of food.

"Welcome," he said, gesturing to seats at the table.

Erin and Alystra each took a seat in docile fashion.

Once seated, the man continued, seating himself, "My name is Alex Scurven. I have been watching your negotiations with some

154

interest, and I thought for certain that we should meet." He paused most deliberately to gather reactions. "Rather, I have been fairly eager in my hope that we could meet. And so, whereas I sincerely apologize for whisking you away with no formal invitation sent, I do believe that the reasons for my doing so will become clear as we talk this morning."

He frittered away a minute with a warm pastry and some spread. "You and your actions led me to some peculiar conclusions. But first, please, let us eat." He proceeded to pass and pour, serve and dote, prattle and cajole. He was an elderly man with short, white hair and a florid complexion, light blue eyes, medium height and build, but in just about perfect physical condition for a man of advanced years, his slight stoop was the clearest sign of age. Despite this, he projected a casual aplomb despite the building evidence that his every motion and word carried brilliance of mind and cunning attention to the most miniscule detail.

"This is our host. I sense no danger in him although he is expectant and curious about us," Alystra thought to Erin as Alex droned on and on about his home, the continent where he lived, local events, and his hobbies. Alystra ate some fruit, which stunned Erin exceedingly.

Alex asked them both some irrelevant questions, about their likes and dislikes, whether Erin had read a certain book or Alystra had seen a play that was a personal favorite of his. His conversation was a droning patter of weaving curiosities, lulling them gently. At about the time they finished eating, two men appeared, suddenly, one behind Alystra and one behind Erin with the last thing you would expect on such an advanced technological planet, basic swords, and they each made a move to attack.

Alystra and Erin reacted as their host had wanted and expected, being suddenly thrown into an unexpected life-or-death situation. They jumped up and turned; Erin producing a practiced and intuitive blade from her dress combat fatigues, and Alystra summoning Brahtenla, which filled the area with dark and cold. The men disappeared even as they jumped up. Erin immediately looked to Alystra for guidance, surprised that the men had been able to appear without Alystra knowing in advance.

A sudden sound led them to turn fiercely to Alex, their posture and swords indicating an aggressive stance in his direction. He was clapping gently. "Excellent." He grabbed a napkin and wiped his mouth, stood up and said, "That was most helpful. Please follow me." He then turned his back and walked away, profoundly confident.

Erin found the situation disconcerting, but Alystra nodded to her and she seemed more settled than before. Her thought reached Erin, "*Now, I see. This is not wholly unexpected.*" And she banished her sword.

Erin hesitated, since none of this had been expected by her and she saw nothing to set her mind at ease. Even so, she re-integrated her sword, nodded, and they moved to follow him.

As they passed in through the doors in his wake, a man was coming out through another door to the terrace with a rolling cart to clean up the meal. Perfect planning and execution.

Entering behind Alex, they found themselves in a study or office. He closed the doors and rounded a massive wooden desk, where he sat in a chair that seemed designed for comfort rather than opulence, and gestured to a couple of seats on the other side of the desk that were made of rich leather.

Alystra took the lead and sat first.

A young lady came in and asked if they wanted anything to drink, and, having taken Erin's request, departed the way she came.

"After our shared meal, we can proceed to business." He sat back and looked at them, gazing for long enough that Erin wondered if she should say something. "You two have certainly caused a stir here on Prevaria," he began with a knowing smile. "I have come to a conclusion, one that I find disturbing and more than a little frustrating. I think that we might be strolling side by side on a path wide enough for only one." He was looking directly at Alystra when he said this. "Before stating conclusions, let me help to paint some context for you." He pulled out a pad or keypad, and a wall of books vanished behind a flat white screen behind him. Pictures appeared on the screen, four familiar pictures, with names attached. "Let's see . . . Marian Thorpe, Dahna Solis, Jedra," he looked up, "we didn't get his last name, although I don't think that would help us to identify him anyway. All in the employ of Chesleth Preller, who," he raised his hand with one finger pointing skyward for emphasis, "with absolutely no prior connections or advance announcement deposited an astronomical cash deposit in one of our banks. No," he stopped himself, "to be precise, he had *you* deposit the funds," pointing at Erin, "and then had you set up in the most ostentatious location on the planet. Quite a show!" He shook his head with a sad smile. "Personally, I . . . always carefully *avoid* the Entrata when I am in Dardel. I find the overabundance of surveillance oppressive."

He paused then and said, "I guess that you already know this, despite being in our *secure* guest room, that Chesleth has arrived at the Epoch, in the capital, and he has already started making purchases. Interesting in dozens of ways. How did he know when to arrive so soon after I had you brought here?" He smiled and appeared distracted by his computer. "I digress. Moving on with our context." He cleared his throat. "Prevaria is one of the top four or five wealthiest planets in the galaxy, and we build ships for, oh, fifty-four or fifty-five percent of the galaxy, depending on the current business cycle. We also have the latest in every technology possible." He put the pad down for a moment, putting his elbows on the desk with his hands up, palms facing toward them, then he raised one hand slightly from the desk. "Speaking metaphorically, most of the executives of the top hundred companies on Prevaria could wiggle their little finger and every government on fifty-thousand planets would hurry to do their bidding." He could somehow wiggle just the tip of his little finger.

Erin wondered if he had practiced this feat or if he had been injured in a way that allowed this odd motion.

"You must admit that your noisy methods were certain to attract attention, which, for myself, *I* think was by design. As it is, hundreds of these executives thought so too, and did, indeed, wiggle fingers, made intergalactic requests, and searched extensively for the four of you in the records of hundreds of thousands of planets, and it is my guess that you knew this would happen." He paused with his hand raised above the pad and looked up at Alystra. "Are you curious what we found?"

Alystra leaned forward in her chair, and she looked both curious and interested. "Oh, yes," she said, with an almost conspiratorial tone in her voice. "More than curious."

"I just *knew* you would be," he responded, pointing the pad at her emphatically and nodding. "So, let's start with the scope of our find. All of these fine executives, looking for answers, were able to compile records for about fifty-seven percent of the populations of the connected worlds, obviously not including worlds with populations of inhabitants who are not aligned. That is hundreds of trillions of records."

At this point, Alystra interrupted. "I don't think that you are implying that these companies actually worked together on this?"

"Brilliant!" Alex said, snapping his fingers and pointing at her again. "Now, what in the *galaxy* would make you think that? They each only had parts of this data."

Alystra smirked. "But *you* have all the data. Who are you?"

Alex smiled and looked back at his pad. "We'll start with your boss: odd name, and rare, Chesleth Preller, and yet, in the galaxy, as far as our data goes, three-thousand, one-hundred-seventy-one people share that name with your boss, and," he looked up, "and just imagine! Every person by that name is accounted for. That is, the records we received located every person with the name." He waved his hand as though dismissing a pungent smell. "Certainly, some people slip through the cracks . . ." He leaned back in his chair, pretending to think for a moment. "But the ones who slip through the cracks don't tend to have such enormous cash resources. At least, that is what so many executives with wiggly fingers are telling them-selves."

Erin was increasingly nervous as she realized that he had been researching their team and unraveling their story. In the Stream, and in her experience, secrecy was paramount.

Alex continued, "Marian Thorpe, personal assistant, my, oh my, yes. *That* name, with alternate spellings of Marian generated a dozen million hits, and thousands even looked like you." He paused and pretended to look thoughtful. "Of course, women do so many interesting things with their hair color. You can almost look like anyone you want . . . I think that you can see where this is going." He then spoke with careful emphasis, tapping the table with each word. "Not one of those executives, with all their wiggling fingers and endless resources, could match you, any of you, to any record, and no government claimed to know any of you. A dreadfully woeful return for the money and resources spent to uncover your identities.

"Nevertheless, I am not surprised that we couldn't find any of you anywhere. Not that it matters much. What you can or can't buy on Prevaria is predominantly about the color of your currency, not whether you are known or not. Although a well-known buyer wouldn't have raised so many questions." He looked at Alystra, tilting his head to the side. "For example, this question: who would have guessed that *you* are an expert at asymptotic drive calculations? If you had entered the stage here pretending to be an engineer, you might have escaped notice, but a personal assistant?"

Erin squirmed a bit, and Alystra was about to raise a protest, but he tapped his screen and a picture appeared of Alystra, as Marian, in the Epoch at one of the many parties they had hosted. He continued, cautiously, sneaking up on something, "I don't suppose it is any secret that the Epoch is a fishbowl where your every movement is seen and every word is heard, which is, perhaps, the reason you took a walk." He paused, glancing at them, waiting for confirmation of his guess.

Erin was feeling increasingly exposed, but Alystra appeared calm and she seemed to be enjoying herself immensely. Erin wondered if Alystra's confidence came from having read his mind.

Alex continued, "The Entrata allows almost all companies on Prevaria to set up surveillance in the Epoch in order to provide an advantage in business deals. Most companies pay a subscription fee, or pay on a one-time basis, depending upon which guest is dealing with which company. The competitive advantage is for the good of whichever company, which is, in turn, better for the planet, which is better for the hotel. Besides, we are a very advanced planet techno-logically, so even if the hotel weren't part of it, spying would happen through other means. On Prevaria we are very pragmatic. The hotel cooperates with the intelligence gathering as a boost to the bottom line. Most companies and their executives knew about everything happening at the Entrata." He paused for a moment to add a calcu-lated aside with an expression of feigned confusion, even covering his mouth in mockery. "Except, for some reason, *your* ship, which has finally arrived. Early efforts, which began immediately upon Chesleth's arrival, reveal that the *Lentoris* is somehow impenetrable to any technology set against her." He hummed to himself in amuse-ment and tapped on his pad absentmindedly. "Chesleth Preller must possess some remarkable technology, utterly unknown on Prevaria." He and Alystra locked eyes for a while.

"No matter." He gestured to the image behind him. "I don't know, *Marian*, whether you remember this discussion, although I have a feeling you could recite it verbatim, but the young lady you are speaking with in this scene is an employee from Gralen's Engi-neering, although she also works for me. I sent her there hoping to ask you some simple engineering questions, and despite your contrived ignorance, careful objections and misdirections to her prompts that would show us whether you understood the drives your boss wanted parts for. She was eventually able to trick you into correcting her reference about the use of Psorfay constants in proximity positioning. I don't suppose that I need to play the entire recording?"

Alystra shook her head, but her smile grew.

Alex continued to gaze at Alystra, steadily. "White hair. Hmmm . . . Did I mention women and their changing hair color?" He mused out loud, then tapped his pad again. "Where in the galaxy, now, hmmm . . . sometimes the facts just reveal themselves when you ask the right questions? Where would a young woman learn about Psorfay constants? Oh wait!" He pretended to search on his touchpad. "Security footage is so," an image appeared on the screen of Alystra in the lobby of a library, "intrusive but useful when you're looking for a woman who dyes her hair." In the image, Alystra's hair was her normal auburn, and she appeared with her normal facial features. "This was a few years ago, right here on Prevaria in Dardel, at the Dardel University's library. I wonder if the young lady in the picture signed in at security . . ." He smiled warmly at Alystra, who added to the temperature in response. "Coincidentally, I have heard that the university's security archives went down about a week ago so that most of the records from this period are currently unavailable."

At this, Alystra slapped her leg, laughing.

"Speaking of these runny coincidences, what is inexplicable to me is that none of the big boys have yet discovered that you aren't quite who you say you are. You have them all fooled, and someone is apparently feeding the fish with a steady diet of misdirection and smoke." He paused theatrically, raising his hand momentarily. "And then there was our meal just minutes ago." He smiled and turned his attention back to Erin. "Now *Dahna* . . . Did I get that right?" He smirked. "I have lived on Prevaria for almost seventy years, and I have sold several million units of tech fatigues of all models and styles, including the rather attractive design you are currently displaying so attractively. Whereas it isn't unusual for a wealthy or paranoid person, or their employees, to wear fatigues for protection or to satisfy some other reason, you are a financial expert, yes?" He paused, pleased with pressing the advantage. He tittered with half closed eyes. "They say that the business world is cut-throat, so perhaps that is where you honed your skill? This morning, with clearly seasoned reflexes, you projected a sword without a moment's thought, from a *dress*, yes!" He chuckled. "From a dress, using, I believe, a five-strand technique." He raised his eyebrows, stroked his chin and mused, "I know a group familiar with tech fatigues of all sorts who uses that technique; a signature style, wouldn't you agree?"

Erin knew that he had identified her Stream training and was finding it hard to maintain her composure.

"So, we have here a financial specialist, with some *deeply* curious connections, who doesn't seem to be who she pretends to be, and, oh yes, *Marian*," he said slyly, feigning mild forgetfulness, "speaking of *swords*, as we were, what we saw this morning makes one think ponderously and work hard to build a surmise. Now, *your* sword is something else entirely, almost magical, wouldn't you think? Sparks, flames, and a strong hint of cold malevolence . . ."

Alystra didn't nod, but her eyes were full of mirth. It seemed that they had already come to understand each other.

"You," he shook his head slowly, "are almost absurdly not who you are pretending to be." He punctuated his comments with another dramatic pause. "As I pondered this and many other things, I came to the inescapable conclusion that perhaps Chesleth Preller isn't who he is pretending to be, although I haven't watched the videos of him, nor have I received any helpful reports on him yet, although I don't think I need to tap that source very deeply. My decades of dealing with people has led me to the final conclusion, and the only one that makes sense, is that your entire *story* is made up, and you are after something other than equipment to use in a salvage company. Which we *all* know would be pointless anyway. Right?" Neither Erin nor Alystra reacted to this, but he continued without giving them time to respond or object.

He tapped on his pad and stood up, rounding the desk to stand on the same side of the desk and view the screen with them. "This is Tergeth's, the galactic registry, you know of this?" The screen showed a running galactic clock and date at the top, rows and columns of different categories of ships, with counts, and a menu system for drilling into the data under numerous headings.

Both Alystra and Erin nodded their assent, at which he smiled and shook his head.

He continued with a tone of emphatic finality, "Tergeth's is a registry of every ship in the galaxy that has an asymptotic drive. For example," he turned to Erin gesturing with his pad controller, "if we wanted to, we could find *Lentoris*, by her builder's numbers, and we might just discover that your fine ship isn't registered to anyone named Chesleth Preller, which is, I am sure, an unfortunate clerical oversight." He smirked a most oily smirk. "As you also know, I am sure, class two drives are registered, but not tracked, the reason being that the singularities in the drives are dissipating rather than collective, but you already know this. Dissipating singularities aren't as dangerous, even though they can be programmed to be just as fast, like the *Lentoris* is, yes?"

By this point, Erin wasn't nervous anymore, since she felt they were already thoroughly exposed, and yet, his tone had no sense of threat. She was powerfully under the impression that he was racing to *his* point, at *this* point.

"Class *one* drives, however, are all tracked, their controllers each equipped with a transponder, as I bet you also know; certainly, dozens of people have reminded you of this since your arrival." At this the screen changed to a galactic map, with a blanket of red dots, too many to see, but the message was clear. "The transponder facilitates that every class one drive in the galaxy is always updated in Tergeth's. The lists are updated frequently, new ships added, destroyed ships put into the archive's appendix; every ship with a class one drive built for the past six centuries, logged, watched, tracked, and every single one can be pinpointed. That is why your story, Flen *Preller's* story, of wanting to outfit a salvage company has the companies here perplexed and adamant. They will *never* sell him a class one controller, and if they did, it would be useless, I think, for your *real* need, because there would always be someone looking over your shoulder. You seem to be surrounded by an air that I breathe frequently. An air of secrecy required for your true mission."

Alex walked back to the other side of the desk where he sat in his chair and leaned back putting his index fingers to his lips. For a half minute he sat with his eyes flitting through an index in his mind, racing to his next statement. "On Prevaria, I," he said, holding the last word in crescendo, "am the release valve. I don't work *for* any of the mammoth corporations here, though I work *with* them through agents, behind the scenes, and they know I exist; we act cooperatively. It is likely that they have guessed that it was I who had you taken off that street and brought here, but they won't say anything." He sat up and smiled, leaning forward now. "Any enormous industry has overflow, or things that slip through the cracks, back doors, or hidden avenues; some items even need to be *pushed* through those cracks. So, when this backdoor pressure builds to the point where it needs to be released, I have an army of faithful employees who recognize the need, learn what I need to know, get what I need, or do what I want, and I have a fleet of ships to carry out what I need to all corners of the galaxy. The corporations smile and nod, the wheels keep turning, the cash comes in, and everyone stays happy; do you take my meaning?" At this they both stared, stone-faced, but he pressed on unabashed. "By way of example, Dahna, those millions of units of tech fatigues sold to that group with *your* signature style? You don't suppose they buy direct, do you?"

He paused and touched his pad once; the screen went blank. "That is the context, and I sincerely appreciate your indulgence this morning as I have reviewed these observations." He stood and walked to the large glass doors, looking out for a minute while they waited. He turned and there was manic mirth in his eyes. "Now the conclusion. I have been in business, and in *this* business, on *this* planet, for half a century. You, the group of you, are up to *something*, with massive resources, and it has nothing to do with a *salvage* company; and please don't insult me with any absurd protestations. Since you arrived, I have been pondering what that *something* is." He paused, holding them in an intense riveting stare. "It would need to be worth the cost and effort, and it would require some combination of the equipment you are buying to effect repairs, *and* a class one controller, *and* the ship you want, which *would* truly be a salvage operation, could not be found in Tergeth's registry."

He looked up toward the ceiling. His facial expression coasted through thoughtful to curious, then struggled past confusion to finally reveal a spreading light as he considered the pieces, laying out the facts in his mind and watching the answer appear as if spelled out in the stars. Then, he whispered, as if he needed to prompt himself, to believe, "Something worth the cost and effort that . . . oh . . . *oh!*" He stood. "I have an idea. Perhaps you should follow me."

He opened another set of large double doors, striding through with a quick and nimble step. "I know what you are after; I know what you need."

After a dozen steps, the short hall they traversed opened to a massive indoor amphitheater, forty meters wide and twenty tall.

He stood aside and gestured. "I know because I have devoted most of my life and most of my enormous wealth in the quest for Prevaria's most precious lost treasure." Hanging from the ceiling was a one-tenth scale model of *Ascension*. Beneath the model was a museum—hundreds of artifacts and articles from the missing ship. "You will never get her working without me!"

"Painfully and with disgust."

After five days of fop, Bendahrin was exhausted of the role. He had concluded that all the wealth and trappings were utterly ridiculous. The energy required to play Chesleth Preller was crushing, but the continued absence of Alystra and Erin was an extra weight of anxiety.

Their arrival was a circus and an interrogation. They circled the top of the Helix while Jedra communicated with the tower to confirm who they were. By the time Jedra had landed the ship, there were a dozen people on deck to greet them including the owner of the Entrata Helix, several mid-level executives from major manufacturers, two dignitaries from the city government, and a handful of the Epoch's servants. There were even members of the city press corps to add that certain sense of deceit, manipulation, and brainlessness common to the media.

Chesleth parried questions about his health and sudden appearance with vague answers. "Simplified, yes, we are fine." And "Copiously, time that we buy what we need and get home." He was asked several times where his colleagues were, and Bendahrin waved vaguely toward the ship and said in his most uncaring tone, coughing, "Diligently, yes, on the ship doing what we need." Eventually he riveted upon one of the more minor servants and seized upon his hand, leading him inside. "So quickly, our trusted helper, we need to see Dorian at Quendrit Shipping, shipping, yes, we need you to call him now, and food." Then he walked off to wander the halls with Jedra following closely.

As the days progressed, Bendahrin made purchases and took tours, sat in meetings, and met with engineers and designers. He spent more money than he had ever known; twice he stopped at the bank to make sure he still had the necessary funds, and both times the bank manager told him he hadn't spent even three percent of what was available. Prantara Enterprises sold him eight different computer cores each with quadruple layered redundancies. Since any of them should work adequately, he bought three of the most powerful, three of the smallest, and two with the sturdiest design.

Jedra was laughing inside, but they were both heady with the freedom to buy whatever they wanted. Two other companies provided their most advanced workstations for navigation, control, systems, everything to outfit two command bridges and complete engineering suites with replacements for everything. kilometers of conduit of various gauges and design, cables and wireless systems for the computers, machines for splicing, and crates of every conceivable connector, adapter, and junction.

To maintain his façade of derangement he planned a meeting with one of the smallest companies in the city that designed what they proclaimed as "agile looping control stations." Their claim was that each of their workstations could be used anywhere since, as they said, "An interface is just what connects you to our software, and our software makes wonderful things happen."

Bendahrin almost gagged when he responded by letting them know how excited he was to know that wonderful things would happen with their controllers in place, and they responded that their software could emulate any need, from command to engineering to communications to tactical and weapons. They threw this out casually, and Chesleth almost forgot to maintain the act in his response. From the beginning Alystra had been worried about purchasing anything weapons related, and a workstation that could emulate anything would slam the door on this problem. Chesleth promptly ordered an even twenty with all necessary cables and connectors and tools, repeating the same tedious shopping mantra. He never did find out what "looping" meant, and he hoped that "wonderful" would be good enough.

At each meeting, tour, visit, meal, and conversation someone would challenge Chesleth about his desire for a class one drive controller. Surely, he understood that he would never need to rescue a ship of this kind. Chesleth Preller would always respond confidently, or in frustration approaching a tantrum, or dismissively, that his dream had always been to be able to rescue *any* ship, *any*where, at *any* time, and that no one could possibly know where the next critical need might be. And to prove his point, he would buy more, but not one company offered to sell him a class one controller.

Now that shopping had begun in earnest, Jedra had the daily workout of dragging pallets of equipment into the lower hold of *Lentoris*. For appearances' sake, Bendahrin couldn't be seen helping as Jedra dropped the rear loading ramp and stowed crates and reels and boxes. The work was heavy and slow, but Jedra was adamant that he had to get everything in and secured before the end of the day.

On the third day of deliveries, as Bendahrin watched, a slender boy came down from the main hatch and talked to Jedra. Bendahrin waited dutifully despite his wonder until Jedra had closed the rear drop ramp and had come and passed the message, "My Flen. We have some critical communications required aboard."

Keeping in character, Chesleth replied, "Evocative. Yes, we will go and face the need; how heroic, but, after all, we pay well for it, yes, well indeed."

He and Jedra glided and walked respectively to where the boy was waiting at the foot of the stairs leading to the hatch. They turned together and ascended, entering the ship and closing the hatch behind them.

The boy immediately turned on them and turned blood red. He raised his hand and mumbled some most unhappy words. There was a faint smell of smoke and Kel-Purim spoke, "Oh yes! You each had a dozen or so nano-bugs on you. I have just burned them up. Seriously, you people," he popped at them, "are so unaware. Spies listening to every word you say. Although I have been listening, too, and you are sickening how tediously you have maintained your façade."

Bendahrin stood closer to Kel, as close as he could without fainting from the smell. "Is Alystra safe?"

Kel-Purim raised his hand and blew across it at Bendahrin, who turned away. "Yes, of course, she is safe. She is busy, and from where I sit here in the mighty command center of our Holy Cause, your timing seems to be amazingly aligned."

Bendahrin quickly remembered that every conversation with Kel was annoying.

"But yes, we have a problem." And he floated back, turning and bowing and also pointing in one fluid motion at two figures lying in the hall, near the starboard lounge.

Jedra ran forward and knelt down, checking for a pulse, for a sign of life. "They are still alive, are we compromised?" Bendahrin was sure that Jedra looked suddenly more alert.

Kel twirled in the air and scowled at Jedra. "Well, yes, now I'm hurt. Of course not. Did you think they would catch me ill-prepared?" He pushed his lower lip forward in the most perfect fake pout in history.

Bendahrin rolled his eyes. "So, you did what?"

"Oh yes." Kel-Purim swelled and grew taller. "As soon as they entered the ship, I entered them, my blood in their blood, and off . . . to . . . sleep . . ." He looked at the sleeping intruders fondly, with a glint of hunger. "I have been holding them since Alystra told *me* that I had to do whatever *you* say if something goes wrong, and she is away." He glared at Bendahrin. "And you know what? She never told me what to do if something goes wrong, and she is away, if it's *your fault.* Why doesn't she ever think of that?"

"Good choice on her part. *You* would just eat them, I suppose."

Kel nodded eagerly, although Bendahrin wasn't sure it wasn't an act.

"How long have they been here?"

"Oh yes, the first, now she entered almost immediately after you left for your superbly boring meeting early this morning. The other appeared just a few hours later. I would say that they will be quite rested when I release them."

Jedra's fatigues had produced a gauntlet that he held out over each of the fallen intruders. He turned and spoke to Bendahrin, "Both of them have sophisticated outfits equipped more for observation and surveillance than combat; also disabled," he added, looking to Kel-Purim.

"Oh, yes, of course!" Kel retorted with a snorting wave of fumes. "What would be the point of leaving all of their little watchy and listeney things sending back information. Oh yes, Alystra was most clear, 'Kel,' she said to me, and his voice turned serious, 'no intruders get out of here with any information. But they all get off alive—do whatever Bendahrin tells you.'"

Bendahrin pondered for a moment, looking down at the two figures lying on the ground. He nodded slowly, coming to a conclusion, then looked at Jedra. "Could you rig their suits to look as if they had a malfunction?"

Jedra shrugged a non-commital shrug. "What do you have in mind?"

Bendahrin started slowly and thoughtfully. "This intrusion is not unexpected. We have been cagey and evasive, and thrown money at sellers rather than telling them what we are *really* after, which they can tell is deliberate deception. We *can't* give them an explanation, so any attempt they make to figure out what we are up to is not a surprise." He looked down again. "These two are hired guns; Stream mercenaries, maybe?" He looked at Jedra.

"Surveillance fatigues?" He waved his gauntlet over the two again. "Possible, though these two don't have Stream insignia, nor any custom components that would identify them as Stream." He paused, making an internal adjustment. "Sometimes Stream mercs, to be untraceable, will remove anything identifiable. That is why nobody in the Stream gets tattoos. Do you want to question them?"

Bendahrin shook his head. "They would not tell us anything of value, and I don't need to find out which of the major companies, or the government, sent them. We certainly have no reason to elicit any information. Besides," he glanced toward Kel, "I assume that you can dance through their minds anyway?"

Kel nodded with a massive, drippy grin.

"No, not necessary. As I said, this kind of effort is totally expected. No, what I am thinking is this, we rig their suits to look like a malfunction, or an unexpected interaction with some unknown security feature on our ship, and we make it look as though the malfunction bumped them to someplace else on the planet, where we wake them up. They have no immediate sense of the time, and they then need to find their way back. No one is hurt, and the cause of the malfunction doesn't, then, look like we were involved. Or, if they suspect us, they have no proof, and certainly aren't going to accuse us of anything that happened as the result of an unlawful intrusion."

Jedra clearly liked this idea, and his full helmet formed to cover his head, enhancing his interface with the suit.

Bendahrin turned to Kel. "Can you move them? I mean, can you move them in a way that won't leave the ship unguarded?"

Kel-Purim looked at him sideways. "Oh, yes, the ship? I could, yes, I could, But, no. No, I am afraid that Alystra was most emphatic that I can't leave the ship."

Bendahrin thought back to remember what Alystra had said, knowing that his memory wouldn't be as perfect as Kel's. She had been at 'Alystra levels' of emphatic that the protection of the ship was paramount, and evidently they were surrounded by people of impressive prowess at spying and infiltration, motives unknown. She had also made it clear at moderate levels of emphasis, for Alystra, that is, that Kel was to follow Bendahrin's instructions on issues that impacted their overall mission. She had followed *that* statement with a string of qualifications and protections so that Kel couldn't sneak around the injunction. Kel had put on his typical appearance of being offended that Alystra felt so certain he couldn't be trusted.

Bendahrin didn't understand the magical constraints outside of which Kel couldn't operate with respect to Alystra. It was a mix of whatever dictated their general relationship in conjunction with whatever specific instructions he received from Alystra for the specific event or context. It was a complicated puzzle, but even though Kel's motivations were far more complex, uncertain, and mysterious than an average person, the puzzle was similar to any other sentient entity, which might be redundant, but all sentient entities could be swayed, cajoled, convinced to think or persuaded to act, and, of course, threatened.

Then it struck him. Alystra's instructions. Her instructions about the ship were highly emphatic, but general in nature to all of them; the ship needed to be protected. Her instructions to Kel-Purim, in comparison, were specific and highly contextual, *and* tied to the urgency of their current endeavors. He also recalled something that Kel had mentioned when they had first met, that Alystra had put around himself a "frosting of protection," that for Kel was an imperative of some kind. If he applied enough pressure to Kel, using the angle that success on Prevaria was critical for his safety, that imperative might tip the scales.

It *also* struck him that he could also pull the plug. Bendahrin could call to Alystra in an instant and draw her back saying that the intruders were, he deemed, a sufficient threat to warrant an emergency, then Kel would be faced with having not helped at a critical moment, jeopardizing their success. Then Kel would face Alystra, although maybe that didn't matter to him, or only mattered in ways that didn't matter, which was a circular trap in this thinking. He almost laughed at himself when he realized that Alystra was *already* listening and was probably thinking, *Get on with it, already!*

Then a different "it" struck him, Kel *had* left the ship, he had *just* left the ship. So clearly this wasn't a magical compulsion tied to the ship. He *could* leave the ship, so what was the issue? It was highly likely that Kel could carry out the magical transfer of the two intruders to safe locations around the planet fast enough that there would be no threat, and Jedra and Bendahrin could guard the ship, well, Bendahrin thought honestly, Jedra could.

Bendahrin shook himself from thought and realized that Kel was looking at him intensely, *had* been looking as *he*, Bendahrin, was *lost* in thought.

He was about to speak, when Kel said, "Is that really going to be your approach, your argument?" He looked angry and fearful at the same time. "I *also* told you, your mind is a stage, I know your every thought. And yes, she does, too. You are right, I will do what you say. I must."

Bendahrin could barely find the courage to pity him, but he asked, "How long have you been here, safe on the ship?" But in that moment, an image of Kel's chalice filled his mind. "Oh . . ."

Even Kel's misty nature failed to hide the fact that he looked like a man at the precipice of disaster. And Bendahrin was struck by another "it" for the final time, but this time the conclusion took no thought. "Kel, I wish I could understand, but I will protect your home while you are gone."

"It is more than my home. Until Alystra finds a way to make me whole, my life and the destiny I contain, are housed in that chalice."

Bendahrin was confused. "But isn't the chalice safe, here, on the ship?"

Kel was downcast, and this was the first time Bendahrin was sure that his appearance was fully genuine. "This ship has no protection. I protect the ship, Alystra protects all, but in you, you could protect my chalice."

Bendahrin nodded calmly. "Yes, I could watch your chalice, I assume this won't take long?"

"Time is irrelevant, an instant is all that is needed to topple everything. And you won't *watch* my chalice; as I said, *in* you, you could protect my chalice."

Now it was Bendahrin's turn to be nervous. "I don't know what that means."

"You don't need to understand, you only need to give assent."

Bendahrin had no guidelines with which to draw a conclusion. So, he rested on the only joint authority he knew. "Would Alystra approve?"

Kel shrunk. "Bendahrin, I know that I am full of mischief and cunning, by nature and by choice. Nevertheless, I would never suggest anything Alystra would not approve with regard to *you*. She has made a pact with me, but you are central to her destiny and deliverance."

Bendahrin snorted an ironic laugh in his ignorance. "Well, then I hope I get it right! What do we need to tell Jedra?"

"He will need to protect the ship from intruders or surveillance from outside."

Bendahrin turned to Jedra, who had been listening intently anyway.

Jedra nodded and said, "They are ready to go now." He gestured to the two figures on the floor. "And I am ready to watch the ship."

"Then, Bendahrin, you must come with me," Kel said.

Bendahrin followed Kel to the port museum and wove through the artifacts til they stood before Kel's chalice. "Pick it up! And you must state that you will guard the chalice, with all the faculties you possess."

Bendahrin picked up the chalice and hugged it to his chest. "It is so. With my life I will guard your chalice."

At that, Kel nodded, no sense of mischief or deceit in his blood-red face.

The chalice turned warm and seemed to shrink a bit but then it passed into Bendahrin, into his chest, and when, looking down, Bendahrin could see the chalice no more.

Kel was gone.

Bendahrin looked around the room and walked to the window to look at the city spread beneath.

At the same time, he felt the fire; fire that surrounded him, and fire that stretched in all directions. But the fire didn't burn; it was a fire of impending doom, a threat, a danger, but also the fire and warmth of life. In that moment, Bendahrin realized that the chalice was joined to Kel-Purim, who, in turn, protected a vast body of sleeping souls. Their minds reached him in gentle song, faint, whispery, but their presence was strong. Bendahrin tried to look, tried to see, he reached to touch, but in that moment, Kel had re-appeared, the fire was gone, and the chalice was back in his hands.

Kel looked at him, and from what they had just shared, Bendahrin knew that although he now knew the reason he could never trust Kel, he knew now that he always would, and Kel made it clear as he danced on the stage of Bendahrin's mind, that he would never be worthy of trust, but he would never fail in it. Bendahrin walked back from the window and put the chalice back in its spot and Kel-Purim spoke, "The intruders are safe, in woods, part way around the planet where night is halfway past so they will find it hard to be certain of the passage of time, starting now, as I leave their veins and they awaken."

Bendahrin, waving to Kel to follow, started walking out through the artifacts. "You are back in charge of the ship." He stopped, closing his eyes after he saw Jedra approaching. He took a deep breath, settling his mind back into his role as the wealthy idiot, Chesleth Preller. He opened his eyes. "Consequently, now, yes. We need to finish our purchases, for which we pay dearly, oh yes." And he gestured to Jedra, who could tell that he was only substantially frustrated.

They exited the ship, and Jedra returned with renewed energy to finish loading their latest purchases. Chesleth Preller, in his flamboyance, entered the Epoch calling out for assistance. To the first hotel employee he found, he announced, "Unequivocally, right now, I need to meet with the representatives of Chardeo Shipbuilders. Please set up a meeting, for which we will pay greatly so, yes, greatly!" coughing thrice, for compounding effect.

The calls and arrangements were made, and two hours later Chesleth and his exhausted bodyguard entered a luxurious transport on the east landing platform of the Extranta Executive Epoch and were whisked at sizzling speed to the offices of the largest shipbuilding company in the galaxy to take part in one of the most ancient dances on the familiar stage where the combat of buying and selling make their home.

16

The Chardeo Shipbuilders' Sky Dome conference room was an awe-inspiring and breathtaking room. Whereas the Epoch atop the Entranta Helix was the joint effort of the city and planet to overwhelm with opulence and spectacle, the Sky Dome was the ultimate expression of corporate power, making it an intimidating and overwhelming location to go head-to-head with a group of CS's top executives. Nevertheless, Chesleth Preller somehow maintained an air of thorough indifference with aplomb, although he kicked himself for the rest of his life for playing his part *so* well. Jedra, in contrast, had the freedom to glance around and build some memories for life.

The Sky Dome tower was only about 300 meters tall, although it stood atop a mountain that had been leveled at about two kilometers elevation to build the base of the tower. A range of mountains to the west swept around the tower in a grand curve with some peaks higher, and some lower. The height of the tower was chosen to provide a view that allowed a visitor the opportunity to either look up at an entire mountain, or down at an entire mountain, and several of each. Since the tower was built on the eastern side of the circle of mountains, the view to the east swept down into the vast Dardel plain where the city was built like a vast plate for all its flatness. Most impressive of all, however, was the endless parade of Chardeo's ships visible from the Sky Dome. A score of ships of all sizes were always in the surrounding sky. Each ship freshly-built, carefully-restored, or dutifully-serviced by the massive CS factories would join the choreography, sometimes hovering with the ship's nose inches from the dome, sometimes passing just overhead in a slow roll, other times joining with other ships in formation, and then each, when done showing off, would shoot off to be delivered in a flash of light, to be replaced by the next ship in the display.

Their transport approached the tower from below, always heading straight in, so the passengers could not see the tower as they approached. Beneath the upper levels that housed the Sky Dome was a hangar for a fleet of corporate ships, and, above that, another hangar for smaller, more private craft. Jedra was looking outside when suddenly they were inside, and the transport stopped in a room that looked more suited for a ball than parking ships. They exited and a single man approached and welcomed them most cordially. He directed them to an elevator and bowed, saying, "Please stand within the rectangle, and don't touch the walls."

There *was* a rectangle on the floor, to keep them from getting too close to the walls, and the reason for the precaution became evident in moments. As the elevator started to ascend, the ceiling of the elevator, which was made of countless hinged panels slid away into the walls, and they looked up to see blue sky far above, but the rectangle of sky was growing as the opening was fast approaching. When they reached the top, the walls now disappeared into the floor like the top of a roll-top desk so that as they passed floor level, they had an unimpeded view in all directions. The top floor of the Sky Dome was about sixty yards square, and they had arrived near the west side, facing the mountains and a sunset panorama. This square area was like the top of a pyramid, stairs and terraces with seating areas and additional open conference space sweeping down in all directions so that, when standing at the top, there was almost nothing to block the view of sky, mountains, city, or, most importantly, the ships.

"Flen Preller," a voice said from behind them, and they turned to see that a small group had congregated nearby. One said, "Would you like a brief tour of our . . . ?" But, Chesleth Preller, true to character, nodded at them and in their direction and then proceeded to walk awkwardly, right through the group, to take a seat at the table with his back to them, waiting for them to join him.

Jedra, without a word, rolling his eyes to show his understanding of their consternation at the odd greeting from Flen Preller, smiled at the group and shook their hands, gesturing to them to join Chesleth at the table, which they did, sitting on the opposite side.

In this way, Chesleth Preller began his meeting with a handful of top executives of Chardeo Shipbuilders, the largest designer and builder of ships capable of asymptotic travel throughout the galaxy.

When they were seated, Chesleth began in earnest, "Gratefully, I want to assure you that we are happily appreciative of your time and attention, and we look forward to making some purchases critical to our plans and operations."

An elderly man, gray hair, gray suit, and stern but twinkling eyes, smiled warmly, but like a predator. "And we welcome you. My name is Marth Porter, President of Chardeo. Our lead engineer, Dr. Dara Timnao, is here to answer any technical questions you might have." He gestured to a middle-aged woman all in tan, who was youthful and exuberant, with eyes that were fierce, intelligent, and penetrating. "Alphous Prensner is our chief of finances, and Torfan Boyd is one of our operations specialists, he will make all arrangements for delivery of your purchases." These two men were both keen and calculating, but whereas Alphous was massive and warm and engaging with soft, round features and mirth in his eyes, Torfan was small and sharp and cold as a pit of winter darkness.

Chesleth, whose eyes slid over them with complete indifference, was certain that the first three were as introduced but that Torfan was joined neither to the name given nor the role described. Chesleth nodded to each in turn and Marth continued, "We have heard, Chesleth, that you have made a large number of purchases already. We must wonder what else you would need to acquire?"

"Affectionately, we have been holding Chardeo in our hearts for our final purchases since our own personal cruisette was built right here, by Chardeo Shipbuilders." In this case, Chesleth was careful to not mention anything about having, "paid dearly," since he didn't want them digging too deeply into the records in this regard.

"Your ship, the *Lentoris*, I believe?" Marth nodded proudly. "A VLX fifty-seven-oh-five series, very fast. I remember the series, not *too* old." He turned to Dr. Timnao. "Were you part of that design?"

Dara nodded efficiently, facing Marth. "Certainly, I worked for Dennis and Mila Tentharsus back then. I helped with engine room ergonomics." She turned to Chesleth. "We could probably do some upgrades to your ship, if you want to leave her with us."

"Again, gratefully, we have no need. We have our own technicians to maintain our stable of crafts." He paused, pretending to be thinking about answering. "Although, if you have a way to transfer all that . . . math to new equipment, it might be useful. I don't want to lose the speed improvements we have made to the drive."

The engineer sat back. "You aren't using the original equations for the drive?"

Chesleth smiled most idiotically, and for an obvious and personal reason, got his next line perfect. "Profusely, I admit, to my shame, that I don't understand the math, but I asked, just in case, and I still couldn't get it, but my man here," and he beckoned to Jedra who was already standing right behind him anyway, "can tell you what our experts said."

Jedra said, with precision, "I have been told the current drive proximity coefficient has a calculated stringency of seventy-one x for delta two-hundred-five at plus ten-point-zero-one-three and rated at one-hundred-seventy-eight Harbens."

Chesleth smiled idiotically, but Dara was immediately engaged and impressed. "Who did this?" she asked with severe intensity.

Chesleth laughed. "I have several technicians who do math for our ships." He placed his fingertips together and gazed at his thumbs. "They are quite accomplished with math and . . ." He couldn't think of anything else to add.

"I would like to meet your team. If this is correct, your ship . . . this is remarkable." And she couldn't think of anything else to say either.

Torfan took a breath, knowing *exactly* what to say, but Marth cut across him, "We would be happy to give your ship a complete overhaul, all new systems? Of course," he added hastily, "we wouldn't alter the drive system's control parameters in any way. With proper care, even they can be transferred to new equipment. We would be horrified to cause the loss of such an advanced improvement to the drive."

"That is very generous, very generous indeed," Chesleth said, holding up his hands and bowing his head, with reverence. "But no, no, we have our own technicians and mechanics, so, we would prefer to have our own team repair and install. Could we agree that my first purchase be a complete package of your upgraded systems? I assume that you know what is needed?" He looked at Torfan directly. "Just deliver everything I need to the Epoch. We will take it from there, of course."

Alphous nodded and smiled. Although this initial purchase was trifling, he had the sense that Chesleth was just warming up. "We can certainly accommodate this easily." He had pulled a data pad from an inside pocket earlier, upon which he tapped and dragged. After a couple of yawning minutes he announced, "I have pulled together what you need, and included all hardware and fittings. We wouldn't want your experts to come up short. I have also included some critical equipment and tools that will help them; is that acceptable?"

Chesleth waved his hand again. "Conditionally, that is excellent, and ideal. Whatever you feel is right, we certainly trust you."

At *that* Alphous' eyes went wide. It was unlikely that anyone had ever said that of a salesman in his experience. Chesleth was certainly warmed up.

"Finally, what I need from Chardeo: a complete outfit of bridge components for all standard stations to fit Chardeo ship specifications, a full engineering suite, computer and navigation systems with all controllers, fittings, hardware, tools and equipment for outfitting and repairing any ship with a class one asymptotic drive system." He coughed into his hand. Bendahrin had now said this same phrase enough times that he could rattle it off without much thought. He folded his hands and smiled, as if expecting to have it all delivered to the table.

Marth nodded slowly and thoughtfully, and dove in, most gently, to the same argument Bendahrin had now heard a few dozen times. "Flen Preller, with all possible respect and regards for your endeavors, why would you want or need a class one system? All ships with class one drives are closely regulated. I, personally, sit as the chair of the oversight board. Because of the transponders encased in all asymptotic singularity clusters in the drive itself, we know where every class one ship ever built is located. We have heard extensively about your plans and appreciate your eagerness to provide salvage support, but we can't imagine a situation when you would ever need a controller, for this reason."

Bendahrin, from tedious experience, knew this was coming, and he had thought through in his mind the perfect temper tantrum to toss at the panel of experts facing him.

So, Chesleth Preller burst out of him with vehemence, "Adamantly, this argument has been frustrating from the beginning!

Heatedly, we must confess that we have never been so obstacled by so many." He stood up, and everyone at the table did likewise.

He turned away from the table and found himself nose to nose with a dreadnaught class military ship. At the sight, his vision somehow became crystal clear and a faint smile danced on his lips that he quickly hid before he turned. The massive presence almost took him off his stride, but he continued the turn, unpausing, and started to walk around the table, speaking with gestures and bows and even a slight, but appropriate, stamping of his feet; all punctuated with a stream of well-timed coughs.

For the first time, Chesleth Preller actually referred to himself. "This salvage company has been a dream of mine since I was young. As a child I read books on rescue tugs saving ships at sea, the glory and heroics, a crew and a ship against the odds to save wrecks and derelicts with their desperate passengers. I was also enamored by the sky and night, the looming blackness with the twinkling stars. My driving passion has long been to join these in a salvage company amidst the stars. As I grew and conquered my way to wealth, I never lost sight of my vision. I want to be able to save any ship I encounter and restore it to life, beautiful life, and bring any people rescued home. And I will get what I want to fulfill that dream." By this time, he had circumnavigated the table. He turned, facing the home team fiercely and finished emphatically, "I will get what I want, and if my only path to my dream is to buy that!" He pointed over his shoulder at the massive combat vessel, "I will purchase one and tear it to shreds to extract the class one controller I want!"

He then straightened up faintly, gazing with empty eyes across the table and continued, "Simply, we have the money we need, and your reticence only makes us wonder what you have to hide; yes, we wonder sincerely." He blinked as his sight seemed to fade to normal.

From this point, the discussion proceeded in a business-like fashion and straight as an arrow to the target. They left with a promise of two complete sets of every possible bridge and engineering configuration *and* computer systems, miles of conduit, crates of connectors, equipment of all kinds, etcetera and so on, with one new and top of the line class one asymptotic drive controller. By the time they were through, they had spent enough to purchase three class one ships, but were promised delivery, in three days, of enough supplies to outfit the progenitor of them all.

17

So again, Chesleth Preller had to wait, suffering many hours in the stuffy opulence and annoying attentiveness of the Epoch. He wondered idly if some people were able to enjoy all the affluent nonsense. As a few other small deliveries trickled in, he did end up reading a book projected up to him from the entire city, which was so distracting he couldn't focus and gave up after a dozen pages. The staff of the Helix approached regularly with requests for an audience from city officials and companies wanting to sell him the perfect whatever for doing whatever task. Since the money was flowing everyone wanted to dip in the stream. He humored some by making a few small purchases, providing Jedra with more work to do. Three other people had attempted to infiltrate the ship, and Jedra and Bendahrin were called to the ship while Kel removed the intruders. Each time Bendahrin saw the fires he and Kel seemed to connect.

One crate arrived early on the first morning, delivered by a young man who insisted that he was required by his employer to make the delivery directly onto the ship.

Jedra listened to his instructions and told him to wait at the entry to the landing pad near *Lentoris*. After a few minutes Jedra re-appeared, coaxing Chesleth to speak with the man. "Flen Preller, this delivery is unusual and must receive your direct attention."

"Annoyed! I am, yes. Deliveries are your responsibility and for their management, I pay well."

The man turned to Chesleth and said, "I have been instructed to make this delivery directly to the hold of your ship from the offices at Denton Street Enterprises, Limited."

Bendahrin gasped, but quickly recovered, "Astonished and inconvenient! But we will accompany you. Maintain security—as needed, which costs us at all times."

Jedra led the way and the man followed him, pushing the dolly with the single crate.

Chesleth Preller followed behind, muttering and gesticulating with stiff and abrupt jerks of his arms.

When the three had entered *Lentoris's* hold the man deposited the crate and slid his dolly out from under it. Heading toward the door, he spoke, "Your manifest," and he handed Chesleth an envelope. "I am told that you should check the details immediately. He hastened to leave the hold and disappeared toward the front of the ship.

Chesleth opened the envelope and read the contents quickly. "The crate is full of Alex Scurven's favorite wine, a gift. Erin and I will transport on board *Lentoris* as soon as the delivery from Chardeo arrives. We will meet you as soon as Jedra is done loading the shipment in order to leave immediately." It was not signed.

As a result, it was no surprise that after the shipment from Chardeo arrived four interminable days later, and Jedra spent most of the day loading it, as he was closing the loading ramp after the last crate was stowed, *Lentoris's* main hatch opened and Marian and Dahna exited, proceeding down the stairs in matching colors. Chesleth, who had been fretting endlessly between the main balcony and the western landing pad, was there when they emerged.

Bendahrin, who wanted to run forward and confront them and greet them, forced himself to stay in character and turned his back, waiting for them to approach.

Dahna spoke first. "My Flen Preller, we have completed all assignments and we need your instructions."

Chesleth turned to the two women, working hard to not make eye contact or express the relief that was flooding through him. "Copiously, we are displeased at how long you have taken, but," he raised his hand, "you have timed your sloth well. We are shipped?" He looked at Jedra, who nodded. "Conclusion, for certain." He folded his hands like a serene pontiff. "Then, final instructions before departure." He nodded to Jedra. "With speed remove all of our possessions from the Epoch." He then turned to Marian and Dahna. "With care, transfer our balance from the bank, and settle with the Helix." He headed for the ship with a sweep of purple, ascended the stairs, and turned his back on the opulence and extravagance of the Extranta ay-po-sh atop the Helix ha-purr tower.

It took Jedra three trips to remove the irrelevant and useful, the Chesleth Preller wardrobe and the wardrobes of Marian and Dahna and himself, a fortune in combat fatigues in bright colors. By the time he had returned to the ship for the last time, Bendahrin had put on his own clothes and was feeling tremendously relaxed. He greeted Jedra with a hand clasp, careful to not be visible through the hatch. Jedra went to his quarters to change as well; the bright yellow, sweat-drenched fatigues were far from his favorite.

Erin arrived next, a sharp two hours later, having finished with the bank. She came through the main hatch where the two men were waiting, at the side, so as to not be visible through the hatch. In her arms she held three medium-sized cases. Handing one to each of the men she said, "Alystra wanted me to provide each of us with a few million in galactic currency, for future use." Then she turned to Bendahrin and punched his shoulder. "Bendahrin, you happen to be the second wealthiest person on Palestre now. I transferred the remaining funds to your account there." She then put her hand on his shoulder. "You! You spent an epic amount here. This will be a measurable bump in their economy. Despite your annoying char-acter, stories will be told for years about those weeks where cash poured from the sky."

Jedra chimed in, "We have a hold packed with enough gear to create three salvage companies and repair scores of ships." He laughed. "I haven't had such a workout in years."

Erin proceeded quickly to her quarters to get into black and gray fatigues, the color of the day clearly wasn't popular.

Jedra and Bendahrin were standing near the hatch, being careful to not be visible, when Alystra appeared minutes later, surrounded by deferential Epoch employees orbiting her and peppering her with questions. Alystra stopped at the bottom of the stairs and turned. She held up her hand, and they stopped. She said something quickly, and they all turned as one to go. Meanwhile she leapt up the stairs, retracted them into the ship, and closed the hatch almost with a single motion. As soon as the door closed, she cried, "Enough!" and her dress was gone, in a yellow flash, and she was dressed all in black. She approached Bendahrin and removed the thick glasses, and in that instant, he was himself again, his face and eyesight restored.

Immediately, they felt the ship move and accelerate.

Alystra swept them up, and they were on the bridge, where Erin was already at the controls, and the sky was creeping quickly to the black of space.

Bendahrin had thought that they would get a break when they left Prevaria, but clearly this was not to happen.

Alystra nodded toward Erin. "Jedra, you are with Erin."

At that, Erin activated her suit helmet and Jedra, seeing this, activated his, and they disappeared an instant later.

Bendahrin sat in one of the bridge chairs, holding a dozen questions between his teeth.

Alystra was busy at the controls, and she had summoned several items that floated in the air around her. After a minute or two she turned to Bendahrin, grabbed his arms, and kissed him on the forehead. "You were fabulous. Your act was amazing, and you kept the top executives of three dozen companies hopping and hopping mad. They couldn't figure you out, and you kept changing plans and demands. They convened together and had a few group meetings to compare notes and strategize, unprecedented in the competitive climate on Prevaria. I spied on these meetings; hilarious!" She kissed his forehead again. "However, we've still a few insanely dangerous tricks we need to pull off." She stopped and closed her eyes for a moment. "We are being followed by about two dozen ships, and, of course, tracked."

Bendahrin cocked his head, about to ask, but she put a finger to his mouth.

"Sometimes you are so simple." She shook her head. "They *told* you, *everyone* told you, at least a dozen times. They know where every class one asymptotic drive in the galaxy is because the *controller* is a galactic transponder. You bought a class one controller, which, by the way, was brilliant! That threat was priceless. I didn't think you had it in you! However, we need to get rid of that controller, so Chesleth Preller needs to die."

Bendahrin's scowled. "But, but I thought the controller was the most important part we needed."

Alystra shook her head. "Our new friend, Alex Scurven,

has provided a controller uniquely built with no transponder. So Chesleth Preller is ready to crash."

She might have kissed him again, but time was fleeing as quickly as *Lentoris*. "Even though no one on Prevaria is sure about our true purposes, we are still being followed. Suspicious, I guess. We need to pull off an impossible sleight of ship at multiple times the speed of light, and we have to do it with only one use of magic, and a big one. But we have a huge problem." She looked Bendahrin in the eyes and he saw it instantly, her eyes were flickering to black, and he felt her sense of urgency. She closed her eyes and clenched her whole body; a cloud of black rose from her. She took a step back. "This will happen fast."

Suddenly Bendahrin found himself enclosed in combat fatigues, and he heard Jedra's deep, calm voice. "Bendahrin, breathe slowly and remain calm. You are in your own fatigues. We need you in the helmet so you can hear us and see what we are doing. Can you see what we are seeing?"

Bendahrin had never been in the isolation of combat fatigues before, but he closed his eyes for a moment and discovered that despite the isolation, the sensation seemed natural. "Y-yes," he stuttered. He opened his eyes and was immediately impressed with the way the display was balanced and even intuitive, when he looked at a specific element in an image, the suit focused there. "I can see what you are seeing. This is—"

Alystra's voice came through next, cutting him off, and Bendahrin noticed that she was in fatigues as well. "Pay attention. The transponder in the controller you bought is transmitting and it's location is being tracked. Once we make our first turn, the transponder needs to maintain a straight path to the crash, otherwise they will see the change in course and suspect something. That controller and transponder is in a crate at the back of the cargo bay where Erin will use mass isolators to float the crate so it is independent from the ship's artificial gravity. That done, we move *Lentoris* down and away from the crate so that it continues on a straight path, independent of the ship. Alex provided us with a derelict ship that we will use as a decoy. It doesn't have power, or our pursuers might detect that too. So, we drag the decoy ship into the same path as the transponder, moving *Lentoris* out of the way at the same time. That way, the transponder crashes with the decoy. Allow me to provide the detailed procedure."

Bendahrin, and the others, were flooded with images and details, a sequence to follow, and tasks that they must each do. They also knew when Alystra would be gone, and the danger they would then be in. Alystra was showing off: she had placed a simple checklist in the display that populated as she went through the tasks.

Erin offered one piece of advice. "The safest way to succeed is to talk through everything you are doing so everyone is confirmed on where we are in the process. Be clear. Bendahrin, don't wander into questions."

Bendahrin could see Jedra and Erin's view of a crate in the hold. Erin was typing into a keyboard attached to a thick mesh of wires and small nodes. "Activating the mass isolators!" Erin said, and, after a few seconds, "Isolators working. The controller is ready to be isolated from ship's AG and become fully inertial after our turn."

"Excellent. Thirty seconds to light speed turn." As Alystra was making adjustments on the control panel, she explained to Bendahrin, "I am sure that you know that this is something you should never do. No ship's system can calculate a trajectory fast enough at this speed to make this safe; you would never know if you were heading right at a planet, and, pow! you're dead. We simulated this maneuver several times and pre-programmed *Lentoris*, and it's still risky."

Bendahrin wanted to ask if field strikes saved you from a crash, and then he realized that the *ship* might survive a field strike.

Suddenly the ship turned and the starfield shifted abruptly.

Kel appeared off to the right. "Oh yes, reporting and present as required."

Alystra glared at him and then returned her attention frantically to checking their new course.

Kel shook his head and rolled his eyes. "Fine. All the ships pursuing us have dropped to calculate a pursuit trajectory."

Alystra scanned the displays. "Perfect, we will pass three hundred, seventy thousand meters off Dredit's moon, aimed at Dorvair, eight minutes. Let's turn the mass isolator on!"

Erin said, "Isolator on. Controller fully inertial. Jedra is also gravity neutral and buoyant. We are ready to move *Lentoris* away." Bendahrin could see that Jedra was floating next to the crate with the controller.

Alystra pointed to a part of the control panel which Bendahrin recognized from other ships but even more from her mental instructions. She touched a single control. "Thrusting down." On his helmet screen, he could now see Erin's view which showed the crate and Jedra floating upward in the hold. Bendahrin had to make a careful mental note, although it appeared that the crate was slowly moving up, Alystra's manuever had moved the entire ship down and away from the unwanted crate. As soon as Erin had mentioned the separation, Alystra had reversed thrust and stopped the relative downward motion of the ship.

Erin's voice cut in almost immediately, "Alystra, we have two feet of separation between the ship's floor and the controller's crate. Evacuating atmosphere from cargo hold. Other cargo is secured, and Jedra is tethered to the controller."

Jedra's voice cut through, "Let's get this ride going!" His excitement was obvious.

Kel piped in, blissfully unconcerned about the tension, but pretending to care. "Oh, yes. The other ships have adjusted, they are following, but they have fallen behind substantially."

"Let's hope that the increased distance is sufficient to make their visuals insufficient."

After a time, Erin spoke again, "Atmosphere evacuated, opening loading hatch."

Bendahrin watched Erin's view, watching as the hold opened, and Jedra's view, who was watching the crate. Bendahrin's breath caught. He felt the odd sensation of his vision becoming hyper-focused, but he ignored it in the tension.

Finally, the hatch was fully open, and Erin confirmed, "Hatch is open, accelerate forward from target."

Alystra moved to activate further controls and they all saw *Lentoris* moving away from Jedra's view, and from Erin's, Jedra and the crate appeared to float out of the hatch into space. "Expanding drive field to four-hundred-and-thirty percent. Get ready everyone, we are about to pass Dredit's moon. I will seize the decoy, but then I will be gone. Six minutes. I can feel it . . ." She stepped back from the controls and Bendahrin stepped up.

He wasn't sure what to expect, but suddenly the small cockpit was filled with swirling dark mists and he was glad he hadn't turned.

At the same time Jedra cried out, "The decoy ship is here, and it is just three meters away. The placement was perfect. Now we need to drag that derelict down to the transponder. Go, go, go!"

"Setting the bow tether," Erin said, and Bendahrin could see that she had used her suit to transport to *Lentoris's* bow. She had a sturdy line that she quickly secured to a cleat on the bow, and then she did a tricky maneuver where she threw the cable and then transported again and again, redirecting the cable to the bow of the other ship. "Time? Bendahrin? Time!"

In his fascination, Bendahrin had forgotten his job to provide verbal cues to supplement the timer visible on everyone's helmet display. "Four minutes forty!" he called out. Then, "Sorry," under his breath, forgetting to save this for after the crisis.

"Bow secured. Heading for the stern." Erin was abrupt but she had good reason. "Bendahrin, from four minutes, every thirty seconds and then every fifteen at two. Setting stern tether." Her breathing was now loud in their ears. Bendahrin's mysterious hyper-focus made the soft sound painfully grating.

At this point, Jedra piped in, "I can see that the bow tether is taut. Erin is at the stern. We're going to make it!" Bendahrin could see Erin in the projected view from Jedra's suit. She was running out another line toward *Lentoris.* He watched her secure the line then remembered what he was supposed to be doing and looked at the countdown clock.

"Four minutes!" Bendahrin cried. He was beginning to sweat and wondered how to get the suit to eliminate the moisture when the suit responded, and the moisture was suddenly gone and he felt the temperature drop a bit. *Wow! Just* like *magic.*

"Stern tether secured. The ships are now connected. Begin downward thrust. Moving to derelict's hold." Erin was in her element. Bendahrin could see her transporting from place to place with precision.

"Thrusting down, three seconds." Bendahrin was glad that Alystra had preset some of the controls.

Bendahrin hit the down thrusters that fired for three full seconds, and in that moment, Erin shouted, "The hold hatch on the decoy is closed." Bendahrin could see that she was in a dark hold, the light from her fatigue's helmet was dim in the enclosed space.

"Three minutes thirty, thrusting up to stop *Lentoris.*" Bendahrin called out. "How are we doing, Jedra?"

"The decoy is closing on *Lentoris.* The bow tether was slightly shorter, so expect impact at the bow first, the decoy is rotating down, but we're about halfway there."

Just then, flashes of light came from Erin's view.

"Cutting the top of the hatch to break the latches, then I will hit a concussive blast to open the hatch. These enhanced power supplies are amazing," Erin added, and Bendahrin smiled at the momentary lapse in discipline; new toys can bring out excitement even in the most disciplined mind. From Jedra's view he could see the laser cutting through the top of the hatch. Vapors and blistered debris floated away from the rear of the derelict ship. He could also see that the derelict ship was slowly approaching where Jedra was, still moving with the controller in a straight line.

Bendahrin heard a deep but low crunching thud as the decoy made contact. He felt a slow series of additional impacts, pounding down the length of the ship as the two ships impacted. "Three minutes!" he called out.

At almost the same time Jedra said, "Bendahrin, the ships are touching, still drifting down slowly. Now would work for reverse thrust, I am almost directly behind."

"Thrusting up," Bendahrin cried, hitting the controls, and he heard additional minor thumps, at least, he *told* himself they were minor. With his heightened senses, they sounded thunderously loud. He wondered if the *targshobe* was already repairing the dents caused by the slow collision.

At almost the same time, Erin cried, "Concussion!"

And they all saw the hold burst open from both sides. Jedra's view was especially disconcerting, since the door seemed to blow out right at him, but the hinges held, and the large loading hatch slammed down.

Erin vanished from Jedra's view for a moment and returned almost immediately with another coil of cable, which she threw to Jedra.

"Impact in two minutes, thirty!" Bendahrin cried. He looked through the force-field glass and the planet they were heading for was just a dim dot of light.

Once again, Erin transported her way along the line to bring it quickly to Jedra.

He took the cable and secured it to a handle on the crate.

Then both he and Erin transported to the hold and dragged the crate the remaining few feet into the hold. This infinitesimal delta in speed wouldn't register from the transponder. There were scores of additional crates in the hold of the derelict ship, so they needed to search for the few they needed to remove.

"Alex insisted that we fill the hold with sufficient junk to look like the rest of our purchases. The other controller should be clearly marked," Erin said, calmly but with frustration in her voice. She and Jedra moved from crate to crate.

"Two minutes to impact," Bendahrin said, quietly, hoping his voice sounded as calm and confident.

"This is the right one," Jedra called out.

Bendahrin saw what Jedra was viewing on the crate. He read out loud, "Marian. One Class One Controller. No Transponder. Pleasure. Scurven." Jedra paused with a sharp intake of breath. "Also, it says, NOTE: Imperative You Remove ALL crates with blue flags.'" Jedra sized up the crate with the controller, then looked at Erin. "I think together?"

They both grabbed the crate and there was a change of view as they transferred to the hold on *Lentoris*.

"One minute, forty-five."

Bendahrin was getting tense. The world they were approaching was still a dot, but time was running out. He could see that Jedra and Erin were back in the dark hold, moving with deliberation. There were three massive crates with blue flags, and Jedra held out his hand. Bendahrin could hear him whispering, "These are quite massive. This will draw some energy," then, to Erin, "These won't fit in the hold. Front lounge!" They moved in position with the first crate between them, then the view changed again and again as they transferred the three crates. "Yes!" Jedra cried.

"One minute, thirty to impact," Bendahrin said, looking back and forth between the timer and the helmet display.

Bendahrin watched as Erin signaled quickly with rapid hand motions to Jedra who nodded, and their views changed again as they each transferred outside the ship; Erin at the bow, Jedra at the stern.

Jedra spoke first, "Stern tether cut."

Almost immediately Erin confirmed that the bow tether was cut. And their views changed again. They were back in *Lentoris*'s hold.

"Bendahrin, get us away!"

"One minute, fifteen. Thrusting down. Five seconds thrust, then we will drift for ten."

"Closing hatch," Jedra said. Bendahrin glanced and saw the hold closing.

"One minute."

Erin said, "Transferring to engineering on the decoy—I need to place an energy source." Her view changed and they could see her place a small but brightly glowing power source on the deck. Erin appeared on the bridge, her helmet went off, and she was drenched in sweat.

Bendahrin counted slowly, and then hit the button. "Thrusting up for five seconds, forty-five seconds left."

Jedra cried out. "I have an idea." As Bendahrin watched, he saw that Jedra had jumped to the starboard lounge on *Lentoris* where most of their clutter from Prevaria had been dropped. He grabbed an armful of Chesleth Preller's gaudy clothes and he appeared in a random room on the derelict ship, he dropped the clothes and was back to the control room on *Lentoris*. His helmet retracted. "Sorry Bendahrin, I thought that would make the wreckage more authentic."

Erin snorted, and she waved her hand in front of Bendahrin's helmet and said, "Just think, 'retract helmet.'"

Which he did, and his helmet was gone.

They looked through the front viewscreen and their target planet was now a disk, and they could see it growing in size rapidly.

Jedra spoke. "Hold secured. Let's make the turn!" Bendahrin could hear the urgency in his voice. They could all see the clock and the approaching planet.

At thirty seconds on the clock, Erin asked, far too calmly, "Bendahrin, do you want me to do this? As soon as we retract the drive field, that ship is going to explode into unprotected space at faster than light speed and slam into the planet."

Bendahrin nodded and stepped back, and Erin and Jedra both stepped up.

Erin commented, "And to finish the deception, we need to do another blind light-speed turn." The clock had mere seconds, and Erin's hands were poised over the controls. At three seconds she punched three buttons in quick succession, there was an enormous flash of light as the decoy started impacting space dust at faster than light speeds, at almost the same moment the starfield shifted left and up as they turned, the planet flashed past, for an instant filling almost half of the window.

Jedra started tapping buttons on the panel, and after a few moments said, "We are good, nothing ahead of us for hundreds of light years, we can maintain this course."

Erin then said, "Pushing to maximum speed. I am glad that we didn't try that at a higher speed; that was close enough. If I ever see Scurven again I'm going to kick him so hard his grandchildren will be unable to sit down for a week. That hatch was supposed to be open." But her face was beaming with a crushing smile.

Bendahrin started to ask who Scurven was when Kel spoke, "The derelict has crashed into the planet. Nice explosion from the power supply you placed. They will find enough debris, but very little to recognize. Except, perhaps for Bendahrin's clothes." He disappeared with a smile, a pop, and an extra dose of stench.

Bendahrin sighed. "Okay, that was tense. Did Alystra tell you where to go next?"

Erin and Jedra both shook their heads, dripping sweat in every direction. Their efforts had outstripped their suits' ability to remove all the heat and perspiration.

Erin said, however, "She was in a frightful rush, but gave me the impression that she would be back soon."

Then it was Bendahrin's turn to shake his head. "Not this time, no. We will be waiting for her; we are on our own for a while." And then it came to him, from a vast distance, and out of shredding darkness: numbers and times. He went foggily to the control console and entered the proper locations into the navigation system. He waited a few moments for the computer to calculate the course, and when it was ready, he executed the command for travel at the fastest speed. Bendahrin was struggling to shake off the connection. "That was dark; this is vitreous." He squeezed his head and turned to them. "Coordinates; two sets; one stop on the way. Travel will take twelve days to the first, then about eight days, but we are headed to the *Ascension*. There is plenty of work for us to do until she gets back." Then he seemed to be released. He walked to the hatch from the cockpit but turned. "We all need showers, and someone needs to tell me how to get out of this suit!"

It wasn't long before Bendahrin was free from his fresh, new combat fatigues and clean. He lay on his bed, thinking about the crashed ship, their harrowing escape, covered by a tricky sleight of ship. He had no specific agenda for his thinking, allowing his thoughts to tumble and bounce around in his mind until sleep tumbled in and bounced his conscious thoughts out. His sleep was peaceful, his dreams darkly pleasant.

18

The dream was silent and murky.

He was in a field of wheat—wheat ready for harvest. He looked around and noticed that this field went on as far as the horizon; one gentle hill beyond the next, stretching in all directions under an oddly violet sky. He began to walk, down one slope and up the next, then down the other side. Although the sun was at the top of the sky, he felt cool, and the air was windy; the waves of passing air revealed in the rippling blanket of wheat. He appeared quite suddenly at the top of a hill that seemed far higher now that he was at the top. Suddenly, yes, and now quite close as if it had just appeared, he saw a fearful black scar of burned wheat. It stretched beyond his vision both left and right and beyond—a wicked slash across the face of the field, broken by occasional patches of regular wheat. He moved toward the slash with the hesitant deliberation typical of an uncertain dream. As he walked, he realized that the sound of the wind was a voice all around him, chanting, singing, sighing. The words meant nothing to him, but the voice was unknown, deep and somber, louder with every step.

The blackened patch opened up before him, the wheat was burned but not consumed, utterly black and yet waving gently. He bent down for a closer look and felt himself falling forward. He tried to catch himself with dreamy slowness, and the wheat became a precipice; an edge leading to a bottomless darkness. Feeling and falling, he fell and flew and stepped through the dark wheat and landed on a ledge with a heavy door built into a stone wall. Opening the door, he found himself in a lengthy hall of stone with doors every few yards. The doors were heavy and bolted *and* from behind them he could hear the sounds of unnecessary suffering; the kind that those in charge call "justice" yet everyone knows is something else. Through the stone walls of his mind, he could see the people jailed behind, but he knew, with the confidence borne by thousands of nights of sleep, that the doors would not open so that true justice would never prevail.

Besides, he was certain which cell Alystra was in.

His confidence led him through halls both narrow and old, turning and doubling and racing tirelessly down stairs. Some corridors opened to a sky of billowing flames and violet, dancing stars, others narrowed until he felt suffocated by walls that he could not reach nor touch. Numerous times he fled through the same vast chamber, once filled with the wreckage of a giant toy box, and then a somber armory, a giant thrashing machine, a gleaming and brilliant warehouse of clothes. Fascinating distractions irrelevant to his confidence.

One room of particular insight forced him to pause. A man dressed as a comic bellhop approached him with a simple face that implied both wonder and perplexity. Matching the bellhop theme, Bendahrin glanced around to take in the lobby of an ornate and aged hotel. The reception desk and the furniture in the lounge were made of a deep-toned wood that gleamed in the light of the crystal chandeliers overhead. Through the large glass windows, he could see the streets of a city covered in snow. Shoppers weaved through the traffic, and the trees and buildings were bedecked with snow and lights. The skies were black and the stars were as brilliant as the decorations.

"May I take your bags?" A voice?

Bendahrin turned back.

The bellhop, smiling, grabbed his elbow, and directed him toward the reception desk where some luggage stood waiting as if it had done so quite properly for a long time.

Bendahrin glanced around at the changing walls; bewildered and frustrated that he had lost control of the dream as usual. He looked at his bags and then up at the clerk behind the desk.

The clerk extended his hand. "May I have your ticket please?"

"Ticket?" Bendahrin leaned forward. The desk seemed to loom

before his mind with wavering obstinance.

"You need a ticket if you intend to board a train for your destination." Another voice!

Bendahrin whipped around and saw that he had somehow arrived at a train station filled with hundreds of shoppers moving, standing, scurrying across a vast marble floor under a lofty glass dome. Rows of trains were aimed away from him into the distance so he knew he was in The Grand Terminal. He tried to read the destinations posted above the countless gates, but they were either in a foreign language or perhaps written in letters of an ancient confusion.

He heard the clerk behind him. "Do you know where you're going?"

Bendahrin took a slow step toward the line of trains and the man behind him said again, "Do you *know* where you are going?" He stopped and knew the answer of *all* dreams; finding your way is always accomplished as an inverse proportion of your desire to get there. Or was it an inverse quotient of your desire? Bendahrin looked at the destinations spread out before him and he knew for certain that he would never find his way as his desire approached certainty because the quotient was also certain to be inversely related to the relevance of finding his way. He wasn't *quite* sure, but he had a feeling that he had known his purpose before he had seen the snowy street.

"Are you checking in?" Incessant voices.

He turned back to the ticket agent to tell him that he knew he *had* a destination if he could find it and he was back in the hotel lobby.

"Are you checking in, or are you checking out?" The clerk smiled.

The snow called and reminded him that he had been going somewhere. "I am checking out!" he said with exuberance.

"Excellent!" the clerk said, with exuberance to match. "Francois, will show you to your room."

"This way, sir!" Insistent voices.

Bendahrin found the cliché debilitating, but turned toward the waiting bellhop thinking, *No, I want to leave.* But he found himself in a long hallway of hotel doors, one every few yards. The doors were typical for a hotel *and* from behind them he could hear the sounds of a *very* necessary snoring; the type that most people find either humorous or annoying, almost a soundtrack for night. Through the ornate walls of his mind he could see the people sleeping behind, but he knew, with the confidence borne by thousands of nights of sleep, that the doors would not open. With happy frustration, he knew those sleeping people were only there to complete their shopping.

Besides, he was certain which room Alystra was in.

He ran down the hall following a familiar confidence in his increasingly uncertain mind, properly leaving his bags behind without a glance. His confidence led him through halls both wide and new, turning and doubling and racing tirelessly up stairs. Some hallways opened to a sky of billowing waves and orange cavorting stars, others narrowed until he felt suffocated by walls that he could not reach nor touch. Numerous times he fled through the same vast chamber, once filled with the wreckage of a memorable toy box, and then a sobering armory, a giant trash dump, a dreary and dimly lit storefront of smiling mannequins. Fascinating distractions irrelevant to his confidence. He knew that mannequins never smile.

He wondered why this seemed so familiar and worried that he had had this dream before. Then he seemed to see a vision of himself realizing that repeated dreams are harder to remember. Then he remembered what mattered, he needed to find the right door. He came to a junction and followed the train tracks on the left, past a river of flowing cement which also seemed familiar. *Something* about trains made him certain that destinations were possible, or at least, quantifiable or desirable.

A somber chanting followed after his steps and caused him to weave as though he were being buffeted by high winds. Eventually he saw The Door in the distance. He was afraid that he would never make it, but the passage was quick, and he braced himself for the impact. When he hit, the door burst open, and he stopped in the middle of an enormous warehouse. This final distraction was the destination he'd been pursuing even though it was finally a place that didn't seem familiar.

Behold, a young boy, surrounded by gray rags but untouched by their grayness. His face was young and timeless, with eyes of blue and dusty blond, explosive hair. Bendahrin locked eyes with the boy, and he sensed a wisdom as ancient as the birth of stars. The boy beckoned.

Bendahrin followed, reminding himself that destinations were often distractions, but sometimes helped you to arrive.

A voice spoke into Bendahrin's mind, "Where did you come from?"

Bendahrin answered, as though hailing from a distance, "I have looted the dungeons and escaped the hotel but then the door opened here."

The boy nodded. "I see. You are traveling through your sleep. Why are you here this time?"

Bendahrin looked around. They seemed to be walking through a warehouse with strangely-curving walls, as though the warehouse floor was the bottom of a steep bowl. Instead of neatly stacked boxes, crates, or pallets, the floors and walls were strewn with a gigantic clutter: pipes and pumps and relays and switches, as though a huge chemical processing plant had exploded, and the debris had been stored haphazardly. Everything was covered with the thick gray dust of the eons and yet, as Bendahrin looked back, there were no footprints behind them. The only light came from streaming shafts of alternating moonbeams and sunbeams that poked through various holes in the ceiling and walls or through broken windows high up the walls. Everything was dusty gray and dim—silent and yet peaceful.

"I don't know why," he whispered with reverence appropriate for the solemnity of the surroundings. "I don't know where we are."

"I see. You did not come here by choice. And yet I sense you are searching with severe confidence. My furtive epochs always attract the one who seeks. But we need to find what you seek." His voice was light and unconcerned. "Perhaps we can help one another." Bendahrin felt as though this boy had done this before.

They walked through the warehouse, passing from cavernous room to cavernous room. They often passed through normal sized doors, at other times the boy slid aside enormous doors that towered to the ceiling.

At last, they stopped before two that were chained and locked with an ancient and rusty chain. The windows in these final doors, dressed in the appropriate fashion, were thick with dust, though some were broken and let in the air from outside. Bendahrin peered through a hole where the window had cracked, and he saw more warehouses across an apron of concrete ten meters wide that was broken by tufts and lines of grass.

He stepped back and turned to the boy who said, "The broken

windows only show you what is between but will never satisfy the cry of your soul's quest."

Bendahrin stared at the boy as the singing continued. He had no idea what he was questing. "And the other windows?"

"Try one," the boy said, holding out his hand toward the windows before them. "But be careful! Choose wisely and with hope."

Bendahrin looked back. There were dozens of windows before him that, dreamlike as expected, counted in the thousands. He pondered for a moment, both sharpened and dulled as is normal for a dream, how to choose intuitively or was it hopefully, he couldn't seem to remember either *or* which. He reached out in a determined and disconnected way, and it passed his mind that this too was normal. He brushed away the dust from what *seemed* a totally random window and the dust tingled pleasantly and burned like acid. Although Bendahrin did not consider this normal in any way, the dusty window revealed a view that was not what he had seen when he peeked through the hole earlier. The boy beside him gave a short gasp of approval.

They moved closer and saw a room, large and cubic, or round—there was no way to tell—everything was uniform gray with no shadows or sense of depth. A figure was suspended or floating in the middle, and although Bendahrin had a shocking sense of recognizing Alystra, he could barely see her through the dusty window. In addition, her whole body was engulfed in frenzied flames of every color pressed tight against her body.

He went to wipe away more of the occlusion, but the boy yelled, "Hurry! Break the glass!"

"What?" Bendahrin looked at the boy, whose serenity had disappeared in exchange for white-faced panic. His explosive hair was scorching through a frenzied wind.

"Bendahrin, I keep telling you to retain direction! I need you to break the glass now—this is the convergence, but yours—and yes, I have felt for decades." His voice was like a whisper, and yet a shower of dust fell all around them as it echoed through the rooms.

Bendahrin wondered why dreams always contained statements that were unclear, ambiguous or misleading. He turned and squinted at the window, gathering the image and hugging it in his mind. He drove his fist to the window with what he hoped was wisdom and hope, as requested. The glass cracked, and Bendahrin felt a pain shoot up his arm; pain enough that he jumped, but not enough to wake him from his sleep.

He cried out in pain, but the voice of the boy's whisper thundered at him again, "Sleep! You must have determination stronger than the glass!"

No one likes pain, and Bendahrin was certain that he liked pain perhaps less than most. Even in his dreamy mind he knew that punching glass was a way to be gifted most generously with incisions at best. Yet, he summoned up his fear and linked it arm in arm to his anger and they danced from his mind and through his arm as he plunged his fist against the glass again. The window shattered with a flash of blinding, sparkling light. Bendahrin was thrown twirling to the floor, the pain in his arm just as blinding. He looked at his hand and arm where a wicked, two-inch dagger of glass had scraped a gouge from the back of his hand for twenty centimeters where it stuck out of his arm covered with his blood.

The boy bent down and grabbed the shard of glass and pulled it out, saying, "I see. This is good, the blood of your sacrifice is powerful."

Bendahrin, even in his most blinded moments knew glass and gashes and blood were rarely used in a thought or statement with the word, "good."

The boy squeezed the glass in his own hand and his blood began to drip; Bendahrin thought that the word good could clearly mean many things, but it sure seemed as though there would now be plenty of power. Then the boy dropped the glass and reached his bloody hand through the hole where the window had been.

Bendahrin saw that there was nothing but blackness through the empty frame.

A hot wind blew through the hole and Alystra's chanting was louder than ever.

The boy had almost his whole arm through the hole, and he seemed to be shaking with cold. Frost began forming on his arm and face, and he turned to face Bendahrin, his peaceful serenity had returned. "Grab my hand," he said, and Bendahrin reached out, realizing as he did so that the bloody wound on his arm had healed, leaving a dark brown scar. He gasped and grasped at the same time and the boy yelled, "Pull!" And this action didn't seem to require any hope to accomplish.

Bendahrin strained, and the boy stretched out sideways with his arm still through the window. The frost by this time had covered the boy and began to crawl up Bendahrin's arm. The boy turned toward him fiercely and commanded, "Don't let go." His face was totally white with frost, even his eyes were white, coated with frost, and yet Bendahrin had an eerie feeling that the boy had no trouble seeing him.

He turned back, and they both continued to strain, but Bendahrin could see that the boy's arm was slowly coming out of the window as though they were pulling something large through an ocean of tar. The progress was slow as of an endless timelessness. In the odd way of dreams, Bendahrin was watching himself from an odd angle high above even though he felt the cold and sensed the effort.

There was a horrible crunching pop, and the boy cried out.

Bendahrin eased off his effort and the boy was pulled back; his arm totally disappeared through the window. A nauseous wave of pain filled Bendahrin's body, and his shoulder was searing, but the boy turned toward him, blood dripping from his eyes.

He cried out in agony, "No! You must pull harder. We need to break the barrier through time."

Another wave of nausea washed over Bendahrin. Somehow the dream painted the pain a color Bendahrin had never supposed, so he hesitated. "But your arm . . ."

The boy spat blood on the floor but continued in painful patience, "Bendahrin, you are wise but lack experience. Sleep, keep! Put your eye on the goal." He panted and dropped his head to his chest. "Nobody is ever redeemed without sacrifice. And my pain, any pain, is worth the ultimate benefit. Even if I die . . ." His voice trailed off for a moment and he whispered, "But not today, again." He looked up at Bendahrin again with a smile. "Now pull!"

Reluctantly, and with inner disgust, he began to pull again. The progress was slow, and now the boy's agony was a throbbing aura that pounded against him. They were still both covered with thickening frost, but beads of sweat dripped from both of them in shards that shattered in the gray dust on the floor. Bendahrin glanced at the window, and he saw a flaming hand holding the boy's arm about to pass through the edge of the window.

"Here it comes!" the boy yelled, and they both fell back.

The doors bulged and creaked as if a massive weight were leaning against them. A flaming arm poked out through the window.

"Be free!" the boy yelled, and the old, rusty chain on the door stretched and snapped, pieces of steel streaking through the room with a passage like screaming streams of bees.

Something huge and brilliant crashed through the doors; glass and dust showered Bendahrin followed by a burning light and tremendous heat.

He woke up with a shout.

At the same moment, a whisper that finally whispered, whispered, "Now *you* see. Separate image and reality."

Some dreams are so vivid that they are stronger than memories, and some memories are so vague that they fade to less than dreams. Bendahrin was sitting up in bed, again, on *Lentoris*. He glanced around bleakly and lowered his head into his hands, attempting to get control of his breathing. He wondered how long he had slept, but it was impossible to tell from the lights or lack of lights; the ocean of endless, eternal star-dotted blackness; and the constant environment on the ship, but he felt painfully rested. He tried to recall the details of his dream, and although certain images presented themselves vividly, the connections and meaning seemed to be utterly muddled. He knew that the dream had been filled with rooms and purpose, but he could not grasp it, the purpose, that is. The only thing he thought he knew for certain was that he had no certainty whether he had ever dreamed the same dream before, or had been there numerous times, yet this time, he knew, his train had reached the correct destination, with the right and proper luggage.

19

Bendahrin woke after fifteen hours of sleep, although he still couldn't tell how long he had slept since the view out his window was unchanged. He took another long shower and donned his fatigues, one of six, that he now owned and kept hung in his closet. Erin and Jedra had previously both insisted or offered that he complete his training in the use of combat fatigues. Whether this training was a kind offer or an imperative was only slightly ambiguous in Erin's statement, "Now, you'll be learning from us how to use this new part of you effectively since there will be daily training." Jedra walked him through the thought commands to get the fatigues on and off. As Bendahrin walked from his quarters to the galley, he activated the helmet and made it go away a few times. Some parts of training would be fascinating, although he wondered about clothes described as "part of you."

He arrived at the galley to find Jedra and Erin eating and reading. They had both been pleased to find that Alystra had a diverse library on board, although, he noticed when he entered, they were reading books on loan from Alex Scurven about *Ascension*; Jedra a history, and Erin a technical manual. Bendahrin sat with them, and Jedra pushed a plate of food toward him.

"Hope you like lunch food for breakfast. On a Stream ship you'd never sleep so late."

Bendahrin shot back, "I needed extra sleep to overcome the awful mindset of Chesleth Preller; may we never meet again. That was ghastly!" He grabbed a glass and some juice. "And although I guess that you two find almost crashing into a planet just a normal day, it took hours for the stress to wash away." As he raised his hand to grab the glass, he noticed, for the first time, a faint scar that stretched from the back of his hand that stretched past his wrist where it disappeared under the cuff of his fatigues. *And now I've been injured in a dream.* He shook his head gently, resigning his will in the depths of his heart that he had taken a few more steps deeper into a totally new life he wasn't sure that he feared.

Erin put her book down. "And yet, you put on the mantle of Preller with ease. It makes me wonder. From our observations, you had everyone fooled. Something, I think, that Alystra and I didn't pull off quite so well." She shook her head and took a drink.

Bendahrin nodded and gestured with an open hand. "Indeed, we'd love to hear about it, if you haven't already told the story. We were somewhat frantic, to say the least."

Jedra laughed, but sympathetically. "*You* were frantic. I was in contact with Erin most of the time, and although there were a few tense moments, she gave me enough to put *my* mind at ease. It doesn't help that I *wanted* to tell you. I couldn't or we might have compromised our cover."

"Another vote of no confidence." Bendahrin took a bite of something frightfully delicious, chewed thoughtfully, then, mumbled over the food, "My mother used to say, 'Mere thoughts don't make a bridge.'" He sighed. "Sometimes I feel like the least 'team' member in this team."

Erin nodded. "Hence your required training." She glanced at Jedra, who raised his eyebrows and produced a single nod. "We won't put you through the full regimen because of your overall," she paused, looking for a word, "seniority, but basic tools and weapons, communications, and thought protocols, situational awareness, and team tactics. We will figure out what role fits you best. The Stream is outstanding at filling roles, and I have matchless skills at task assignment as a result."

Bendahrin snorted, pretending to roll his eyes. "Seniority, thanks. But I support the limitations. I don't really want to be a combatant under any circumstances. But if I can help with communications or organization, who knows?" He took another bite and grumbled through the food, "So, do we get to hear your story from Prevaria?"

Erin stood up. "No, not yet, we will have idle time later. For now, and for the next few days, we need to prepare for our pickup and get this ship in shape."

Shaping the ship kept them busy and tired, and Bendahrin had little time for questions. They unpacked the treasures from Prevaria that stuffed the hold and distributed the content to different parts of the ship as an exercise in overawed inventory assessment at all that Bendahrin had purchased. They opened crates, carried what they discovered and organized, computer components and workstation controls in the front lounge, tools and diagnostic equipment in the shop on the lower deck, drive, and engineering parts to the engine room. The main deck of *Lentoris* ended up looking like a warehouse.

Both Erin and Jedra dedicated time in between to Bendahrin's training. Jedra focused on teaching Bendahrin hundreds, out of the thousands, of actions his combat fatigues could do, along with the trigger thoughts: safety, avoidance, evaluation, surveillance, and most importantly, team communication and coordination. Jedra restricted some functions of Bendahrin's collection of combat fatigues because of the inherent danger they represented: transport, weapons, and defense. Even so, Erin worked with Bendahrin on some basics of weapons and combat skills.

They also spent hours studying. Even with Alystra's ability to perform magical repairs, a fixed volume of the technical work would require hands-on installation and testing, much of it requiring arduous physical labor. The more they knew in advance, the easier the work would proceed. Their rendezvous on the twelfth day was done, in part, to help with this arduous task.

After breakfast on that day, Jedra was at the auxiliary controls in the front lounge, Erin and Bendahrin standing in front of the huge force-field glass. They had arrived in the right planetary system and needed to set their watch for an approaching ship.

"Orbits!" Erin barked. "And show me top and wide." A projection replaced the starfield on the main force-field glass; planets with their orbits mapped in multicolor lines with two projections displaying coordinates of the central star and the fourth planet. "Jedra, mark the rendezvous." A single crosshair appeared on the starfield and on each map. Then she called, "Kel-Purim, can you identify anyone in the system?" Nothing happened. She rolled her eyes and looked at Bendahrin.

"Kel!" Bendahrin shouted.

"Oh yes. Here I am," Kel said, appearing between Bendahrin and Erin, with his back to her. "And there is no reason to yell. I can hear your thoughts across the ship or across the system. What do you want?"

"Is this the way you are going to play this? You know what I want."

"How would that be? You have not made a word of request."

Bendahrin sighed. "Erin did, and you heard it. Besides," he narrowed his eyes, looking at Kel, "you just bragged that you could hear my thoughts."

"Oh, Erin called?" Kel twirled in place, spraying out swirls of red vapor, to face Erin. "Yes, oh yes, perhaps I did hear something. But," and he turned back to Bendahrin, "I am not required to listen to her."

"Your choice," Bendahrin said, but he pressed on. "The system around this star, within a light year distance. Are there any other sentient beings, and without quibbling, you know what I mean; people, anyone watching, nearby, sleeping, on a ship, in a ship, or on any asteroid, planet, or moon, or floating in space, or any technological devices of any kind watching, probing, gathering data—?"

But Kel interrupted him, "Oh stop, Benny! You know I know you can't trust me, but I know you know I can't betray you into danger. Besides, you know I know the threat to the ship, so yes, I know there is no one in the system . . ." then he added, "you know?" He was enjoying the situation sufficiently for all of them.

Bendahrin turned and nodded to Erin. "You won't get any better than that."

Erin had carefully ignored Kel's pronoun play, but she knew she could trust Bendahrin's trust, which was sufficient trust to move ahead.

She pointed. "Grid seventeen C, anything there?"

"Asteroids, other interplanetary debris," Jedra replied, after a moment consulting the console.

"Then show me the top angle view of the asteroid."

Jedra tapped on the console. Maps rotated and lines appeared. "Thirty-eight degrees, angle facing out." He spoke.

Erin walked closer to the display, looking left and right. "We don't have any reason to think this is a trap." She pointed. "How about below the asteroid's orbit. Anything there?"

"Nothing beyond dust and background radiation," Jedra replied.

Bendahrin wondered what the conversation meant, but he said nothing.

Erin gazed at the screen for a few seconds, then pointed. "We put a communication and observation node in four B, the exact location is not critical, then we move to this asteroid," she pointed and Jedra nodded, "land, power down, and listen. Keep it simple. I will stand in the airlock to place the node. Tell me when we arrive at the drop."

Jedra nodded, and Bendahrin grabbed a book. They were early by most of a day. Erin had been suspicious and careful, that seemed to be a constant in the tapestry of her character.

Although Erin felt there was no reason to expect the rendezvous to be a trap, she wanted to be ready if Alex Scurven had a last-minute change of heart and decided to try a double-cross, this was his last chance to try; even the most sincere and honest people might be tempted when their deepest dream was at stake.

Jedra and Erin performed the node placement and maneuvered to the asteroid in a score of boring minutes while Bendahrin read. They landed the ship on the chosen asteroid, then turned off everything that could possibly be detected and modulated the force-field glass throughout the ship, save in the front lounge, so that light couldn't pass through; and even so, they dimmed most of the lights. In the halls and front lounge, all lights were extinguished.

Bendahrin went to the galley and brought back some food and drink to accompany the wait.

Jedra sat in a chair near the auxiliary console; Erin stood in the middle of the floor between the chairs and piles of equipment doing some isometrics and stretching. Bendahrin was standing close to the force-field glass. Kel hovered at the back of the room, across the hall. Time passed.

They had landed *Lentoris* near the pole of the asteroid Erin had chosen. The pole pointed at about forty-five degrees away from where they had placed the communications node. This meant that as the asteroid rotated, the location of the node moved with the sky from directly overhead to straight ahead. The asteroid's "day" was about seventy minutes, and Bendahrin was fascinated to watch the starfield as it moved across their view as they rotated.

Nevertheless, typical to form, he turned to Erin and asked a question, "Can you tell us about Scurven now? Who is Scurven, who you, uh, wanted to kick so hard?"

Erin laughed. "You remember that? No, Alex did all right. His help was pivotal and critical." At this she recounted their capture and time at Alex Scurven's estate. She told them about his clever way of revealing that he knew their true intentions on Prevaria. She described his efforts and assistance and his passion about *Ascension*.

Bendahrin had been both listening and eating attentively. He held his next question until Erin had finished. "Alystra *trusted* him?"

"Now, *that* is not the question I would have expected. Why do you wonder at her trust?"

He snorted. "Prior to her meeting me, she hadn't trusted anyone for more than a decade. This seems abrupt, for her."

"That is true, but she took you on rather quickly. Besides, don't be naïve; it doesn't matter whether she trusts him, she can decide to use him for no return, and it would look the same on the outside. She later told me that she *had* read his mind, a bit, to discover his true intent, and she uncovered his sincerity."

It was Jedra's turn to snort. "A person can be utterly sincere in what they believe, but that doesn't mean he won't cut your throat. Some beliefs, he recalled, even encourage the cutting of throats, so sincerity doesn't mean much."

Erin nodded. "Always better to be safe; however, in this case we hadn't found only sincere *belief*, but sincere *passion*. He is an *Ascension* fanatic, descended for many generations from the brother of the navigator, from a family that never gave up looking." She walked over and sat down. "It turns out that, despite the *official* cessation of searching for the *Ascension*, there have been scores of groups that have kept searching, primarily among descendants of original crew members. Alex's ancestors have been searching for six centuries, and there are still several branches of his family tree involved, independent of his operations. Alex Scurven spent about thirty years in the search, and he now owns eight ships that do nothing else—all too close to Prevaria and in the wrong direction; they can't conceive of the speed nor of the field strike that sent the ship so far off course. Two of his sons have lived on ships for twenty-five or more years, looking everywhere; several descendants from his family are also in their little fleet."

She stopped and looked at the rotating stars, reflecting on what she had said. "Did I say fanatic? It is his driving love. The central room of his massive home is a three story-atrium planetarium with a one tenth scale model of *Ascension* hanging from the ceiling: huge! He showed us the display. At nights he can project a moving starfield onto the ceiling and he immerses his imagination watching *Ascension* on the move. He has artifacts, and every book written on the ship, but more helpful for us, partial blueprints, engineering notes, design specifications, even technical repair manuals. He loaned us some of his annotated historical records and technical manuals, and some of the early classified reports.

"Over the week following our unscheduled visit, while you were buying piles of supplies, he had his agents sneak in tools and pre-cut templates to make the equipment you were buying fit in the existing consoles, along with adapters, power supplies, even keys to panel doors. He was particularly thrilled when you bought those agile systems, and he had some of his experts hack those systems to build a backdoor in the software of those consoles so they will be able to control the weapon systems. He advised us on ways to do every imaginable repair; he has had teams working through what they imagine would be needed to repair every system on board for years anyway. We couldn't have asked for better help.

"In the end, the only thing that Alystra wouldn't tell him was how she had found the ship, what had happened in the accident, or, especially, the location of *Ascension* now. Interestingly, he didn't get angry, but rather, just intensely sad, like someone experiencing a death in the family. He and Alystra went off for a private conference, and when they returned, he was exuberant, and you'll find out why.

"Alex has infiltrated every company of consequence on Prevaria with people whose first loyalty is to him." She stopped and shook her head. "Calling it 'infiltration,' isn't quite accurate. It's an odd situation because the companies all know about the employees who have these dual roles, and even have a name for them, *'fhasprez,'* which means, 'silent bridge.' Silent in part because no one talks about it, but it's something of a coveted status because of the recognition, extra pay, and the influence and secrecy afforded those who are able to handle the additional effort without compromising either loyalty or their responsibilities. They are a bridge because they are the ones who close the gap to meet needs on both sides. Everything is handled with the appropriate level of secrecy and accuracy, and most importantly, buyers get what they want, and the money flows to the producers. It seems crazy, and would probably be illegal elsewhere, but it works on Prevaria. Perhaps I should mention that Alex isn't the only facilitator of this kind, but his network is undoubtedly the largest and most utilized for meeting those delicate needs that are too dirty for the public companies to touch.

"This network of *fhasprez* was of special significance to us because they kept Alex up to date on everything you did, what you purchased, and more particularly, what the differing companies thought you were up to. His network even helped to spread some misleading suggestions to keep anyone from making a connection to *Ascension*. Not that you needed much help; you rained money and confusion upon them with extravagant liberality, and they just thought you were a misled fool, but they were glad to take your money.

"But then you obliterated all expectations and forced Chardeo into a corner, and they agreed to sell you a class one controller—we still can't figure why they caved, probably just for the money. This left Alystra shredding herself in quadruple tangents between anger and wonder, panic and delight. We already had a controller without a transponder, and this threw us off. The last thing that we wanted was to provide our location; if we started out in the direction of *Ascension*, far too many people would start putting the pieces together and forming a picture of our designs. Fortunately, we were able to contrive a plan that would free us from being tracked; in fact, it provided most of the companies on Prevaria a welcome opportunity to close the books on the mysterious and annoying Chesleth Preller and his interfering salvage company. They will retrieve what they can from the wreckage, and hopefully not fuss too much with any inconsistencies they find. After all, they made a fortune because as we all know too well, Chesleth always pays very dearly, yes, very dearly indeed." They all found the freedom in the moment to laugh, though Bendahrin's laugh sounded more like a groan from the grave.

Kel-Purim interrupted, "Oh, yes! A ship has entered the system, a single ship. Thirty-eight members of blood."

Jedra turned to the console. "The node has picked up their transponder. Ship is identified as *Prestaria*. This is what we expected."

Kel made an insulting noise with his tongue. "Yes, your node. Yes. But I bet your node isn't telling you about the wonderful taste of conflict on the ship. There is a lot of tension on the ship. Delicious! What fun!"

"Conflict?" Erin said, moving toward Kel. "Jedra, what is the ship doing?"

"The ship has slowed, but it is moving to the rendezvous point," he replied.

Bendahrin said, "Kel-Purim, can you tell me any more about the conflict?"

"Oh yes! Delightful! The agitation on that ship is great. I have a feeling that the disagreement may lead to violence." A leering grin sprawled across his red face. "Not that I care, much, for them, but this could interfere with our rendezvous."

Bendahrin spoke quickly, ""Kel, can you intervene?"

"Oh yes, but to influence anyone I need to be in contact at some point, and there are many, so no, this is not my time."

Bendahrin was confused.

Erin turned suddenly to Jedra. "Blow the node!" She pointed at him and he turned to the console.

"Wait! What will that do? Don't we need the node to monitor them?" Bendahrin said.

Jedra turned to look at Bendahrin and Erin.

Erin ignored Bendahrin. "Jedra, now!"

Jedra turned again and tapped at the console.

Erin turned her attention to Bendahrin, but slowly, rubbing her chin. "I am not accustomed to explaining my orders. I guess I will need to learn to adapt." She frowned, then continued, looking at Bendahrin. "Discipline! On a ship, boring routine and living with nothing but the expected will cause speculation, questions; channels break down. Throw in the unknown, and the crew will find their feet again."

Bendahrin replied, "I'll need to learn to contain my curiosity."

Jedra worked at the console for a few more moments. "Done. It will take six minutes for the signal to get to the node."

"Do we need to move the ship? Do we need to see?" Bendahrin asked, his curiosity already betraying him.

Erin walked forward and sat down. "I don't see why. Kel can tell us everything we need to know in an instant, the node was just a communication safeguard," she said, leaning back and closing her eyes. "We just need to wait."

Bendahrin sat beside Erin. He looked out the window, wondering if he would see the explosion. He picked up his book and tried to read, but his mind kept turning to the other ship.

What is going on over there?

He turned to Erin and was about to ask her a question, but she looked so serene. He scowled for a moment.

How can she be so relaxed?

He sat back and closed his own eyes, wondering if he looked serene, and doubted it. He opened his eyes and watched the turning starfield, wishing he could *be* serene.

Eventually, Jedra broke the silence. "That's it, the node is gone." Then, without knowing, he answered Bendahrin's question. "At this distance, of course, there will be nothing to see when the emanations from the explosion eventually reach us, again in six minutes, at least not without a very powerful telescope. *Prestaria* will sense it in four."

Erin responded quietly, without opening her eyes, "Acknowledged."

Bendahrin looked out the window again for as long as he could, then asked, "Should we move the ship? Or *prepare* to move the ship?"

Jedra took a deep breath. "Not until *Prestaria* leaves. If they stick to the plan, which we hope they do, the ship will depart, leaving behind the three people we are picking up in a habitation pod—or what would be even nicer would be a large shuttle."

Erin sat up. "Since we don't have one, I'd like *any* shuttle." She stood and looked out at the stars. "I have a feeling that anyone coming from Scurven's search fleet will have nothing but the best. How much room in the hold do we have for a shuttle?"

"We can probably fit anything up to a class three or four, depending on the manufacturer," Jedra said. Just then the timer he had set finished the countdown. "They will be detecting the node now."

Erin continued. "I don't think we need to worry about the shuttle. Alex knows our ship, and he will have provided detailed instructions. Bendahrin?"

"That fast?" Bendahrin replied.

Erin looked grim. "Discipline on a ship in space is an absolute for survival, by now the entire crew knows."

Bendahrin turned to Kel-Purim, who didn't even wait for the question. "Oh yes! Very, very sad. They are now all very alert. The tension hasn't changed, but now it feels like a storm all rushing through a funnel."

"Not sure what a storm through a funnel means. Let's hope that the funnel is pointed in the right direction," Bendahrin said.

The next few hours were prolonged, a typical waiting mix of boredom and tension. They sat mostly in silence, and Bendahrin flip-flopped between dozing and reading. Periodically, when he was awake, Bendahrin asked Kel for updates, who indicated a ship with an increasingly calm crew but a ship that wasn't going anywhere. Eventually their wait was amply rewarded when Kel announced that the ship had suddenly gone and was quickly leaving the range at which he could detect them. "Oh yes. They aren't a happy bunch," he added, quite happy himself, and happier to report it.

Erin jumped up. "Do we deploy communications, or just go get them?" she asked, looking more to Jedra for the answer, but Bendahrin answered.

"Enough security and sneaking. Let's go get them."

"Concur! If their ship comes back, we have a standoff, or we outrun them. Best to clear the system."

At this Erin took command. "Jedra, cockpit, go." Jedra's helmet popped on, and he was gone. "Bendahrin, we will go to the hold."

"Aye, aye," he said, activating his helmet for communication purposes. "But, we'll *walk* to the hold," he said, forgetting that Jedra had turned off the suit's teleport function.

They walked together.

The next forty minutes included some delicate and technical communications, a deliberate and direct rendezvous, and one of Slaintyth's Paragon series' shuttles was welcomed into the hold as Bendahrin and Erin watched. Erin managed the controls to pressurize the hold.

On the bridge, Jedra picked a random course for *Lentoris* to follow and set the ship for the fastest speed it could handle. He then jumped to the hold and stood with Bendahrin and Erin to welcome the guests.

"Helmets off!" Erin ordered, however gently.

The shuttle's side hatch opened, and three people stepped out.

Erin greeted them with a half smirk, half smile, but warmly.

The man in the middle was older than Bendahrin by at least a decade, short, tough looking, alert; he carried himself like a military commander, and indeed, his clothes were a kind of uniform, with insignia that Erin would have immediately identified as the Scurven crest. The man to his right was a generation younger, out of shape, unkempt, bland, and thoroughly distracted. Although he wore the Scurven uniform, he would need to depend heavily on some hidden area of expertise to find himself a place in the corporate promotional poster.

To the left was a woman even younger; she was on the taller side, with short, blonde hair and a perpetual smile, but what was striking was her eyes—they were full of feverish curiosity, mischief, and sparky intelligence. In all three Erin could see family resemblance to Alex Scurven, which, at least, put to rest her concerns; these were the three people she had expected.

As expected, the elder took a step forward to shake hands with Bendahrin. "My name is Marcus Scurven." He gestured toward the woman. "I introduce Mandy Sharma, my niece, daughter of my sister, Wherdle, and this," he gestured to his right, "is Prescott Scurven, my nephew, son of my brother, Trent." He turned back to Bendahrin and you could almost hear the click of his heels as he focused his attention forward. "And you must be *Flen* Chesleth Preller? My father, Alex Scurven, was distressed that he could not make your acquaintance on Prevaria. He chose us to join you, and I must express, for all of us, our eager enthusiasm and humble gratitude to be included in your most singular endeavor."

Bendahrin was immediately uncomfortable and relieved by the excessively formal greeting. Without conscious effort, he found himself equally stilted in response. "Yes, well, I must apologize immediately for some required security precautions, for which I hope you take no offense, especially since we want to welcome you and your worthy companions into our cause with openness and trust, of which, I confess, we are the only party requiring an apology on account of our duplicity. In short, for security reasons, we need to perform some quick checks." He nodded to Jedra and Erin, who moved immediately, Jedra to the rear of the shuttle and Erin to the front. Spreading their arms, their suits immediately formed a weave of threads around the shuttle. "Your shuttle—" he began, but Marcus interrupted him.

"No, this is *your* shuttle, now." He bowed his head a small measure.

"Thank you, that is not necessary, but we welcome the kindness."

Erin and Jedra were done, and Erin shook her head to Bendahrin who continued. "That was a technical check of *our* shuttle, and now we have a more in-depth check required. Please don't be alarmed, this will be disconcerting, and will likely raise many questions and concerns that we will discuss immediately following. Kel!"

Kel-Purim appeared behind the three, and he reached out his arms to envelop them in a red mist. Their reactions were interesting: Mandy looked around to face Kel with a smile of wonder; Prescott cowered and fell to his knees, crying out; and Marcus merely stared at Bendahrin at first with a slight scowl, which transformed quickly to an uneasy spreading smile of growing insight. The hug of blood lasted only seconds. Immediately Jedra rushed forward to help Prescott to his feet, and Kel slithered to face Bendahrin. "Oh yes, my *Flen*," he said as mockingly as words can be twisted to such an end. "No deceit beyond what is normal, and nothing hidden, although we could talk details later."

"No details needed." Bendahrin said. "Kel, we are grateful, and you are released. Go find your measure of rest."

Kel stuck his tongue out and disappeared, carefully wafting a stench of rotting blood at Bendahrin.

Marcus approached Bendahrin. "Father warned me that we might run into magic here." He shuddered. "I hope we won't be spending much time with that red fellow."

Bendahrin coughed and shook his head. "If you are here long enough you grow acclimated to him, all but the smell. But I do apologize, and please," he gestured to the door from the hold, "let us proceed to a more conducive setting for discussion, and we will pass out explanations along with a meal, to welcome you."

Bendahrin led the way, weaving through the ship from the hold to the starboard lounge. He was talking with Marcus, who nodded and responded in a warm, yet direct and gruff manner.

Mandy looked around in wonder, as though the old ship was something special, and she fully stopped and looked with interest at the frightening and ever-changing wall outside Tored's Room, the room next to Bendahrin's. Bendahrin noticed that she was neither disturbed nor repelled by the palpable aura of evil pouring from the manifestation. As far as they could tell, Prescott spent his attention on his wrist computer. They arrived at the starboard lounge where Bendahrin and Jedra had pushed all of the clutter against one wall and had moved a table and chairs from storage.

Bendahrin turned to the newcomers. "We will be eating here, please make yourselves comfortable."

But Marcus grabbed Bendahrin by the arm and placed his hand on the wall. "Your ship is from Chardeo, correct?"

Bendahrin nodded.

"A V-series, fifty-seven, fifty-eight hundred, maybe?"

"I'm impressed, did you sneak to the engine room to read the construction plaque when I wasn't watching?" He laughed.

Marcus humpfed. "I've spent forty-five years on ships and grew up on Prevaria. What *impresses* me is your drive; I can hear and feel your drive; you're pushing triple digit multiples of spec. I'd love to know how you pulled that off, Preller."

"Then let's get you to your seats and let the questions commence." He returned the favor and grabbed Marcus's arm, leading him to the table where Prescott was already sitting, fully engaged by the computer on his wrist.

Mandy was looking out the window, appearing utterly fascinated, as if she had never seen stars before.

The table was perpendicular to the window. Marcus sat at the short end, facing the window. "Mandy!" he called. "Let's find out what our new friends mean when they greet us on their fine ship with the word, 'duplicity.'" He didn't seem particularly bothered, but no one could miss the implicit challenge.

Mandy sauntered to the table and sat to his right; Prescott was already seated to his left, typing into his wrist computer.

Bendahrin felt jabbed in the heart but nodded mildly in assent. "Yes, again I apologize. And so, I begin with the obvious, I am not Chesleth Preller, and I have no intention of starting *any* kind of salvage company. My name is Bendahrin Casthay, and I am a resident of Palestre."

Marcus nodded and Mandy looked excited.

"To sum up our time on Prevaria, it was all a façade to mask our true intentions."

Prescott still looked bored, but he rallied his voice sufficiently to grumble at the rest, "Your money was real enough; I've never even been inside the Entranta."

Bendahrin laughed. "Yes, because our true intentions, which are the reason *you* are here, required us to purchase what we needed, we hope, to resurrect the *Ascension*, and outfit it for our use."

The air in the room relaxed palpably and yet, was electrified at the same time. Mandy shook as she rubbed her hands together beneath the table, Prescott, raised his eyebrows and tapped something into his wrist computer.

Marcus sat back in his chair, and said, speaking in a sloppy, informal way, "I, for one, am so hoppin' glad that we got that straight! I was thinkin' for a minute that we got dropped at the wrong secret interstellar rendezvous." He gestured to Bendahrin. "It makes sense. You were on a clandestine operation on Prevaria to bring back the biggest prize in the planet's history. Personally, I can't believe you pulled it off." He chuckled. "Father knew, and he helped to throw dust in a few eyes. So," he said, waving his arms toward the rest of the ship. "D'we get to meet the rest of the crew and get to work?"

Mandy giggled. "Uncle Marcus has a reputation for his constantly changing modes of speech. They are a source of endless amusement amongst the crews of the ships on which he has served."

Marcus feigned offense and quipped, "Me hasn't no clue, what you speak!"

As if on cue, and it might have been, the ship changed course sharply, the starfield turning wildly as the ship turned and pitched "up." Immediately Jedra appeared in the lounge and moved to stand behind the seat to Bendahrin's right.

Marcus promptly commented, "Father hadn't met you on Prevaria, but I guess we have *two* ex-B'Tarks in this crew." Marcus looked at Jedra's fatigues and nodded. "Hey, you'll, uh, really like those new fatigues, the new weave and faster migration will speed up a lot of your basic moves."

Jedra looked at Marcus and then his suit. "And it looks like you have the latest, too."

Marcus smiled. "All Scurven uniforms are made from the latest."

"This is Jedra Corbick, and, yes, he was B'Tark until very recently," Bendahrin said, and then Bendahrin became suspicious about the timing, for Erin immediately came into sight from the direction of the galley, pushing two carts loaded with food and drink, so Bendahrin continued, "And this is Erin Flesson, lately Ver Tark of the Stream."

Marcus stood to greet her, clearly showing his age. "A captain! Your own ship? Which I am sure you left behind. You will need to tell me all about it." Jedra started transferring food and beverages and tableware, but Marcus didn't skip a beat. "As I heard, there were four people on your ship. We are missing," he paused, pretending to recall something, "your personal assistant . . . Marian, was it? Certainly, that misty red apparition was not somehow playing her part."

Having transferred all of the food, Jedra sat, and Erin rounded the table.

"Our fourth crew member is not on the ship at the moment," Erin said, sitting and making eye contact with Bendahrin, wondering how he would handle this.

Marcus continued, baiting them, and enjoying himself immensely; just as his father did. "Not on the ship? Now, there is *another* story. Father informed us that you were heading here most directly, after a little diversion." He paused dramatically, pretending to examine his fingernails. "He did mention that she seemed somehow beyond tech, almost magical."

Bendahrin smiled. "As I had said, this is the time for complete honesty. We have no intention of hiding the identity of our missing companion. She is magical, as your father knew fully, and, no doubt, already informed you. I am sure you have already seen enough magic on this ship to verify its presence here. She is Alystra Alsatia, also of Palestre."

Mandy gasped and stood up slowly, her eyes ablaze with awe. "The Destroyer?" she whispered. "I'm going to meet the *Destroyer*." Her expression was that of a six-year-old who had just been presented with a most highly-desired gift.

Bendahrin was palpably surprised by this reaction; it was like a person living on ocean-front property welcoming a hurricane or tsunami. "Yes, she will be here. I see that you have heard of her. But I want to assure you that the stories tend to overstate the wanton destroyer aspect of who she is."

"When will she be here?" Mandy asked, quivering with excitement.

"We aren't totally sure, and this is probably a discussion for another day, but I have a feeling that she will be back before we arrive at the *Ascension*," Bendahrin answered.

Marcus spoke up, his voice at a higher, questioning pitch, musing aloud, "Father sent the images. Alystra. Alystra. Well, when ya live in a galaxy with a population of trillions, y'expect to see people ya think ya recognize from time to time. She, ummm, did look familiar, but I was thinking maybe someone from my youth. Very pretty." He nodded, and then added hastily, "Not to diminish the beauty of anyone at this table, of course." He smiled, his gaze bouncing between Erin and Mandy, then he started working on his food, stopping part way through something that might have gotten his attention under other circumstances. "I know!" he blurted out. "She did something with her hair, didn't she?" He looked at Erin. "Changed the color? That's it! Women have such an advantage when it comes to going incognito, they can look like anyone." Then he allowed his attention to truly return to the food. Erin wondered what had happened to the Scurven men that made them so attentive to women's hair.

For a few minutes their attention turned to food and drink. The only conversation was appreciation and logistics; passing items when requested.

Eventually Erin stated, "Before your ship left, there was quite a commotion with the crew."

Marcus stopped eating and looked at her; they held their gaze for a while. Bendahrin imagined that some kind of ship captain thing was going on—sizing up and evaluation. Jedra and Mandy were certain. Then, "You were monitoring us somehow? Oh!" He nodded to himself, and Erin could see his mind putting the pieces together just like his father. "Magic of some kind." Then, "Oh!! You knew, so you detonated some hidden device. Oh excellent! Very clever. Your idea?" Erin nodded, and he matched the nod. "Figures," he finished. Then he looked away. "And it worked. Command's the same every-where, isn't it? Yes. We, each," he gestured to Prescott and Mandy, "come from different ships. The Scurven fleet has hundreds of ships, but eight are dedicated to the search. All ships are led by a Scurven family member, and there are forty-three family members total amongst the ships, not all descended from Father; lots of cousins and second cousins; some of the family connections go back a dozen generations." He took a drink.

"*Urgent* orders came down that *Prestaria*, my ship, was to rendezvous with *Dorstaria* and *Centaria*. Prescott and Mandy were to transfer off their ships, and then we were being dropped off, in a shuttle, in the middle of an unknown system." He took a bite and chewed. "You can imagine, the eight search ships are a tight bunch: competitive, fiercely loyal, dedicated, determined . . . and gossipy. Also, with good reason, only the best and smartest get to work for the Scurven organization, and the best from that pool are chosen for the search fleet. In the end, despite our commitment to, and attempts at, secrecy, everyone's guesses and conjectures piled into the same corner and congealed into the right answer. We had to keep pretending that we were doing something else, but, you know this," he nodded to Erin, "on a ship, trust is life, and you can't lie and get away with it. Everyone knew we weren't telling the whole story."

He stopped, and his face turned emphatic as he clenched his teeth and the beginning of tears grew in his eyes. "My crew, every crew, they have dedicated their lives to finding *Ascension*, and they are devastated." He took his napkin and dabbed his eyes. Then he started laughing. "I can tell you that I am not going to be invited to *any* family reunions with my brothers and sisters for years. Kenny," he put his hand out to Mandy, "Mandy's dad made a secure ship-to-ship and begged me, offering me seven kinds of wealth, to sneak him on board.

"Anyway, your little trick did the job. On a ship, discipline is the other side of trust, and we were able to persuade my crew to leave us. Just wait 'til we come back. Phew, we are gonna need to show something for this. As far as I know, Father is having the search fleet stand down, but if he gets his way, there's gonna be a celebration; I hope we can share the find."

Bendahrin felt the weight that they all felt. Even Mandy looked somber.

"You don't yet know the full scope of what is ahead of us, but you will when Alystra returns. I think that we have agreed to give your father a ride." Bendahrin looked at Erin, who nodded. "But even with the path ahead of us, we might be able to arrange a rendezvous with your search fleet, and perhaps some visits. In fact," he looked at Erin, "we might need additional crew, but the way forward is dangerous."

At this Prescott spoke up, as if he hadn't heard any of the previous conversation and didn't care anyway. "Where is *Ascension* now?"

"We are on our way there now, although our route will be circuitous. Nevertheless, our agreement was that we will take you to the ship, you will help us to effect repairs, and then, if you wish, you may join us, or we will find a crew elsewhere. I am pretty certain that Alex is eager to provide a crew, but we will see."

"How many days do we have?" Marcus asked.

"We will be at the location of the last *Ascension* sighting in eight days, taking an evasive and circuitous route that I have pre-programmed," Jedra answered.

"What is our plan? What equipment do we have, supplies? Provisions?"

At this Erin and Jedra jumped in and the discussion turned technical and tactical; plans were discussed, assignments made, details argued, and priorities laid down.

Bendahrin listened loosely and enjoyed the food. He learned that Marcus had masterful training and experience in every part of ship operations; he had worked as a designer and engineer for two different shipbuilders on Prevaria, commanded several ships, and had worked on every conceivable ship system. Mandy was an encyclopedia of ship design and construction; she had memorized almost everything known about *Ascension* and had extensive knowledge about most of the systems they had purchased. More than all the knowledge, her intuition and creativity were expansive. Prescott was almost a cliché—the ambivalent computer expert, but his degrees in computing and ship's systems made him more than a match for any computer issues they would face. Their collective knowledge of the *Ascension* was well-nigh comprehensive, although in that area Jedra could hold his own, which impressed the Scurvens again and again.

Their plan included an overhaul of *Lentoris* on the way to *Ascension*, and when the discussion turned that way with renewed vigor after a few hours, Bendahrin excused himself. Erin assured him that she would arrange quarters for the Scurvens. Bendahrin returned to his quarters, where he changed into something comfortable and slept. He was certain that he would never learn to find comfort in combat fatigues.

That first morning at their planning breakfast, they discussed their first obstacle: getting at the computer core. Prescott had started early by looking for it. On most ships, and indeed on *all* Chardeo V-series, the computer and control systems were in a room at the back of the main deck. He had gone to that room and found it not only empty, but there wasn't any evidence that a computer core had *ever* been in the room; no holes for cables, no access panels, it was empty. He had immediately moved all of his personnel to claim the room as his quarters. After getting this most important task done, he had then crawled between decks and found that all conduits and power had been rerouted to a room on the second deck—the locked room on the starboard side near the front.

He had then reported that the door had what *looked* like a key-activated lock, but closer examination, which he had carried out immediately, revealed that the lock was an apparition, magic in the surface of the door. He had examined the room from all sides and through every access tunnel. The door was the only way in, short of cutting through a wall, floor, or ceiling. After completing the meal and making a precariously large and ambitious list of plans for the day, all six congregated around the door to consider the puzzle.

Marcus, Erin, and Jedra each rubbed the spot in turn and could only feel the smooth door; their fingers passing right through the image of the lock. Mandy's experience was surprising, and left her wide-eyed, and giggling. The lock-image moved to avoid her touch, and nothing she did could pin it down. "It doesn't like me!" she cried, looking at the rest of them with a smile. "No lock has ever done *that* before!"

But this sparked a thought in Bendahrin's mind, and he approached the door with his palm face up. When he was about a foot from the door, his palm throbbed, and the white key appeared on his palm, and started to shape itself into a long thin stiletto shaped key that Bendahrin was able to grab and insert into the lock. He turned it, and the door swung in to reveal what appeared to be a standard computer room, consoles with displays and controls, a massive trunk of conduit and power, and a computer core gently humming. The only unusual element was the marble pillar next to the computer core that was topped with a glowing cylinder made of metal, crystal, and lights that came from great depths and moved as though passing through moving water. They all walked in and circled around the pillar, as soon as the last of them entered, the door closed behind them. Erin said, "I guess it goes without saying that we would find magic on Alystra's ship." The key disappeared back into Bendahrin's hand.

Attached to the front of the pillar was a piece of paper taped to the front of a plaque that was mounted to the pillar. Jedra grabbed the paper and held it up for all to see, across the top was written, boldly, *READ THIS FIRST.*

Jedra handed the letter to Bendahrin, who looked at the page. He had never seen Alystra's handwriting before and was surprised to find that it was neat and fluid, delicate, and close to perfectly-spaced with straight lines. He wondered if she had used magic to write it but decided that she had just taken the time on this note because it was important. He read aloud, "What you see on this pedestal is an extremely powerful *Targeshobe* that I created to maintain the integrity of the ship. Bendahrin saw it work when Erin and Jedra tried to destroy the ship when they first arrived."

Marcus looked at Jedra and Erin. "Now *that's* a story I am sure I want to hear."

Bendahrin continued, "The destruction their explosion caused was repaired in about twenty minutes. A *Targeshobe* is a mechanical device that uses and directs magic—in this case, the magic restores the ship. You will NOT be able to make any upgrades to the ship until you have set the *Targeshobe* properly. If you try to, any equipment you install will be destroyed and the original will be restored."

"Port and starboard shimmies!" Marcus exclaimed. "Can y'imagine how much people would pay for this? Why hasn't anyone thought of this before?" Nobody ventured an answer, and Marcus nodded back to Bendahrin to continue, and besides, nobody had an answer to offer in response; although Prescott was imagining how much buyers would pay . . .

"Use is simple but MUST be done properly. You damage my ship and I will *banish* you all to a thousand-year torment. Ask Bendahrin if he thinks this is an idle threat. Pay attention to the following three settings and steps for use. Currently the *Targeshobe* is set to active; the knob is at the top."

They all looked up to see the metal knob that had three settings, clearly distinguishable.

Bendahrin continued, "The center setting captures a new image of the ship—*only* after you have been in repair mode, and the bottom setting is required for you to do repairs and upgrades. The knob clicks out toward you in the center setting to force a stop before clicking to the bottom. You will need to push the knob *in* to move the knob to the bottom."

Jedra chuckled at this. "Good safety design! She thinks of everything."

Bendahrin nodded in agreement.

Mandy was fairly jumping up and down, and this room had finally grabbed Prescott's interest.

"This is how the *Targeshobe* works. When you are in repair mode, ANYTHING you move or change anywhere in the ship other than what is in this room or the other safe zones will be considered a repair and will become a permanent part of the ship's new template when you move the knob to image capture. These examples will help: In repair mode, you remove a console and replace it, placing the old console in the hold. When you move the knob from repair to capture a new image, everything in the ship is now remembered and becomes permanent. Or, in repair mode, you move a crate across the room. Its new position becomes part of the new template. On the other hand, anything you *don't* move is ignored. This is helpful because everything in the ship at the time you move the knob from active to image capture that wasn't part of the previous image will be ignored until you move it during a repair mode period; at which time it becomes a permanent part of the new image. I would suggest you don't move any of your personal belongings or the furniture, or food in the galley, in sum, only move items that you want to become permanent. Although, don't worry, I can do an override and make a master template when I arrive to make any adjustments. Oh, and put all of the debris in one place for later removal or throw it out of the hatch; anything that leaves the ship is ignored or deleted."

Bendahrin stopped and shook his head, looking around, he asked, "Does this make sense to you?"

He was somewhat dismayed that they all nodded affirmatively but also enheartened.

"We will just need to have strict work zones, careful procedures, and probably a fourteen-hour work period, not a problem," Marcus said.

Bendahrin finished the page. "I have added a safety measure; you can only move the knob if all of you are in this room. The port lounge, Tored's Room, and the area around the drive are safe zones that are not part of the changeable locations and should not be entered in repair mode. The library is on its own system, so although you can enter, it is wisest to stay away. The following steps for use will help you to not make any mistakes. First, plan your work time carefully to do tasks that can be completed in blocks so you can create images periodically. The corollary is that you need to finish these blocks of work so that everything is finished and tested before you make an image. Second, bring anything you want to keep out of the template into the room with you when you move the knob. A good example would be any food you want to eat. Third, and this is redundant, but important, don't move anything that isn't a repair when you are in repair mode. Obviously, *you* can move because you were in the room and will be in the room and won't be included in the image update. Finally, set time aside to test everything carefully. Although you can make additional repairs that will become permanent in a subsequent repair period, the ship might not *work* if you don't test carefully. I think that the five of you, sorry Bendahrin, understand what this means. And this means that the computer core can be replaced at any time, but DON'T DAMAGE MY SHIP!"

"This is amazing!" Mandy said, looking around in delight. "I really can't wait to meet her."

Prescott scowled and turned to Mandy. "You are such a flit." His tone was surly, and might have been playful, but no one else could tell. With cousins, an acceptable style of communication can only be appreciated from within the relationship. "From what little we know and all that we have heard, she is evil and terrifying! And dangerous! What is this blind attraction of yours?"

Mandy's face went slack, and her smile fled. She glanced at her uncle and then at Erin, Jedra. When she spoke, her words seemed to be caught in a mire of shame. "I . . . I, ummm, have always wanted to meet someone who knows how to, how to use magic."

Prescott shook his head in barely feigned mockery, mere baby steps from actual disgust. "Then have the family hire a mage from one of the magic planets so you can have a kiddie show."

Mandy was about to protest when Marcus, sensing the need to protect Mandy and divert attention, cut in, "So, Bendahrin, you've seen this work?"

Bendahrin was looking at Mandy with sympathy, and he turned slowly to Marcus. "I saw the repairs to the ship, as they happened, but I didn't know how, and this is the first that I have seen this device."

"But it seems that its use is straightforward, and we should be able to do what we need to do. Agreed?" Marcus turned to Prescott.

Prescott was still looking at Mandy, with something less than sympathy, but he quickly averred, saying, "It works like programming version control. You can't write over anything by accident, and you check in your changes. Simple enough."

"So! Great! This is excellent," Marcus added, then looking to Erin. "The discipline, teamwork, and experience we work out here will make our efforts on *Ascension* more effective. This ship is just a refit."

Erin added, "We need to re-think, re-organize, and plan in detail before we start. I suggest we take the rest of today to get ready, rest, and then tomorrow we commit to a full day."

Mandy was quickly moving past Prescott's rebuke, and her mind was racing through the possibilities. "This could be really helpful if we need to duplicate something; it could save us a lot of time. Listen. Imagine we need a few identical copies of a specific length of RX-seventy-two conduit with full connectors. We build one to spec and drop it outside the door, then we come in here, switch down to repair mode, someone steps outside and moves it. We make a new image and set the, uhh, *Targeshobe* to active. Then we step outside and move the cable. The *Targeshobe* will then be forced to make a duplicate. We could do that as many times as we want!"

Marcus laughed out loud and clapped his hands slowly. "Genius, but, yes, it would certainly work that way, it seems. However, I don't think we want to use that shortcut unless we run out of raw materials—we don't know what the operational limits are, but we will keep it in mind."

For the remainder of that day Marcus and Mandy wrote detailed plans that were posted in the computer room. Crates were moved to make sure that the items needed sooner were not behind others that would then need to be moved. Bendahrin was kept busy moving crates, posting instructions, and serving the others with food and drink.

Prescott worked frantically with Erin and Jedra to switch out the computer core, along with upgrading the connection cables. The ship had to be stopped a few times, and power turned off from various parts of the ship, but after ten hours, they had not only replaced the core, but Prescott had integrated the old core into a cooperative processing design using one of the agile consoles and had somehow more than doubled the power of the new core. The ship came online in the early evening, and Jedra resumed their course, again, at best possible speed.

The four days following were long and mentally exhausting more than physically demanding. These ships were designed for easy, modular repair, and the replacements were, after all, made by the same ship builder *for* this very ship. Even so, thousands of connections had to be made, diagnostics run, each system tested, and then on to the next. Their planning helped, and so did the *Targeshobe*. Since the cables had been magically maintained for the past many years, in most cases, only the control panels themselves needed to be tested. The ship only had to be stopped nine times in four days; proof that planning paid off.

They finished the last replacement near mid-day on the fourth day, and they congregated in the computer room to reset the *Targeshobe* to active the last time. They all cheered when this happened, and then Prescott hurried them all out of the room in order to run the final system diagnosis. The ship could not run during this process, but none of them cared very much; they talked and laughed, and Bendahrin, Erin, and Marcus gathered in the galley to pull together a celebration dinner.

As they worked, Marcus raised the question that had not been *specifically* asked to this point. "Have we worked out a chain of command?"

Bendahrin looked up at Erin, who smiled and returned to cutting vegetables. "By that you mean to ask, 'who will command the *Ascension*?'"

Marcus nodded swiftly. "I don't imagine I need a quote for you Darren's first rule of survival in space?"

Erin smiled again and shook her head. "We both know that command is held by one, *and* experience is the weight that tips the scales," she said, paraphrasing Darren in order to poke fun at him. "But, *experience* is such a challenging and subjective quality to evaluate fairly, don't you think?"

Marcus looked grave. "I think we would both agree that it isn't just about the miles and the years, but the opportunity to show leadership, discernment, or even the tenacity to stick to a difficult assignment."

"Or perhaps the ability to adapt and think quickly in diverse and dangerous circumstances, getting your crew through adversity to safe success." They both stopped, as if on cue, and they looked up, their eyes meeting, fencing, locking in combat, feverish, but full of disgruntled respect.

Bendahrin observed this with amusement, this gentle battle had gone on without letting up since the first day they had met, and now that *Ascension* was the next meal on the menu, Bendahrin sensed that the showdown was coming. "This is largely academic. When Alystra is on board, she will be in charge, and maybe even when she is not. Furthermore, she promised the ship to Erin, and if that is her choice, her choice will stand. Either way, at this point, Erin is a member of *Ascension's* crew, and you are a guest contractor, a *highly esteemed* guest contractor with extensive experience. Nothing is final, but that is probably the way Alystra will see it."

Neither Marcus *nor* Erin were satisfied with this answer. But it was Marcus who gave voice to their thoughts. "You have mentioned and hinted that she is this mystical Issachon, but how can you be sure? I admit that on Prevaria we don't encounter very many mages," at this he looked bothered, "but the point is that even being a very clever or powerful mage isn't the same thing as being some creature out of ancient and largely unreliable legend."

Erin jumped right in again. "I spent a good bunch of time with her, planning my escape from the Stream, and on Prevaria. I have also known a lot of mages through the years, and many of them were powerful enough to do the things Alystra did."

Bendahrin stopped and looked from one to the other, contemplating what to say and knowing that nothing would answer their questions. "That is the problem of faith, isn't it? At some point you believe, and then, once on the other side, everything makes sense. What I have seen and experienced is mine, and I have no power to help you see without some other source of authority that can call to you from some other realm to open your eyes. I have to tell you that I stood beside her, when we first met, and I saw her hold in her hands the power of suns and storms, wind and wonder, but you will each, probably, need to see this for yourselves, although I hope that you never do. Faith *is*, after all, the path of innocence."

"And what will we see?" Marcus asked. "What will change our minds?"

Bendahrin trembled. "Fear. Utter, incapacitating terror that you can't escape. Not fear that she casts on you, but fear that pours from her being. You will see fear that will strip your heart away and leave you naked before the ghastly probing. But then, you will understand." He stopped for a minute and leaned on the counter. "I hope that you will come to her out of loyalty, or love, or for any motivation rather than fear because she is fairly irresistible. Sadly, that will not likely be your choice." He paused for a moment. "But the answer to your first question is still hovering because she will still be on *Lentoris*; *Ascension* has another mission, not as dark but potentially as dangerous."

–|–

Their celebration dinner was festive and filled with technical discussions and humorous recollections, much of it seemed to be at Bendahrin's expense since he was the only non-technical person on board. Mandy recalled her own story on the heels of Erin. "I agree with you on that! Jedra and I had been in the cockpit for hours; we had replaced *all five* of the panels that morning. At about lunch time, Bendahrin comes in, carrying a drink in his hand and he greets us. So

Jedra asks, 'What do you think?' Bendahrin looks around and says, 'Is it different?' and Jedra just about hurt himself laughing. So, I told him that we just spent seven hours working in that room, and he says, 'Sorry, it looks the same to me, but as my mother used to say, "If you clean the kitchen enough, nobody notices when you mop the floor."' Jedra threw his work gloves at him."

Bendahrin raised his glass to respond, but at that moment there was an enormous crash and the ship lurched physically, toppling glasses along the table.

They all jumped up in time to see an enormous black cloud pouring around the corner of the hall from near the front lounge.

"Fire!" someone cried, but Bendahrin knew better.

"No!" he shouted. "To the library, quickly!"

The first plumes of the blackness engulfed them, and Erin and Prescott screamed; Marcus called out.

They felt as if their souls had been poured into a canyon filled with dripping and circling terror.

Bendahrin had the slightest edge of experience and was barely holding his thoughts together. As the first rush of blackness passed, his mind cleared sufficiently that he was able to grab Erin and Prescott, both of whom had fallen to the floor, and half-lead, half-dragged them to the library shouting all the way for the others to follow. His eyes were burning, and his mind was pounding with fear, and after he had pushed the first two through the library doors, he went back for the others. He passed Marcus on the way, and he heard the library doors open again behind him. *Where did he find the courage to move?* Bendahrin thought. He found Jedra still seated in his chair, a dazed expression on his face. Mandy stood looking up the hall with wide eyes and wider smile. He grabbed their hands, yelling at them to move, and again he forced them to the library where he pushed them into the receiving hands of the others.

He was about to speak to them when there was a sound like a roar and a scream mixed in horrid harmony, each painful voice distinct yet joined, with neither voice compromised the least in its ability to carry on its waves the pounding beat of fear. Everything went dark and cold, and they all cowered to the floor, except for Mandy who was standing and staring. After that wave had passed, Bendahrin yelled, "Close the door and lean the table against it. Don't come out. You will be safe. In fact, it might be better if you get behind the shelves of books.

"Don't open the door 'til I knock and call!"

Marcus, who had the longest years of facing the unknown, had gained his composure more than the rest. He stood and looked to Mandy, who was leaning left and right to see out the door past Bendahrin. He said, "Bendahrin! What are you going to do?"

"Who knows! Just close the door now." He stepped into the hall, and Mandy closed the doors, still trying to peek past Bendahrin. Moments later, Bendahrin saw the table through the glass, leaning against the doors. He turned to his right and muttered, "Where is Kel when I *really* need him?" He walked away toward the front of the ship.

To those in the library the next several minutes were a dance with confusion and fear. As soon as the doors closed the horrid screaming roar echoed down the hall again, only slightly quieter from being within the library. The ship shook, and at times, blasting waves of iridescence tore through the room, waves that erased the ship so they could see into space and gaze upon the stars where the deck of the ship should have been. For periods of time the lights went out, which was almost *worse* since at those times they could see that some of the books glowed with an unwholesome fire as if they were a permanent doorway to places of evil and darkness and torment.

Time passed for the five hiding in the library. The sounds and shaking of the ship subsided, and still they waited. After a time, the lights stayed on for long enough that they walked around talking in whispers. Eventually they moved near to the door listening, and when it seemed that the ship was *deathly* still, there came a knock and Bendahrin's voice. "This is Bendahrin, open the door."

They scrambled hastily to lower the table away from the door and pulled the doors open.

Bendahrin stood in the hallway, alone, exactly one half of his face was as black as space. He walked in and held his hands out to Marcus and Erin. "That was the fear I had mentioned, and, as promised, understanding will follow."

Mandy was behind Marcus on the left. "I wasn't afraid," she said happily.

At that, Alystra walked in from the left and entered behind Bendahrin. "Excellent work all of you! You didn't damage my ship! Would you like to go back and finish your dinner?"

Jedra was the first to speak, his voice unsteady. "I, um, think I could use some wine right now."

They all began to move, but Alystra put out a hand and stopped Mandy. Under other circumstances the rest might have continued, but the action seemed both personal and threatening, so they stopped and turned to watch. They had all passed Alystra and were standing in the hall, behind her, and Mandy faced Alystra with her exuberant smile, beaming with excitement, and, if possible, her smile was even more eager.

Mandy quivered; this was rapture. "You're Alystra the Destroyer! I am so excited to meet you!" She started to approach Alystra, who held up her hand to stop her, her expression was one of crushing hatred and fury, mixed with painful curiosity.

Bendahrin moved back a step to see them both, and Marcus followed suit on the opposite side. The recent rampage of fear and the world of unanswered questions had left him severely leery of Alystra, and her actions made him concerned for his niece.

Alystra nodded slowly and a smile began to adorn her face. This put Bendahrin at ease at once, but Marcus opened his mouth to speak. Both Mandy and Alystra raised a hand to silence him. He took a timorous, small half-step back and raised his hands in resignation.

"I can see that you weren't afraid." Alystra asked.

"Yes! Why would I fear you?" Mandy piped, her voice a bit higher than normal, her exuberance fit to explode.

Alystra looked down for a moment and held her palm out

toward Mandy, their eyes locked, and time seemed to stop.

Bendahrin felt as though he was suddenly viewing two statues as the two women assessed each other.

Alystra nodded in confident consternation, having concluded her evaluation. "Truth. Deep truth. Honest truth. You *weren't* afraid." Alystra whispered, but this time it was a statement, an affirmation, and after she had sensed and confirmed what she already knew, her confirmation became a conclusion. She took a sudden step back, mentally and physically, her mouth open in wonder and anger. Then she made a sudden throwing motion; Mandy's eyes engaged on something unseen by the others, and her hand snapped up to grab something invisible right before her left eye.

She lowered her hand and opened her palm, there was nothing visible to the rest, but she looked at Alystra and nodded toward her hand, grinning. "Did I pass?"

At that, Alystra nodded, and Teela, her dagger, became visible in Mandy's hand. Alystra raised her hand beside her head. "Don't move your hand. Throw my dagger back to me."

At that, Mandy smiled, and the dagger jittered, turned a bit, then shot from her hand to Alystra's where she caught it.

Alystra put the dagger back into its sheath, and she gazed across at Mandy. "You," Alystra said, almost a whisper, but it was like a breeze through the room, in fact, their hair moved as if a wind had just passed through the door. "You are a natural adept." Mandy nodded, and Alystra continued, "You can *create* magic like a song of virtuous beauty, filling any void, stretching through ages and distance, with nothing but your voice, but, but there," she paused, closing her eyes in concentration. Then she continued, shaking her head in disbelief, "there is not one note of magic in your life symphony."

Alystra moved to put her hand on Bendahrin's shoulder as if she needed him to steady her. She looked at Mandy again, who was still beaming, and they all felt the warmth coming from her. Mandy was a flame. In fact, as if Mandy somehow knew in the deep worlds of her unconsciousness, a wave of confidence flooded the room and the fear most of them held was pushed back. The sigh of relief that followed was chased from the room by Alystra's growl. Warmth and goodness were mortal enemies to her.

Alystra scowled in anger for a moment but continued in

wonder, "I can sense your entire life like a thread before me. You have never uttered a single magic word, *ever*. Like a newborn, your eyes have just opened, and you've seen, *me!*" Mandy nodded, but Alystra continued, "This is amazing, unprecedented . . ." She shook her head, an expression of horror and tortured disbelief upon her face. "It's not possible. You are totally empty, but as pure and clean as light itself." She looked at Bendahrin, their eyes locked, and whispered again, "Unblemished, free of malice or design, untainted, directionless. Bendahrin . . ." She turned back to Mandy, but then looked to Marcus. "How can this be?"

Marcus spoke gravely. He seemed to have landed on his feet, and Mandy had washed away the fear, though not the wisdom bestowed by fear. "On Prevaria, technology and science make up the driving current of the culture. Anyone who shows signs of magical skills is sent to one of the great magic centers because they just don't fit in. We . . . can't train them, and they have no use on our technological world. Although, if we could start outfitting those *Targeshodes* on ships, we could revolutionize the shipping industry."

"*Targeshobe*," Alystra corrected. "It took me years to figure that one out, and I'm afraid just being a mage isn't enough. Maybe when I want to retire someday." She turned back to Mandy. "How did you hide it? How old are you?"

Mandy danced in a circle. "I'm twenty-six, and I have known for most of my life. My mother can do magic too."

Marcus scowled and took an unsteady step away from Mandy.

Mandy looked down at the ground. "Sorry, Uncle Marcus. She never told you. She taught me to hide my skill, and besides, our family had the money, so I had the means to hide my ability on Prevaria. But mother also taught me discipline and hope; hope that one day I would find something, the right person or place, and then my magic could be unleashed, and here I am." She twirled around again, her arms outstretched.

Alystra watched Mandy with her mouth open, then she shuddered and ran her fingers through her hair. She turned to Bendahrin and noticed his blackened face for the first time. She shook her head and said, "Didn't I tell you not to look at me in that state?" Her voice was devoid of any sympathy.

Bendahrin pointed at her, his hand also as black as night. "*You jumped into view faster than I could turn away.*"

She looked closer at Bendahrin. "Can you see out of that eye?"

He nodded. "Everything is gray, but yes."

She shrugged and spoke to Mandy. "So, you are almost my age." She paused and pressed her fist against her lips, then dropped her hand and continued, "Mandy, I don't think you understand the full importance of this. Most mages *use* magic; it is a tool, an ability that they have to use something that is essentially external to them. For them, magic is controlled or channeled through spells and stored in devices like staves or wands or rings or books, anything." She rolled her eyes in disgust. "But as a natural adept, you can *create* magic. You are not a *source*, not exactly, but you will be able to originate and create and control magic as an act of will. One in a *billion* mages is like you, but," and she paused, the wonder pummeling her, "You are an adult, and you haven't been trained. This situation has *never* happened. *Never!* Natural adepts are too powerful. This situation is, and you are, totally unpredictable. But you, you have *perfect* control and no design. You are a wonder. What are you?" She was asking Mandy, herself, and the universe.

"So, I am like you!" Mandy said, her enthusiasm not diminished the slightest bit by thinking that she was like Alystra.

"Uhhh, well, yes . . . and no. I also create magic, but I am also something totally other, but you will understand that atrociously soon. I can't *wait* to meet your mother."

"But this is perfect, *you* can teach me!" Mandy cried, her eyes held Alystra in an embrace of adoration. "This is the moment I've been waiting for my whole life!"

Alystra looked horrified, but she walked to Mandy and took both of her hands, shaking her head. "I don't know. I . . . You are so . . . I don't know if it is possible."

Mandy was undiminished in her enthusiasm.

Alystra looked at Mandy, perplexed and undecided. "You burn me, just standing there." But she nodded her head decisively and spoke to Bendahrin. "Explain it to the new folks, two minutes."

And they were gone.

There was a collective gasp, and Marcus said, "I think it is far past time for some explanations." He held his anger behind the practice of command, for in his heart he was concerned for Mandy and surprised by the revelation of her magical abilities, and his *sister's*.

Bendahrin sighed deeply. "I know this is very hard." They

returned to the lounge and resumed eating while Bendahrin began his explanation. Apparently, the recent fear from Alystra's arrival and Mandy's subsequent washing didn't deter hunger. "I understand your concerns and doubts. Magic, because of *what* it is, is mysterious. For those of you from Prevaria, but even Erin and Jedra, who were exposed to some rather plodding magic users in the Stream, magic, and Alystra, can be distant, fantastic, even hidden in legends. I was born and raised on Palestre, which is one of the twelve great centers of magic, the home of the Entaparion, a fountain of magic that wields influence over a sphere twenty-thousand light years around."

Prescott looked up. "What does that even mean? Influence. It isn't alive, is it?"

Bendahrin pondered for a moment. "No, not alive, but interactive, or . . ." He paused. "No, the word I need is reflective." Bendahrin bit his lip. "Although I grew up on Palestre, as a non-magic user, my understanding is purely theoretical. As I understand it, a power center grows from the collective efforts and input of all mages who interact with it over thousands of years, thousands of centuries in the case of the Entaparion. In time, the relic itself gains a character or presence that impacts the surrounding area. Apparently, the Entaparion's influence is a sense of balance." He shook his head. "I can't really say much more.

"Nevertheless, with respect to magic, living on Palestre, magic is everywhere; we all use it, pay for it, dodge it in the streets. For you, any hint of the Issachon was nothing more than a fable or footnote. On Palestre, in the capital, there are a dozen temples to the Issachon, and so we know more about the stories of the ancient primal force." He paused, lost in what to relate. "The legends from the past, the stories, the hints, the dark understanding are a mix of fears known and unknown. That woman, against her will, was transformed into this metaphorical and legendary embodiment of evil, about a dozen years ago." He paused to gather reactions, and to take a short swipe at wondering about Alystra's return. "However, in direct defiance to every conceivable destiny and expectation, she has set herself against evil. For this reason, Alystra, more than anyone, is aware of her innate evil and doesn't want to expose Mandy, so teaching her is out of the question for Alystra. Fighting evil is her cause, my future, and may even be our deaths. If any of you are to join us, you need to know that you will be in alliance with the embodiment of evil in order to destroy that very evil. Erin and Jedra have committed, although perhaps tonight was their first real taste of the full measure of what this commitment entails?"

Erin had felt the fear and the cleansing but was still subdued and thoughtful, and yet she raised her head. She spoke firmly, but clearly shaken. "I begin to understand, now, and I will face the fear to bask in the power. My commitment stands."

Jedra nodded his assent.

"But Marcus, Prescott," Bendahrin nodded to each, "you signed on to see a ship, to repair a ship, and we hold you to no commitment of any kind beyond the promise of assistance, which, after all, was a promise made by your father." He sighed. "Beyond the ship, I can only promise you the adventure of a lifetime, and a chance to save the universe from a future too dire, if you want to continue."

Marcus had been eating as he listened. He looked at his son. Prescott still seemed to be in shock. "Bendahrin, I can't understand your part in this, and I don't know how we *can* help. We will need to think this through." Marcus then raised his glass. "At the very least, we are committed to *Ascension*, which is the next adventure ahead of us, and that has always been *our* desired destiny."

At that moment there was a wail from behind Bendahrin, and Alystra re-appeared with Mandy, who was on her knees, her body shaking. Alystra knelt beside her, her arms wrapped around Mandy.

Everyone jumped up.

Erin rushed to Mandy, looking at Alystra with concern. They held each other in a huddle for a gaggle of seconds while the men watched.

In time, Mandy composed herself and stood. With a tear-streaked face she gazed into each person's eyes. Suddenly as if a switch had been thrown, she shook her head and threw her hands down. It seemed that a tremor flowed out from her that they all felt in their feet. She took a deep breath, and her smile returned, brighter than ever.

She walked over to Marcus and hugged her uncle. She held his hand and reached out her other one to Prescott. Holding both of their hands firmly, she announced, grinning fiercely "I just completed my first step into magical wonder!"

She stepped back to Alystra and grasped her hand, which Bendahrin felt was more dangerous than anything else that had happened that evening. "We have decided, Alystra *will* teach me, and I," she said nodding to each of her kin, "will follow Alystra and will serve on *Ascension* or *Lentoris*. Now that I have seen her, I know with certainty, my life has always been directed to this end. To stand against the Issachon."

Then she stood and spread her arms. "I need to do one thing." She raised her arms and swept them down and forward and cried, "Goodbye, Fear, as I name it!" and there was a rush of laughing wind, which flurried over them, and they all felt the remaining crushing weight of the earlier fear swept away in such a cleansing roar that it wasn't even the faintest memory.

"But now, let's eat! I'm hungry; it has been almost two days since we left and then we will sleep!"

Alystra said to Bendahrin, "I understand her now; she and I have come to terms. Her years of discipline and indifference to magic have made her impervious." She looked over at Mandy who was talking with her usual bright animation to Marcus and Prescott. "I think that she has found the perfect magic of love, joy, hope, I don't know, faith maybe? There is something insanely providential going on here, and so, I will be able to teach her with no evil effect." She paused and drew him aside further. "Bendahrin, she's close to my age. She is so *perfectly* good."

Their eyes met, and Bendahrin shrugged.

Alystra and Bendahrin turned to face the table.

All seven were standing, some uncomfortable, others at ease, uncertainty, confidence, confusion were present, amusement, all alert, tired headed toward exhaustion, but apathy and disinterest were nowhere to be found. The room was silent save for the normal sounds of a ship in space. The moment lingered; they all looked from face to face, as if meeting for the first time, new impressions over-writing first impressions or adding new contours.

Alystra swept through their minds, except for Mandy's, reading impressions, seeking dissent, feeling for fears. What she found was what she expected.

Then the moment passed.

Jedra moved to sit, saying something about wanting to finish dinner.

Erin sat, asking for the bottle of wine.

Prescott took the hint and seated himself.

Marcus helped Mandy to her seat, and then joined them.

Finally, Bendahrin did the same, with Alystra standing behind him.

But Mandy stood up immediately and walked slowly to Bendahrin. "I'm sorry," she said, looking at Bendahrin's face.

"What are you sorry for?" Bendahrin asked.

"I noticed your face before, and I want to help. This doesn't hurt does it?"

Bendahrin shook his head. "No, it doesn't."

"Bendahrin, you face the danger and the fear. Your skin isn't damaged; it is a sign of your defense." She touched his face and flinched. But she shook her head and put one hand on his shoulder and the other on the top of his head. She slid her hand down his face, and after her hand had passed, the blackness was gone. She continued down his arm, to his side, all the way to the floor. In her hand was a black blob which hissed and exuded wisps of black smoke. She tossed it up in the air and caught it, laughing. "We don't *want* this anymore!" she cried, and she threw it toward the force-field glass, where a hole opened briefly to let it pass, and it was gone. She turned back with a smile and patted Bendahrin's face. "That's better." She danced back to her seat.

Bendahrin reached up and touched his face. "I didn't even know there was anything visible."

Jedra laughed out loud.

Erin spoke through her food. "So now, Marcus, we're all here. The next stop is the *Ascension*, and then on to the next adventure."

At this comment, Prescott raised his hand, as if he were in school, he looked around the table a bit jerkily. "What if, after *Ascension*, I just want to go home?" He lowered his hand slowly, along with his gaze, "I came here to fix *Ascension*. I'm not interested in evil adventures and danger." He glanced at Alystra and then at Mandy.

"You, or anyone else, can leave at any time," Alystra said, "You will be rewarded for your assistance, and you can go home with the *Ascension* after it is ready to travel."

Prescott started to reply when Mandy jumped up and rushed to the window.

Alystra nodded knowingly and waited for Mandy to speak. When she turned from the window her eyes were wide. "That was me, out there. Right? I could feel it from *here*."

Alystra nodded again. "And notice how clearly you could sense your power and your newness? Even from this distance. Pay attention, that ship will land a thousand miles away."

Mandy turned and closed her eyes. "Yes, there it goes." She turned back and said to the others, "That was something Alystra and I did while we were away just now." She proceeded to describe her experience; questions and answers washed over the table in colorful wonder.

Her story and the subsequent questions took some time. When she finished there was a wave of quiet as each person turned to inner thoughts.

Marcus cleared his throat. "Obviously we have many decisions and plans to make," he glanced at Mandy and Prescott, "but, I have an, uhhh . . . kinda personal question, if you don't mind." He stood, formally, looking a bit embarrassed, or, at least, doing a good job *acting* as though he was embarrassed. "I just want to know, and really, it's Prescott who wants to know," Prescott rolled his eyes as if he had endured *this* type of joke a thousand times, "when you were Marian, on Prevaria, I, uhh . . . was that your natural hair color, or is the current *auburn* the real you."

"Erupted with laughter," immediately became the gathering's middle name. After this, the laughter flowed, ideas were exchanged, plans were discussed, even Prescott had his moment when he acted out some of his favorite comedian's routines. They all rolled into bed later than they had wanted, having eaten and drunk more than they had wanted, a new group born in the safe cradle of a shared meal. Save Alystra, who first cleared up the mess from the party with a whisk of magic then nestled herself into the engine room. Feeling the ship, sensing the sleepers and frantically calculating millions of digits of detail into the drive; *Lentoris* was renewed, *Ascension* was ahead, but Alystra was racing frantically into the future.

22

Bendahrin knew that their chase was winding down, and he sighed inwardly with relief. Being surrounded with enthusiasts and their endless accolades of expectation, ejaculations of excitement and dazed stargazing had grown grating on him. His further sigh of relief was drowned in a feverish rise of enthusiasm from everyone else when Jedra turned from the control console in the forward lounge and said, "That should be the final course correction." He paused. "If all of the calculations are correct, we will see the *Ascension* in about fifty minutes."

Bendahrin rolled his eyes when everyone, but Alystra turned exuberantly toward the massive force-field glass as if they would see the *Ascension* by looking hard enough. He sighed a third time, nodding silently to himself and remembering that, whereas he had little interest in *any* ship, most of the rest of the people in the lounge were utterly devoted to the fast-approaching discovery.

Prescott turned. "Wait! If? Shouldn't we be certain? Don't we know where we are going?" His gaping mouth revealed his astonishment.

Alystra snorted. "Don't be absurd. I last saw the *Ascension* more than eighteen months ago. It was moving slowly enough by interstellar standards, but since I last noted its course and speed it has traveled almost four million kilometers each day, which is more than a billion kilometers since then. If I was off by a tiny fraction of the *Ascension's* course or speed, we could miss the ship by a vast margin."

She moved to the center of the lounge. "So, let's find the ship!

Everyone on your feet."

When the six of them had stood, the furniture slid back so that the main section of the lounge was clear.

"Sit on the floor around me, and don't move." When they were seated, she said to Mandy, "*Shavla,* and if you could collect the darkness."

Prescott started to get up. "Wait! Darkness?" But he fell back to the floor as he suddenly found himself surrounded by space. He was falling swiftly through blackness and stars. In a moment of astonished discovery, his awareness was a sphere of vision allowing him to see in all directions at once. His falling motion suddenly stopped, and he realized that his body had hit the invisible floor.

The voice of Alystra was soft and ethereal in their minds. "The Strentrian Bubble duplicates the universe around me for a radial distance of two parsecs, or about sixty-four light years. For the math challenged, Bendahrin, that means sixty-four light years in all directions or a sphere of one hundred twenty-eight light years. I contain that representative universe into a sphere of whatever size I want, which in this case is about three meters, enough for all of you to sit within. Your location in the universe is analogous to your location in the bubble, which is why you can't see each other. Right now, Prescott is about one hundred light years from Jedra, who is sitting on the opposite side. As Prescott found out, if you move in the bubble, your perspective changes within the contained universe at impossible speeds. As for your concern, Prescott, yes, this spell uses a moderate amount of magical power, but the evil released is slight. Either way, Mandy can collect it and contain it.

"I can manipulate time in here, so let's have some fun before we find the current location of the *Ascension.*" The starfield shifted slightly to compensate for the passage backward in time. "We are now viewing space as it was on the day of the *Ascension* accident. Of course, the *Ascension* is infinitesimally small in this view, but with a little practice and a bit of magic . . ." She paused, and a line appeared that cut across the sphere and stopped slightly ahead of them and to the right. "This line is the path the *Ascension* followed that day. When it hit the star, the field strike damaged the engines, bouncing it in a different direction and slowing it down to a mere forty-four thousand meters per second. This is incredibly slow from our perspective within the Bubble now. Let's come back to our time." The starfield moved again, and they saw a bright dot tracing the continued course of the ship, which, given the scale didn't appear to move at all. "There it is, and Jedra, I have already fixed our course for the intercept."

The starfield view disappeared, and the six sitters released a rushing sigh.

"That was amazing!" Jedra said immediately, and his words were met with a murmur of agreement. They all stood and moved about the lounge, most looking out through the massive force-field glass.

Mandy stood more slowly, holding a sphere of blackness a few inches in diameter.

Alystra approached her and said, "Why don't you take that down to the lower hold and chuck it into space?"

As Mandy moved off, Jedra hurried to Alystra. "That view of the universe in the bubble was amazing."

Alystra nodded, waiting for him to say something that required her attention or a response.

"Do you want to change our approach speed?"

At this she shrugged. "What do you suggest?"

"We are in open space and the ship is pretty large. We can continue at multi-light speed until we are right on top of it, then pursue it for the last few million kilometers at about six times its speed. Upon visual, we can decelerate using just our thrusters." Alystra nodded, smiling carefully. It was distinctly positive to have competent support. Jedra headed toward the auxiliary controls. She turned and walked over to Marcus and Prescott.

Prescott asked, "What happens to that thing when Mandy tosses it into space?"

Marcus looked interested.

"The universe is already full of evil, and that ball of concentration that Mandy has will dissipate and find its metaphysical way back to those who love it, use it, or want it." She lowered her voice. "What *I* want is your opinion about Mandy, which is why I sent her to the hold."

Marcus nodded, raising his eyebrows in curiosity.

"The *Ascension* has been tumbling through space for a long time and we need to stop that tumble. Now . . ." she began but stopped herself upon interruption.

Marcus was nodding and jumped in. "Yes, tumbling." He

turned to look out into space. "That's a couple hundred tons'a tumble. You have any ideas how you want to stop it?"

Alystra chuckled. "Marcus, stop. You don't need to be so deferential when we are talking about *your* area of expertise. I would imagine that you have *done* this more times than I have *thought* about it. Jedra and Erin have probably done this more than all of us, but I don't really want to mess around with the time required to attach thrusters or try to grapple the thing or whatever you spaceship experts do. My original plan was to just stop it myself, but now I'm thinking that this would be a profound moment for Mandy to really let her be creative with her magic in a critical situation. Having her do it would also have the advantage of her purity over my intrinsic evil." Alystra was tempted to make a fake yawn as she reiterated the evil of her magic, again.

"Oh, yes! Interesting, but are you sure? Isn't she still fairly new at magic? Could she damage the ship?" Marcus asked.

"Not in any way that I couldn't fix. I *will* scan the ship and remember its state before we let her go at it." She stopped and reached out, pulling them closer. "This is more than just the ship. This is for Mandy, look! Magic forms the mage as much as the mage uses magic. This task would be a substantial anchor to her confidence. The challenge for us is deciding *how* to present the problem. On the one hand, we could jolt her with the challenge as an emergency, and she could blast her new magic as a reflex. She might not fall for that, of course; she is far too smart. On the other hand, we could tell her in advance and allow her to put her brilliance into the task. You can probably imagine the difference in what this would teach her. Thoughts?"

Decades of command had made Marcus decisive, but with regard to magic, he lacked confidence, and uncertainty started pushing into his mind.

Alystra sensed this and added abruptly, "Marcus! Stop! Think! This isn't about *magic*; this is about *people*—how would *Mandy* handle this?"

Marcus nodded slowly as his mind switched the direction of his focus. "Abrupt challenge versus carefully thought-out procedure, yes. In light of where you're taking her, shooting from the hip has a highly charged appeal. She also might like the change of pace; she has always been careful, thoughtful, and disciplined. That kind of thinking is imperative in an emergency." He stopped and rubbed his chin, looking out the window again as though seeking guidance in the darkness.

Prescott shook his head. "No, I don't like it. Mandy is thoughtful and gentle. A false emergency won't actually teach her to be decisive. It will make her edgy, as if somehow you can throw some critical test at her at any time."

Alystra replied, "Good point. However, I threw a massive test at her, and she was, quite simply, magnificent." Alystra added no more, not wanting to influence the flow of insights.

Marcus nodded. "We're kinda in the same spot, hey? Is it better for us to make a snap decision, or think this through?" He paused and looked at Prescott. His eyes narrowed. "Prescott is right. Let her think this through. Her future is likely to be packed with emergency decisions and learning in that crucible will probably perfect her even better than a contrived test."

"Okay, I will set her mind to it." And she disappeared.

Marcus turned to Prescott. "I will never grow accustomed to that."

"I don't even *want* to grow that way," Prescott replied, wrinkling his nose as though the air was putrid.

Meanwhile, Mandy had entered the lower hold where Alystra was already waiting, leaning against the shuttle. "If you want, you can try out your solution to being in a vacuum in space, or just chuck it through the hull. Or the force-field glass like you did before."

Mandy stopped, looking at Alystra out of the corner of her eye. Alystra could sense how quickly her mind was racing even without magic. "Oh! I see. Sending me down here was an excuse so we could talk together." She turned to her left and tossed the black blob through the back hatch causing an opening as before. "Bye."

"Almost." Alystra smiled. "It was a distraction to get you out of the room long enough to get an opinion so that I would know what to say to you if I came down here to talk to you." Mandy nodded eagerly and Alystra continued, "As you know, the *Ascension* is tumbling through space, roll and pitch at the same time. I'll get right to the point. We want *you* to stop the motion."

Mandy's eager face showed a moment of concern, then excitement. "I think that Jedra and Erin would be the best at placing thrusters or . . ."

But Alystra stopped her. "We aren't using thrusters to do this;

you will stop *Ascension*, and you know what we are asking."

"Are you sure? This is really important. I don't know—I can't—I'm—"

Alystra snorted. "Don't be absurd." She jerked her head toward the door, and they started walking together. "Imagine that we were all about to die. Could you do it then? Think! This isn't about ability. The *Ascension* is about a *hundredth* of the weight of *either* of the ships you used to thread that needle. The question for you is *how*, not *if*. You have time, you know the ship, you *know* everything you need."

They walked in silence up to the main deck and stopped at the starboard lounge.

"You have some time. So, let's go back and watch the end of the chase." Alystra put her hand on Mandy's shoulder and sighed. "Remember that magic isn't just about making things happen; it is a natural part of you ... like breathing or using a muscle." She paused, putting her finger on her top lip. Then she smiled broadly with more than a hint of mischief. "And, for you, this is more a reminder than advice: Magic is an adventure. Just—" She bit back "don't screw it up" and said instead, "Have fun."

When they had arrived back at the front lounge, they discovered that the furniture had been rearranged so that everyone could have a good view through the forward force-field glass. Bendahrin was off to the right side, Jedra was at the auxiliary controls, but Erin and the Scurvens were seated, having pulled their seats far forward.

Mandy stopped and stood, thinking, at the back of the lounge.

Alystra sat near Jedra.

Bendahrin was watching the Scurvens more than he was observing the view. As interesting as the *Ascension* was, as a historical relic, he was keenly interested in his crewmates and their reactions.

Prescott and Marcus were leaning forward, almost touching the force-field glass, as though the extra inches would get them to their desired destination sooner.

Erin's expression was eager, even hungry.

"The Stream is still deep in her," Bendahrin thought.

The silence in the room seemed to quiver with tense expectation as the minutes passed. In contrast, outside the force-field glass, the stars were steady and unmoving against the soothing blackness, so slow was their passage. Bendahrin gazed for a moment into the depths, then closed his eyes, calling upon the greater darkness that closing ones eyes provided. He took a deep slow breath, enjoying the moments of slow calm. He couldn't tell whether he should be reflecting on the past to enjoy the peace he remembered, or probing toward the future, where paths of uncertainty lay. He shook his head slightly, perturbed that his old well-worn paths that led to thoughts of comfort seemed to be lost amidst new broad avenues of trouble and tension. He shook his head again in slow dismay and brought his fingers lightly to his lips.

And he jumped when Jedra spoke. "I am going to slowly taper our speed, so we don't overshoot our target." He looked at Erin, whose eyes had gone wide, and he shrugged. When the Stream hunted down ships, their approach was aggressive to maintain the edge that surprise provided.

If anything, the Scurvens leaned in further. Hopes and desires wrestled with anticipation so that time seemed to slow along with the ship. Eventually Jedra's voice cut through the tension, "The sensors are showing a faint return. We should have a visual any moment."

At this, Prescott, Marcus and Erin stood.

Bendahrin watched the others to see who would react first, or point.

Keep breathing, everyone! he thought.

Then Jedra called out, "About fifteen kilometers! We have a firm return." He looked through the force-field glass for a moment. "Nothing but starlight here so there won't be much to see until we are very close and our lights are on it."

This didn't dampen the enthusiasm in the room in the slightest way. After a tense minute, a vague shape, tumbling end over end, appeared in the darkness and in an additional minute they had matched the other ship's speed and pulled in close enough that as it tumbled, the bow and stern of the ship disappeared beyond the top and bottom of the view in the window.

Jedra's voice cut through one more time. "Keeping station five hundred feet from the *Ascension*. Speed forty-three thousand, nine hundred seventy-six feet per second."

The Scurvens erupted; they danced and cheered, hugged and shook hands, tears streamed down their faces, and they all ran over to Alystra who suffered herself to be hugged. They thumped Bendahrin on the back, surrounded Jedra and Erin, hugging them, too.

The din continued for a few minutes.

As the excitement passed, Marcus sat down again in a chair facing the window and said to himself, "If only father could have seen this. There are a lot of people who will be frantically upset that they missed this."

Jedra, slightly breathless, mentioned, "I captured the forward view and recorded the last few minutes. You can forward the event to your dad."

All of them were now talking quietly, savoring the moment and allowing the tension and excitement to fade. None noticed that Mandy had not joined in the celebration but was standing slightly apart from the rest in the center of the lounge, her legs spread shoulder length apart, and her hands clenched at her sides. She was whispering to herself, thinking fiercely, and maybe waiting when suddenly, she raised her hands and shouted, "Stop! Now!"

Immediately, obediently, *Ascension* stopped tumbling and spinning, her bow pointing directly at *Lentoris*, revealing what she had been waiting for.

Marcus jumped up and turned with the rest of them to look at Mandy, who was staring with the happiest and most successful grin in her life.

Then Alystra laughed and walked forward slowly clapping. She ambled over and grabbed Mandy by the shoulders, who grabbed Alystra's arms in return. "I must tell you," she said, laughing again, "don't *ever* say anything like that in front of a real mage. They would be *so* embarrassed. The words and language don't *matter*, but it looks so much more impressive when we dress up incantations in some unnecessary ancient language."

The next morning, they gathered in the starboard lounge in preparation to search *Ascension* for the remains of the crew. The task was to be gruesome, but they had all decided to make the arduous search and remove the deceased crew through a collective effort rather than through magic to uphold the humanity and dignity of the wretched experience.

"While you were asleep, I took the liberty of making some magical upgrades to the *Ascension*," Alystra began. "While I was on Prevaria, I walked through the minds of the countless engineers, designers, and technicians we had invited to the Epoch, discreetly, of course. I only searched for technical content. In this way I gathered the latest in shipbuilding technology, metallurgy, structures, and numerous systems, I won't bore you. The result is that structure and hull of *Ascension* is lighter and sturdier now with the accumulated expertise and knowledge of six-hundred years of technological advancement. Stronger and lighter means faster."

Marcus was about to make a compliment to her efforts, but Prescott interrupted, "And you painted *Ascension* black." His voice was clearly disapproving.

Alystra's voice snapped coldly in return, "It's my ship, and it is a *combat* ship."

Marcus continued, ignoring the tension, "But there are still plenty of unknowns." He waved to the team and they gathered around a table covered with blueprints of *Ascension*. He placed his finger on each location and traced directions as he spoke. "Erin and

I will start on the lowest level at the front and proceed toward the engineering spaces to begin an evaluation of the power, propulsion, and environmental systems. Prescott and Mandy will start at either end on the upper deck and proceed room by room. Alystra and Jedra will begin at the back of deck two and search towards the bridge. Bendahrin will remain on *Lentoris* to record where we find the deceased, although suit cameras will make continuous records." His voice tiptoed down in pitch. "With the mysterious unknown woman on the bridge, we are looking for the remains of 23 people. Any questions before we go?"

Mandy's voice was far brighter as she lifted a mug from the table. "Just one! What is the secret of this amazing coffee?"

There were some chuckles in response.

Jedra was the one who spoke up. "That would be hidden in the brain of the now captain, but once Ver-Tark, Erin, who drove her cooking staff to jitters with her endless forays into the galley to cook. I remember many days on patrol where the day duty crew would be awakened to find that she had cooked for all of us. And her coffee, well, that is one of the Stream's most sought-after secrets."

"I have always found cooking relaxing, but if you call me Captain Cook, or the Cooking Captain, I may be forced to retaliate." Erin was smiling but put on a threatening leer. "I don't think that Captain *Marcus* was asking for questions about the food."

"Always a good idea to praise the chef," Marcus said, raising *his* mug. "And I appreciate Mandy lightening the mood a bit. Now, remember, even with the repairs Alystra has done to the ship, we have no environment yet, no heat, no air. We are entering the cold of space. Also, without power, field gravity will not exist, so turn on your boots to detect and connect to field panels." He turned and winked at Erin, who scowled back. She had wanted to give a similar pep talk.

Marcus turned to Bendahrin. "Too bad we don't have our ol' buddy Chesleth Preller here with his team of salvors to help us." Marcus grinned.

Bendahrin pretended to scowl back. Marcus seemed to be on a roll.

Prescott and Mandy were ready to go. Their helmets deployed and lights came on. Mandy waved to Bendahrin and they disappeared.

Bendahrin noticed that they were holding hands. Good technique, according to Erin. It allows one person to manage the jump through the suit contact, while the other focuses on weapons. Not that anyone was likely to need weapons on *Ascension*.

Marcus and Erin left next without any pretense of making suit contact, although they were looking at each other and both nodded and disappeared.

Alystra wasn't wearing combat fatigues, although she had a headset and boom mic for communication with a camera and light on a headband. When asked why she was not wearing fatigues, she had made a vague statement about something she and Mandy had discussed, and she claimed she wanted the challenge. She waited for Jedra to go and then followed him.

"I see all images." Bendahrin mentioned, as six different views appeared faintly in his visor. He was still new to the use of technology as clothing and was therefore both fascinated and bewildered by the multiple moving images that were visible on his display. By default, they were dim so he could see through the helmet glass. However, the suit tracked his eyes and thoughts so that when he focused on a specific image, it was enlarged and brighter. He quickly learned that looking away, or thinking away, restored the multiple view or enlarged another image.

As he watched the searchers, Bendahrin was reminded of his own experiences exploring ancient tombs and ruins. He recognized the slower pace and hushed voices that reverence or trepidation enforced upon people exploring the unknown and unexpected. Each door concealed mysteries, each turn revealed something hidden. Despite the novel experience with the suit technology, he found the scenes he was observing oppressive. Hallways disappeared into distant grayness from the light from the searcher's helmets, open doors were dark holes, and closed doors had a sense of sudden foreboding. He shuddered.

He jumped when Mandy's voice cut through the silence. "Nothing in the first two rooms," Bendahrin could see that she was looking into a closet with clothes. "Crew quarters. It looks like most of the soft materials are intact." She turned and the view from her camera swept across an ancient desk, chair and bed. Simple quarters in a faded tableau.

The views from the cameras continued their quiet display of

the ongoing investigation. Bendahrin scanned the blueprints on the table before him. *How many rooms do we need to search?*

"Contact." Erin's voice. "We just found our first bodies, two. They're mummies or petrified, space frozen." Bendahrin could see one corpse was under a massive console and the other was somehow caught to the top of the same console where it floated. "We are in the computer room."

Bendahrin made notes on the diagram to reflect the location of the first two corpses. The searchers moved on.

More doors. More rooms. More silence.

"Nothing but empty rooms here," Prescott said.

Suddenly Mandy giggled, and Prescott whispered, "Stop it."

"Nothing here either. These are all quarters for the command staff." Jedra's voice seemed thin. His already taciturn nature was unable to maintain much enthusiasm in exploring *Ascension* for dead bodies.

Nevertheless, Bendahrin noticed that the searchers were moving less slowly and talking more. Now that the first bodies had been found, the mystery and fear had been removed and the sense of new purpose was born, a desire to get the arduous job done.

"Here's another." Marcus's voice cut through. "This looks like the communications room." Another mummy against the front wall of the room, under the console.

Suddenly Mandy laughed. The image from Prescott's camera showed Mandy running out of the room.

Bendahrin responded, "Okay, that's three." *Twenty to go.*

"All of the crew quarters on the port side are empty," Alystra said. "As expected, moving forward."

A minute passed. "Same here, the rest of the command quarters on this side are empty as well," Erin said shortly. "It will be interesting to see how many of the furnishings and clothing are still intact. We could outfit a museum here."

Bendahrin wondered if Erin was still having thoughts of the value of what they had found. A life of mercenary thoughts could become a profound enslavement. Then he wondered, *And what obsessions do I serve?*

"Oopf," Prescott said. From his camera Bendahrin saw that he had just entered another one of the crew's quarters and Mandy had clobbered him with a six-hundred-fifty-year-old pillow. "Mandy!"

He hustled over to her and the views from their cameras were confused and bounced around. There was the sound of a scuffle and laughter and giggling.

Marcus chuckled, too. "It seems like the cousins are enjoying the search. I imagine they are reliving some encounter from their childhood."

Bendahrin imagined Alystra and Erin rolling their eyes.

The search progressed room after empty room. Progress was slightly slower for Prescott and Mandy who had the added distraction of ongoing combat. Even so, at about the same time, the other search teams reached the end of their halls. Bendahrin saw four views of the two large hatches to the bridge and engineering. "These hatches require power to open. Do we try to force them or make a blind jump to the other side?" Marcus asked.

"I've got this!" Alystra said.

Bendahrin had multiple images of the hatches sliding open.

Meanwhile Prescott had found another pillow, which he promptly used on Mandy. The images from their cameras showed scenes of a fierce and fluffy battle, but in silence. They had cut their mics, or maybe Erin had.

"Oh, no," Marcus said. Bendahrin saw that the scenes from the bridge and engineering were horrid. With no gravity to hold them in place, mummified corpses were floating in these larger rooms. On the bridge, two of the corpses were locked together as if in an embrace, slowly spinning in a gruesome mockery of an eternal dance.

"We have seven more in the engine room." Erin sounded choked.

"Nine here, but something is . . ." Alystra began, her voice suddenly commanding. "Everyone back to *Lentoris*! We have a *survivor*. Jedra, can you transport her? To the medical room."

Bendahrin watched as, one by one, the images blinked from various locations on *Ascension* to the small medical room on *Lentoris*. He watched Jedra's view which drew close as he bent down to pick up the survivor, a woman who looked as though she were merely sleeping. Bendahrin moved quickly from the starboard lounge back along the corridor and he entered the crowded room.

Jedra placed the survivor's body on the examination table. The survivor was surrounded by a faint blue and yellow glow. He immediately stood and addressed the group. "This is unbelievable, but I know who this is."

Prescott jumped in. "Doctor Talia Themblen."

Jedra nodded.

Bendahrin moved in close, his eyes wide.

Alystra motioned to Mandy. "Come here and see, probe the spell. Bendahrin, you stay. Everyone else clear the room."

Mandy chucked the pillow she was holding at Prescott as he exited and turned to gaze at the woman. After a moment she said, "I see the web, threads of magic. Weird, it's like they are alive and growing, do you want me to . . . ?"

Alystra shook her head. "This woman has been locked in this spell for more than six centuries. She might have been subjected to stray magical currents, so this could be tricky. I will remove the spell and also kill off any viruses or diseases she is carrying. Stand on the other side of the bed, you will know when to help." Then she held up her hand, a glass of water appeared. "Always remember water, otherwise . . ." she trailed off. "Headaches or worse." She handed the water to Bendahrin. "This will be kinda sloppy. Breaking through starts with careful spell work, then it devolves into brute force."

Alystra leaned over the woman and placed her hand on the blue glow. After a few moments, she was pushing her hand down into the glow, until she was touching the woman inside. Upon being touched the woman started to move slightly. Alystra immediately reached with her other hand and started pulling the hole open. She looked up quickly at Mandy, who also thrust her hands in, and they both pulled and tore at the blue glow, until it fell apart and disappeared, exploding gently outward with a windy sigh which dispersed through the room leaving a smell akin to lavender and turpentine.

Once freed, the woman sat upright and screamed. She kicked out with her feet frantically, sliding herself toward the top of the examination table as she looked around the room in panic. Alystra jumped back, but Mandy immediately moved close to her, embracing her, and Mandy started singing.

The words, if they were words, were lost to all but Alystra, who immediately disappeared from the room with a ripping pop, leaving behind a smell of burned leaves and smashed maggots.

Mandy's melody was lilting and soft, but as she sang, a warmth spread out from her, whirling around and filling the room, leaving no particular smell, though if it had, everyone effected would have claimed it had been delicious.

As she sang, Talia relaxed, and the terror passed. Her frantic movements slowed, and she calmed. Eventually, she closed her eyes and the pace of her breathing slowed to a normal rate.

Mandy stopped singing, and she spoke softly to Talia who nodded gently. Mandy released her.

Talia looked around the room, eyes stopping on each unfamiliar face.

Alystra returned silently, thankfully releasing no new smells.

Bendahrin moved closer and said, "Welcome Dr. Themblen, to *Lentoris*. Before you start asking your questions, I suggest, from painful personal experience, that you take a drink of water." She took the glass.

"All of it," he added, nodding.

Mandy moved back. Bendahrin continued, "My name is Bendahrin, and Mandy sang for you. I suggest that you need to prepare yourself for some surprises. Although Mandy seems to have calmed us all." He looked around at the others, who had now opened the door but still stood in the hall peering through. "There is probably no good place to start, but perhaps one quick question: what do you remember?"

"I . . . just a moment ago, I was on the bridge of module nineteen, preparing for the first full engine test. Telemetry was nominal, every reading within expected parameters. We had a go ahead, so we engaged the new eight-six-zero-zero drive. I was monitoring at the time because my systems," she paused, "None of you are cleared for what I was doing. We engaged, there was a lurch, or bang, and . . ." She paused. "I remember time, passing time, but no change. Like my mind was stopped in a long moment that never changed." She looked around at the strangers. "Who are you? Where is the ship?"

Bendahrin pointed past her, toward the window.

She turned and gazed at *Ascension* through the force-field glass for a moment, then turned back, her eyes narrow. "I don't understand. That's Nineteen, but how is it black? Where is the rest of the crew? Why am I here? What happened?"

Alystra spoke. "When you were on the bridge, was there someone there with you? Perhaps behind you." Bendahrin thought that was a stoutly leading question.

"Oh, yes." She shook her head. "Director Stries insisted, emphatic. He had that tall, dreary woman follow me everywhere. She wouldn't even leave when I dressed! What is happening? Where are we? How did I get here?" Then she slapped her hand on her knee. "This is impossible, just answer my questions!"

Bendahrin raised his hands and bowed his head slightly. "I am sorry. This is distressing." He took a slow breath. "Dr. Themblen, there was an accident. As I understand it, the controller on the *Ascen* . . . on your ship's proximity drive failed in some way—we will be looking into that most carefully, I hope—something about the singularities being forced too close. The *Ascension* ended up traveling . . . what was it?"

Alystra took over the narrative. "The *Ascension* blasted away from the space near Prevaria and covered one thousand seven hundred light years in the first three seconds. We assume that the crew died instantly, but the woman following you around must have been a mage who cocooned you in magical stasis, so you survived. That is a guess since the mage didn't survive, or at least we didn't find her alive on the ship to greet us, but we found *you* in stasis. The last element of the story is what will be the most difficult. The *Ascension* accident took place over six-hundred-fifty-years ago."

"Six-hundred-fifty-four to be exact," Marcus added. "Some of us have families that have been searching for your ship, *Ascension*, ever since the accident. It has been my single occupation the last half of my adult life."

Talia sat for a full minute, unmoving. As these scant details had been relayed to her, she had focused on each speaker intensely, her expression hovering between astonishment and fierce concentration. The others watched her with sympathy.

Far too soon for the circumstance, Alystra broke the quiet, "Dr. Themblen, I imagine that this is overwhelming, but we have work to do; we need to get the *Ascension* working again. We will leave you with Bendahrin." She started to leave the room but stopped and turned back. "Doctor. You will need to reconsider your perspective on what we are cleared for. We are repairing the ship and you can be part of that effort. Module nineteen needs to be ready for war. Your expertise would be welcome." She departed; the others followed.

Bendahrin turned. "I am sorry that you have been thrown into this disconcerting predicament."

Talia scowled at him, "Why are you sorry? You had nothing to do with what happened."

Bendahrin opened his mouth to speak and paused. "Umm . . . I am not apologizing; I am expressing my sympathy to you for being shunted through hundreds of years magically. You were clearly upset."

Talia pursed her lips. "From what your colleague indicated; the rest of the crew is dead. I will build a new foundation with the mindset that I was the fortunate one." Suddenly she laughed. "What an irony!" She turned and got down from the examination table, laughing again. "Six centuries on magical hold, and I feel as though no time has passed at all! I would expect to be stiff and unsteady."

"Magic has some drawbacks, but often it makes the unexpected normative. Even so, I am not sure how that is ironic."

"No!" she snapped at him. "The irony is that Director Stries put out the effort, very annoying and costly effort, to keep me alive and protect his investment. And here I am, hundreds of years away from his clutches."

Bendahrin spoke slowly, "Not to be indelicate, but your use of 'investment' seems to imply . . ."

Talia's hands snapped up and her left hand gripped Bendahrin's shoulder. With her right hand she pointed at his face. "Bendahrin is your name, correct? Let's be clear. I am a scientist *and* a mathematician. I do *not* imply; I state facts, clearly and precisely."

Bendahrin smiled. He had met with numerous serious academics like this in the past. He wasn't sure whether she was truly as precise as she hoped, or if she was hiding some insecurities behind bravado. Nevertheless, since he was on firm ground, he decided to unbalance her some. "I understand, Dr. Themblen. Allow me to express my sincerest apologies." He paused and raised his left hand, gently pushing her finger down and away from his face. "On Palestre, my academic rank, so to speak, is *Frethant* which is similar to your honorific. "My disciplines," and he stretched the "s" in disciplines to emphasize the plurality, "are Galactic Archaeology, F.L, Artifact Dating, Integrity, and Preservation, F.R.L, and Archaeolinguistics, F.L. In the midst of all those long titles full of capital letters is a wealth of languages to draw upon from which I can assure you that your use of the word, 'clutches' is a vivid metaphor, but perhaps not as clear and precise as you would wish." He held his smile at length.

Talia glanced down and her shoulders dropped from their previous tense height. A slow smile appeared on her face as she looked back at Bendahrin with a mild nod. "It seems that you see me clearly. In that case it would be foolhardy to engage you on my eminently valid excuse that a metaphor is often clearer than a page full of details. I will therefore claim the alternative excuse that I just spent centuries under a spell from which I am suffering aftereffects." She loosened her grip on Bendahrin's shoulder and she ran her hand gently down his arm.

Bendahrin released her other hand. "I would love to hear about this investment that you are. But first, I will show you the ship, and find you some food." He exited the medical examination room.

Talia nodded slightly and followed him into the hall.

–|–

The rest of that day, the three teams scoured *Ascension* until they had seen everything in cursory form. They found the final three of the deceased crew in the massive front lounge beneath the bridge. No evidence could be found of the mage who had saved or trapped Talia. They concluded that she had probably done her job regarding Talia and had escaped to live out her life in unknown obscurity. Nobody felt any desire to try to unravel that mystery.

Alystra conjured caskets of ornate wood with steel insides into which they placed the twenty-one people who had died.

Jedra and Mandy welded the inner boxes shut, maintaining the vacuum inside. Although they needed to keep their discovery of *Ascension* a secret, they knew the secret wouldn't last, and eventually the remains would be returned to their descendants. Until that time they would be hidden somewhere on Prevaria under the Scurven's protection.

Once the remains of the previous crew were carefully stored, Alystra conjured a *Targeshobe* and installed it on *Ascension* and they began to transfer supplies in preparation for the task of repairing and rebuilding the derelict ship.

–|–

Eighteen days of work later, Jedra woke slowly to hear the sound of chimes ringing through *Ascension*. He sat up, wondering at the sound in a partial, sleepy way, but his training took over quickly and he shook himself to alertness; nothing on a ship in space was accidental. He dressed quickly and stepped out into the hall. He had chosen quarters on deck four along with the rest. He started walking toward the sound that was coming from up the hall toward the bridge.

As he passed a door on his left, it opened, and Marcus stepped out. "This is new."

Jedra nodded and they continued together.

They discovered that the sound was coming from the bridge. When they entered, they saw that the force field glass was displaying a view of the front lounge in *Lentoris*.

Alystra was on the viewscreen looking uncharacteristically patient. "So, the chimes generate a response in about a minute," she said tersely.

"Okay. So, this looks different from standard ship-to-ship communication," Jedra said. He yawned and rubbed his eyes as he sat at the navigation console.

Marcus took a seat in the captain's chair.

"Yes, I installed this last night while you were sleeping. Instead of relying on tech, this is a direct magical link between the ships through the *Targeshobes*. It is then integrated into the forcefield glass on both bridges, in the computer rooms, and in the communication room on the *Ascension*. The communication works in the same way as a tech viewer only better. This system is thought activated at magical distances."

At about this time, Erin walked in and stood next to Marcus. She was carrying a pot of coffee and a tray of mugs. Erin had been up for a while but had been on the deck below when she heard the chimes.

"I chose the chimes because they are distinct from any other sound on a ship. If we want to, we can create unique tones for different people or situations. But for now, an example, Jedra, if you could think, just think, 'Urgent! Assistance required.'"

Jedra nodded. What followed was an awful blaring klaxon.

"Perfect," she said, and the noise stopped. "For emergencies, this thought trigger will work *anywhere* on either ship. It will set off the alarm on both ships. Notice that Jedra's name and location were displayed on the screen as the initiator of the alert. It isn't worth reviewing at this moment, but the magical interface has countless other useful features and applications."

In response to the klaxon alert, it was mere moments before everyone on both ships were assembled. Mandy, Bendahrin and Alystra in the front lounge on *Lentoris*, and Marcus, Prescott, Talia, Jedra, and Erin on the bridge on *Ascension*.

Bendahrin was, as usual, the last to arrive, just as Prescott was finishing his update. For the duration of their efforts to repair and refit the *Ascension* they had started each day with a short meeting to review the status of the work and confirm plans and next steps. Bendahrin had found these meetings tedious since he was not technically competent enough to join the discussions or much of the work. As a result, he never hurried to these meetings. He took a seat near Alystra and observed the screen lazily, noticing how vivid the image of the *Ascension's* bridge was, perhaps too vivid. He closed his eyes for a few seconds and listened. His hearing, too, seemed overly acute. He opened his eyes again and looked at the screen, thinking that Alystra must have done something magical to enhance the connection. Despite how bright and clear everything seemed, he only paid half attention as Prescott finished speaking, hearing only the words, "complete" and "success." Jedra and Marcus nodded. When they agreed, the words, "Every test" seemed to blink in his mind, but he shook his head slightly to focus on what Erin said next.

"We have followed and completed every procedure and test on Dr. Themblen's list. The *Ascension* is set to go. And, thanks to the special blue crate supplies from Alex Scurven, combat ready."

Bendahrin heard "ready," and his mind seemed suddenly fuzzy *and* painfully alert. He sensed a distant but approaching triumph. The view screen suddenly went off, revealing the view of space through the force-field glass, *Ascension* in full view. With a snap, he was thrown back in his chair, but his mind became clear. He looked at Alystra who was suddenly alert. She had summoned Brahtenla.

The image of *Ascension's* bridge re-appeared. Bendahrin gasped and stood slowly. A dozen B'Tark pirates were standing with weapons drawn, most aimed in the general direction of Bendahrin's friends, who were kneeling. Each was accompanied by a pirate who held one hand on the side of the head of each kneeling captive. Bendahrin scowled as he recognized Rish, the mage from his captivity with the B'Tark, standing behind the captain's chair, where another man sat.

"Surprise!" Rish said, and his face broke into an evil grin.

24

The figure in the chair looked over to Rish then back toward the front. "Well, look at this." His voice was as uncaring as his eyes were cruel. A scar stretched from above his left eye down through the center of his lips and chin. This old injury added a minor rasping hiss to his voice which made him come across as even more sinister. Bendahrin wondered if this man had smiled in years. Despite the general intensity of his countenance, his pale blue eyes seemed strangely indifferent as he examined the fingernails of his left hand. He was sitting sideways in the chair with his left leg over the chair's arm, his foot bouncing slightly. He glanced up, "You are Alystra, I am told. I am Tark Theman Drell."

Alystra started to move, and the man continued, "Listen, sis. Before you do anything rash, I want to pass on what Rish here says." He pointed his thumb over his shoulder at the mage behind him. "Rish, Rash. Get it? Yah! Rish says that the spell is *treh'quar* or something like that. He described it as a kind of 'dead man's switch.' If my people remove their hands from your friends, they die . . ." he paused, the barest hint of a cold grimace on his lips, "your friends die, that is."

Alystra opened her mouth slightly, then closed it, she nodded slightly and lowered Brahtenla to her side, leaning on it like a cane. "Yes, I am Alystra." Bendahrin noticed that she was oddly calm rather than combative. "And if Rish is saying so many useful things to you, I assume he also told you some specific things that should matter to you right now."

Drell nodded, looking back at his hand. "Well, hell, girlie, Rish says all kinds of things. Mages! Blah, blah, blah. And it looks like you have things to say to me, too." He looked up at her with bland eyes, turning his head only slightly. "Go on, mage. Speak your mind."

Alystra opened her mouth as if to respond but stopped. She raised her head, looking up in thought. "No," she said, looking back at the man. "Nothing I say is going to change what you do. Can I have any assurances of my friends' safety?"

Drell barked a short coughing laugh. "Ha! Rish did tell me at least one 'specific' thing about you, as you might call it. You don't have friends, you somehow can't have friends, and then, blah, blah, blah—magic nonsense. I won't bore you. There will be no negotiations, no talk, no discussion of demands. I refuse to provide any insights into our plans." He paused for a moment. "No, there is one little threat that I have planned, for your delight. Rish is particularly attuned to all of us, and if you, oh, cast any spells, try to enter our minds, or play any magical tricks, he gives the order, and bye, bye, all five." It seemed to Bendahrin that Alystra nodded slightly.

Bendahrin's innocence overcame his judgment, and he said in wonder, "I spent months with Rish, he demonstrated no extraordinary magical power whatsoever."

"Ah! Ha ha." Drell barked his laugh twice. "Fell for that, did ya? Ol' Rish here, master of befuddlement, I hear. Auras, or some such. Very tough to see through his deceptions. His fake stutter is particularly disarming. And I mean, literally disarming. His stutter is a confusion spell." He scratched his head. "I admit it's strange, when he jumps into idiot mode, it even confuses us. No, I assure you that Rish is sufficiently powerful for this situation."

Bendahrin was about to counter by saying, "I wouldn't count on that," when Drell laughed, almost pleasantly. "Surely you don't think we needed two months to prepare for a Presentation. All those meetings in your cell? Rish was penetrating your defenses, slipping his weave of control between the, what did you call it, Rish? Formidable magical protection around you. It took time, but it was worth it. We have been looking through your eyes and hearing through your ears for months. How do you think we found you?"

Then Alystra laughed, and Bendahrin felt fear because her laugh was soothing and warm, at least to him it was. "Drell, you don't need to reveal any of your plans; they are clear. Petty pirates.

You want my ship, and you have taken hostages. Did Velven send you?"

Drell cocked his head in thought. "You see, darling, there is no doubt that Velven doesn't like you very much. Even mountains of riches are an insult to him. But hell, we all knew a good thing when we saw it, and Rish thought he could pull it off. Certainly worth the effort, and the prize." He turned to glance at Erin and Jedra. His voice turned colder, if possible. "And imagine our surprise to find Erin, the ex-Ver-Tark, alive and well. That'll be an enjoyable bit of treason to bring to Velven when we return."

As this discussion proceeded, Bendahrin looked at the five captives.

Jedra and Erin were concentrating and focused, like athletes waiting for the start of a competition.

Talia looked bored, which Bendahrin found perplexing.

Marcus was tense, and Prescott was trembling with fear.

Alystra lifted Bratenla and pointed it at the screen. "There can be but one alternative, now."

Drell sat up for the first time, facing forward. "Hell, missie, I don't need alternatives. All this talk was merely a distraction until we confirmed your repairs. Ha! I have the faster ship." He nodded to another pirate at the navigation console. "And you are gonna be busy."

At this the screen went off for a second time and Bendahrin, Alystra, and Mandy gazed for an instant at *Ascension* visible through the force-field glass. For a moment nothing happened. Then, in that odd silence that the vacuum of space affords, the ship disappeared in an instant as it transitioned to motion at hundreds of times the speed of light.

Immediately, another ship appeared where *Ascension* had been, bow pointing directly at *Lentoris*, but Alystra shouted, "Five ships!" There was a lurch and an explosion of sound as *Lentoris* was battered from many sides.

Bendahrin dropped to the floor in time to see the forcefield glass in front of him glow for an instant then it exploded outward. The air escaping through the gaping hole blasted the three of them into space along with the furniture in the forward lounge.

Bendahrin immediately felt himself surrounded by the vicious cold of space. As he tumbled, he glimpsed the foggy shape of *Lentoris*, surrounded by expanding debris from multiple holes blasted in the hull, enemy ships to the left, above, below, and angled behind.

Mandy was flailing near him, but she quickly put up the helmet for her combat fatigues.

Then, just as suddenly, he was back on *Lentoris*, sitting near the back of the front lounge against the wall.

Mandy was seated next to him, but Alystra was standing, again, just in front of them, facing toward them. Bendahrin looked up to see her face, determined with concentration, her eyes holes of blackness. She held her sword before her, and she was drawing upon the power stored within it, the transfer of dark rage was a blistering cold in his eyes.

A moment later, Bendahrin felt, or felt he saw, five massive streams of blackness shoot out from Alystra. One was headed at the ship that Bendahrin could see through the hole in the front of the ship, and the others headed off in different directions. In his mind, Bendahrin imagined the other ships as he had seen them, surrounding *Lentoris* in the distance.

In that same instant, Mandy jumped and shouted, and the blackness stopped as though the flow of blackness had hit an invisible, semi-spherical wall. It drew back in and coalesced around her.

Alystra shouted, "Mandy! No!"

Mandy instantly fell to the floor and Bendahrin started to move toward her, not sure what to do. She had curled into a fetal position, trembling violently in the center of a swirling black cloud. He stopped as if held back by a hidden compulsion. Mandy was wrestling with the writhing mass of black turmoil. Her eyes were closed, and her jaw was clenched. She struggled to get her knees beneath her, seeking to cover the blackness with her body. Instead, she jerked and screamed in an echoing, smitten voice, her arms and legs suddenly flung wide as though the black mass had exploded from her body.

Indeed, Bendahrin felt, or felt he saw, that the five streams had become a turmoil of black raging motion that shot out from her along the paths Alystra had originally sent them.

Mandy was thrown against the ceiling of the lounge, her body surrounded by an eerie orange glow that seemed to bounce her from the ceiling, diminishing the impact. She tumbled to the floor, where she lay moaning.

Bendahrin was also thrown back from the explosion to skid along the floor to impact the wall. He noticed that he, too, was surrounded by an orange glow, and hitting the wall didn't hurt as much as he had expected. He turned quickly and gazed through the hole at the front of the lounge to see the black torrent smash against the attacking ship, shredding and blasting it away into the distance in a ball of gasses, flame, and flying debris.

Bendahrin turned from the scene of distant destruction and crawled to assist Mandy, who was speaking softly to Alystra who had moved and knelt next to her. "I'm sorry, Alystra, I couldn't contain it."

"I didn't ask you to. We will talk. Now, you must heal yourself, then guard the ship."

She stood and shouted, "Kel!"

Kel Purim appeared and started his normal oily subservience. "Oh yes, you called . . ."

"Not now!" Alystra shouted. "Kel, five ships. Search for survivors. Secure them here."

"Oh yes, five beautiful . . ."

"Go!" Kel Purim disappeared.

Alystra turned to look at Bendahrin, and immediately he found himself floating in space, but knew that he was again in the Strentrian bubble. He heard Alystra's urgent thoughts. *"That ship is fast!"* Next, he sensed a powerful pulse that rippled away in a growing sphere. *I've already broken the spell, treh'quar, but that only releases them.* In an instant he sensed when Alystra found *Ascension*. Then he was moving through the stars at a terrible speed. He saw *Ascension* rushing at him and then he was standing on the bridge.

The battle lines had been drawn, but the combatants, indeed everything in the room, were frozen in place. Talia was hiding behind a console to the right of the bridge, near Jedra, who had somehow acquired a weapon, and Erin was by his side. She was shooting parts of her fatigues as sharp projectiles, one of which had just left her upper arm and was suspended in the air a few feet away, aimed at one of the assailants.

Six armed pirates were behind other consoles on the opposite side of the bridge, two of them frozen at the perfect moment so that the blasts from their weapons were blazing in bright white shafts of phosphorescent plasma.

Four other pirates were prostrate on the floor around the bridge.

In the middle of the bridge, Marcus was on hands and knees, facing toward Erin, clearly in motion, but motionless in the frozen moment.

Prescott was on the floor, flat on his back.

Rish and Drell were at the front of the bridge. Rish had raised a shield so that the two were hazy and dim behind it.

As always, Bendahrin watched Alystra to see how she would react. At first, she looked around the room slowly, as if she didn't already know exactly what she would see. She turned slowly to Bendahrin. "Why am I here?"

Bendahrin's eyes went wide. He felt this was an odd time to discuss the nature of existence. "I . . . umm. What do you mean?"

"A ship? Actually, two ships. A team? Why?" As she talked, she walked toward the pirates. Reaching into one gun blast, she grabbed a nasty looking projectile and moved to the other firing pirate where she did the same. "I'm a danger to everyone," she said, turning to walk to Erin. She grabbed the projectile that Erin had just released. "But that is a general danger, one that I can control or work around." She took a few more steps back toward Bendahrin and paused to lean against another console facing partially away from him. She shook her head.

"Look at this." She pointed with open palms to the room in general, then pointed specifically. "Prescott is dead. Mandy has been wounded, and although she will be okay, in time. She destroyed five ships full of pirates, which is bound to darken her heart. Killing people always carries that cost." She paused and turned to face him. "But me, I am now *putting* people in danger. The risk is no longer just mine, but I need to somehow weigh this beyond the confines of my malice."

Bendahrin, like so many, sought to offer a reasonable explanation. "You are asking good questions. It seems appropriate that you care, so if the cause is just then . . ." Alystra interrupted with a snarl.

"Just?" She snorted and looked up sharply at the six pirates. A shimmer of blinding blackness surrounded them like a raging halo and then, in an instant, they were gone, along with the four on the floor. "How can I be just?" she murmured. "Justice demands that a person weigh merits in a balance under the pervading light of a firm principle that rightly divides between right and wrong." She turned to face him fiercely. "And care? I can't care. If I cared for any of these, even for an instant, even you, the Issachon would lash out as you just saw." She leaned back against the console that Talia was crouching behind.

Bendahrin trembled in fear, but spoke nonetheless, "And yet, against your nature, you *have* asked the proper question. And allow me to emphasize that I think you know the correct answer as well, even if you can't speak the words. Apart from me, everyone here is moving under the onus of their own choices. The vision, as far as we can tell, stands in solid affirmation that this team, your team, is not only right, but maybe inevitable, and probably imperative. Whether you care or not, you can't question your purposes, your destiny, or our place in it. No one expects you to coddle us, even if we have every reason to hope for your protection."

Alystra looked at him for a moment, her eyes narrowed. "It is ironic that you put it in those terms. She pushed off from the console and walked to Prescott's body, where she knelt. Her face was expressionless, and her voice carried only the barest hint of sympathy, "Here lies the only one who refused my protection and sought to get away. Perhaps the Issachon moves in mysterious ways to destroy those who would escape?" She stood and walked to face Talia, Erin, and Jedra. She stood and turned to looked at Marcus. "I will release these."

There was an immediate flurry of motion. Jedra fired, but he was aiming to Alystra's left. His head snapped to see Alystra and he quickly pointed his weapon to the floor. Erin launched another projectile that Alystra caught with a snapping motion of her hand inches before her chest, and Marcus scurried across the floor until he realized that the sounds of combat had ceased.

He looked around quickly then turned then and crawled to where Prescott lay, seizing the younger man's arm and pulling his body toward him. He began sobbing. He fell to a sitting position and rocked slowly.

Erin approached Alystra and Bendahrin. "You probably know, but it was only twenty, thirty seconds ago." She shook her head. "Maybe a little more. The ship was moving, Rish and Drell were talking quietly when suddenly Rish went stiff and shouted something I didn't understand. Then he turned fiercely toward us where we were, standing at the back of the ship. Nothing happened. I guess you broke his spell?" Alystra nodded and Erin continued. "I felt it go, and attacked instantly, Jedra and Talia, too. She had a wicked looking knife hidden somewhere that she used immediately, stabbing one mage and throwing it into the eye of another across the room. That's a surprise from our distinguished doctor."

Alystra turned to Talia, who smiled grimly. Erin continued. "So, the mages holding us died quickly, I guess they weren't expecting a physical attack. Marcus, meanwhile, had pushed off the mage holding him and rolled toward us. Prescott just stood there, and the mage looked me in the eyes, mocking, and stabbed him in the neck with a dagger. I killed him an instant later with a projectile from my suit."

Alystra gazed around the familiar room. "I need you and Jedra to get this ship back to *Lentoris*." She grabbed Bendahrin and steered him gently to move in the direction of Marcus.

Bendahrin's mouth felt dry, and the room seemed filled with a painful buzzing tension. He looked at Alystra for guidance, but she had stayed back a few yards. He knelt quietly near Marcus and spoke softly, "Marcus, I am so sorry. This is a horrible and unexpected turn of events."

Marcus didn't speak or move, the only sound from him was his breathing. He continued to rock slowly for minutes, then he moved his leg and lowered Prescott's head so it rested on his thigh where he could look at Prescott's face. Bendahrin reached out and put his hand on Marcus' shoulder. Marcus took a deep breath, his left hand clenching and unclenching into a fist that trembled.

He looked up to Bendahrin for a moment then back at Prescott. "My . . . sister is going to be so very angry . . ." he began, but stopped, closing his eyes.

Alystra spoke softly but coldly, "We have those responsible before us. We can pass judgment and exact punishment. May I suggest first that you allow me to summon a casket for Prescott? And, if you would feel so disposed, we can honor him with a permanent place on the bridge. His contribution toward creating the complex computer system for the *Ascension* will always be the ship's heart."

Marcus looked at Alystra and his eyes narrowed. He gazed at her, unmoving, as he appraised her, probably correctly for the first time. "In the beginning I doubted the claims of evil against you. Now

I see that death follows you, surrounds you, and walks with you, arm-in-arm. Although his death is not on your head, is it?" He laid Prescott's head gently on the floor, standing to face her. "Yes, I'd like him off the floor at the least. If you get a casket to cradle his form until we reach home, my sister and her family will decide about your offer." He turned to face Drell and Rish who were still unmoving. "I think I have some ideas about a proper form of justice."

Alystra looked up, muttering, "I wish Mandy were here to mitigate. But I have an idea that will honor our fallen computer genius." The room dimmed and a hint of cold air swept through the bridge causing all who felt it to shudder. The next moment a casket appeared upon a low table that appeared at the same time, both at the far back of the bridge. It was shaped like any casket, but it was made of a polished silvery metal. The metal glowed with a colorful iridescence, patterns of shape, color, words, and images moving over the surface.

Alystra spoke. "In honor to Prescott, this casket is punctuated with trillions of microscopic lights that can create endless patterns and images that will never duplicate the same pattern until the end of time as we know it, a computational feat in keeping with his skills and passion for the science."

Marcus moved to lift Prescott, but Alystra intervened. "A moment." She touched the side of his neck where he had been stabbed and when she removed her hand, the wound was gone, and all the blood had vanished. She stepped back and gestured to the rest. "Please help to lift him."

Talia and Bendahrin moved forward to help Marcus and they lifted Prescott carefully into the casket, and then stepped back. Marcus stood with his hand on the opened lid. He didn't look up as he spoke. "I never served on the same ship with Prescott, we, uh, rarely spent time. Mandy . . ." He cleared his throat. "He and Mandy were, they were very close growing up and they served together for two years with Mandy's father." He hit his fist gently on the edge of the casket and turned to face toward the others. "This is going to hit her hard. And it will hang a dark shroud over the victory of finding *Ascension*. This ship," he looked around the bridge, "comes at a very high cost." He took a few steps toward Drell and Rish, his face hardened as he gritted his teeth. "Let's talk about justice."

Jedra and Erin remained at the navigation console but looked to the front of the bridge.

The other four moved toward the front of the bridge and stood facing the two unmoving pirates.

Suddenly Alystra laughed and the room seemed to brighten. "This is the second time that I have caught two pirates on my ship." She turned for a moment to look back at Erin and Jedra. "This time, in contrast, my patience is spent for pirate ilk."

Bendahrin felt a passage of cold that wasn't carried on the air. The magic shield that Rish had raised disappeared, and the two pirates were released. Rish froze again, his eyes wide with terror.

Drell looked around the room dispassionately then sighed and spoke, "Ahh, hell. This is why you *never* build a plan around promises that mages make."

Alystra shook her head in disgust. "So, Rish came up with this absurd plan to steal my ship?"

Drell rolled his eyes. "Your other ship generated a lot of high-level interest, so there were many, many powerful Tarks involved." He shook his head. "The opportunity was euphoric. Priceless, magical artifacts, mysterious entities, and, of course, nobody thought that Erin had been able to kill you. So, we were suspicious. Even the most casual investigation of you led us to the conclusion that you pulled some mage trick to fake your death. Of course, we had no idea what you would do or how or when you would come back. We decided to see if we could penetrate your defenses on Bendahrin and see what we could exploit whenever you revealed yourself. Once we had him, we orchestrated to release him on the pretense that Rish wanted that mage trinket you gave him." He paused for a moment. "You can imagine our surprise when we discovered that Erin had turned, but that was nothing to learning that you had found the *Ascension* and were going to restore her; utterly priceless. But clearly our brilliant mages underestimated you by far."

"You don't seem to possess much respect for mages," Alystra noted, with the hint of a smile.

He shrugged. "Life in the Stream. Capture a ship, ransom the captives, sell the loot, raid a planet, mercenary work. Good solid certainty, and a return on the effort and risk. Magic, bah! Any plans that include magic always come with excuses and disclaimers and then turn to chaos."

Alystra snorted. "Then you should be pleased that I will help you to change your perspective about magic. Unlike other mages, with me there is no ambiguity, uncertainty, confusion, or even, ironically, chaos. Malice has such a way of maintaining a tight focus, especially when compared to greed." She clapped her hands. "You will *most* certainly pay for your attack on my ship and the death of my 'friend.' For even though Rish was correct to say that I don't have friends in the usual sense of the term, I understand loyalty and those who deserve to be avenged."

Rish, who boldly showed no sign of stuttering despite his quite evident fear said, "How did you, I mean, we had seventy mages on each of five ships. The containment was perfect! We followed the precise five-sided *tello-dorehn*. That is unstoppable!"

Bendahrin felt the violent mirth cascading from Alystra's laugh. "Seventy whole mages on each ship! Imagine!" Her lip curled in a snarl, and she spoke in measured disdain, pointing her finger toward his chest. "I . . . didn't . . . notice . . ." She said with contempt.

Bendahrin knew full well that she had counted them all carefully, but he said nothing.

Alystra turned her attention back to Drell. "Certainly, you must have felt some doubts about this venture?" Drell rolled his eyes and nodded. Alystra's eyes were grim. "You should have listened to those doubts. Underestimated? Was that the word you used? Ha!" She shook her head and Bendahrin sensed a mix of painful sadness and welcome hatred. He felt the familiar twist in his gut as he realized, again, how attuned he had become to her.

Alystra turned to Marcus. "We will be back to *Lentoris* soon. I want these two disposed of before we arrive so we can restore our focus. I have a simple plan for Rish."

Marcus frowned as he spoke and his voice was stern. "I have an idea for Tark Drell that might work. Can we contain him?"

Alystra shrugged. "I can make him sleep in stasis as long as you want, or I can just make a simple cage in the corner. I suppose I could convert one of the many crew cabins into a cell."

"Any of those would work. Although if we had him sleep in one of the crew cabins, we wouldn't need to put as much effort into his care while we travel to Prevaria, where he will face Scurven family justice."

"Sleep it is," Alystra cried, and Drell disappeared from the captain's chair. "I put him in a cabin on the lowest deck. Not that you need the space. And he will wake up with the worst headache he has ever had—because he deserves it," she added with malicious delight.

Then she turned to Rish, who had forced himself to stand up straight in an attempt at contempt or courage. "You have affronted me in many ways. Attacking Bendahrin was enough alone, but the death *of my friend* is also on you. And I have what you might consider a fitting punishment." Her voice contained no anger but dripped with fearful malice. She held up her hand, and a shiny duplicate of a Telterran trough totem appeared. "You're the *expert* here," she said to Rish, her own expression of superiority on her face, unassailable in the contempt it displayed. "But I did a little quick research when I was bored." She held the item up as if examining it. "The experts say that the merciful totem, used as a cage, was to be made of wood, porous enough for the, and allow me to quote an ancient to assuage your pride, porous enough for the 'residue of confinement to escape from the eternal presence of the mage thus contained.'"

She paused and looked at Rish, whose eyes began to move slowly about the room. "I am not really sure why that is the merciful option, but it seems to me that an apt punishment for you would be this fine totem." At this, she pulled off the lid and turned the bottom section upside-down so that the figurine inside fell out onto her hand. She handed the figurine to Bendahrin, who took it with multiple levels of horror. "This totem, for your comfort, has been made with the most non-porous steel, titanium, glass and gold in layers to provide the finest protection with *no* pores to allow for the escape of anything." She looked Rish in the eyes, "Who knows, maybe after a few years I might allow Bendahrin to convince me to release you in order to glean your insights into totem design."

At this, Rish's body fell to the floor, and Alystra restored the lid, where she ran her finger around the gap between the lower section and the lid, sealing it magically.

She turned to Bendahrin. "I can't believe you trusted him."

"What would cause me to think anyone could break through *your* protection?"

Alystra scowled at him suddenly and he caught his breath. But she relaxed and almost smiled. "As soon as I am bored again, I will tighten your protection, using the inspiration of steel, titanium, glass, and gold, in multiple layers!"

She turned toward the navigation console where Jedra and Erin stood, and Jedra spoke, anticipating Alystra's question. "We are about eight minutes out." He hesitated. "We didn't want to push the ship as hard as they did."

"Good enough! I will take Bendahrin and return to *Lentoris*. We will confer when you get there."

And in an instant, Bendahrin found himself standing near the back of the front lounge on *Lentoris*. The force-field glass at the front of the lounge still displayed an eight-foot hole, but even as he gazed out into the blackness of space through the opening, he could see that the *Targeshode* was quickly closing the hole.

Mandy was seated on a restored chair to the left of the lounge and she stood slowly and started toward Alystra, who glared at her and held out her hand to stop her. "I will talk to *you* in a minute," and she was engulfed in the misty semi-sphere of a Strentrian bubble.

Bendahrin moved quickly to Mandy and led her back to the chair where he directed her to sit again. He then pulled a chair close and asked her, with a slight hesitation in his voice, "How are you feeling?"

Mandy looked at the floor as if searching. Then her head jerked up and she smiled at Bendahrin brightly. "It was amazing! A lot of pain, truly painful, and I was seriously injured, but I asked, and *Pfrail*, that's magic, helped me and let me see exactly what I needed to do to control the pain and to heal myself. I could both feel and see exactly what I was doing when I put my bones back together. I was even able to close up wounds and rebuild little blood vessels and . . ."

Despite his astonishment, Bendahrin interrupted her. "I'm more concerned about destroying those ships."

Mandy flinched as if by painful reflex. "I tried desperately to stop Alystra's spell."

Bendahrin didn't respond at first, but instead, he patted the back of Mandy's hand, absently. Then he grabbed her hand, gently and said, "Yes. Yes, you did try." In his mind, however, he knew something was amiss.

They sat silently for a few minutes, then Alystra was back. She said, "I have checked excessively thoroughly for anyone else nearby." She nodded slowly. "By nearby, I mean dozens of light years. The pirates must have converged on us at enormous speeds, for their ships, but now, there is nothing alive out there. My pursuit of the *Ascension* will have caused a burst of magical noise, but so far nobody is investigating."

She paused to look at Mandy and Bendahrin, scowled at Bendahrin's supportive affection, then continued, "The *Ascension* will be here in moments so I will keep this simple." She looked directly at Mandy, and Bendahrin leaned back from her, releasing her hand. "*My* spell would have merely pushed those five ships back two-thousand light years, leaving them and their crews intact and unharmed."

Bendahrin's eyes went wide at the enormity of this revelation. He caught his breath and allowed Mandy the time to think and respond.

As expected, she put the pieces together quickly and her hand flew to her mouth. Almost instantly she dropped her hand and was about to speak when Alystra held up a hand. "I can't hear your confessions or remonstrances and I have no absolution for you. Nor can I help you with this dark burden. You will need to find solace with the others." She stepped back from Mandy. "However, I can give you a rule to follow." She paused, waiting for Mandy, who nodded. "I will tell you when I want you to contain the darkness. Otherwise, *you* are choosing the danger."

Bendahrin was surprised at the harsh tone Alystra took with Mandy. Normally she was far more tolerant and patient. He felt a sudden trembling absence of warmth as Mandy looked down, gazing at the floor, her hands clasped in her lap and her shoulders drooping. He reached out and placed his hand on her shoulder, but she didn't move.

Alystra walked from the room as the hole at the front of the ship disappeared and the ship was whole again. Bendahrin wondered if Alystra had upgraded the *Targeshobe*, the repairs to the ship seemed much quicker this time.

–|–

On *Ascension*, the mood was equally somber. Marcus was again standing with his hand on the edge of Prescott's casket, his head bowed in thought.

Talia, Erin, and Jedra were huddled around the navigator's console, talking quietly.

Talia broke away and approached Marcus. She hesitated for a moment until he looked up. "We have arrived back with *Lentoris*," she said simply, gesturing to the massive viewscreen at the front of the bridge where *Lentoris* appeared.

Marcus moved forward and sat in the captain's chair, mumbling, "Let's try the new communication system," and he thought, *call* Lentoris. Immediately the viewscreen showed the *tardeshode* room on *Lentoris*, and Alystra walked in moments later. She was soon followed by Bendahrin and Mandy. Marcus wondered why the communication had connected in the smaller room rather than the front lounge. Maybe he needed to be more specific.

Talia moved to stand behind Marcus, while Jedra and Erin remained at the navigation console. They were silent and somber, waiting for Alystra to speak.

"Kel!" she called, and the reddish, smoky figure appeared, hovering conspicuously near to Bendahrin, who flinched away, holding his nose. Alystra growled at him. "This is *not* the time for your usual antics."

"Yes, well, with you it is never time for my antics." Kel slowly turned away from her as if he hadn't heard her. She ignored his impudence.

"Deliver the prisoners to the other ship."

Three men and two women appeared at the back of *Ascension's* bridge. They appeared to be in a daze, although only one of them showed signs of injury and hasty care.

The four turned to look at them, and Alystra continued, "Marcus, I think that these can also be tried by your family, but perhaps Erin can interview them to see if . . ."

There was a loud thudding noise and a screech like the call of some excited animal.

Alystra stood up and shouted, "No!" They all heard a chattering sound that might have been words. "Are you nuts?" Alystra started to disappear looking upward, but then reappeared and flew against the wall as if she had been slapped aside by a giant hand. "No, you don't!" She ran from the room, and her shout diminished into the distance as she ran.

Mandy jumped up to follow her.

The chattering became a chant and the viewscreen on *Ascension* went dark, quickly replaced by the view of *Lentoris* steady in space.

Talia walked closer to the front, as if to garner a better view of *Lentoris*, but she was also confused as the sound continued, coming from everywhere. Jedra and Erin stood as well.

The chanting continued, and the chattering gave way in their minds to a song of ancient words, deep and wonderous. As they watched, the chant came to an end and *Lentoris* shot away at top speed.

The four on *Ascension* looked at each other for a lingering string of ensnared moments, seeking solace, direction, or answers. Their eyes repeatedly retreated to the force-field glass full of stars but empty of *Lentoris*.

Time stretched on as a chain of increasing tension until, Erin said, nodding slightly to Marcus, "Jedra, we have our orders. Let's set course for Prevaria."

To learn more about this author, please visit:

www.DarkAscensions.com
www.Issachon.com

To subscribe for updates on upcoming
releases, sign up at:
www.NStreetPublishing.com

www.ingramcontent.com/pod-product-compliance
Lightning Source LLC
Chambersburg PA
CBHW030418310726
48979CB00007B/1099